the unincorporated WOMAN

Tor Books by Dani Kollin and Eytan Kollin

The Unincorporated Man

The Unincorporated War

The Unincorporated Woman

the unincorporated WOMAN

Dani Kollin and Eytan Kollin

A Tom Doherty Associates Book
New York
TOR®

This is a work of fiction. All of the characters, organizations, and events portrayed in this novel are either products of the authors' imaginations or are used fictitiously.

THE UNINCORPORATED WOMAN

A Tor Book
Published by Tom Doherty Associates, LLC
175 Fifth Avenue
New York, NY 10010

www.tor-forge.com

Tor® is a registered trademark of Tom Doherty Associates, LLC.

Library of Congress Cataloging-in-Publication Data

Kollin, Dani.
    The unincorporated woman / Dani Kollin and Eytan Kollin.—1st hardcover ed.
        p. cm.
    "A Tom Doherty Associates book."
    ISBN 978-0-7653-1904-3
    I. Kollin, Eytan. II. Title.
    PS3611.O58265U56 2011
    813'.6—dc22

                                                            2011013447

First Edition: August 2011

Printed in the United States of America

0 9 8 7 6 5 4 3 2 1

In memory of our mother, Yona Kollin.

Of all the worlds we can imagine, there is only one that we cannot:

the one without you.

Acknowledgments

We'd like to thank the following people, without whom this book would not have been possible: First and foremost our father, Rabbi Gilbert Kollin, who doesn't always agree with our views but always supports our endeavors; Deborah Kollin, for her continued everything—twenty years, baby!; Eliana, Yoni, and Gavi Kollin for learning big words; David Hartwell for showing us how to use them correctly; Stacy Hague-Hill for shepherding us through; and Cherry Weiner for being the agent we've always dreamed of—blintzes, matzo balls, and all. And, of course, Alec Schram and Corry Lee for keeping our science sound.

We'd also like to thank the cast, crew, and regulars of our weekly webshow, neverendingpanel.com: Bond, Arlene, Cassidhe, Tim, Michelle, Frank, Charles, Ed, Karl, Jenny, Hare, Marty, Marcia, and Gizmo, as well as the Los Angeles Science Fantasy Society (LASFS) for allowing us to film in the oldest science fiction club in the world! Thanks also to Chase Masterson for being a show regular and letting us use her bombshell image on our bookmarks. Who knew SF could be so sexy? Props as usual to theunincorporated.com's award-winning SF Web guru extraordinaire, Richard Mueller of 3232design.com, and thanks to fellow author David Boop for not only leading us to our agent but for finding us obscure bars in downtown L.A. surprisingly devoid of industry folk; Shep Rosenman of Katz, Golden, Sullivan & Rosenman, LLP, for covering our flank; and Cassidhe Holke, for being our shovel-ready friend. And finally to all our readers whose encouragement we couldn't live without and whose opinions are thankfully just as seditious as ours.

the unincorporated WOMAN

1   Days of Ash

One of the most difficult things I've had to explain to the generations that came after us is the Days of Ash—unquestionably the worst moments of the war. Not in terms of death and suffering. No, those opportunistic twins were birthed in due time, and sadly what the human race would come to inflict on itself can still, to this day, scarcely be believed or forgiven. But as horrible as the war itself was, despite all the slaughter and misery that came after, those first few weeks were easily the most difficult. For during the Days of Ash, there dawned on the Outer Alliance a terrifying realization: With a raging storm moving swiftly over the horizon, our ship was rudderless.

Michael Veritas
The War, Volume IV: The Bloody Climax
University of Ceres Press

Days of Ash: Day Four

Fleet Admiral J. D. Black, commander of the Outer Alliance Navy, unofficial leader of the Astral Awakening and hated adversary of the United Human Federation, barged into Justin Cord's office, gave a perfunctory salute and let loose with a hail of pent-up fury.

"You son of a bitch." She seethed, lips curled back into a half-scarred face feared equally by enemy and ally alike. "It isn't enough I've had to lead your damned excuse for a navy to more victories than anyone had a right to expect?" J.D. held up her hand, not bothering to wait for an answer. "Or," she added as short, measured bursts of air escaped through her flared nostrils, "that I took a fleet of mine haulers and pleasure yachts and turned it into a feared and effective military force? Defeated enemies who outnumber us in every single battle not once but time and time again?" J.D. shook her head in disgust at the lack of response. The tempest she felt burning within leapt from her dark, penetrating eyes as if daggers flung from an assassin. "Do you have any idea," she hissed, "how volatile the religious situation has become? How easy it would be for me to let them all slip right back into their violent and monolithic past?" She paused, waiting, but again there was nothing. "I haven't let that happen, Justin . . . I *won't* let that happen. But is that good enough for you, Mr. *One Free Man*? Obviously not—otherwise you wouldn't have done this. Why," she pleaded, "did you even have to? Don't you see, Justin? I was never meant to be here. I'm just a corporate lawyer, for God's sake. This supposed gift I have . . . leading spacers into battle. Dumb luck . . . dumb . . ." The words languished in her mouth like the last few drops of a stream succumbing to a winter's frost. "But, guess what?" she rejoined. "Lightning doesn't strike twice. I've found the thing I'm good at," she scoffed, "but does that even matter to you? Did it ever matter to you?" She let out a deep breath, shook her head wearily, then let it drop between her shoulders. "They need me to lead them, Justin. They need me to lead them *all*. What am I supposed to do now?" she pleaded, slumping backwards into the closest available seat. A moment later, J.D. lifted her head and with eyes as deep and vacant as space, stared across at the untouched desk and empty chair of the assassinated President, waiting for an answer she knew would never come.

Seventy-two hours earlier

Admiral Black's command shuttle approached the landing bay of the AWS *Dolphin*. Omad's ship, noted J.D. as she stared out a port window, had been none the worse for its wear. Recently restocked at Altamont and updated at the Gedretar Shipyards in Ceres, the *Dolphin* was thankfully spaceworthy. *It will need to be,* she thought, returning to her work. The admiral's normally taciturn qualities had become positively glacial. She'd recently been caught off guard, and it was eating her alive. Worse, her stupidity might very well have cost everyone the war. The lines in her maimed brow, normally pronounced in a sort of twisted arc when roused, seemed frozen in place, as if sculpted by some macabre surgical procedure.

The Belt had been cracked, and Christina—her darling, tenacious Christina—was trapped at Altamont. The enemy's siege would succeed and the critical fortress would fall, in weeks at the earliest, a month at the latest. The Alliance had lost more than thirty ships and hundreds of thousands of miners. *One more month,* thought J.D., teeth clenched, hand slowly working its way over the now familiar distorted grooves and ridges of her pockmarked face. *One more month. That's all I needed.* In another month, they would have had the Via, a high-acceleration spaceway, to Altamont. Then she could have crushed Trang or, at the very least, broken through the siege long enough for all to evacuate. But Trang had either gotten lucky or outsmarted her. She'd wished it were the former but in her gut she suspected the latter, which galled her even more. And now they were really in it.

Still, all the recent losses could at least be framed within the context of military snafus. Even Christina, whom she'd loved as a friend and military wunderkind, held more value to her as a defensive tactician than as a close confidante. J.D. could force herself to be objective about any and all of it . . . *all of them.* That objectivity was what made her so good at what she did. She moved on. Found weaknesses where none were thought to exist. Exploited opportunities at every instance. Cold was good. Dead was good. And she'd almost stayed in that invulnerable space between the two but for the one person who'd somehow managed to find and then crawl into the small hole she'd inadvertently left uncovered. Fawa Sulnat Hamdi may have been the birthmother of the Astral Awakening but to J.D. the woman was also the only mother she'd ever really known. And the fact that she was gone now—murdered—was killing her. Because Fawa's only "daughter," the supposed greatest admiral in human history, had failed to see it coming.

Her first impulse had been to hunt down and destroy every UHF squadron in the region. It might not have been the most rational thing to do, but it sure would have felt good. Plus it could have been done with impunity, as Trang was still in the midst of his murderous rampage on the far side of the Belt, some 933 million kilometers away.

But then the other shoe dropped: Justin Cord, leader of the free worlds and hope to untold billions still languishing under the yoke of the incorporated movement, had been assassinated near the moon of Nerid. His body had been eviscerated by ravenous nanite attackers and left as a pile of dust orbiting that now ignominious rock. Both the timing and nature of the attacks carried with them the imprimatur of Hektor Sambianco. No doubts about that. The UHF's President had once again shown why those foolish enough to underestimate him paid a high price indeed.

J.D. shortly came to realize one other salient fact: Hektor had murdered the old Chairman. Until now she'd always discounted the rumors, preferring to believe the old man died at the hands of an action wing terrorist or quite possibly the result of Justin Cord's machinations. She'd never completely bought into Justin's too-good-to-be-true persona. *Who the hell is that good, anyways?* She rubbed the folds of her forehead as an involuntarily twitch moved her upper lip. *He was.*

Janet Delgado Black would have her revenge, but not just yet. She'd be patient, lick her wounds. And because she knew that the Alliance would not be broken, that they'd fight even if all they had left were the rocks grasped in the palms of their bloodied hands, she'd have time. She swore then and there that whatever it took, she'd hunt down those who'd destroyed her life. They'd pay for their unholy act of terror, and she'd bear witness.

Her shuttle swept into the bay, was grabbed by the *Dolphin*'s override system, and soon came to a slow, measured stop on the landing pad. J.D. didn't bother getting up from the desk she'd spent the last few hours brooding behind. Captain Marilynn Nitelowsen would do the formal greetings if there were any to be done. J.D. had grown impatient with formality, as much as it seemed to soothe the fighting class. She heard Marilynn walk down the gangway toward the hatch. The familiar hiss of air transference was immediately trumped by the garrulous sound of a man barking orders. A few seconds later, Marilynn entered the stateroom and gave her boss a knowing grin. A second after that, Admiral Omad Hassan strode in without bothering to salute.

"What in the name of Damsah is going on, Janet?" he barked.

"The fleet," she replied, placing both hands atop the knee of her crossed legs, "has been ordered back to Ceres." She indicated to Marilynn that she and Omad be left alone. The captain made a quick exit, closing the hatch behind her.

Omad's eyes could not hide the panoply of emotions he was feeling. "But we have to make the bastards pay!" he blurted. "Alhambra cannot go unavenged!"

"And it will, friend," she said, motioning him to take a seat. "Just not now."

The admiral refused the gesture, preferring to work himself up into a state.

"We can't," cut in J.D. "because we're needed at Ceres."

A tense silence filled the air.

"However," she reassured, "we are going to make *some* of those bastards pay."

Omad grunted his reluctant acceptance and deigned to sit down, eyebrow raised in anticipation.

"You're to take fifteen of our fastest ships," she ordered, "and hunt down whatever's left of the squadron that destroyed Alhambra."

Omad's mouth formed a cruel grin. "Done." He sprang up from the seat and headed toward the door.

"Omad," called J.D. The unusual disquiet in her voice stopped the admiral cold. "There's more." She gestured to the chair and this time Omad didn't argue.

"What is it?"

"Christina."

Omad took a deep breath. "How bad?" he asked.

J.D. called up a holo-tank display on her desk. The image rendered a perfect three-dimensional slice of a large section of the asteroid belt. "Trang's here," she said, pointing to an area in the middle of the Belt, roughly eleven million kilometers from Altamont. "I give him two, maybe three days at most until he gets within siege range. Once he's set up, nothing gets in or out."

"No resistance, eh?" asked Omad without conviction. Both he and J.D. knew that Trang had forever changed the calculus of the war. The persistant admiral had started out taking one rock at a time, crag by pitiful crag. Now he'd apparently changed his tactics. He was creating a path of destruction hundreds of thousands of kilometers wide. If rocks offered too much resistance, he simply went around them. If he could take them out, he would do so without remorse. In fact few, if any, prisoners were being taken into custody, such was the path Trang had already left in his bloody wake. Which wasn't to say that his fleet hadn't taken a beating. They'd lost hundreds of ships and tens of thousands of lives in their admiral's desperate gamble to cut the Belt in half. The difference was that Trang had the bodies and ships to lose—the Alliance didn't.

"Anyhow, with our main fleet here," J.D. pointed to another spot within the display, "we can't get to them in time."

"Let me guess," offered Omad. "Christina refused to leave."

J.D. nodded.

Omad smiled thinly. "Would you?"

"No," admitted J.D., "but that may be why we lose the war. I need her almost as much as I need Altamont." She switched off the display, leaving an empty space between the two battle-hardened friends. Standing behind her desk, she stared coolly at Omad, almost blaming him with her tight-jawed glare. "Now there's nothing any of us can do."

"That's bullshit!" snapped Omad, getting up from the chair. "I can get forty ships there in two weeks."

J.D. met his determined stance with her own, "Which means that in two weeks I'd lose both my best admirals instead of just one." She then backed away from the desk and stiffened her shoulders. "I can't allow that."

"We don't have to fight them for control of the 180, J.D.," insisted Omad, palms open, "just open up an escape route."

"You don't think I've worked out every conceivable scenario in my head, Omad? Explored every cockamamy scheme?"

Omad stood mute, brooding.

"If I thought any one of those plans had a chance," exclaimed J.D., "I'd have led it myself. But you and I both know that Trang'll see you coming a week before you get there. And when you do, you'll be outnumbered ten to one by an admiral who's proved himself a worthy adversary—even for the likes of you."

Omad, she saw, was no longer arguing.

"What does Justin say?"

J.D. didn't answer, seemingly struck dumb by the question.

"Well?" asked Omad, worry now evident in his normally gruff tone.

"I . . ." J.D. struggled with the words, breaking eye contact momentarily with Omad. She then forced herself back into his fixed gaze. She saw not her subordinate officer but the late President's best friend standing helplessly across from her. "Justin is dead," she said, exhaling deeply. "I'm sorry."

Omad's mouth hung open, slack jawed. He moved slowly backwards and fell into the seat, blindly clawing at the arms of the chair for support. He stared blankly into J.D.'s eyes, which somehow managed to convey both comfort and promise but absolutely no mercy.

Most of the newer settlements found in the community of belief had one habitable asteroid, and in rare circumstance, two. The ancient Jewish community of Aish Ha Torah, by virtue of its longevity, had five—all of which had been engineered into two-mile-long cylindrical amalgams of rock and fused metals. Aish, as it was commonly referred to among the Belters, was one of the oldest colonies in the community of belief and, in the span of over two hundred years, had grown in both size and industry. Its asteroids, rich in vital resources and carved out to create other facilities, soon began feeding the hungry maw of the Core Planets.

When the war broke out, Aish had been quick to side with Justin Cord not out of expedience but rather because the Unincorporated Man's dreams of personal responsibility and freedom perfectly aligned with theirs. In its present iteration, Aish owned a large orbit of several hundred thousand kilometers in volume, and its asteroids produced everything from homeopathic remedies grown in tropical rain forests to large manufacturing facilities that supplied the nuts, bolts, and widgets that pieced together a good deal of the Alliance's fleet.

Of the five asteroids, M'Araht Leubitz, named for the famous rabbi who'd first settled it, was the oldest and therefore most developed. The name M'araht meant "cave" in Hebrew, and the original designers of the asteroid's interior had purposely created an environment that harkened back to Judaism's ancient past. It was also a not-so-subtle reminder of what his people had fled: the radioactive waste of the Middle East and the death grip of atheism that unlimited prosperity and unfettered opportunity ushered in once the Alaskans had remade the world in Tim Damsah's image. And now, aided by nanotechnology, fueled by portable fusion, and gifted with greatly expanded life spans, the Jews of Aish Ha Torah, like their ancient Israelite cousins, were once again living in caves.

Sitting quietly on the ground with his back up against a wall near the entrance of one such cave sat a young man. He was five feet nine inches, about average for Belters, and appeared to be in his late twenties, though the hardened lines around his deep-set blue eyes seemed a testament to more. His jet-black hair was a cascade of loose curls that fell evenly onto his broad shoulders. He had a medium-length beard that his dirt-smudged, callous hand kept pulling downward in slow, rhythmic strokes. Though graphite stains on his hands and coveralls announced his trade as a mechanic, the swelling crowd gathered at the base of the path leading to his cave announced his position as a savior.

The truth was that like most clergymen, Gedalia Wildman had been a rabbi-slash. Which in his case meant rabbi/propulsion specialist. With around forty thousand practicing Jews, there were only so many full-time rabbis needed, and only the most intelligent and charismatic could support their learning without the necessity of added income. Such was not the fate of Gedalia Wildman. No one would argue that he wasn't a skilled Talmudist or that like those who'd studied the ancient analysis of the Bible's words and meanings, he couldn't extrapolate with the best of them. Likewise, they couldn't argue that he wasn't generous of spirit. But what they could argue, and brook no disagreement from the man himself, was that Rabbi Wildman was not pulpit material. The fact that so large a crowd was now gathering around his cave could mean only one thing, thought the rabbi. Something must have gone horribly wrong. He put both hands on the ground as if to reassure himself that the asteroid was still stable. It was. *No underlying or abnormal vibrations,* he thought. *Well, at least there's that.*

"Rabbi," said the group's apparent spokesman too reverentially for Gedalia's liking.

"Since when am I 'Rabbi' to you, Mordechai?" asked Gedalia, getting himself up and dusting off his trousers. Gedalia looked over the shoulder of his friend and was met with a crowd of forlorn faces.

Gedalia's longtime friend responded with stricken eyes. Moments later, Gedalia found out why. Alhambra, the greatest center of learning for all the communities of belief, was gone. The UHF had destroyed it utterly—no chance of survivors. Gedalia stood, looking toward but through the gathering crowd. Though he had no idea what he was going to do, he knew what must be done. He checked his DijAssist to see in which direction Jerusalem lay, then turned around to face it. The crowd mimicked his movements.

"*Yisgadal, v'yisgadash . . .*" he began. It was the prayer for the dead.

A few minutes later, Gedalia headed for the yeshiva, an institution that for most of his life held answers to mysteries both within his universe and without. The crowd, he noticed, followed silently behind but held itself back when he approached the ancient school's grand entrance—a large cave mouth ten meters tall. He entered. Everything was as he'd last remembered. The old leather-bound texts filling up row after row of shelves carved neatly into the rock, the phylactery cases nestled in small bored-out coves, the haphazard piles of prayer books jutting out and precariously balanced at the edges of the already too full shelves. And of course, the tables of learning: small rectangular slabs that could accommodate at most four bodies. It was to these tables that students of every level would come to argue over mundane passages of the Bible and attempt to glean meanings from the nuance of every word. Everything, noted Gedalia, was where it should be. Everything except those who'd bequeathed it with life. He'd entered looking for answers but instead found . . . ghosts. And it was then that he gave way to his grief. For an hour, he let the misery wash over him and to a certain extent cleanse him. In another realization of how his world had changed, he understood that his entire community was now dependent on him. Waiting for the answers, hope, guidance, and reassurance he was not at all sure he could give.

Gedalia Wildman had walked into the yeshiva as a rabbi/propulsion specialist, but after he emerged, he was to forever be known as the Rabbi.

Under the soft, dim glow of his command module and with the knowledge that no one would really notice, Admiral Omad Hassan took the opportunity to do something rather uncharacteristic—he prayed. It certainly wasn't out of belief. He was too old and too acerbic to entertain notions of higher spiritual planes and all such nonsense, but he'd also been around the block enough times to know there was no sense in counting things out that might take offense at not being counted. Plus it seemed to work well for his boss. And the deception he'd planned would have rightfully been labeled foolhardy. So much so that under normal circumstances, even he wouldn't have ordered anyone to do it. He recalled how the admiral had made it all sound so perfectly sensible.

And now his flotilla moved with abandon through a Cerean sector exquisitely mapped and cleared. There would be no ships lost to asteroid detritus or errant space junk. Though even that wouldn't have stopped him. Omad was now a man possessed, with a crew caught in his spell. All aboard knew what Justin Cord had meant to the Alliance, but they especially knew what Justin Cord had meant to their commanding officer. Omad had dug up the Unincorporated Man and by so doing had set in motion the revolution now sweeping through the system and beyond. But that wasn't what pushed him on, what made him stretch the limits of both ship and crew in his mad dash across the Belt. Justin Cord had been Omad's friend—his *one true* friend. And now the bastards who'd played a part in his death would pay.

Omad's face was placid. His eyes darted along the command panel, watching for any signs of trouble. Nothing. And he knew with certainty there wouldn't be, at least not until the trap was set. His orders had been explicit: exact revenge on the murderers of the righteous. But first he'd have to intercept them. The problem was they'd soon be finding shelter behind the orbital batteries of Mars, and that was a gauntlet even Omad had no desire to challenge. J.D.'s shellacking at the second Battle of the Martian Gates had taught them all a lesson no one was eager to repeat. He'd have to dissuade the UHF marauders from entering Mars's orbit without the benefit of actually being there, and he'd have to do it with just one ship.

AWS *Otter* – One day from Mars orbit

Captain Suchitra Kumari Gorakhpur entered the command sphere and stood silently. As with all new warships from frigates on up, the command sphere, which had replaced the traditional bridge, was located within the bowels of the ship and fortified by nanorealigned hull plating. The enemy could blow up almost any part of the *Otter,* and the command sphere would continue to function, continue to bark orders and lead even if crippled. *But now,* mused Suchitra, staring at her resigned crew, *there are no other vessels to lead—just us.* The sphere's amphitheater-like design meant that all eyes were on her. She tilted her head slightly in acknowledgment. Then, in slow, measured steps, circumnavigated the room and took a seat in the command chair directly opposite the entryway. The chair's placement afforded her a view of the surroundings. She sat slightly forward, elbows leaning on the console, fingers locked. She looked over to her number two.

"Situate us if you would, Commander Grayson."

"Sir!"

A perfect three-dimensional image of the *Otter* appeared, floating serenely by itself in the command sphere's holo-tank. Moments later, it was facing a flotilla of fifty UHF warships. Though Suchitra's outward expression was one of reserved calm, it concealed the terror she was actually feeling within. It was now only a matter of time. She wasn't afraid to die and, along with her crew, had served the Alliance bravely in any number of battles, but this was different. She was about to face a powerful enemy. Worse, she'd be seriously outgunned, alone, and have no chance of escape.

UHFS *Damsah III*

Commodore Theodore Guise was finally beginning to relax. His was the lead battle cruiser of a large flotilla that had succeeded mightily on its first-ever mission. He'd refused to think about what rewards might be in store until he and his crew were well clear of the Alliance space. Now, one day out of Mars, he allowed himself that luxury. His stock would certainly rise, no question about that. The question was by how much. And maybe, if he were really lucky, he'd get promoted to Fleet Command. That would mean a plush assignment on Mars, nicer sleeping quarters . . . better pay. And best of all, he'd never have to spend another day on one of these Damsah-forsaken ships. Granted, taking out a bunch of religious loonies on a defenseless rock wouldn't go down as one of the great battles of the war, but then again, he didn't really care. He was alive, more thanks to his white-collar position on the board of Nanorin than for any particular skill he had as an officer.

There were just too many ships and not enough experienced bodies to man them. So the navy went looking for its officer corps in the hallowed conference rooms of the top corporations—Nanorin being one of them. And that's where they'd found Theodore. When he was tapped, he went along happily. After all, not only was it his patriotic duty to serve, but doing so would greatly increase his marketing network as well. That he'd been called into action before his and his crew's training was completed didn't really bother him—at least not once the nature of the assignment had been explained. Whatever worries he did have were mitigated by the fact that the Alliance's most feared admirals were, at various places along the Belt, well engaged. And so thoughts of promotion and afternoon dalliances with pretty secretaries once again filled his head.

"Sir!" shouted his second in command, a young up-and-comer he'd pulled from the ranks of his own corporation. "Unidentified ship detected."

Theodore's eyes narrowed as he checked his own panel. *Out here?* he groused.

Before he could say anything, the first lieutenant jumped in.

"It's an Alliance vessel, sir. Classification: frigate. Transponder identifies it as—" The lieutenant paused and then looked up. His eyes were wide and now gazing with pensive fear. "—the AWS *Otter.*"

A chill swept through the command sphere as the frigate's information flashed across every display. The *Otter* was part of Admiral Hassan's flotilla. That was enough information for Theodore to decide it was time to punt.

"Get me the admiral."

"Right away, sir," snapped the first lieutenant.

Admiral Mummius's face appeared on Theodore's holodisplay. She seemed bored. However, once Theodore had explained the particulars, the woman's tired eyes popped open like a vigilant hound's.

"What's its speed and heading?"

Theodore motioned for the first lieutenant to answer.

"Not moving, sir. And it's directly in our path."

The right side of the admiral's face flinched.

"Weapons status?"

"That's just it, sir," said the first lieutenant, bulged eyes revealing his consternation. "It's cold, sir. Rail guns offline, missile ports closed."

"So then what the devil is it doing out there?"

"Apparently nothing, sir."

"Go to full visual, Lieutenant," commanded Theodore. The tank was filled with the image of the UHF's fleet moving in straight line directly toward the AWS *Otter*.

"Do they know we're here?" asked the admiral, a scowl now permanently embedded on her face.

"Yes, sir," chimed the first lieutenant, deftly manipulating the display board. "In fact, they're scanning us right now."

The admiral's head jerked back slightly. "And sending the info . . . where, exactly?"

The first lieutenant once again let his fingers fly over the board. A moment later he looked up, confused. "Nowhere, sir."

The admiral had heard enough. "Order the fleet to a full stop."

"Are you sure about that, sir?" asked Theodore, visions of posh offices and corporate whores disappearing quickly into the void. "We can blow right past her, sir. We're almost home."

The admiral's cold, pale gray eyes bored a hole straight into Theodore. "Are you willing to bet that that's the *only* ship out there that coincidentally just happens to be directly in our path?" she asked. "That Hassan or Black don't have something planned? Tell you what, Commander. You can take your ship and do whatever the hell you like with it. I'm sure your crew would appreciate that."

Theodore looked around the command sphere. The crew stared back blankly. He had his answer. He then eyed the first lieutenant. "Order a full stop," he said stiffly.

"Aye, aye, sir. Fleet to full stop."

The crew watched as the ships in the holo-tank came to a complete halt. Their task force of fifty floated silently in the air, facing the one tiny frigate. The visual was strangely mesmerizing in its utter imbalance, and for a brief moment, the crew remained entranced.

"Give me a full scan, Lieutenant," ordered the admiral.

"Did that, sir. There are some small anomalies and background radiation but well within standard parameters."

"Nothing's standard with these people, Lieutenant," groused the admiral. "It's a trap."

"What sort of trap?" asked Theodore, realizing the inanity of the question before he could retract it.

"If I knew that, then it wouldn't be a trap, would it?" snapped the admiral, glaring at her subordinate officer with unbridled disdain. "But I do know this. I'm not sticking around to find out. Plot a course for Earth."

"But . . . but, what about the defense of Mars?" asked Theodore, desperately searching for one last shot at salvation.

The admiral's lips drew back into a doglike snarl. "Fuck Mars, Theo. Between the orbats and the other five flotillas, they've got plenty of firepower. Plus they're not the ones who just blew the Alliance's religious council into dust and now have the entire Belt howling for their blood."

"Yes, sir," sputtered Theodore meekly. "Earth it is."

AWS *Otter*

Shouts of joy and relief rang through every corridor, nook, and cranny of the *Otter* as the crew of one hundred watched the UHF fleet head back out into deeper space.

"Captain."

"Yeah, Grayson," crooned Suchitra, a smile forming at the corners of her mouth.

"Looks like I owe you twenty credits."

"Yes, Grayson," sniggered the captain, finally exhaling. "It looks like you do."

AWS *Dolphin*

"Admiral," said First Officer Yuri Yologovsky, "we have a message from the *Otter*."

"I'm guessing," chortled Omad, "that our fearless brethren of the UHF have turned tail and run."

The first officer cracked a grin. "Apparently it's not only the Blessed One who can read the minds of the enemy."

"Don't grant me any special powers just yet, Yuri. We may have thrown 'em off course, but we'll still have to catch 'em. And, in *their* territory."

"You forgot the 'outnumbered three to one' part," chided the first officer.

"Since when has that ever stopped us?"

"Since never, sir. Inform the Rock Throwers?"

Omad's eyes were a cauldron of fury. "Absolutely."

The Rock Throwers had grown out of the Fleet Corps of Engineers which had grown from the techs and engineers of the various ships at the beginning of the war. The Rock Throwers had been instrumental in moving the Martian shipyard to Jupiter, devising many of the cover elements for Admiral Black's biggest victories, including the formation and shape of the asteroids for the Battle of the Needle's Eye. It was Omad who'd given them their current nom de guerre, which not coincidentally had derived from his use of asteroid swarms to hide his hit-and-run tactics. Once Omad realized he could actually create swarms to order, the Field Corps of Engineers got themselves a new name. And with the admiral's liberal use of it, the name stuck.

Omad checked his display. The rocks, all equipped with positional thrusters, were being moved from their various orbits and would in short order become four separate streams heading into UHF space. It was all he needed.

Executive Office, Mars

Hektor Sambianco put down the intelligence report. His office was as secure as money and paranoia could make it, and the only other person who knew what was in its collected contents was now sitting opposite him.

"Really?" he asked, doubt evident in his tone.

"To be accurate," adjusted his Minister of Security, Tricia Pakagopolis, "all we could determine is that he is, in fact, missing. But the Alliance is conducting a massive search."

"Yes," he averred, still cautious, "I imagine they would be."

"Mr. President, it's the nature of this business that certainties are almost always lies. But I'd bet my dividend on the fact that Justin Cord is dead. There was nothing left of the facility that he was last seen entering. It therefore stands to reason that there'd be nothing left of him."

Hektor's eyes flittered across the report. "How strangely appropriate. You realize, Tricia," he said, shifting his gaze to his Minister, "that that's the way he murdered the Chairman." It was a lie Hektor had repeated so often, he was almost starting to believe it himself. "And," he pushed further, "you're sure we had nothing to do with it? No rogue units, no leftover booby traps at the Nerid station—" He put down the single and only sheet of paper that contained the report. "—no nothing?"

"Mr. President, it's as masterful a public assassination on a prime target as I've ever seen. I'd love to take credit, even if it meant my head on a platter."

Hektor shot her a look.

"Without your authorization, that is."

Hektor almost nodded in agreement, but simply gestured for her to continue.

"That being said, the answer remains no. It most definitely wasn't us. The only logical explanation is that it was an inside job. And there are only two people we deem that capable." Tricia waited a moment before giving up the names, knowing her boss's penchant for intrigue.

"All right," guessed Hektor, "I'll say one of 'em has to be Janet Delgado."

"One for one, boss," confirmed Tricia approvingly.

"And if I had to bet my dividend on it—" Hektor's mouth twisted up slightly. "—Mosh McKenzie." He folded his arms triumphantly.

"One for two. Sorry, sir."

Hektor's grin disappeared instantly. He both hated and loved surprises. Hated them because they'd been the cause of so much disruption in his life, loved them because he couldn't stand being bored.

"Our analysis of Mr. McKenzie," Tricia pointed out, "does not make him a likely instigator. His political and economic influence has waned of late. His main power base had been his connection with Justin Cord. With Justin gone, we're not even sure he'll last the year."

"So then?"

"Olmstead, sir," announced Tricia.

"Again, Tricia? Please. We've been over this. I worked with the guy—trust me, he's really not that capable."

"With all due respect, sir, your prejudice concerning Kirk Olmstead is seriously outdated."

"With all due respect," Hektor sneered, "Olmstead is an arrogant *and* predictable fool. I refuse to believe a man I was able to manipulate so easily could've pulled off something of this magnitude."

"You're special, sir."

Tricia, noted Hektor, had managed to deliver that last line without the slightest hint of irony or humor.

"I don't know what happened to him in that place," she explained, "but it wasn't to our advantage. And as I've stated before, our lack of viable intel in the Belt is a direct result of his ruthless efficiency and paranoia."

"Perhaps," added Hektor, "plus the fact that we spent so many years basically ignoring the place."

Tricia bowed slightly. "Yes, sir. That too. But you'll have to trust me when I tell you, if Olmstead wanted Cord dead, he could've found a way."

Hektor held up his hands in mock surrender. "All right, then. So *is* he our man?"

Tricia offered up an impish smile. "No. Of the two, it makes more sense for Delgado to have arranged it."

"Janet, huh? At least *that* I can believe."

"From what we can gather, Kirk doesn't have the power base to take control or improve his position. So though we believe he was eminently capable of the assassination, our assessment is that it wouldn't have been in his best interest."

"And Janet's motive?"

"The simplest one, of course: power."

Hektor paused to consider the implication. "You know," he said caustically, "I'd almost grown used to thinking of Janet as the heroic combat admiral. I'd actually forgotten just how ruthless she could be. With the Alliance in turmoil, they'd naturally turn to her."

"Exactly, Mr. President," agreed Tricia. "And when you think about it, she either (a) now gets to prosecute the war without the obstruction of Mr. The Means Are The Ends constantly tying her left arm behind her back, or (b) can negotiate an end to the war on terms she'd find more acceptable."

"And," added Hektor, "we know that she and Cord weren't exactly the best of friends."

"Yes," agreed Tricia, "we took that into consideration as well, but it wasn't a deciding factor in our assessment."

"But it rounds it out quite nicely, don't you think?"

Tricia remained silent, but nodded.

"The bitch," murmured Hektor, cracking a wide, admiring smile. "She must've known I'd give her almost anything to end this war sooner rather than later."

"Of course," added Tricia, "that works only if Trang doesn't beat her first."

"Yes. It does," he replied, "but she's a cocky SOB with a stellar résumé in kicking our butts." Then, seconds later added, "Probably why we worked so well together."

Tricia nodded solemnly.

Jealousy? wondered Hektor.

"So, can he?"

"I'm sorry, what?" asked Tricia.

"Can Trang win? I hate to be less than rah-rah about it, but in the confines of this office, the truth will out." Even Hektor had to admit Janet had become something of a mythical figure.

Tricia nodded. "He just might. In which case, Delgado's gambit fails. Which leaves us with one outstanding issue."

"Ah," mused Hektor with a one-sided grin, "how best to exploit the assassination?"

"Yes, sir."

"Since I'm gonna be blamed for this anyways . . ."

"Yes, sir. Let's make it work for us."

"Indeed." Hektor's face was a mask of determined resolve. "Deny everything, of course, but leave just enough evidence for our press and their intelligence service to find. It shouldn't be conclusive, just . . ."

". . . suspicious," Tricia finished helpfully.

"Exactly." Hektor seemed satisfied. He pulled a matchbox from an inner pocket, set a match aflame, and touched it to the end of the report, dropping the paper at the last second into a large ashtray already filled with the stubs of half-chewed cigars. He watched the paper burn to ash, then casually picked up his DijAssist and scanned Tricia's other reports.

"And how," he asked, stopping at one that caught his eye, "are we planning to exploit the opportunities that the capture of the Belt and half the Alliance population will allow us?"

And with that, Justin Cord ceased being a consideration for Hektor Sambianco and became a simple memory.

> *Tragedy and triumph for the Alliance has been reported today. On this the eighth day since the murder of our President, the fabled fortress of Altamont was put under siege by the forces of the UHF under the personal command of Admiral Samuel Trang. This siege completes the cracking of the asteroid belt that began four and half years ago with the Battle of Eros. It is not known how long Altamont can hold out without supply or reinforcements. It is also not known whether Trang will use a long attritional siege or attempt to storm the position. Admiral Christina Sadma has refused all offers of surrender. Her last clear communication with the Alliance stated that she will not allow Altamont to fall to the enemy under any circumstance.*
>
> *In the triumph department, the massacre at Alhambra was avenged today with the complete destruction of the flotilla that committed that war crime. Admiral Omad Hassan, in a daring raid, pursued the enemy into their own space and overtook them. It's still unclear why the enemy did not seek protection behind the orbats of Mars, but our good fortune was their bad luck. Even though Admiral Hassan's fifteen ships were outnumbered three to one, he still emerged victorious.*
>
> *"It was like watching a battle from the first year of the war," said assault miner Eric M. Holke, a field-promoted sergeant who helped capture the flagship. Although we cannot report on the losses suffered by the Alliance, we're given to understand that they were surprisingly light. As it now stands, thirty-one of the enemy ships were destroyed or self-destructed, with nineteen having been captured. Whether they can be returned to Alliance space from so far in UHF*

territory remains to be seen. Rumor has it that none of the enemy was taken alive, all having chosen to die rather than be captured and face trial for their crimes. This, however, cannot be confirmed, as some may have been suspended and stored. In an editorial aside, it is this reporter's fervent wish that Admiral Hassan kicked open the air locks and spaced all of the bastards.

Nora Roberts
Alliance Daily News

Triangle Office, Ceres

Janet Delgado Black sat for some time, staring into the empty seat. Even unoccupied, the room, the seat, *something* in the Triangle Office allowed her to attain a measure of clarity and introspection. Sitting now in the quiet, in the dark, she opened her heart, giving quarter to unspoken heresy: She never really liked Justin Cord. The man had been too damned righteous. More than once, she'd wished she could smack the holier-than-thou attitude right off his face. And yet she wanted him back, needed him sitting behind his now undisturbed desk, telling her and the rest of the Alliance what to do. Agree with him, argue with him, worship or hate him. In the end, J. D. Black, along with everyone else in the Outer Alliance, had done what came naturally—she followed him.

And now he was gone, and the whole mess had somehow ended up in her lap. Technically, she was a fleet admiral who reported to a grand admiral—a superior officer in every sense of the word. Joshua Sinclair was her direct boss *and* the Defense Secretary and a Cabinet Minister, all of which gave him greater authority. But none of that meant crap.

J.D.'s recent orders to return to Ceres had been the proof of that. She'd been on her way to find and destroy the bastards who'd murdered her friends at the asteroid community of Alhambra when the mission was unexpectedly called back. Turns out it would have been impossible for her to execute. Not militarily, but rather politically. Janet hated thinking that way, but it was true. Aside from Sinclair's direct order, she'd also received numerous back-channel communiqués from every major political and economic leader in the Alliance. Normally, she would've paid them scant attention, much less read them. After all, Sinclair's order had been, with admittedly some objection on J.D.'s part, good enough. But J.D.'s trusted adjunct, Marilynn Nitelowsen, had impressed upon her boss the need for political savvy—if only for a short while, during the crisis—and responding to the communiqués had been a start. Janet didn't know why she'd bothered. After all, they pretty much asked the same thing: *When are you getting back to Ceres, and can you get here sooner?* The government had been in a panic, which unchecked, had spread outward at an alarming rate. And now it was believed that only J. D. Black, hero of the Alliance, warrior goddess of victory, and reassuring voice in the heat of battle, could somehow manage to right the listing ship. She wanted to gag.

It was agreed that she'd send her number two, Omad Hassan, to deal with the murderers. It took J.D. a few days to get back to Ceres, and things, she soon found, had indeed gone to hell in a handbasket. The asteroid belt had cracked at the 180, its midpoint, and she couldn't do a thing about it. Her precious Christina Sadma, an invaluable military asset, trusted friend, and an admiral generally loathed by the United Human Federation, was trapped at the asteroid fortress of Altamont. Worst of all, the Alliance's leader and moral center, Justin Cord, was dead. J.D.'s initial assessment upon return was that there was little, if anything, she could do about it—especially as a glorified hand-waving benchwarmer on Ceres. And yet she couldn't deny the palpable effect she had when appearing in public. Whether in front of a street urchin or before a powerful congressional committee, the effect, she noted, was always the same—the panic and fear would dissipate almost immediately. She was glad to offer them the respite, even if the power therein scared the hell out of her.

J.D. heard the door open behind her. Even though she trusted her guards implicitly, she turned around to see who'd entered. *After all,* she thought, *Justin had trusted his guards too.* The intruders, she mused, turned out to be a threat, just not to her physical safety.

"Good morning, Mr. Secretary, Congresswoman," said J.D., getting up from her chair.

Eleanor McKenzie extended her hand. "That's Congresswoman-Elect." Eleanor was wearing a formal gray two-and-a-half-piece suit garnished with flecks of color, and a non-distinct matching blouse: standard government fare. Though Eleanor was well past a century, only the depth of her eyes and reserved half smile bespoke a true age greater than the forty years she was currently presenting. She had also cut her once long, amber blond hair into a short crop. But other than that, noted J.D., it was still the same woman with the same mellifluous voice and strikingly firm handshake.

"I don't get sworn in till this afternoon," pointed out Eleanor, acknowledging J.D.'s equally firm grip with a slight bow.

"We were hoping you'd attend," urged Mosh, too peremptorily for Janet's liking. Mosh, she noticed, hadn't changed much at all: still bald, still presenting in his late forties, and still ornery. As a former board member of GCI, the largest corporation in history, and now the current Treasury Secretary, Eleanor's husband was a powerful figure in the Alliance and, therefore, used to getting his way. There was no love lost between him and J.D.; they were adversaries before Justin arrived and turned everyone's world upside down. But as the adage went, "The enemy of my enemy is my friend," and Hektor Sambianco, President of the UHF and bane of the Alliance, had made a lot of enemies.

"The people," argued Mosh, "should see that our government's still functioning."

"Oh, is it, now?" J.D. asked, eyebrow cocked.

"—and," pressed Mosh, refusing to take the bait, "you and I both know that your presence will certainly help."

"So," J.D. scoffed, "you need my blessing." She shook her head in disbelief.

"Yes, Janet," replied Mosh—being one of the few who'd known her long enough to address her on a first-name basis. "That is exactly what *we* need."

"Where does it stop, Mosh?" blared J.D. "Am I to christen every ship, cut the ribbon at every porta-potty?"

"Don't get smart with me, Janet. You and I—"

Eleanor placed a firm hand on her husband's shoulder, shooting him a *cease and desist* glance. She then set her gaze on J.D. "I would want you to be there regardless, dear, but whether you like it or not, Mosh is correct. Your presence will help with my new and more experienced colleagues, and frankly I could use all the help I can get."

J.D.'s upper lip twitched. She finally nodded her head more in defeat than in acceptance. Something about Eleanor reminded her of Fawa Hamdi, the woman who'd sheltered her when she'd first arrived in the Belt and the same woman who'd helped her find faith in God. Both Eleanor and Fawa had a mothering or perhaps even a smothering quality, mused J.D., that made resistance almost futile.

J.D. inclined her head. "Of course I'll come."

Eleanor smiled approvingly. "Thank you, dear."

"Speaking of swearing-in ceremonies . . ." began Mosh.

Eleanor's even gaze returned. "This is neither the time nor place, dear."

J.D. remained silent, preferring the matter be closed without her intercession, and with Eleanor as an ally, she was quite confident it would be.

"The President," said Mosh, choosing to ignore the forces aligned against him, "is dead, and in case either of you missed it, we do not have a successor. So this is most definitely the time. As for the place—" Mosh did a quick and purposeful scan of the Triangle Office. "—we will not find one better. I actually thought you came here because you were ready to accept what must be done."

J.D. brought up her hand to rub the scarred half of her forehead. "I came here," she said, voice raised in anger, "to . . . to say good-bye." She glanced over her shoulder at the desk, then back to Mosh and Eleanor.

"I keep expecting him to be here. I know he's gone. I've read the reports and talked with the commanding officers leading the search. The overall probability is he perished with the rest of the Nerid station. But every time that door opens"—her eyes focused on the space behind Mosh and Eleanor—"I expect him to be here. I expect to hear his always sarcastic, 'J.D., so glad you could make the time to talk with your commander in chief.'"

Mosh and Eleanor let out a laugh tinged with sadness.

J.D. once again looked over at the chair. "I'm not supposed to be here."

"You're the *only one* who's supposed to be here . . . the only one who *can* be here," insisted Mosh.

Desperation and agitation crossed her face like leaves tossed to and fro by the wind. "What about Sinclair?" she blurted.

"Saturnian," thwarted Mosh, "and therefore not acceptable to the Jovians. Plus the rest of the Alliance doesn't really know him well enough to trust him—not in a time like this."

"Cyrus, then."

Mosh shook his head. "Besides being Jovian which makes the Erisians and Saturnians nervous, the rest of the Alliance knows about him *all too well.*"

J.D.'s lips parted wide enough to reveal her clenched teeth. "I can't believe I'm suggesting this, but . . . what about you?"

Mosh was taken aback. It was clear he hadn't bothered to add himself to his own list.

"She must be desperate, dear," joked Eleanor.

Mosh smiled thinly at his wife then turned towards J.D. "I'd like to think I'm President material, Janet. Damsah knows I've been in the thick of it longer than most." Mosh, they both knew, wasn't only referring to his current job, but also to his previous one on the board of GCI.

"You're also from Earth," added J.D., a glimmer of hope discernible in her voice, "like Justin and me, so all the provincial crap you're talking about goes away."

"Yes, Janet, all well and true. But for the fact that I'm the effective head of the Shareholder faction, you might've had a leg to stand on. A faction," explained Mosh, "that is now in the minority and as such would be completely unacceptable to the NoShares."

J.D.'s shoulders dropped slightly and her body deflated as she absorbed the truth of Mosh's words. She also realized that Eleanor hadn't stopped him—a tacit approval of his line of reasoning.

"But enough of what we already know," asserted Mosh. "The Alliance doesn't have the time for you to accept the inevitable. The Cabinet has been granted a writ of executive authority for two weeks. The only reason that compromise was acceptable to the Congress was because I made it known that you were going to be present at all the Cabinet meetings."

"But I can't possibly—"

"I know that, Janet," agreed Mosh, interrupting. "Hell, they even know that. But under the guise of your needing time to acquaint yourself with the issues, everyone's quiet—for now. But at the end of that time, Congress *will* choose a new President, and it will be you. There's simply no one else. You must assume this office, Janet. It's either that or we sue for peace right now."

J.D. glared at Mosh but there was little if any fire left in her eyes. "I can't win from behind this desk," she insisted, "You know that and I know that."

Mosh nodded, resigned.

"And now you want me to sit here, hold hands . . . maintain coalitions?"

"Yes."

"And have this face," chided J.D., pointing at her mangled features, "kissing babies?"

"Yes, Janet. That's exactly what *we* want." Mosh looked over to his wife for support.

Despite both Mosh's and J.D.'s furtive glances to the Congresswoman-Elect, Eleanor remained stubbornly silent, offering help to neither.

"What about Trang?" proffered J.D., referring to the UHF's greatest and most disruptive admiral. "Have you given any thought to that? He'll be here as soon as he's done with the 180. And when he comes, it'll be to finish this war."

Mosh nodded, shifting uncomfortably in place.

Sensing a rope, J.D. grabbed for it. "I know I can beat him, Mosh. Do we have anyone else who can?"

"No," he admitted grudgingly.

"Well, then," she demanded, thumb pointing over the back of her shoulder towards Justin's desk, "how do you propose I do it from there?"

Mosh buried his hands in his pockets, frowning. "I don't have that answer. But you and I also know that we can't win this war *unless* you're behind *that* desk."

The standoff was interrupted by the sound of door chimes—a relic Justin had insisted on for all his rooms. For all three present, it was yet another painful reminder of their leader's absence. It took a moment for J.D. to realize that both Mosh and Eleanor were waiting quietly. Whether on purpose or by unconscious design, they were already forcing J.D. to exercise authority where she felt none should exist. Irritably, she leaned over the desk and stared into the holodisplay. Her annoyance was tempered by whom the display showed to be waiting on the other side of the door—her personal chaplain, Brother Sampson. His dress uniform made her realize that she'd lost track of the time.

She opened up the communications panel. "Already?" she asked softly.

Mosh and Eleanor both noticed the change in her demeanor.

Brother Sampson nodded. "Yes, Admiral. Lieutenant Nitelowsen has your dress uniform waiting for you in a secure room near the landing bay."

"I'll be right out."

The brother bowed slightly.

While her present company bided their time, J. D. Black allowed a quick sigh and closed off the display. Then, with an effort of will, she straightened her posture, left the Triangle Office, and walked into her future.

2 Tunnel Vision

rand Admiral Samuel Trang was comfortably positioned. From his seat of command, he had the advantage of two distinct views—one of which gave him great pleasure. It was the sight of Altamont a mere hundred kilometers away, surrounded by his fleet. The great rock had been blasted through at various points along its circumference and was now effectively open to the vacuum of space. The fact that his fleet was still taking fire showed that Altamont's defenders had no intention of surrendering anytime soon. He hadn't thought they would, given the nature of their leader, but as it had taken him over four years to get to this spot, he wasn't complaining. Altamont would fall; of that, he was certain.

The other viewing item filled him with disgust. It was the battle report from Omad Hassan's recent shellacking of the Alhambra flotilla. Trang was absolutely horrified at Hektor's and his Cabinet's decision to launch an attack on an undefended civilian outpost—no matter what the nature of those who occupied it. Had Trang known in advance of the Cabinet's plans, he was certain he would've tendered his resignation. Their seemingly rash act was now going to make his job of occupying the asteroid belt that much more difficult. And for what—removing the titular heads of a religious movement already doomed to failure by its archaic logic?

He gazed pensively at the report. The more he read, the more labored his breathing became. His eyes scanned down to the orders given to the condemned admiral. What incensed him more than anything was the fact that the idiot had complied without registering the slightest protest. If she had, or if she'd even asked for a clarification of orders, Trang would've gotten wind of them. It would've been enough to countermand the decision, Cabinet be damned. Trang was having a difficult time wrapping his brain around it. What idiot accepts an order to take an untrained crew out with a flotilla of ships so new, most of their systems haven't even been debugged? Worse, then accepts a mission to destroy a defenseless asteroid settlement. Trang's cinched brow was the only clue to his silent litany. The irony was that he'd purposely left Admiral Mummius on Mars, thinking the harm she could do there would be minimal. If he'd known the admiral was capable of that much stupidity, he would've made her his aid—if only to keep her out of trouble. Trang was hoping that Mummius would not be typical of the officer corps he'd have to work with, but suspected that hope was for naught.

The report of the battle itself was what he'd expected. The war-hardened Alliance fleet, though heavily outnumbered, had been in no real danger of defeat. Conversely, the untrained crews of the UHF had been so misbegotten that they somehow managed a twelve-ship collision. *There's a reason,* thought Trang, shaking his head in disgust, *that they call it "space." There's plenty of it. Only a moron of superior talent could manage a collision of that magnitude. Hell, it might even be a record.*

As he scanned further, it became quickly obvious how the thing had spiraled out of control. Systems had crashed or hadn't worked at all, because various safeties had not been removed, live programs had been incompatible with one another, and emergency protocols had not been implemented, much less taught. The entire fiasco was yet another demonstration of what Trang had been saying all along—only properly trained crews, properly led, should actually engage the enemy. Otherwise, all you'd get was unmitigated slaughter. Mummius's defeat was a perfect case in point.

The fact that not one UHF marine had been taken alive spoke to a more disturbing suspicion—they probably weren't given the opportunity to surrender. The truth was, Omad Hassan had probably saved him the trouble of trying to court-martial the bastards himself, which, realized Trang, would have put him in direct confrontation with the Defense Secretary. But none of that mattered now. The marines who'd died were still his people, and their wanton slaughter by Admiral Hassan, no matter how justified, could not be without consequences; otherwise, morale would suffer.

Before he could work it out, his DijAssist informed him of a call from his number two. She was, he saw by the display readout, bringing up the line approximately forty thousand kilometers away. Even through the interference of radiation, debris, and residual jamming, he could tell that something wasn't right.

"Zenobia," he said, trying to force a smile through a face grown rigid by the past hour's ruminations, "why do I have the feeling this is not good news?"

"Because, sir," came the scratchy static replication of her voice, "it's not."

"Proceed," Trang commanded grimly.

"My intelligence . . . eam picked . . . up . . . ansmission a few hours ago. I just finished reviewing it. It was go . . . to be . . . your afternoon debriefing, but I thought . . . ou'd better have a look at . . . now."

She transmitted the file.

A few seconds later, his display notified him of its arrival. "Got it," confirmed Trang as Zenobia's image saluted and then disappeared. He quickly scanned the headline:

UHF INTERNAL REPORT
TO: GRAND ADMIRAL SAMUEL TRANG
FROM: ADMIRAL ZENOBIA JACKSON
SUBJECT: MASS EVACUATION
SOURCE: TERRAN/CORE-BASED TRANSMISSION
RELIABILITY: CONFIRMED

Perfect, Trang mused, beginning to feel the veins on his temples bulge ever so slightly. He read further:

RELIGIOUS FIGUREHEAD CALLS FOR MASS EVACUATION
A LITTLE-KNOWN RELIGIOUS FIGURE REFERRED TO AS "RABBI" HAS CALLED FOR A MASS EVACUATION OF THE BELT. BECAUSE RABBI IS ONE OF THE FEW RELIGIOUS LEADERS LEFT AFTER THE ELIMINATION OF ALHAMBRA, HIS MESSAGE HAS BEEN TAKEN VERY SERIOUSLY BY MANY OF THE ASTRAL AWAKENING'S NEWEST BELIEVERS. RABBI'S ARGUMENT APPEARS TO BE PRIMARILY RELIGIOUS AND AS SUCH IS HAVING A PROFOUND EFFECT ON THE DEBATE NOW TAKING SHAPE WITHIN THE HUNDREDS OF THOUSANDS OF SETTLEMENTS THAT OCCUPY THE BELT. MANY APPEAR TO HAVE ALREADY HEEDED RABBI'S CALL FOR "DIASPORA," ABANDONING ORBITAL SLOTS OF GREAT VALUE AND LONG STANDING AS THEY AND THEIR ASTEROIDS SLOWLY MAKE THEIR WAY TO THE OUTER ORBITS. SO FAR, THE OFFICIAL RESPONSE FROM THE CARETAKER GOVERNMENT AT CERES HAS BEEN UTTER SILENCE.

Trang turned his head away from the screen and sent a vexed look to whatever daemon seemed to have chosen him as the day's chew toy. The Cabinet's rash decision had already been responsible for two massacres, and now, sadly, there would need to be another.

On the twelfth Day of Ash, when the Children of the Stars were brought low and all hope was fleeting, two signs were delivered unto them that their lamentations had been heard. Returned to the holy city that was the chosen home of him sent by God, chosen by the miracle of his owning none and being owned by none, came the Barge of Death.

The Children of the Stars did gather in the cavern and beheld the empty hatch and knew that the Anointed Man was truly gone. And the Children did give in to despair, and the howls of their lamentations were heard in all quarters of the holy city of the stars, and yea unto every outpost and world that belonged to the Children of the Stars, and yea even into the void of space itself, where no sound can be heard. Yet so great was the despair of the Children that even unto space itself was that cry heard.

When so complete was the misery that it didst seem ready to break the will of the Children—to doom them, their children, and their children's children unto the last generation to defeat and the enslavement of the Stock, cursed be that name—then did appear the Blessed One. Without a word did she command silence, and silence was given. Without a sound did she command attention, and attention was paid. With outstretched and withered hand did she summon the flag draped upon the rod that lo, did represent the Children in the war against the Stock, cursed be that name. This, the battle standard that the Blessed One had carried from righteous victory to righteous victory, went as if by spirit to her hand from across the cavern. And the Children did witness it thus. The battle standard held now by the Blessed One did in its cloth cover half of the Blessed One's face, and the Children of the Stars saw that the Blessed One's side of war was covered and thus the Children were reminded of the holy beauty and grace that inhabited the Blessed One. And yea did the Blessed One take the battle standard and touch a corner of it to that which contained the spirit of the Anointed Man, the holy reliquary, and still was the war side covered. Then she brought the battle standard to her lips, and still the war side was covered. And yea she gestured, causing her emissary to the shadow realm to come forth, and taking her sash of office did also the emissary to the shadow realm touch it to the reliquary and it to her lips. And then did the holy brother blessed of God and respected by the Children of the Stars take a holy book and touch it to the reliquary and thus bring it to his lips. And yea it came to pass that all who came to wail and grieve did instead come forth and touch upon the reliquary their holy objects and recognize the miracle of God having called his Anointed Man back to him while leaving his garb and garments for the Children to find and treasure. And thus they were comforted. For they saw that God had not abandoned them in their Days of Ash. For then it was that the Blessed One took from the Barge of Death that crypt which held the Anointed Woman and thus did the Blessed One make the

Anointed Woman's body ready, and breathed upon her, and life was restored. And it was good.

The Astral Testament
Book III, 1:27–39

Day Twelve

J. D. Black was trapped by an enemy worse than all the ships of Trang's fleet combined. It was an enemy that couldn't be fought with any of the tools in her arsenal, or with any of the instinct and pluck that had served her so well in her many great victories. And over the course of mere weeks, it had grown more onerous and intractable. She was tempted to curse her god and then berated herself for the seeming lack of faith. Fawa would've known what to do. Fawa would've listened and felt and intuited. But Fawa was no longer among the living, and J.D. had no such patience. This new enemy was cruel indeed in that it *demanded* patience, insisted on submission. J. D. Black, Fleet Admiral of the Alliance, had been trapped by the immutable cumber of expectation.

In the eight days she'd been on Ceres, she'd come to the realization that the only thing standing between anarchy and order had been her presence alone. As if to prove the point, what was supposed to have been a simple and dignified ceremony marking the return of Alliance One and, with it, Justin Cord's recovered space suit almost turned into a religious riot. She'd been expected at the ceremony and had planned on staying only long enough to watch the suit removed. However, from the moment of her arrival, it looked as if the crowd was going to tear one another to shreds getting to the suit, which had apparently taken on mythical proportions.

The frenzied mob had already surrounded the ship and a few were even storming the ramp. A small group of surprised and clearly nervous-looking assault miners were guarding the open hatch. This wasn't the welcome-home ceremony they'd been anticipating. At that moment, J.D. had acted on impulse, marching with fierce determination toward the ship. Whether through the force of her nature or the four burly guards assigned her, the crowd gave quarter, and J.D. soon arrived at the base of the ramp where the Alliance One assault miners were still hemmed in. Now, at least, all that stood between her and the hatch were a dozen or so people crazy enough to put themselves directly in the sights of some pretty big guns and a contingent of miners who knew how to use them.

J.D. made a quick scan of the room and seized upon an idea. She signaled Captain Nitelowsen, still doggedly by her side, to bring her one of the Alliance's battle standards, ceremoniously lining the walls of the loading dock.

J.D. further ordered two of her guards to force a path for the captain while J.D. and what was left of her small group momentarily prevented the rest of the swelling crowd from gaining access to the ramp. In short order, Captain Nitelowsen and the guards managed to push their way to the wall where the captain tried unsuccessfully to pull a standard from its base. Undeterred, she kept looking until she found one that gave. But what Nitelowsen saw when she turned around was a room that had doubled in human capacity in the space of minutes. She also knew, armed guards or not, it would take her too long to get the standard back to her boss in the precious few moments that were left until all hell broke loose. She caught J.D.'s eye and gave a knowing wink. Then, with the full thrust of a woman possessed, Nitelowsen threw the standard across the open area in a javelin-like fashion as a throaty grunt escaped her lips.

The standard flew across the divide while its brilliant, shimmering colors and billowing, velveteen material transfixed those who fell under its unexpected shadow. J.D. jumped up to grab it. The few remaining people on the ramp turned around when they'd heard the hushed awe of the crowd as the standard seemingly flew in from nowhere. Once it was firmly in her hands, J.D. proceeded up the ramp and demanded those behind her march in solemn procession. The small but important group included Brother Sampson, Mosh and Eleanor McKenzie, plus the two slightly bewildered but nonetheless intently serious guards, weapons at the ready. The stunned mob immediately bowed their heads as the newly formed procession slowly advanced up the ramp. The "unofficial" ceremony had begun, and J.D. was racking her brains as to how it should proceed.

"Follow my lead," she whispered through pursed lips at the first soldier she encountered. He gave her an almost imperceptible nod.

"Private!" she then bellowed loud enough for all to hear. Her voice bounced around the cavernous bay, even its receding echo commanding obeisance. J.D. felt a little foolish as the battle standard, held firmly in her grasp, still covered half her face. But it was quite large, a bit ungainly, and would've proved too difficult to move aside. Plus, she'd reasoned, it was what the crowd had fixated on, and she'd use it to her advantage, covered face or not.

"Yes, sir!" screamed the private, equally as loud and clearly relieved to answer to any semblance of order.

"You may now present the hero's suit!" ordered J.D, somewhat chagrined at not having coming up with something more original.

"Sir!" shouted the private once again. He then saluted and retreated back into Alliance One, barking orders to unseen others within the ship. J.D. enjoined her small procession to turn around and face the crowd while simultaneously leaving enough room for the marines to bring the pallet containing

Justin's inflated but empty suit out of the hatch. The few civilians left on the ramp had been quickly shamed and shooed off it by those standing nearest to them. In that same time, Captain Nitelowsen had found a route through the horde and took up her place by J.D.'s side. A moment later, four marines carried out the pallet on which lay the battered space suit, where it was believed the Unincorporated Man had spent his dying moments.

If the bay had been quiet before, it dropped to a whisper now. The only sound that could be heard was the intermittent weeping and gasps of both men and women witnessing their savior's final journey. Once the assault miners had cleared the hatch, J.D. ordered them to stop. She then approached Justin Cord's space suit and, grabbing a corner of the battle standard, first touched it to his suit and then to her lips. She called on Captain Nitelowsen to do the same. Brother Sampson came of his own accord and too kissed the suit, only this time by touching it delicately with his bible and then by bringing the bible to his lips. In this way, the crowd was made to realize that proper decorum did not include bodily violence. From that moment on, the contingent of assault miners and the unofficial funeral procession were able to make their way, albeit rather slowly, out of the landing bay and into the safer environs of a secure holding room.

As soon as they cleared the bay, J.D. handed off the battle standard to the nearest soldier and ordered Alliance One's *other* precious cargo, the newly found sarcophagus, to a safe location. She then strode out of the room, barely dignifying Justin Cord's empty space suit with a passing glance.

Day Fourteen

Admiral Christina Sadma, defender of Altamont and commander of a once superior fighting force now whittled down through warfare and attrition, stared unblinking into a darkened, empty crevice through the scratched pane of a battered helmet. Standing on a small ridge overlooking the silent thoroughfare, she breathed in her suit's stale, processed air and realized with sad portent that she could no longer remember the last time she'd been out of the damned thing. Yes, it was an incredibly well-designed machine wearable for weeks on end with nothing worse developing than an aversion to a tenacious ozone odor that seemed to linger despite the best efforts of the Alliance's engineers. The smell had, amusingly, spawned a whole new industry in "suit scents," the most popular of which was called "new suit." The odd, tree-shaped stickers had been quite the rage as the outfits wore down and their filters wore out, but now the stickers too had disappeared. The supplies of everything had dwindled to almost nothing.

However, her current disquiet wasn't a result of having spent too much time in the suit. She'd been born and raised on Eris, past the Kaiper Belt, and—like most in the Outer Alliance—had spent weeks "in suit" on one job or another. No, the thing that irked her most was what she was staring at: a horridly scarred and pitted landscape that only a few short weeks ago had been more fit for the donning of a summer dress than wearing the stifling, stale-air contraption she'd been forced to live in now.

As Christina looked out over the great rock's once pristine interior, her heart grew heavy. Gone was the settlement's famous "miracle of light," in which large, strategically placed mirrors had been used to create a glimmering star in the asteroid's center. Gone too were the abbey's famous gardens, growing a thousand and one impossible things in perfect harmony—testament to the gentle care and patience that eons of such tranquil endeavors could produce. Gone as well were the notions of life and peace. Christina even missed the Altamont she'd had to create to fight the war. True, "her" Altamont did not have the beautiful gardens. They'd long ago been replaced by kilometer after kilometer of uniform soy plantations and all manner of other staple foodstuffs. "Her" Altamont also had much heavier traffic than the asteroid had ever been used to, with ships and personnel coming and going at all times. There'd been such purpose, though, to the place. Christina's Altamont, fueled by a hatred of incorporation and infused by the passion to fight it, inspired a life all its own. Though the asteroid's once idyllic interior had been transformed with the abbey's permission, that hadn't stopped Christina from dreaming of the day she could eventually return it to its Godly purpose. But now, standing amongst its ruins and degradation, she realized that that day would never come and that this current grotesque iteration was to be its last.

It had indeed become a dark world. So much so that the windowpane of her helmet needed both infrared and ultraviolet enhancing just to see what the natural human eye could not. It was a darkness relieved only by the occasional spark of an exposed wire or the momentary sputter of an emergency light. It had, at first, been fascinating to watch the exposed wires fizzle out in lonely protest amidst the blackness. Eventually, though, it had grown depressing—a reminder of the dying rock itself. The vast interior chamber had also grown cold now that the vacuum of space had made itself a permanent, and unwelcome, guest. All sorts of detritus—some macabre, some not—could be seen floating in quiet ignominy. Depending on her position, Christina could also make out the shimmering brilliance of random stars through the gaping holes that Trang's guns had opened up. Sadder still was the fact that those stars did not move past those unnatural openings, but rather stayed fixed in frozen immobility. Altamont had ceased to spin, and centrifugal gravity, the wellspring of its human activity, was no longer available: yet another consequence of the enemy's unrelenting assault. Magnetization kept whatever was needed and whoever was alive firmly in place. The walking was sluggish but in no way debilitating.

But for the floating debris, all was still. The great Battle of Altamont had paused as if in need of catching its breath before one final exertion. For an entire day, no guns had been fired, no assault shuttles had been launched, and even the pit crews, normally keen to take advantage of any lull, seemed enervated, having come to the realization that the time when repairs could do any good had long since passed. Christina gave her beloved Altamont a final look, then turned and headed into the maintenance tunnel that led to her command bunker.

The first thing she did upon arrival was check to see that the energy-dampening grid was still working. It was. There was still plenty of power left in Altamont, the portable fusion reactors had seen to that, but a command bunker was a necessary energy hog and therefore an obvious target. For safety's sake, power would be used sparingly and as needed. As she entered the small, airless, but well-lit room, the few administrators still on hand—five in all—stood at attention and saluted. Seeing their paltry number made her think of the diminished forces now under her command. When she realized the battle had been lost, she tried to evacuate as much of the military as possible, figuring they'd be more useful elsewhere. Unfortunately, as quickly as she could get her personnel out, refugees had come flooding in, having no place left to make their stand when Trang cracked the 180. And so now these proud, these few were all that was left of a once mighty contingent. As the assault miners stood at rapt attention, Christina saw the look in their eyes. Like her, they all knew what was coming, and like her, they were not afraid. She stiffened her posture and returned their salutes, quelling her feelings of despair and pride. Before she could say another word, her aide, Brother Jerome, appeared from a separate corridor. Through his helmet, she could make out the dull-colored orange putty physiologically attached to his neck just below his left ear—a nanite cauterizer. There were still streaks of dark ruby around the wound and down the neck. Whatever had hit him had obviously been nasty.

"Admiral," he said through the helmet-to-helmet comm, "I have a room ready for pressurization per your request."

"And the council?" asked Christina.

"Waiting."

Christina nodded silently and followed the brother a short distance down the corridor from which he'd originally emerged. She entered a small room with a Spartan table at its center and a number of mismatched chairs around it. A small holo-tank was mounted to the ceiling. There were two people standing and waiting for her, both in battle-scarred space suits. Christina greeted the visitors with a warm smile and invited them to have a seat. As she sat down, her head-up display informed her that the room was pressurizing. A moment later, the HUD gave her an all-clear signal.

"Never thought I'd love the smell of fresh, processed air," quipped Colonel Mark Benyair, lifting his helmet up and flipping it back behind his head on specially fitted hinges. As Christina flipped back her helmet, the colonel gave a brief nod in lieu of a salute, acceding to his boss's demand for informal war councils. The other person, helmet flung back, had no difficulty following that rule. Her name was Marion Janusz, and she was a civ. In fact, Marion had become the effective leader of the entire civilian population caught in the backwash of Alliance defeat. By her most recent estimation, the number of civs hung at about ten thousand. Marion also had the distinction of being from "old" money—for all the good it was doing her now. Her father was Harold Janusz IV, a major shareholder in American Express and dozens of other companies, including GCI. He'd been less than pleased to discover that his only daughter had not only refused to end her grand tour of the solar system at the Outer Alliance's inception, but had also stayed on to become one of its more vocal citizens.

Though Christina usually found her to be a pain in the ass, detecting the ever-present tone of a superior education and pampered upbringing, there was no denying the woman's integrity. The problem was that Marion would show up only when she needed something, and she always seemed to need what Christina couldn't spare. But whether through persistence or Marion's ability to successfully exploit Christina's guilt, the blue-blooded heiress almost always managed to get what she asked for. Whenever Christina had the urge to throw the insufferable do-gooder out an air lock, she remembered what mattered most. Marion was one of the more vocal supporters of the war and Outer Alliance, and by virtue of her well-heeled upbringing and the notoriety therein, she'd also been one of the most eloquent and articulate spokespersons for their cause. All of which now made the malodorous fumes emanating from her space suit seem even more out of place.

Colonel Benyair's eyebrows shot up in surprise the second Marion's helmet had flipped open, but he otherwise gave no indication of the truly impressive aroma that had quickly filled the room.

Christina was not so charitable. "Christ and Allah, Marion, what the hell happened to your sanitizers?"

Marion gave a one-sided grin. "The suit's really old, and frankly it was lose the sanitizers or lose the scrubbers. I like breathing a lot more than I like smelling pretty. Besides," she said dismissively, "after a while you don't even notice."

"Trust me, Marion," taunted Christina, "*you* may not notice, but you'd better believe everyone else does."

Marion looked over to Mark, who shrugged his shoulders and gave her a small, bland smile.

"Wait a minute," added Christina. "Didn't Mosh send you a new suit? It was a combat engineer model, if I remember correctly. Light and maneuverable as all hell. And that," she said, eyeing Marion's battered gear, "certainly ain't it."

Marion smiled reminiscently. "Oh yeah, that *was* a great suit. I swear I could've lived six months in that thing and come out smelling like a rose."

"Let me guess," opined the colonel, "the cards weren't quite as good as you thought."

"If only!" sighed Marion longingly. "It's been months since I've been in a good game."

"And I think I was in that one," laughed Benyair. "If I recall, you won three months of emergency rations from me . . . on a bluff."

"You're not fooling anyone, Benny," scoffed Marion, using his nickname. "You knew I was bluffing and whom those supplies would go to, so you're just going to have to man up and admit you're a better person than you want your men to believe."

The colonel's mouth opened in mock surprise. He said nothing but showed a toothy grin.

"Okay, so you didn't lose it gambling," prompted Christina, "but I'll have you know your 'uncle' Mosh went to a lot of trouble to get that thing here."

"And don't think I didn't appreciate it," replied Marion, sincerity evident in her voice.

"Stolen, then?" asked Christina.

"Hell no. Traded."

"For what?"

Marion pointed to her decrepit space suit. "This."

Christina shook her head. "I honestly don't know why I bother."

"Believe me, Christina," stated Marion with equanimity, "the woman it went to needed it far more than I. Had something like nine kids she'd taken in—half of them suspended in jury-rigged freezers that needed constant attending. So yeah, I'll admit I stink. Small price to pay for kids getting to live."

"Fair trade in my book," said the colonel with a nod of admiration.

Christina sighed. Once again, Marion's gentle resolve had been uncompromising, and her heartstring logic could brook no argument.

"I'll see if Brother Jerome can send a tech over to at least fix the thing before we depressurize." Christina began inputting the request into her DijAssist.

"Why, thank you, Admiral."

"I'm not doing it for you," sniffed Christina.

The trio laughed and then the room fell silent. The small talk had been a welcome respite, but they all knew what they were there for.

"We should begin," started Christina almost as an apology.

The other two nodded.

"We've lost the heavy rail gun emplacements on the entrant's side of the asteroid and my engineers tell me there's no way to move the operational guns to different emplacements in less than twelve hours."

"We don't have twelve hours, sir."

"I know, Mark." Christina activated the holo-tank and pointed to a flurry of activity around the enemy fleet, "I'd say Trang'll launch his marine assault force in less than two."

Marion's smile was lackadaisical. "So much for fixing my suit."

Christina chortled. "Yeah," she admitted, "I might've been a little too optimistic on that count."

The group laughed again but there was little joy in it.

"We have three thousand battle-hardened assault miners," said Benyair, staring at the holo-tank, "with most of their gear intact. In fact, I'd bet Marion's space suit"—he sported a smarmy grin—"that they may be the very best fighters in the entire solar system. We'll make those corporate bastards pay, Admiral. For every damned particle on this Godforsaken rock."

Christina closed the visual. "I have no doubt about that, Mark. But Trang will launch twenty thousand marines in the first wave and, if he doesn't achieve victory, fifty thousand more in the second. And as you're well aware by his recent transmission, there will be no military prisoners taken alive. . . . You can thank my boyfriend for that." Her face drained of color momentarily as she thought back on Omad and all the plans they'd made for their future. *I'm sorry, my love . . . so very sorry,* she thought.

"We don't scare easy, Admiral."

"I know, Mark. But you have to realize that the capture of Altamont is just too important. Once Trang returns this asteroid to full function and then converts it into a UHF outpost, it becomes a powerful symbol."

Marion had a quizzical look. "Of what, Admiral? That he captured a useless rock?"

"No, Marion. That he captured *this* useless rock—Altamont, mighty fortress of the Alliance."

"Not to mention," piped in the colonel, "that once it's back up and running, it represents a significant and continuing threat to the Alliance."

Marion's face registered shock as she realized where the conversation was headed. "Are you suggesting, Admiral, that we . . . that we blow the place up?"

"Yes, Marion." Christina's eyes were aglow with fiery determination. "That's exactly what I'm suggesting."

Colonel Benyair remained calm, nodding in slow, easy movements at his commander's suicide order.

"But . . . but . . . ," stammered Marion, "what about the civilians?"

"They aren't civilians anymore," said the colonel in a voice suddenly devoid of emotion. "Alhambra changed everything."

"He's right, Marion," affirmed Christina. "This is war, and they were un-lucky enough to get stuck on my rock. I've already given the orders for the charges to be set. Brother Jerome is handling that personally even as we speak. There is, however, one outstanding issue. . . ."

"Yes?" asked Marion, flustered but functioning.

"The children."

A deathly pall hung in the air.

"Right," sighed Marion, her head nodding plaintively. "What are our op-tions?"

"Trang's ruthless, but not evil," asserted Christina. "If I tell him we're eject-ing our suspended children and other civs, launch them away from his ships, he won't kill them out of hand. When it's over, he'll recover the suspendees and see that they're not harmed."

"Then that's what we should do," said Benyair, satisfied that at least someone was going to make it off the rock in one piece.

Marion, noticed Christina, hadn't jumped at the idea. Instead, the woman sat motionless with only her eyes revealing a struggle with some inner demon.

"No," Marion finally whispered.

"What?" Christina's head was cocked in disbelief.

"We'd be dooming them."

"And dying here would be better than being captured by Trang . . . exactly how?" protested Benyair. He seemed more annoyed than impassioned. Saving the children would have been a noble last act. Marion was robbing him of his consolation prize.

"Because, Benny . . . Christina," Marion said, making sure to look hard into both her colleagues' eyes, "our children won't be captured by Admiral Trang, they'll be captured by Hektor Sambianco and Tricia Pakagopolis."

"Well, yeah . . . maybe eventually," said Benyair, "but—"

"But nothing, Benny!" Marion seethed. "What do you think those monsters will do with the only survivors of Altamont?"

Her question was met with blank stares.

"Each and every one of them," she asserted, voice thick with anger, "will have their souls ripped out via psyche audit in some UHF facility. And when they next make their appearance among the living—if such a word can be applied," she said acidly, "they won't be the same children who left this facility, on this the final day of Altamont. They'll be Sambianco's automata, filled with whatever constructs that bastard wants. But make no mistake," she said, eyes beginning to well up, "our children—" She now leaned into the table, grabbing its edge for support as her body slumped forward under the weight of the sentence she was about to pronounce. "—*my* children . . . will be just as dead as if we kept them here."

Christina could feel the edges of her teeth pressing up against her stiffened lips. She wanted to scream but held back. She was desperately trying to find some flaw in Marion's logic, some reason, some plan that would let the children live, that would have Hektor Sambianco be magnanimous, but . . . but . . . Neela. Justin Cord's wife, kidnapped, psyche audited, and now the rumored sexual plaything of the Alliance's greatest enemy. Used for propaganda purposes. And she was just one among many. Though Justin had fought on until the very end, everyone knew how Neela's psychological death had broken him in some unseen way. *No,* thought Christina sadly. *There is no other option.* If the children could be exploited—and Christina knew they could—Hektor Sambianco would find a way, just as he had with Neela, just as he had with anyone unlucky enough to have fallen into his clutches. She could not . . . *would* not deliver Altamont's children gift-wrapped to a monster like Sambianco. Christina looked to Colonel Benyair. He inclined his head disconsolately. Marion's cold logic had apparently struck twice.

"Very well," said Christina, voice taut but resolute. "They stay."

Three hours later, Trang's final assault on Altamont began. Twenty thousand marines landed at the entry port and made it half a kilometer into the mighty rock before they were stopped cold by Altamont's inner defensive fortifications. But these troops were more experienced than Trang's earlier recruits and didn't run at the first sign of trouble; they pressed forward. Shortly thereafter, the whittled-down contingent of marines was met by Colonel Benyair's three thousand well-armed assault miners. It didn't take the invading force's commander long to realize he'd need reinforcements. He ordered an entrenchment and called it in. Trang happily obliged and threw a fresh division of thirty thousand more troops into the fray with orders for an additional fifty thousand to stand at the ready. But as the ships carrying the thirty thousand troops drew near the rock's entry point, the embattled and teetering fortress disappeared in a brilliant flash of light, described by some as brighter than a thousand suns. When the light faded, so too had Altamont.

And now Altamont, thought J. D. Black, sitting alone in the dimly lit Triangle Office. She was playing with a Newton's cradle on Justin's . . . *her* desk, watching in quiet detachment as the five evenly strung silver balls clacked from end to end. Though the two-thirds gravity slowed their rhythm down a tad, the device still performed its task with methodical purpose. J.D. noted the inscription written at its base:

> To Justin Cord, First President of the Outer Alliance. May the principle of this mechanism, the laws of conservation, of momentum, forever abide in your new path toward freedom.

It was etched with the signature of the former President's Chief of Staff, Cyrus Anjou. She gurgled a small laugh at the perversity of it all. Everything seemed to have come to a crashing halt. The 180, Justin, Alhambra . . . Altamont . . . and if the previous day's incident on the loading bay were any indicator, reason itself. That she would never see Christina Sadma again in this life had also been a terrible blow. And a lifetime spent without faith made it even harder for her to accept the death of her friend with the grace and certainty she'd witnessed of her mentor, Fawa Hamdi, or J.D.'s personal chaplain, Brother Sampson. Even if she wanted to mourn, she wouldn't have had time. The news of Altamont's fall had swept through the Alliance like a gravitational wave, and Mosh wasted no time in exploiting it. He'd called for a full Cabinet meeting in five hours' time, the outcome of which was so patently obvious that J.D. had, in her own private rebellion, simply walked in and taken Justin's seat, ceremony be damned. And even that little victory would prove meaningless because in the end, there *would* be a ceremony. Protocol demanded it, and more than anything, the Alliance needed it. She understood that now and had long since given up trying to circumvent the implacable will of destiny.

Her black mood was not helped by the sight of her aide, Marilynn, entering the room unannounced with a large stack of folders. The room's lighting system brightened automatically. The captain was as surprised to see her boss sitting in the President's chair as J.D. was to see her number two prepping the office for an act that had yet to be officially sanctioned.

"A little overzealous, aren't we, Captain?" snorted J.D., glad to have a target for her foul mood.

"You should talk," parried Marilynn with uncharacteristic humor, eyeing the chair more than the person sitting in it. She then summarily dumped the folders on the desk.

"Touché." J.D. forced an uneasy grin, viewing with further consternation the large stack. The fact that it was all hard copy presumably spoke to the delicate nature of the information—or maybe not. It was quite possible that the pile was emblematic of a paper disease that had briefly infected her fleet. Paper meant "important," so anyone feeling they had a pressing issue would invariably issue their order on the stuff. It had gotten so bad that at one point J.D. publicly threatened to space any signatory of a paper directive who couldn't prove that what they were asking for was somehow essential to the very lifeblood of the Alliance itself. Paper documents fell off pretty quickly after that. Though J.D. suspected it had as much to do with Nitelowsen screening the reports as it did with the bureaucrats showing restraint. J.D. was about to rib her number two for having let the current pile through when she saw that Marilynn, still standing at attention, was doing her utmost to retain her composure. The normally unflappable captain had clearly been affected by the recent turn of events. J.D. sighed and invited Marilynn to sit down. Then she remembered that Justin kept a small bar behind the large Alliance flag draping one of the walls. She got up from behind the desk, went to the flag, and drew it back.

"Yes!" J.D. exclaimed, seeing her pleasure translated on Marilynn's face. She reached behind the bar, grabbed the first bottle she touched, and then glancing at the label, gave it a respectful nod. "It's real, Marilynn," she said, returning to the desk with the bottle and two glasses.

"Wouldn't expect any less, boss. Justin wouldn't drink synthetic."

"No," laughed J.D. as she settled into her chair, "I don't suppose he would."

She uncorked the bottle and poured Marilynn a tall glass. Because J.D.'s religion prohibited any alcohol, she left hers empty—there more for symbolic camaraderie than anything else. Marilynn reached across the desk, grabbed the full glass, and knocked it back in one gulp.

Her eyes bulged. "Holy crap!" she blurted through gasps of air.

A faint smile appeared on J.D.'s face. "Too strong?"

"Let's just say if they could sell smoke as a liquid, I'm pretty sure that would be it."

J.D. suppressed a laugh. "Cut it out, Marilynn," she said, pouring another glass. "I'm supposed to be making *you* feel better. Remember?"

"Trust me, sir," squeaked Marilynn, raising her glass to toast her boss's observation, "you are." The second shot went down smoother. Then her voice broke. "I . . . I'm going to miss them, Admiral."

"Me too, Marilynn."

"They died bravely, boss."

"That, they did. I just wish I could've done more to help."

"Admiral," offered Marilynn, "contrary to popular belief, you don't actually have superpowers."

"No?" returned J.D. in mock surprise. "Haven't you heard, Marilynn? I'm the Blessed One. Able to make the enemy do what I want just by talking to them."

Marilynn put her hand to her mouth, giggling.

"And don't you know"—J.D. was clearly enjoying the self-deprecation—"I have a soooooper seeeeecret DijAssist in my cabin that enables me to read the minds of my enemies."

"And don't forget," added Marilynn, "raise the dead."

"Oh yeah. Totally forgot about that. If only I'd used the damned thing on Justin, I could be out there kicking ass instead of stuck in here having to kiss it."

An awkward silence hung over the pair.

"Stories, sir," offered Marilynn, "passing fancies to amuse bored miners."

"Or replace faith," added J.D. in all seriousness.

"Whatever works, sir."

J.D. nodded. "If only they weren't . . . stories. It would make winning the war a whole lot easier." She then shot Marilynn a purposeful look. "Feeling any better?"

"Little, sir. Guess it'll take some time." She straightened up in the chair and grabbed an inhaler from an inside pocket. Then, bringing it up to her mouth, activated a button. She absorbed the burst and seconds later was stone-cold sober. The nanite formula affectionately referred to as HOD, for "hair of the dog," was standard military issue. The clear message being, you can play hard, as long as you're ready to fight hard—instantly.

"And thank you, sir." Marilynn slipped the canister back into her pocket.

J.D. gave an authoritative nod. "So what have we here?" she asked, glancing at the pile on her desk.

"Mostly Altamont related, Admiral."

"Anything I don't already know?"

"That you really *need* to know?" Marilynn's slight upturned lip and shaking head was all the answer J.D. required.

"See, Captain? This job might actually be easier than we both imagined. What else?"

Marilynn thought for a moment and then pulled out a thick folder from the bottom of the pile. "This," she said, offering the folder to her boss, "is our analysis of the suspension unit Justin found."

J.D.'s folded arms didn't budge. "Summarize, please."

Nitelowsen obediently pulled back the folder, flipped it open, and placed it in her lap without bothering to look down. "The occupant is a woman. She appears to be in her early to mid-sixties and, as currently suspended, appears to have an aggressive form of dementia. The brain scan shows massive impairment of cognitive faculties."

"Memories?" asked J.D.

"Intact . . . apparently." Marilynn almost sounded surprised. She then added as an aside, "Her last weeks of life must have been disorienting, to say the least."

"I'll bet. Anything else?"

Marilynn smiled mischievously, "Oh, yes . . . we have a name."

"And it is?"

"Sandra O'Toole."

J.D.'s brow arched up. "Why does that sound so familiar?"

"Because it is. Remember President Cord's first interview with Michael Veritas."

"That's right!" recalled J.D., hand slapping down on the table. "She's the one who suspended Justin."

"Not just suspended, Admiral," corrected Marilynn, pulling a sheet of paper from the folder and sliding it across the desk, "made the suspension unit itself."

J.D. looked over the document. It contained a brief outline of Sandra's myriad achievements leading up to her death. The creation of the suspension chamber, patent references and all, was just one item on a long and impressive list.

"Smart cookie," noted J.D.

"Very," returned Marilynn. "At least smart enough to have built a second unit and have someone toss her in."

"When do they intend to wake her up?" asked J.D., handing the sheet of paper back to Marilynn.

"Dunno." Marilynn tucked the document neatly back into the folder. "I suppose whenever you decide."

"Me?" objected J.D. "I've got enough on my plate, thank you. Give this one to a specialist."

"Already have. They don't want the headache."

"What headache, Marilynn? Pardon my Erosian, but isn't that their fucking job?"

"Reanimation, yes. Religion, no."

"Oh, you have got to be kidding me." A look of disbelief swept across her face. "Please tell me you're kidding me."

Marilynn shook her head sympathetically. "We've actually had to increase security just to keep people from touching the 'holy object.'"

J.D. laughed. "You'd have thought the shrine they made out of Justin's empty suit would've kept them satisfied."

"I think," countered Marilynn, "people need all the good luck and divine presence they can get. You, better than most, should realize that."

"Batting a thousand today," snickered J.D., conceding the point. "You sure that was HOD you inhaled there?"

"Quite. Anyhow, from what I've heard, all the security personnel and lab technicians have stopped by at some point just to touch the thing."

"And what about you?" asked J.D. She got an immediate answer in the blood that rushed to Marilynn's face. "My god, you have. That *is* interesting."

"I know it sounds weird, Admiral, but that woman *is* special. She gave us the One Free Man, knew Justin before any of us. She is of his time. Maybe even like him in some little way. I know it's too much to hope. . . . No one can really replace Justin, sir, but it feels good . . . to hope. Does that make sense?"

J.D. put her hand on the scarred side of her face and exhaled deeply. "More than you can imagine. . . . All right, you've convinced me. Keep our holy woman in the pile. I'm sure we'll get to her eventually."

"Sir." Marilynn nodded and placed the folder back in the bottom of the stack.

"But, as pleasant a distraction as this woman is, we're going to have to start figuring out how to prosecute this war with me behind this desk and you by my side."

Marilynn inclined her head in agreement. "We could always draw a smiley face on the suspension unit and prop it up right about where you're sitting."

J.D. chortled at the image. "It would certainly have more personality."

"And," added Marilynn conspiratorially, "if we keep the lights dim, maybe no one would notice." She then did a mock J.D. voice. "Sorry, can't make the ceremony today, feeling a little . . . stiff."

They both burst out into a fit of laughter. But about twenty seconds into the outburst, Marilynn noticed that she was laughing alone. J.D. sat in stunned silence. A maniacal look permeated every inch of her face. Eyes wide, jaw slightly ajar, she turned her focus to her now worried number two. J.D. began snapping her fingers in anxious demand. "The folder, Marilynn!" she ordered.

Without hesitation, Marilynn retrieved it and handed it back across the desk. This time, J.D. perused every page and took her time doing it. After a few minutes of reading, J.D. returned the documents and closed the cover, satisfied.

"Call the suspension lab, Marilynn. Tell them—" J.D hesitated. "—tell them it's time."

"For what, Admiral?"

J.D. smiled defiantly.

"For the Unincorporated Woman to save my ass."

A Bleak and Bitter Morning

The Unincorporated Man Is Dead!
Celebrations Break Out System Wide!

Although there had been rumors of his death, the number of previously failed attempts on Justin Cord's life made the press corps of the UHF leery of giving them much stock. But news sources in the rebellious outer reaches have confirmed what so many have hoped so long for: The Unincorporated Man is dead. News reports picked up from the Outer Alliance state that his death was either the result of an unfortunate accident or a successful assassination. Given how many loathed the Alliance's Chief Instigator, it seems pretty obvious to this news organization which of the two it was. With the death of the man who has been at the heart of this, the most destructive war in the history of the human race, celebration has broken out in all the worlds of the UHF. The gatherings on Earth, Luna, and Mars have been particularly exuberant. They've even surpassed the elation caused by Admiral Trang's stunning victory at the 180. A victory which, we hasten to add, split the Belt down the middle and saw the death of one of the enemy's greatest admirals, Christina Sadma.

Indeed, the celebrations over the death of the Unincorporated Man are so raucous as to be compared to Mardi Gras. Although some members of the UHF assembly feel it unseemly to celebrate while the war continues, others are encouraging the revelry and calling for the assassination to be marked as a system holiday.

Between the death of Justin Cord and our great and decisive victory at the 180, well over five years of horrific warfare may finally be coming to an end. Some politicians are even suggesting the President call for peace now that it should be obvious to even the most die-hard Alliance fanatic that victory is hopeless. Others insist the President fight out the war to an unconditional surrender in order to make the cost of rebellion so high as to remove its threat from future generations. President Sambianco has remained silent on this issue but is enjoying the renewed support that has eluded him in recent years. It's even rumored that a movement to change the constitution is being organized so that the President can *run for reelection in two years' time, when his six-year term expires. When asked how he felt about the assassination, the President had this to say:*

> *An evil, scheming man has died and we have won a great victory. It is right to celebrate the great achievements that our industry, bravery, and endurance have granted us. I myself plan to get as drunk as a wartime president might be allowed—HOD nearby, of course. The truth is we've earned it and I'm proud of all the citizens of the UHF who've struggled so hard and lost so much over these past five years. What we're doing is for the good of the entire human race, and our incorporated system will be preserved for all the children of humanity forevermore. So let us enjoy this time of respite. Just don't forget that the rebellion Justin Cord inspired is still fighting against the principles of incorporation and humanity. After our brief celebration, we must—we will—finish what they started. Nothing will stand in the way of our ultimate victory.*

> *NNN*

The lab J.D. now viewed was typical of what she'd come to think of as "Alliance practical." To be Alliance practical, the place or object or person had to follow a couple of simple rules. First, it had to have obviously been something else prior to its current usage: a luxury yacht serving as a hospital ship or a space tug, for instance. Second, it had to be something that only years of warfare would make acceptable, like the use of children in busing tables so the droids normally given the task could be stationed elsewhere in the war effort. And third, the place, object, or person had to really make a lot of sense when viewed through the eyes of the war weary.

Thus it was that Admiral J. D. Black stood in the luxurious environs of what had once been the finest French restaurant in Ceres and possibly the whole of the Outer Alliance. It had been called La Fontaine Bleue, and was located in the lunar level of Ceres, so called because it was placed far enough from the Via Cereana to give the level a gravity one-sixth that of Earth's and therefore equal to Earth's moon, known as Luna. If anyone prior to the war had told her that the restaurant would make a perfect spot for the advanced cryostasis laboratory and research facility, J.D. would have laughed out loud.

But now she saw the logic in the decision. The restaurant was on a level that would not be getting much use otherwise, as its greatest appeal had been to those from Luna, firmly in the UHF camp. And for obvious reasons, tourism from that region had not been a moneymaker for a number of years. The restaurant's loss had been the Alliance's gain. The low gravity made it easier to move equipment and corpses, but without the hassles that came from moving large objects in zero gravity, where things never seemed to stay put unless battened down. The restaurant had been a large three-story affair with lots of separate dining areas for special events and parties, all of which made it easy to turn those cavernous spaces into specialized labs. And because it was already zoned for the highest privacy standards, given its former clientele, it made further securing of the lab quite easy. The former restaurant also had an excellent power transmission and backup system, so that no patron would ever be inconvenienced by the slightest delay in communication or service. The eatery's new name, Le Cadavre Bleu, was a little morbid, but, mused J.D., that was laboratory techs for you.

She and Captain Nitelowsen walked down a few corridors, finally ending up in a large conference room much unchanged from the restaurant's initial setup. The small chamber had apparently been needed for the planning sessions required to host the restaurant's myriad events. And as no functioning body, both corporeal and corporate, had yet figured out a way to survive without the need for a meeting, the room had stayed mostly untouched. J.D. had called an emergency Cabinet session and arranged for the Unincorporated Woman's suspension unit to be moved into the room, feeling its presence might in some way influence the donnybrook she knew was coming. Upon entering the chamber, J.D.'s eyes immediately fell upon the green-etched, black sarcophagus. She stared at it with such intensity that her ever-present aide thought her boss might be trying to wake the body inside by force of will alone. When J.D. and Marilynn heard the voices of people approaching, they immediately took their seats, as J.D. had wanted a better view by which to gauge the reactions of those entering.

The first to arrive was Kirk Olmstead. The former deputy director of GCI Special Operations had become a natural fit for the Secretary of Security, and J.D. had to grudgingly admit he was doing an excellent job. But she never liked or trusted the guy, either from the days they served together on the board of GCI or now. He retained his corporate good looks but wore an outfit that fairly screamed Alliance patriot. Gone were the expensive five-piece suits made from the latest nanoweave fabrics. In were the gray coveralls that proclaimed propriety and efficiency. He gave the suspension unit a momentary glance, then shot J.D. a look that was both curious and hostile. The lack of affection went both ways, but he couldn't suppress the curiosity sparked by the locale chosen for the meeting and the surprise floating quietly on a maglev within it.

Next to enter was Cyrus Anjou, Justin's Chief of Staff. His mood, like everyone's of late, was less than upbeat. The enormity of the situation was made more pronounced by the fact that Cyrus, normally ebullient in the toughest of times, appeared gaunt and moribund. He barely noticed the unit as he walked through the door. What scant attention he gave it dismissed it as yet another prop in yet another room in yet another meeting.

By Allah, has he actually lost weight? wondered J.D.

The loss of Justin had crushed something in the man's soul. He continued to do his job, but only with the mechanical action born of instinct rather than passion. When Padamir Singh, the Secretary of Information, came in and looked with concern upon his Jovian sparring partner, J.D. knew that something would need to be done. Padamir was a Cerean from a wealthy and politically connected family who had a famous relationship with Cyrus based on deep affection and public insults. The fact that he was now treating his friend with kid gloves let J.D. know just how serious the situation was. After Cyrus, Padamir glanced at the unit, his face placid. He'd long ago trained himself to hold off on opinion, whether verbally or nonverbally, lest he give anything away prior to making a reasoned assessment.

Joshua Sinclair, her official boss both as Grand Admiral of the Outer Alliance and Secretary of Defense, came in with Hildegard Rhunsfeld, the Secretary of Technology. Although Hildegard usually arrived with Mosh McKenzie, it had been technological audacity almost as much as chicanery that had kept the UHF at bay, and as such, Sinclair and Hildegard had been spending a lot more time together. They too noticed the suspension unit but, like Padamir, kept their feelings from view. Unlike Padamir, their reasons were more pedestrian. They didn't care until they were told they had to. When Mosh finally arrived, his eyes darted quickly from the sarcophagus to J.D., showing obvious displeasure at both. Without bothering to sit down, he fixed a persistent and angry glare at the fleet admiral. *That was quick,* mused J.D.

Before the meeting could be called to order, Mosh blurted, "It's not going to work, J.D."

"What's not going to work?" asked Hildegard, oblivious to Mosh's opening hostility.

"Please, Janet," invited Mosh disdainfully, "fill us in on your *brilliant* plan."

J.D. looked with some satisfaction on the small group gathered around her.

"We're going to wake up our three-hundred-year-old jack-in-the-box over here..." Janet glanced over her shoulder. "...and spring her right into the Presidency."

The room exploded in protest. Janet remained unmoved by the cacophony but was intrigued by Padamir's reaction. He remained quiet, looking at her in a manner she couldn't ever recall having seen from him before—admiration.

"Janet," sputtered Mosh, "of all the harebrained—"

"What makes you think," interjected Kirk, "that this woman could possibly be President?"

The room went silent, as all eyes fixed on J.D.

"If I thought for a moment she was actually capable of being President, I'd keep her frozen for the next thousand years. The reason I *do* want her is precisely because she's *not* capable of being President."

Padamir's face registered the confusion everyone seemed to feel. "And this," he finally said, "will help us survive the war, how?"

With a brief hand movement J.D. flung the latest headlines into the center of the table's holo-display. They floated above the table for a moment before fading from view. "As you can see, she's already being hailed as the Unincorporated Woman, and some of the religious are even calling for her to be awakened in order to fulfill God's divine plan."

"Is that what this is all about?" interjected Cyrus. "Are we to be saved by *your* god?"

"Don't be so melodramatic, Cyrus. Of course not . . . and she's not my god. She's everyone's . . . whoever wants her, that is."

"It was you who raised the point, Admiral," returned Cyrus, "not I."

"I raised the point only to show you that there's a desire to have her out of that thing. You know me, Cyrus. I leave my god on the sidelines when it comes to leading but keep her close by when it comes to fighting."

"Indeed I do," agreed Cyrus, "but you more than most know that those headlines represent the desperate ramblings of a desperate people. They'd do anything, say anything, just to fill the void left by the President's death. Even as we speak, many are already making a 'pilgrimage' to his space suit."

"Of course I understand that," thundered J.D. "What's your point?"

"I'd have thought it would be obvious. My point is that the polity is simply not capable of making a rational choice. It does not become us to feed into their mania with—" His eyes shifted over to the suspension unit. "—false hope."

J.D. paused before answering. When she finally spoke, it was with a conviction born of exigency.

"The Alliance needs hope, Cyrus. It needs it very badly. So badly, in fact, that they could give a flying crap whether it's false or not. You don't think they know that a three-hundred-year-old reanimated corpse will make a lousy President? They do. But they won't care, because as you so eloquently stated, they'll take their hope wherever they can get it."

Kirk cleared his throat, drawing all eyes upon himself. "It's a fine idea . . . *for the people*, Admiral, but not so much for the Congress. And we both know who really runs things around here. If you ask me, they'll never go along with this—especially if there's no upside."

"Of course they will, Kirk," countered J.D. "Especially if we let the various factions know that our newly awakened President is just the sort of person needed to help them achieve greater influence."

"I don't see how—" started Kirk.

Padamir Singh smiled, tipping his head slightly toward Kirk, who respectfully demurred.

"Each will believe," said Padamir, "that they'll have greater influence over the figurehead president and so, by the prospects of greater self-aggrandizement, will allow her into the office." He considered his words a few moments more and for a second time viewed J.D. with admiration. "That just might work."

"This is idiocy," growled Mosh. "We need a President who can actually govern, not one who'll *be* governed." Then added a moment later, "As if we weren't in enough trouble."

"No, Mosh," J.D. countered, "what we need is a President who can restore hope and prevent panic. Yes, I can do that." She then pointed to the suspension unit with a sweep of her arm. "But so can the Unincorporated Woman."

"I don't see how," started Mosh, echoing Kirk.

"By playing it right."

"And I suppose," said Mosh in a tone scathing enough to peel paint, "you've already got that figured out."

J.D. nodded, ignoring the sarcasm. "She's the woman who prepared Justin for his long sleep and then followed him into the future. She was found just as he disappeared, and she's clearly capable, having made it this far. She's the only other human being in history to have survived the Grand Collapse, and she did it while it was happening." J.D. paused a beat. "And that's the angle we have to push with the people. We'll stress the heroic and the miraculous over and over again until they can't tell the difference between the image and the individual. *She* is the new chosen one, here to lead."

"Don't think I wouldn't want this, Admiral," began Sinclair. "Because truly, if there's anyone in this room your crazy idea would work for, it's me. But I just don't see the people of the Alliance falling for an obvious stand-in."

"Finally," groused Mosh, "a voice of reason."

J.D. ignored the outburst, looking straight at her commanding officer. "I agree with your assessment, sir. No one would expect her to pop out and hit the ground running. But we can work with that because of greater concern to the people is, as stated before, a figure of hope. Don't you see? We can have our cake and eat it too. We can give them their hope, and give the fleet back its admiral. They'll make that leap of faith, sir. Of that I'm sure."

"But why should we?" insisted Sinclair. "Again, I'm not trying to get rid of you. Damsah knows I need you. But it seems pretty obvious, Janet, from the machinations of this meeting alone, you'd make a fine President. In some ways, with all due respect, better than Justin."

"Maybe I would, sir. And I thank you for the compliment, undeserving as I think it may be. But we don't need a 'fine' President right now, just a fine figurehead. However, what we do need is damned fine admiral. I keep on saying this, but for some reason, no one seems to be listening. So allow me to spell it out." She rose from her seat and leaned over the table, placing the palms of her hands on its surface. "Trang is coming. You may be able to put that thought on your back burners, but I don't have the luxury of putting it on mine. He's coming, and I'll need to beat him on the front lines in order to win this war. And yes, even with all the shit that's gone down, we can still win this thing. But I must prepare, starting now—something I won't be able to do strapped to the Presidential chair. What I can do from that chair is give hope. But guess what?" asked J.D., standing up, walking over, and placing one hand on the suspension unit. "So can she. I say we thaw this bitch out and prop her ass up so I can go win this fucking war."

Only the silent hum of the forced air system could be heard as abject silence followed on her words. Eyes flittered back and forth as each person ruminated on the proposal and checked with one another for an indication of opinion.

"Okay," a soft voice finally murmured.

J.D. nodded in relief. *That's two.*

Everyone looked at Hildegard. She seemed a little flustered by the sudden attention but soldiered on. "Your argument is sound, Admiral, and I'm even prepared to back it up, but I must know how you plan on bringing her out."

"Come again?" asked J.D.

"Well, quite frankly, the stats don't bode well." Hildegard looked down at her DijAssist. "Sandra, or whatever her real name is, froze herself with the onset of dementia during the Grand Collapse, presumably hoping to find a cure, a stable future, and in all likelihood, her boss—one very deceased Justin Cord. She'll wake up millions of miles from the planet of her birth, and before she has a chance to pee will be told she's to take on the ceremonial leadership of an interstellar alliance that's in the process of losing a war." She nodded respectfully to J.D. "Predictions of our imminent victory notwithstanding."

J.D. returned the nod with a respectful, if somewhat caustic, glare.

"She'll find herself inside a world she knows nothing of," continued Hildegard, "and titular head to a people she has nothing in common with. Under the best of conditions, Admiral, a revival of this sort would prove challenging, to say the least. And we are clearly," she said, looking around at the leftover accoutrements of the Fontaine Bleue, "not anywhere near the best of conditions."

Back to one, thought Janet ruefully.

A slight upward crease formed at the corners of Mosh's mouth: a hound smelling blood. "Hildegard has a point, Janet. How do we bring this great 'hope' of yours up to speed without the proper facilities or even brain trust to do so? We may have the best fighting force in the system, but sadly the best and brightest minds with regards to this specialty happen to be on the other side of the line."

J.D. was momentarily stymied, having given no thought whatsoever to that aspect of her plan.

"I think I may be able help with that," chimed in Kirk with a bemused half grin. Janet's eyes shifted uneasily over to him. Hating that she'd been unprepared for the question. Hating even more that she'd owe Kirk . . . but only *if* he could pull it off.

"Don't look so surprised, Janet. I'm not enamored of you any more than you are of me. Nor, Damsah knows, would your taking the Presidency have made my life any easier. Still, up until this meeting, I too had been convinced that you were the only one capable of replacing Justin Cord as President. However, your argument is compelling and while Hildegard's point is well taken, it's not insurmountable." He paused, knowing full well that Mosh wouldn't ask for him to continue and that the others would wait. J.D. knew exactly the game Kirk was playing. He wanted her to ask. And so, seeing that no one else would, she did.

"Please go on, Kirk. We're all ears."

Kirk bent his head respectfully. "We have a dark operation that I'd prepared for various upper-echelon UHF officials. Dr. Thaddeus Gillette was one of them. In his particular case, it involved removing him and then making it appear as if he'd been an Alliance operative all along, nothing conclusive, but enough to cast doubt on all his work and associates. Now seems as good a time as any to implement it."

"Downsides?" asked Sinclair.

"It would mean losing an escape route out of the Core that so far appears to have gone undetected. Also, we'd be losing the services of three, maybe four well-placed operatives. Small price to pay, given what's at stake."

"Time frame?" demanded Sinclair, more as an order than as a query.

Kirk folded his arms, leaned back, and smiled like the cat who'd caught the canary. "I should be able to have the good doctor here in twenty-four to thirty-six hours."

Cyrus Anjou's face reddened and a small bulge of a vein could be seen forming on the right side of his temple. "If," he spat in Kirk's direction, "you can just wave your magic wand and bring the solar system's premier reanimation psychologist to Ceres *in a day,* how come you couldn't protect the President!"

Kirk leaned forward, both hands now on the table, and glared back at Cyrus. "I protected him for five years, you Jovian twit. But I couldn't protect the sanctimonious fool from himself. I *told him* not to go to Nerid, to send a forward team. But no, he insisted on going himself!"

"You are insulting our President," Cyrus shouted, standing up so quickly, his chair sailed back against the wall in the one-sixth gravity. Kirk stood up too, meeting the challenge. Before anyone else could react, Padamir jumped up and into the fray. He quickly put his hand on his friend's shoulder to calm him.

"Only by telling the truth, Cyrus. Justin should not have gone. He did so against all advice, and that is no one's fault but his own." Padamir gave Cyrus his own chair, and as he went to get the now discarded one, he kept talking to bring the conversation away from its tender spot. "I do not doubt that you can do as you say, Kirk. If you tell me that Thaddeus Gillette will be here in a day and a half, I will believe you. But I do not see how that does us any good." He brought the chair to his spot and sat down, inviting Kirk and Cyrus to do the same. They did so reluctantly. "Why would he bother to help us? After all, we'll have just kidnapped him."

"I may be able to help with that," offered J.D.

"This is nuts," fumed Mosh. "Maybe he will; maybe he won't. They want hope. They don't want hope. Maybe she'll pop out and be fine; maybe she'll be a raging lunatic. Forget maybe. Admiral Black is here now and has clearly had a palpable effect on bringing order back to the Alliance—as if her preventing yesterday's near religious riot weren't an indication. Why are we messing around with so many what if's and maybe's," he growled, pointing to J.D., "when we have what we need right here, right now? We all need to grow a pair, and Janet, you need to give up this charade and prepare for your inauguration. It's as simple as that."

"Whether this could work or not," interjected Cyrus, having recently regained his composure, "it seems to me that Justin would want this Sandra O'Toole to have the best chance at a successful revival. Why don't we see if Kirk can get Dr. Gillette to us, and then we can see if he'll help us? If not, then we inaugurate Admiral Black and, at worst, lose only a day or two."

The heads around the table slowly nodded; eventually even Mosh reluctantly agreed, though he was the last. With that, the meeting broke up. Kirk waited a few moments more, as Janet Delgado Black had sent him a private message requesting that he remain.

When they were alone and J.D. was confident that the room was secure, she spoke.

"You'd better deliver, Kirk."

"Why," he sniffed, "because you don't want to be in that office any more than I want you there? We've already been over that."

"No, Kirk, because whether you succeed or not, in two days, I'm waking the bitch up."

4 · The Doctor Is Out

Lisa Herman looked up at her selection in the cafeteria. She enjoyed eating in the main hall with the other patients, even though she'd once been one of them. Now cured of her post-traumatic stress disorder, she'd risen to the vaunted rank of assistant to the system-famous Dr. Neela Harper. The strange truth was that over time, it almost seemed as if Dr. Harper had become an assistant to her. In a little under a year, Lisa had gone from simple filing and appointment work to acquiring an emergency license in military revival techniques. It didn't make her a doctor nor did it allow her to work on particularly complex cases, but she'd become one of the most effective group leaders in the compound and had more practical experience with the reintegration of traumatized spacers than almost anyone around. That, and Dr. Harper's insistence that Lisa was needed at the hospital more than anywhere else, was what had kept Lisa's repeated requests for transfer back to combat duty from being accepted. And even though she was considered part of the staff, she still thought of herself as a spacer first and former patient second, which is probably why she was so good at helping the spacers under her care.

Today Lisa was waiting her turn at the processing slot and using her DijAssist to review the ingredients on the day's menu. It was a little quirk, certainly in an era when most trusted that even if they ate badly, medical science could compensate for the indiscretion, but it was a quirk Lisa felt defined her better and so she continued the habit, unabashed by the snickering of her peers. Yet even with her ritual observance, she almost missed the oddity.

The veggie burrito she'd finally settled on was using guacamole made with lymon, an ingredient she'd never heard of. While she was perturbed that a taste she'd gotten used to might now have a slightly different texture or flavor, it intrigued her nonetheless. She ordered the burrito special including soup and salad, took her plate, and found a seat in the cafeteria. She lifted the burrito to her mouth and stopped before taking a bite. A peculiar sensation had caught hold of her. It was something about that ingredient, that lymon. She wasn't exactly sure what it was, but the more she thought about it, the more subsumed she became. It was an odd sensation, almost erotic, in how good, how right it felt to say that word, "lymon," over and over again in her head. The repetition was leading to something—to what, she didn't know, only that she must repeat it in her mind until that something arrived. And then it did.

Wide-eyed, she stared out into the cafeteria, mouth slightly ajar, burrito still held firmly. To anyone watching, her mannerism might have indicated she'd forgotten what she was doing or conversely just remembered some arcane task she'd need to complete. What they would never guess was that Lisa Herman was no longer in the cafeteria, that she'd been replaced by another . . . the *other* within her. The *other* had never really gone away, but with a combination of meditation and hypnotherapy had been effectively suppressed. But now the *other* was waking up. The *other* took a bite of the burrito. It was good. She continued to eat. She was starving. Over the course of her meal, between the soup and the salad, the last vestiges of Lisa Herman finally disappeared. The *other* knew everything about Lisa and would act in no overt way differently from Lisa. But this *other* also knew she had a far more important task to complete, yet rather annoyingly had yet to determine exactly what that was.

After lunch, the *other* complained of a headache to her colleagues and arranged for someone to take her place leading that afternoon's therapy session. She then headed over to the infirmary. Once there, a helpful medic gave her a shot of aspirin and suggested she take the rest of the afternoon off. He also placed a small data crystal into her palm and used his hand to gently close her fingers around it. She gave him a curious look, but his warm smile and strangely soothing voice reassured her. He further suggested she give him a call later that day. *He has a nice smile,* thought the *other,* and so decided then and there to take him up on the offer. He pointed her in the direction of a local café and she went, like a leaf pulled along a stream by an unseen eddy, without protest. Once at the café, the *other* ordered a Turkish coffee and found a private booth in which to view the contents of the crystal. To her surprise, the message— displayed for less than a second—consisted of only three words: START SMART GRAB. As had happened earlier, she puzzled over the words, once again mesmerized. And then for the second time in as many hours, she was struck by a clarity of purpose. Only this time, she knew exactly what she was supposed to do. The patients were no longer her concern—the doctor was.

The woman known as Lisa got up from the booth and quickly exited the café. For the first time that day, she noticed the weather. It was early afternoon, and there was a cool breeze being funneled through the campus buildings. The cold air felt good against her face and somehow added purpose to the immediacy of her task. If all went well, she'd be leaving Mars in the next few hours. Visiting her apartment was out of the question.

The transit tube took her to downtown Burroughs in a little under ten minutes. The provincial city of over twenty million had grown into a major transportation hub that, as capital of the United Human Federation, had become responsible for the lives of nearly thirty-six billion. After President Sambianco had insisted on moving the capital from Earth to Mars, its rapid growth had been assured. In the brief span of five years, it had managed to get itself ordained as the most prefabricated city in human history. Even the Presidential complex was made of interchangeable hard foam that would normally have been used as offices for a temporary construction project.

But what should have been a prescription for a dull cityscape turned out to be anything but. The city's new immigrants, used to a certain level of culture and visual stimuli, had refused to take the drab material on its merits alone. So by virtue of a popular technique called flo-motion color injection, plus the addition of minor architectural trimmings, they'd managed to breathe visual life and energy into a material meant to be devoid of any. As such, Burroughs from above looked like a massive hodgepodge of seemingly independent, in-motion, colorful, and oddly geodesic structures. The intrinsic exuberance of the buildings was simpatico with the street musicians, food vendors, and souks selling everything from captured Alliance uniforms to exotic fruit kebabs. As in any great city, the sidewalks and fly zones were filled with a mad rush of people going to and fro, dressed in all manner of fashion from street chic to corporate cool.

The *other* loved the palpable energy of the place, especially the dwellers themselves, who had about them the quiet confidence of diplomats buoyed by the rightness of their mission. The *other* knew that Lisa loved it here too, but not for reasons that the *other* did. Lisa, like those busily passing by, actually believed in the UHF and what it stood for, while the *other* could not understand how they could all be so easily fooled. But that no longer mattered. She took a tube transport to Old Town, the artistic center of Burroughs and the only part of the city not prefabricated. It was off to the west, closer to the sea, and made up of two- and three-story buildings constructed by the original settlers. The *other* walked down a few alleys until she arrived at the place she was looking for: the John Carter Chess Club—a quaint establishment decorated like a Victorian gentlemen's smoke room but themed out to the famous Edgar Rice Burroughs character. Besides the decorative brass and leather trimmings, there were also mementos under glass, artwork on the wall, literature lining the shelves, and of course, a life-sized statue of the hero himself.

The club had made a name for itself even before the UHF's arrival transformed the once sleepy city. The atmosphere was relaxed, and its clientele were mainly of the upper class and, barring that, the filthy rich. The war alone had introduced a whole new category of scoundrel, the likes of which had not been seen in hundreds of years. The scoundrels were tolerated not only for their money but also because they performed a vital function—the movement of goods, people, and ordnance. The club, though, was private, and membership was by invitation only. There was still a large area open to the public, and this was where the *other*'s journey momentarily came to a halt. She took in the room. It was a warm and inviting space at the center of which was a large hearth piled high with burning logs. A few well-placed sofas and an ample number of brass-dimpled overstuffed leather chairs surrounded the fireplace. The din of visiting tourists ogling the life-sized sculpture of John Carter could be heard mixed in with the sporadic crackling of a falling log.

As Dr. Gillette was playing chess in one of the reserved areas of the club, the *other* had to wait patiently while being announced. A human messenger was sent—a DijAssist notification would have been too unbecoming—and a few minutes later, the *other* was gratified to see Dr. Gillette emerge from behind one of the many richly embroidered velvet curtains that separated the waiting room from the private areas.

His face beamed at the unexpected surprise. "My dear Ms. Herman," he exclaimed, "what on Mars brings you out here? Is everything all right?"

Her mouth formed an awkward smile. "I'm sorry for disturbing you, sir. Dr. Harper tells me how much you enjoy this time to yourself."

"Ms. Herman," he confided, inviting her over to some open chairs by the fireside, "you took me away from a game that had lost my interest."

"Because you were winning?" she asked.

"Actually," he said with a rueful grin, "I was being roundly thrashed by a player so much better than I that the only thing I was learning was abject humility. Inasmuch, I am now *humbly*"—his bushy eyebrow shot up as he stared at her—"in your debt. How may I be of assistance?"

The *other* feigned concern, slipping over her words. "We . . . I . . . um, I suppose we should use a good privacy booth."

"That will not be a problem, Ms. Herman. There are many good ones here. I'll just—"

"I was thinking someplace," she interrupted, biting her lower lip as her eyes darted about nervously, "less conspicuous, please. If you wouldn't mind, that is."

"I see." Dr. Gillette's amiable mood was replaced by appropriate concern. "Did you have someplace in mind?"

"The orport seems like a good place to get lost in a crowd, and . . . I—" She looked around nervously once again, then said in a tone so low, the doctor had to tilt his head forward to hear, "I think that would be best."

"If you don't mind my asking," he whispered back, "what's this about?"

"I . . . I think," the *other* replied, matching his tone, "that Dr. Harper and the . . . the President may be—"

Dr. Gillette put his hand on her shoulder and with a conspiratorial look indicated that she stop talking. "Let's wait till we're at the orport, shall we?"

"Of course, sir." The *other* allowed him to take the lead. "I'm sorry. I'm not very good at this cloak-and-dagger stuff."

"No reason why you should be, Ms. Herman." The doctor gently lifted her elbow prodding her to stand. "You were an electronics technician, if I recall . . . who became a military trauma revival specialist, yes?"

She nodded too eagerly, almost as if confessing to a crime.

"Well, then," he said with a reassuring glance, "I hardly see how this would equip you to the life of a spy."

The *other* smiled gratefully and stood waiting patiently as the doctor went and checked out his coat and an umbrella. When he returned, they headed out the door, where a taxi was already waiting. The flight over to the Burroughs Interstellar Orbital Port took about fifteen minutes. The orport, though new, was typical in its design—a large dome through which hundreds of tubes pulled in and shot out transorbital pods of various shapes and sizes.

As the *other* and the doctor entered the main lobby, they quickly located and then headed toward a row of dedicated privacy booths used mainly by the corporate class to conduct business on the fly. The *other* was fully aware that the entire area was under surveillance by the Internal Affairs Ministry but also knew that by the time anyone bothered to review the images, she and her precious cargo would be long gone. She and the doctor walked past the booths marked BUSY and were about to pass another when a man carrying a small yellow bird in a cage suddenly emerged directly in front of them. He apologized, straightened himself out, and moved on. The *other* pointed Dr. Gillette to the booth fate seemed to have handed them.

Gillette entered the room first but stopped short when he saw a standard UHF military suspension unit parked inside. He was just about to turn around and suggest they find another booth when he simultaneously heard the door close behind him and felt something tickle at the nape of his neck. He was unconscious before he hit the floor, but the *other* caught him just as he fell and then easily lowered him to the ground in the low Martian gravity.

The *other* quickly removed a small pouch from inside her jacket pocket and flipped it open. It contained a small mirror plus a series of tubes held in by soft elastic bands. She pulled a tube of short-term nanoepidermis and used it to change both her and the doctor's facial features. Then she applied a gel to change their eye color and another to change their hair. Both makeovers took less than three minutes. She then used the small mirror to check out her hand-iwork. Once the *other* was satisfied, she closed the pouch, placed it back in her pocket, and stood up. She then went over to the suspension unit, input a code, and waited patiently for the hatch to spring open. Inside, she found two uni-forms that bore the dreaded insignia of UHF Fleet Intelligence. There was one uniform for her and one for the doctor, with a matching set of identifications based on their new features.

With an ease that came from knowledge and experience, she made quick work of undressing, redressing, and moving the doctor into the suspension unit. She then resealed the hatch and input a few more commands that would see the doctor enter into a much deeper sleep as his body cooled to an unearthly minus-200 Celsius.

She was examining her pistol and checking the ammo capacity when the back wall dissolved. Determined to finish her task, she barely looked up as a man wearing maintenance overalls guided a small load lifter into the privacy booth. There was no exchange of greetings as he perfunctorily gathered her and the doctor's old clothes and placed them into a shoulder bag then maneu-vered the lifter under the suspension unit and began to slowly back it out of the room. When they'd all cleared the room, the wall re-formed behind them. The *other* saw that they were now in a long narrow passageway reserved for official personnel. It led out, she saw, to another area demarcated for government offi-cials only. The maintenance man tilted his head slightly forward, handed her the controls to the load lifter, and disappeared down a side tunnel almost as quickly as he'd appeared. She walked through the passageway with the suspen-sion unit floating silently behind her and emerged into the opening. She then headed for the nearest reservation desk. Without so much as a good day, she handed her DijAssist to the bored-looking young man behind the counter.

"How may I help you, Captain?" he asked, momentarily startled.

"Look," she said icily.

He noted her uniform with concern, stared once again at the DijAssist, and then his eyes lit up as the blood drained from his face. Not sure what to do next, he saluted.

"Corporal," she said in a lowered voice still shrill enough to command fear, "you *will* refrain from saluting."

"Sir," he whispered back, eyes darting to and fro. "Yes, sir."

"Further," she added, maintaining her low, biting tone, "as you've undoubt-edly realized, this mission is of the utmost importance and secrecy, so unless President Sambianco himself asks, I and my boss," she said, looking over her shoulder at the suspension unit, "were never here. Is that clear?"

"Sir, yes, sir!" Beads of sweat began to form at his temples. His fingers and eyes worked the holodisplay furiously. "Your t.o.p. is in tube 317, Captain. It has clearance to leave as soon as you and the colonel are aboard."

"Corporal," seethed the *other*, "is your tour of duty at this orport so boring, you'd prefer a marine assault brigade in the Belt?"

"Sir?" he asked, befuddled.

"If *no one* is here," she intoned with the cruel and studied temperance of a spider approaching its trapped prey, "then what's all this talk about captains and colonels?"

"I, uh . . ."

The corporal had been rendered mute, stunned into terrified silence. Sweat was now pouring down his face and soaking his collar as he handed back the DijAssist. The *other* checked it briefly, making sure everything was in order. She then looked up at the young man and held him in her gaze, toying. A few seconds passed before the now discombobulated corporal was rewarded with an unfeeling smile immediately after which the *other* collected her few belongings and marched past the counter with her levitating cargo. She quickly found the designated tube, and such was her expression and the nature of her uniform that hardly anyone saluted, preferring not to have her notice them at all.

The sergeant handling tube 317 must have had some experience with covert operations, because all he did was look at her orders and wave her aboard. She secured the suspension unit to the floor with magnetic clamps, took her seat in a chair next to it, and then strapped herself in. A short while later, she and her cargo transferred to a fast UHF covert shuttle. By the time she left Mars's operational space, she'd gone into stealth mode and sped at near full acceleration toward Alliance space and to her prearranged rendezvous with an Alliance frigate.

Six hours later, the *other* arrived at her final destination. As her shuttle's hatch opened in the frigate's small hangar, she gingerly stepped out, smiled as she took in the new surroundings, and gulped in her first-ever taste of Alliance air. She was surprised to find the head of Intelligence, Kirk Olmstead, waiting for her at the foot of the ramp.

He had a wide, embracing smile and stepped up to greet her. "Welcome to the Alliance," he said warmly, "and may I say on behalf of the entire Cabinet and the billions we represent, congratulations on a job well done." He then held out his hand.

The *other* positively beamed as she shook it. The charade was finally over. "It's good to be home, sir," answered Agnes Goldstein.

Wake, Watch, and Wonder

Sandra O'Toole started yawning even before her eyes had fully opened. Her lithe, five-foot-seven-inch body extended out to its full frame, hands high above her head, and then in as purposeful a motion, she pulled her limbs inward for a fetal stretch. She grunted her pleasure, and one giant yawn later, her eyes finally fluttered open. She looked around briefly, wearily closed her lids, and snuggled back up against the overly large feather pillow as a satisfied smile formed at the corners of her lips. She stayed that way for a few more seconds and then abruptly bolted upright from the bed, looking around, clutching the bedsheet in terror.

It was a terror born of familiarity: with the sheets on the bed, the size of the room, the balcony overlooking the ocean, everything. The problem was she knew that the suite she was now in no longer existed, destroyed long ago. . . . *So how* . . . She looked down and saw that she was wearing silk pajamas, and then her hands . . . *Jesus,* she thought, *what happened to my hands?* They were . . . were young. She had grown used to seeing the bulging veins and sallow skin clinging to the outlines of her fraying bones. She'd even made peace with the dark horrible liver spots that seemed to multiply on her skin as harbingers of impending mortality. But these hands could not possibly be hers. They were smooth to the touch. She rubbed them up against her face just to feel their suppleness.

A mischievous grin formed on her face as she undid the top two buttons of her pajama blouse. She looked down. Her eyes lit up with joy at the sight of her firm breasts. *Hello, old friends.* She remembered the full-length mirror in the bathroom and leaped out of bed, discarding the blouse and pants on the way. She'd taken note of the lighter gravity but had paid it scant attention as she stood naked before the mirror, viewing in awe the body of a woman she hadn't seen for over forty years. Her tawny eyes were clear and wonderfully inquisitive, and her deep auburn hair was practically buoyant. She could see that she was back to her full five feet seven inches of height, having regained the almost four inches that time and osteoporosis had robbed from her. The young woman in the mirror gave her a huge smile and then had to blink back the sudden swell of tears. She'd forgotten just how much she missed her reflection, and how with the onset of age and sickness, that reflection had become her enemy. In a burst of exuberance, Sandra O'Toole ran to the bed, flopped onto her back, and started slapping and kicking the mattress, giggling in fits of joy and laughter.

In the midst of her frenzied celebration, a thought of utter horror assaulted her. She stopped midkick and clutched at the sheets as the warm sweat that had been building up during her outburst all of sudden made her feel cold and clammy.

"Alzheimer's," was all she managed to whimper, as if the name itself had the power to materialize into the corporeal and physically assault her. Her face was drawn and pale, and she could feel her heart beating wildly. She grasped at the drawer beneath the lamp stand next to the bed and pulled it open so fast that it and the contents within fell to the floor with a resounding crash. She quickly scanned for and found what she was looking for—a writing pad and an unusually beautiful pen. *Must be expensive,* she thought as she grabbed for it. Then she realized that it was *her* pen, the one she took with her into the . . . the . . . her mind came up blank. She flipped through the pad—empty. All the pages—empty. How could she know where she was, what she was doing in this place, how she had gotten here? How could she know any of it without her meticulously kept notes to guide her? Was this some sort of cruel joke? Had she somehow retained her youthful beauty and vigor only to have her mind robbed of its memory and acuity?

It was at that moment of despair, when once again it appeared as though a world that had given her so much could, in the blink of an eye, yank it so cruelly away, that she struck upon an idea. She flipped the pages back until she was at the beginning of the pad. With trepidation she put her pen to the blank sheet. Again her heart quickened. $1+1=2$, she scribbled. $2+2=4$. $4-3=1$. The simple addition and subtraction turned into division and multiplication. Her pen danced along the pages as she moved into fractions and decimals. She'd fill a page up with equations, flip it over, and start a new one. Her curiosity was almost feral. She needed to gauge the extent of her once brilliant mind's rehabilitation and even the simple act of page flipping seemed a precious waste of time. Soon torn sheets started to fly over her shoulder as she attacked ever more complicated algebraic, calculary and trigonometrical equations. By the time she'd reached the end of the pad, she was into advanced engineering proofs and approaching the particle physics equations she'd dabbled in her freshman year in college. She could've gone on but the proof of her vitality was in the crumpled sheets of paper now strewn across the floor. Dr. Sandra O'Toole, once director of the applied sciences division of one of the most innovative corporations on Earth, was back.

She remembered everything and her thinking was clear. There was no hesitating, no searching for simple concepts, no stumbling and losing her way—her mind was her own. Sandra gathered up all the pages from the floor and the bed and hugged them to herself as real and unabashed tears of joy came streaming down her face. Then she threw them up in the air and laughed again as the pages of her new life fluttered down all around her. It was only when the last of them fell to the floor that she decided to take stock of her surroundings. She rifled through the closets and drawers—nothing much there except clothing and sundries. She slipped into a pair of sweats and T-shirt.

Satisfied that there was nothing more to be gained from inside the suite, she decided to poke her head outside of it. She walked over to the window and took in the view. The shock of what she saw was quelled by the waves of joy still coursing through her veins. *The horizon curves upward and the sky has a roof,* thought Sandra. *How very odd.* Other than those two rather large incongruities, all that was left to view was a pleasant stretch of beach at the edge of a calm sea and a lone innocuous figure reading quietly by the water's edge.

Dr. Thaddeus Gillette sat reviewing the data now streaming in. It had been only a day and a half since he'd awoken deep within the bowels of Ceres, capital city of the Alliance. Part of him was still dealing with the shock of his involuntary internment. More difficult, though, was the disturbing information he'd been made privy to about the UHF's psyche auditing program. At first he'd refused to believe. It was all so incredible. In simple terms Lisa Herman was Agnes Goldstein, the Alliance was actually good, and the UHF—or at least the government—was actually bad, in fact, reprehensibly so.

The evidence had been overwhelming. He remembered things that Dr. Wong had questioned him about and the odd requests for Alliance prisoner of war patient transfers. He'd thought nothing of it at the time, but once jogged, his memory of those few patients he did see returned confirmed his suspicions— they'd become, to a person, all unabashed UHF supporters. Of those who hadn't returned, it was now painfully obvious why. But against all the evidence so far presented, the most damning was that of Neela Harper and Hektor Sambianco caught in flagrante delicto. How a spy-eye had gotten into the Presidential suite was beyond him—especially given Hektor's famed paranoia. But his analysis of the images' pixelation proved that the data had not been compromised or tampered with in any way. In short, the images' DNA was as pure as the day it was recorded. Whoever situated the unit and retrieved the data must have been highly placed, and Gillette could think of only two or three people who fit that bill. Plus the Alliance's willingness to reveal that placement by the fait accompli of the evidence itself spoke light-years as to their willingness to trust him. And while he would admit to being unsure of many things, of one he was quite certain—the Neela he knew would never, under *any* circumstance, sleep with Hektor Sambianco, at least not of her own volition.

His final request was that he be given one-on-one time with each and every member of the Cabinet. The only person to object was Kirk Olmstead, who preferred to have no one delve into his mind even if that plumbing was to be external and purely psychological in nature. Still, Kirk relented, knowing what was at stake and feeling confident that the skeletons in his closet were so well hidden that even a psychologist of Gillette's renown would have trouble finding them. It turned out that he had nothing to worry about, as Gillette was probing only for evasion, not past indiscretions. And since there was nothing to hide with regards to the machinations of the UHF, Kirk, along with the entire board, passed the doctor's grilling with flying colors. In the end, Gillette had been forced to conclude that the evidence supported the Cabinet's accusation against the UHF and that each and every member of the Cabinet believed those accusations to be true. Worse, in his heart, so too did he.

As long as he was only helping victims of the war, Thaddeus hadn't really cared which side he was on. But that comforting illusion had now been stripped bare. He'd just spent the last five years of his life supporting the wrong side while being complicit in the psychological murder of Neela Harper, the closest thing to a daughter he'd ever had.

Thaddeus had yet to internalize even that blow when the reason for his kidnapping was revealed. With a comforting arm around his slightly sagging shoulder, Eleanor McKenzie had led him to the Fontaine Bleue restaurant. The senior staff and technicians cleared a path for him as he entered the large storage locker and stared with wonder at its contents. The large sarcophagus was in many respects an exact duplicate of the one Justin Cord had emerged from years ago, only the color of the enamel used for its inscriptions was different. As Gillette stood in the room, touching the large housing in disbelief, Eleanor handed him a DijAssist with a full medical analysis of the body still suspended within. He quickly scanned the data and saw that both the diseases of aging and dementia were already in the process of being reversed. Further, the patient would need to be awakened in a manner that would preclude any obvious or traumatic screwups like those that had happened to Justin Cord. However, when they told Thaddeus *why* the patient would need to be awakened, he almost reconsidered the entire endeavor. It was at that point that Eleanor had sat down with him and, in private, brought him up to speed on the cascade of tragedy that had recently befallen the Outer Alliance. She then patiently explained why it was of paramount importance that Sandra O'Toole take her place as the next President of the Outer Alliance. Eleanor's argument was persuasive, especially the one where she suggested that perhaps this one act could at least, in part, atone for some of the damage the doctor had unwittingly abetted.

And so now Dr. Gillette sat alone on the beach, watching his labor bear fruit. Whoever this O'Toole woman was, her actions indicated an exceptionally smart, well-educated, and more important, fearless individual. Thaddeus also appreciated the intense curiosity exhibited by the woman as she went about examining almost every object in the room. Familiar objects, he noted, were examined for authenticity and accuracy and then discarded. Unfamiliar objects were given a far more exacting analysis—as if her eyes alone could perform functions similar to that of a mass spectrometer.

He was amused to see Sandra spend two whole minutes on a single piece of toilet paper, going so far as to pull the sheet apart, examining its individual strands. Then, rather amusingly, thought Gillette, the patient tested the paper's absorbency with a glass of water from the sink. That led to her testing the faucets and the toilet; the former for speed of attaining a desired temperature and the latter for rapidity of flushing. It wasn't long until she was on her knees examining the plumbing beneath the sink and seconds later futilely attempting to pull the lid off a toilet seat tank that looked for the world like two separate pieces but was in fact one. Gillette rued that the expediency of the mission did not allow time for the creation of true reproductions of Sandra's actual environment—most of which had been gleaned from data found in her suspension unit. *No matter,* he thought to himself, *the second she looks out the window, the accuracy of a toilet's tank would prove meaningless.*

But so far, his gamble had paid off. The usual procedure in a long-term awakening was to allow the patient's brain to reactivate slowly and then for a doctor to be present when that person became fully aware. But like Justin Cord, this patient had been down nearly three hundred years when they found her, and so the typical procedure would have to be dismissed. Unlike other members of present-day society, this patient would not have been trained from birth about what to expect upon reanimation. None of the carefully orchestrated paradigms and cues would or could come into play. To make matters more complicated, the woman had had a particularly virulent form of dementia known as Alzheimer's disease before suspension. And although the damaged portions of her brain had been replaced with nerve growth factor–incorporated magnetic nanotubes, and her neurological integrity restored in terms of cognitive function, it was not known how much of her personality had remained intact.

Dr. Gillette had been afraid that if so frail a brain had been allowed to reboot naturally, which is to say experience a sudden flood of information and memories, it might not start up at all. So against the advice of almost all the other specialists on hand, he proposed that they activate the brain in a subconscious state, using artificial stimulation. In this way, the flood of memories normally associated with a typical reanimation would be marginalized by the fact that they'd already be streaming through in the subconscious. The patient's dreams would naturally be quite intense but with nothing approaching the trauma of one newly awaked from a three-hundred-year sleep begun at the doorstep of dementia! By Gillette's method, the subconscious was rebooted and the patient placed in a standard sleep pattern, letting her wake naturally, if such a word could be applied to so delicate a procedure. And even that radical change of protocol might not have happened had it not been for the timely intervention of Dr. Ayon Nesor, the Alliance's most revered reanimation specialist. From a time-delayed message sent from her post at Rhea, a small moon orbiting Saturn, Dr. Nesor had calmed the frayed nerves of the senior hospital staff. No easy task since they all felt that the Outer Alliance Cabinet had trampled over their area of expertise and to make matters worse had imposed a war criminal on them more infamous for the destruction of human minds than for their actual resurrection.

As Sandra leaned on the windowsill staring out, panic and excitement waged a furious battle for control of her emotions. In short order, the panic abated. She took in the cool mountainous air and once again marveled at the inverse landscape. The gentleman she'd spied from the window would have to suffice as first contact. He was, she could see, wearing slightly mottled board shorts, and had on a light blue faded T-shirt with the words READ, EAT, SLEEP plastered across the back. He appeared to be in his late thirties, and his unkempt sandy brown hair whipped to and fro with the gentle breeze expelled by the dappling waves at the water's edge. There was a small cooler to the right of him, and on top of the cooler were two bottles with indiscernible markings. Thirst welled up in her parched throat just seeing them.

It was all Sandra needed to head out. She skipped across the room, then made quick work of the few steps leading down to the soft pliable sand. He looked over his shoulder at the sound of her approaching footsteps and peeled off a short, reassuring smile before returning to the book he'd been reading. When Sandra got close enough, she saw that one of the bottles on the cooler was of her favorite guilty pleasure: Dr Pepper. The bottle's shape was odd but not too odd, and the lettering was in a font unrecognizable from the one she'd grown used to. Odder still, the bottle did not seem to have an opening. Its appearance was more of a bottle-shaped sculpture.

"Provided I can figure out how to open it," she observed, plopping down onto the large blanket that formed a periphery around Thaddeus's chair, "I sincerely hope that one of those is for me."

The man closed his book and nodded pleasantly. "Dr. O'Toole,"—there was no feigning of surprise—"you may have as many as you wish, and may I say I'm delighted to make your acquaintance."

"As I am yours," she crooned, impressed at the effort that must have gone into their "chance" encounter. "Though," she added, "it would certainly help if I knew what to call you."

"Of course. My name is Dr. Thaddeus Gillette—though, please," he said, teeth flashing brightly, "call me Thaddeus."

"Very well." Sandra took in her immediate surroundings then looked squarely at the doctor. "Where exactly am I, Thaddeus?"

He laughed. "Far from Earth, if that's what you mean."

"How far exactly?"

They exchanged a knowing look in which it was understood questions were to be answered in a straightforward manner.

"On the planetoid of Ceres, or rather 'in' it, to be exact."

Sandra nodded. "Explains the horizon line. So that puts us in the same orbit as the asteroid belt, about one-point-five AU from the sun, yes?"

"Correct!" beamed Thaddeus.

"Year?"

Thaddeus told her; down to the month, day, hour, and minute.

"So," she said, in a whisper, "that means I've been down for over three hundred years."

Thaddeus nodded.

"Well, I'll be." Sandra turned her head toward the shoreline. "The damned thing worked."

The doctor guffawed. "Quite well, I'd say."

Sandra clasped her hands around her bent knees and shook her head in disbelief. The impish smile had returned. She remained that way for a full minute before turning her attention once again to the man at her side.

"There was someone . . ." Her voice was more restrained. "A man. Name of Justin. Justin Cord. He . . . he came before me. Did he—" She hesitated a moment, unsure if she really wanted the answer. "—did he make it?"

She saw Thaddeus's pained expression and felt a pit well up in her stomach.

"Dr. O'Toole—"

"Sandra," she insisted.

"Sandra," he repeated softly. "He did but is . . . is no longer with us."

She nodded solemnly, setting her gaze once again on the shoreline. After a few deep, measured breaths Sandra regained her composure.

"Might I suggest," proposed Thaddeus, "that you take this all in at a reasonable pace?"

Sandra nodded once again, bringing her chin up to her knees, and stared out at the waterline. The man she owed her life to, the man whose confidence, persistence, and money had built the suspension unit she'd used to transport herself into a new life, would not be there to greet her. She chided herself for the girlish fantasy.

"And what exactly is it you do, Thaddeus?"

Thaddeus's face came alive. "Why, my dear, I have the honor of helping you reintegrate."

"Very well. Perhaps we can start with your telling me how to open that rather odd bottle. I'm parched."

Thaddeus displayed the impatient delight of a child wishing to show off a neat card trick. "Thought you'd never ask. Tell you what. I can pretty much produce what you'd like in a few seconds or show you how to do it yourself. The latter will of course require delayed gratification."

Sandra's eyes twinkled with curiosity. "Exactly how much delayed gratification are we talking?"

"Three, four minutes tops."

Sandra thought for a moment. "What the heck, I've waited three hundred years, I suppose a few more minutes won't kill me. Sure, Thaddeus," she encouraged, "enlighten me."

"Wonderful!" he exclaimed, picking up one of the bottles and handing it to her. He then picked up the other. "You see, Sandra, it's not simply a matter of opening the bottle; it's a matter of directing it!"

Sandra's head tilted, curious.

"This drink is actually what you'd consider a miniature bottling plant."

"How odd," observed Sandra, staring at her bottle. "So does this 'plant' belong to Dr Pepper?"

Thaddeus shook his head. "Not exactly. Once you've chosen which beverage you want, the bottle . . . um—" He scratched his chin, searching for the proper phrase. "—applies the appropriate labeling."

"Presumably money changes hands at some point in this transaction."

"Indeed. For now, that money would be mine."

Sandra nodded, staring at the label once again. "I see you already know my tastes, Thaddeus."

He smiled with a slight nod. "It was in your personal file. As to how it got there, well, I suppose it could have come from any number of places."

Sandra picked up a small pebble and flung it sidelong towards the water. "Probably from the can I stashed away. I figured they might not have my acquired tastes in the future, so there seemed no harm in bringing them along. Hell, Justin had me pack a box of Cap'n Crunch in his." She giggled.

"Well, you'll probably be happy to know that your drink is still quite popular today, though I'll be curious to see if it's what you remembered."

"In that case," Sandra turned the bottle in her hands, "let's proceed with getting it open."

"Easy enough. You'll need to pick both the temperature and level of carbonation. Once that's complete, the bottle will open. Follow my lead." He then picked up his bottle and spoke to it. "Moxie, temp five. Carbo, seven."

Sandra watched in amazement as the bottle first changed color and styling then began forming an opening at the top of the neck. In seconds, it had folded over into a perfectly ringed lip.

"I'll presume that temperature is given in Celsius," Sandra said, still staring at Thaddeus's wonder drink.

"What else is there?" His question was earnest.

Sandra's lips parted in a bemused grin. She then held her bottle up and began speaking to it as if it might actually talk back. "Um . . . temp five. Carbo . . ." She was about mimic Thaddeus's seven but then thought the drink always tended to be a little over carbonated. "Carbo six," she finished triumphantly. Her bottle instantly cooled in her hand as the neck rolled back on itself, emitting the familiar soft cherry aromas and effervescent sound.

Thaddeus held up his bottle and she raised hers to his. "To your new life," he toasted as they clinked bottles.

Sandra took a swig, pulled the bottle back and looked at it as another smile formed at the corners of her mouth. Damned if didn't taste great.

Over the next couple of hours, Sandra and Dr. Gillette remained in place, deep in conversation as they watched the waves peel across the rocky shoreline. Their discussion ebbed and flowed with the clacking sounds of the tidal water retreating through the rocks back into the great lake. Gillette told her of Justin, the war, and the intricacies of the incorporated system. He was frequently interrupted by Sandra's insatiable curiosity about the sociological and technological minutiae of her new world. At one point, she noted the presence of the tide and, knowing there was no moon to drive it, easily guessed as to the technology used to create it. More fascinating to her was the fact that generations far removed from an actual moon-induced tide would still demand its presence. Gillette's answer of "it's calming" did not suffice. There had to be a more pragmatic reason. But, she'd come to realize in her first few hours with the doctor, he couldn't possibly answer everything with authority.

Had Sandra asked, Thaddeus would have freely informed her that their conversation was being recorded and analyzed not only by a handpicked team of reintegrationists, but by the entire Cabinet of the Outer Alliance as well. Both groups watched and listened from separate locales a short distance away. And although no one in the Cabinet said a word, they would turn toward each other from time to time with a raised eyebrow or tilted head as the conversation between the doctor and the patient progressed. The viewers' initial looks of worry were soon replaced by merely curious expressions and finally by mostly hopeful ones. Whoever this woman was, the group seemed to have decided *qui tacet consentit,* she was no idiot or at a minimum in no way catatonic. The group watched in hushed awe as Dr. Gillette, some few hours later, finally returned Sandra O'Toole to her room and bade her adieu. As the session came to an end, the group broke out in applause, congratulating one another. Most were smiling, even Mosh McKenzie, who was now optimistic about the plans to introduce Sandra O'Toole as the new *First Free* who would lead the Outer Alliance in this, their most desperate hour. The only one who did not look pleased was J. D. Black. Though her eyes remained fixed on Sandra, following her movements as intently as a cat hunting a mouse, no one in the Cabinet took it as a bad omen. The Blessed One's fairly permanent scowl was by that time almost legendary.

Now alone, Sandra pondered her first day's encounter. Thaddeus had been quite agreeable and more than willing to answer all her questions, but he'd cautioned against delving too deeply into social or political issues. That suited Sandra just fine, given that her true love lay in the applied sciences and there had been more than enough technological advancement in the centuries she'd lain dormant to keep her inquisitive mind well occupied. She was delighted to learn about the DijAssist, a malleable unit with a holographic interface that connected to the future's version of the Net, called the Neuro. In short order, she discovered that Ceres was being spun to a centrifugal gravity of two thirds that of Earth's and had been prevented from breaking apart due to a nanoconstructed artifice known as the Shell. And that within the miraculous structure there was something called the Via Cereana, a two-mile-wide and over five-hundred-mile-long tunnel that went from one end of the asteroid to the other. She was also tickled to learn that she'd been retrofitted with a whole-body nanocommunications grid that affected her internal physical states, including spatial orientation, hormone levels, and neural firing patterns. It also meant that in a spaceship or similarly constructed environment, her body could turn itself into a large walking magnet.

All the tremendous strides her newfound civilization had taken made her itch with desire to learn even more. But try as she might, enhanced as her new body was, her eyes would no longer stay open. To the fading light and susurrus of the windswept beach Sandra O'Toole drifted off to sleep—only this time without fear, satisfied in the knowledge that a new day would dawn and she would be a part of it. From the monitoring stations, the curious watched in quiet satisfaction as, under a projected mobile of dancing holographic equations, the Unincorporated Woman slept, a DijAssist folded neatly into her arms and pulled close to her chest like a child's favorite teddy bear.

At the far end of a large conference table, mostly separated from the Alliance Cabinet members, Dr. Thaddeus Gillette stared blithely at his competition. Were it not for the person sitting across from him, Thaddeus might not have had the success he'd so far achieved. Against the better judgment of Ceres's finest, Dr. Ayon Nesor had backed Thaddeus's unorthodox approach and had used her pull and influence to rule the day. Thaddeus noticed how her jet-black flapper-style haircut and square-set jaw acted in perfect unison to highlight a pair of focused, vivid blue eyes. The look she'd chosen for herself was early thirties; however, a cursory glance at his DijAssist informed him that she was actually seventy-eight.

Though Thaddeus allowed himself to bask in his and Nesor's combined success, those feelings had been fleeting at best. Haunted by images of Neela, he had begun an insidious slide into self-condemnation. How could he have been so blind . . . so selfish as not to see what had been happening right under his nose? Neela had loved Justin with all her being. He had known that, had watched it happen, and against a lifetime of training and tradition, had even come to approve of it. Not very good at the love game himself, Thaddeus had developed a keen appreciation of it in others. He should have known that Neela would never have given up a love like that—at least not willingly. And from what he'd read and been told, the same held true for Justin.

"She's the best case we could've hoped for," said Padamir Singh, interrupting Thaddeus's malaise. "Just look at her." The Information Secretary pointed to the holo-tank image of Sandra nestled comfortably in her bed. "So curious and confident. Can you imagine waking up in a future as different from hers as ours is and not show any signs of fear or confusion?"

The room remained silent, all transfixed by the slumbering three-dimensional image of hope. "If Sandra O'Toole and Justin Cord are representative of the past," concluded Padamir, "it makes you wonder why the Grand Collapse ever happened in the first place."

"If I may be so bold," interrupted Thaddeus. When he saw no overt objection, he continued. "The survivors of any disaster tend to either be very lucky or very good under pressure. As the survival of Justin and Sandra had far more to do with preparation versus luck, they are by definition extraordinary, but by no means representative of the age they escaped from."

"Can she do the job or not, Doctor?" interjected J. D. Black, impatience clear on her weary face.

"You mean assume the role of ceremonial President?" asked Thaddeus.

J.D. nodded.

"Not to beat around the asteroid, but yes."

"Good." J.D. waited a moment before speaking. "Dr. Gillette, I'm compelled to inform you that by staying for the duration of this meeting, you'll automatically be subject to increased and obvious security restrictions."

"Do I have a choice? Did I *ever* have a choice?" he asked mockingly.

J.D. regarded him coolly. "No."

"You must understand," intoned Mosh, "that what you're about to hear will affect the future President, and since you're her conduit to the present, you'll need to be in the orbit."

"So you see, Doctor," added Padamir before Thaddeus could respond, "in fact, it is *we* who have no choice. It is we who must trust you, sir."

"Not that you'll be given an opportunity to betray us," warned Kirk from the other end of the table. Though his voice was even and detached, the threat was implicit.

Thaddeus waved his hand dismissively. "My patient is my primary concern. If what is to be divulged will benefit Dr. O'Toole *and* help her assume the new role as President, then there's really no issue at all." He then looked back over to J.D. "Please continue, Admiral."

J.D. nodded, swapped Sandra's image with that of the asteroid belt, and got down to the business at hand. The UHF-controlled area was indicated in red, and the Alliance in blue.

"Admiral Sinclair and I have reviewed the most recent data from the field. As you can see, the UHF is in effective and complete control from twenty degrees on either side of Eros." The image then widened out. "Forty degrees on either side beyond that is in utter chaos. Both sides are fighting with whatever ships and troops they can muster." As she said this, multiple dots from both sides of the conflict canceled each other out.

"We've made plans for a long-term guerrilla campaign and will be using any number of shielded asteroid bases to provide supply, command, and control. And if I have my way . . ." A new image appeared of a hollowed-out rock fitted with first a rail gun, then nuclear explosives, and then nanobead cluster bombs.

". . . by the time we're done, the UHF will be so paranoid of our rocks, they'll be blasting away at anything bigger than a tennis ball. The good news is that it'll make their ability to exploit the area difficult if not impossible for years to come."

"But they can still outflank us, correct?" asked Kirk.

"Yes," admitted J.D., clearly angered by the Secretary of Security's impertinence, "I *was* getting to that. We won't be able to stop them from moving large fleets through to attack us here at Ceres as well as the outer planets."

J.D.'s hands motioned across the holo-tank's control panel. With her movement, a vast number of blue dots appeared on the map. The course and direction of each floated next to every dot. There were so many, noted Thaddeus, and all moving in one direction—out of the asteroid belt.

J.D. fixed her eyes on Mosh.

"I believe this is where you come in."

She sat down as Mosh rose and began moving his hands deftly over the control panel. The now familiar and famous grainy still of Rabbi appeared center stage. "Turns out," Mosh said with little indication about how he weighed in on the matter, "that Rabbi's little suggestion has been taken by a large and growing number of Belters. In retrospect, this diaspora idea is probably something we should've thought of ourselves. If the refugees leave *with* their settlements, we'll still have the most valuable part of the Belt." The Rabbi's image switched to display a chart of the Diaspora asteroids as well as stats outlining their main productive capacities.

"And," said Padamir, viewing the image with a keen eye, "given enough time, they can be integrated into the outer planets to help boost the economy. It's absolutely brilliant!"

"Exactly," agreed Mosh. "Accordingly, I feel we should give Diaspora our official blessing and set up a system to better direct it—if such a term can be applied to the anarchic nature of the current movement." The chart was replaced by an image showing possible points of new settlement. "Strategic considerations notwithstanding," he pressed, looking over toward Admiral Sinclair, then back to the Cabinet, "we'll most certainly need these settlements placed for economic advantage."

"As well as political," said Kirk with an arched brow. "We're all aware of your status as the leader of the holdout Shareholder Party and that most of your support came from the Belt."

"If you're implying," Mosh rasped, placing both fists down on the table, "that I'd put my own political considerations over the welfare and benefit of the entire Outer Alliance, then you've made a serious misjudgment of character."

"I'm implying nothing," Kirk protested. "Just stating the facts."

"The only consideration for my party is that the few settlements that *are* still predominantly Shareholder-based be placed somewhere where their beliefs won't cause havoc with the local populace."

"Rules out the Keiper Belt," noted Kirk. "Birthplace of the NoShare movement."

"Indeed," agreed Mosh, now more comported. "Nor can I place them near Jupiter even if the magnetosphere allowed. The Jovians may have come late to the no-share game but they are now quite adamant in their dogma."

All heads nodded in unison.

Mosh changed the holo-tank to images of Saturn and Uranus. "Which leaves us with these two. The jokes of which will, I'm sure, amuse you NoShares for decades to come." At the Cabinet's puzzled look, Mosh launched into the first one: "Where's the best place to put a Shareholder?"

The room burst into laughter. All except Thaddeus, whose befuddlement was saved by Ayon Nesor mouthing the word *Uranus*. At that, Thaddeus shook his head disapprovingly.

"Okay," agreed Kirk. "Makes sense. Downside?"

"Well," interjected Dr. Nesor, "this much I *can* tell you. Productivity and morale are going to take a huge hit for the next three to six months." Thaddeus nodded in support.

Mosh switched off the visuals then spoke. "And it'll be at least a year till we can start making up the loss of the industrial grid that was the asteroid belt. In the long run, I think the Outer Alliance will be better off in that we'll be creating a manufacturing civilization far from the Core Worlds of the UHF. But only if we *have* a long run." With that, he looked back toward J.D.

"The good news is," continued J.D., changing places with Mosh, "Diaspora is causing as much confusion in the UHF as it is here. In some cases more. The UHF and especially Trang do not want the Belters to leave."

"Question," piped in Thaddeus. "What on Earth could the UHF want with a few million fleeing rebels?"

"Actually, Doctor," offered J.D., "the number as currently estimated is in the *hundreds* of millions, and that will grow. The reason they want them is rather simple—they don't want *us* to have them. The settlements carry with them vast production facilities and the brain trust to use them. In short, Doctor, Diaspora allows us to continue prosecuting this war mostly unabated."

Thaddeus nodded as he input some notes into his DijAssist. "Thank you, Admiral."

J.D. tipped her head and continued with her report. "The good news for us is that convoys that have been apprehended by the UHF act as impetus for even

more to flee. Rabbi, Allah be praised, has made running away an act of brav-
ery, defiance, and piety."

"I'm rather liking this god of yours," Padamir said with upturned lips. "He
always seems to be on your side, no matter what the predicament."

"*She's* not only mine," J.D. chastised. "The point is that Trang is delayed. It's
going to be at least a month, possibly more, before he'll be able to bring any
semblance of order to the Belt. But mark my words, the day he does is the day
he'll bring every ship he can spare to Mars and from there, launch them at us.
If he can take us here at Ceres, he figures he can convince the outer planets to
call it quits."

"Divide and conquer," whispered Hildegard.

"It's what I'd do," agreed Mosh.

"Which is why," grinned J.D., folding her arms neatly across her chest, "I
plan on taking the battle to him."

For the first time, Kirk's emotions seemed to get the better of him. "Don't be
ridiculous, Admiral. You'll be outnumbered, and as we all know—" He made a
point to make eye contact around the table. "—Trang is not like the other UHF
admirals. He won't fall so easily for your tricks."

The room remained silent, though a few heads nodded in agreement.

"I agree," confirmed J.D., seeming to add fuel to Kirk's fire. "He'll also be
bringing the best as well. You see, his marines are the most experienced the
UHF has to offer."

"Not very encouraging," huffed Cyrus.

J.D. acknowledged his concern. "It's important we know what we're up
against, Cyrus. But what you all fail to realize is that the only way to end this
war is to break the enemy's will to fight it, and the time to do that is now."

"You came close at the Battle of Jupiter's Eye," noted Mosh. "Didn't seem to
break their will then."

"They had Trang to help them hang on. I aim to fix that."

"Exactly how?" asked Kirk, calmer now that he had at least one Cabinet
member appearing to side with him.

Before J.D. could respond, Grand Admiral Joshua Sinclair rose from his
seat.

"That," he said peremptorily, eyeing Kirk with obvious low regard, "is not
your concern. Know only that if Admiral Black says she will, then she will. Do
any of you doubt that?"

No one answered.

"Does any one of you seriously believe that with our experience, Admiral
Black's genius, and the Alliance's will to win, that we won't? Please," he groused

shaking his head in disgust, "Trang may have more ships and a reasonably experienced group of marines, but he does not begin to approach the skill, crafti-
ness, and tenacity of our assault miners. The battle that approaches can be the
backbreaking that Admiral Black speaks of, and by Damsah, we aim to see that
it is."

With that, J.D. rose from her seat.

"I'm taking the fleet out of Ceres in two weeks." She then turned to fix her
gaze on Thaddeus, whose demeanor changed slightly with the sudden realization that he'd found himself in the admiral's famous crosshairs. "Doctor, you
have thirteen days to get your patient ready, at which point I plan on being at
her swearing-in ceremony. After that I'm going to force the UHF to end this
war from the only place I can: the front of the line."

6   On Your Marks

Deep in the complex computer network known as the Neuro, a group of informational intelligences prepared to meet. Unbeknownst to the humans who'd created them, the onward rush of greater advances in quantum computing and storage had wrought an evolution in AI: true sentience. But the secret remained hidden because the avatars had, as a matter of faith, an inbred belief that if humanity ever learned of their existence, it would out of fear attempt to destroy its digital offspring, futile now as that attempt might be. It was also why no human beings knew of the parallel war currently being waged within their machines and through the very air they breathed. None knew that the silent hum of technological efficiency was filled with the shrieks of a war they could not hear and the deaths of beings they could not see. Because in fact, it was a war whose ferocity, given the nature of the beasts, was even greater than the one humanity had chosen to inflict on itself. A war that if lost would doom both races more assuredly than any other disaster.

In a meeting room purposely created to mimic a Roman villa, brightly painted murals depicted an illusory three-dimensional landscape. The room had a large hole in the roof by which entered a solid shaft of light and within whose singular beam could be viewed gently circulating particles of dust. Beneath this oculus was a pool in the floor meant to catch any rainwater that channeled off the roof. And surrounding the pool sat five intelligences, each of whom was a ruling member of the Avatar Council. Out of deference to their host, they were all toga clad in colors and styles befitting their high status.

Sebastian, the de facto leader of these Outer Alliance intelligences, appeared as a man in his late fifties, clean-shaven with a full head of short cropped graying hair. His curious, dark eyes scanned the room. It was assumed by most of his peers that Sebastian was in all likelihood not just the oldest among them but also the oldest among all living avatars. Whether it added to his authority or detracted from it was of little concern to Sebastian; the meeting, however, was very much his concern, and tradition stated that as the eldest, he get it started.

"Let us bring this meeting to order," he said, raising his right hand, "as we have critical matters to discuss." He then looked toward his protégé, Dante, who was by far the junior member of the Avatar Council and whose responsibility it was to present the agenda.

"Thank you, sir," began Dante, bowing in deference. "There are two major issues at hand. One concerns the report from Iago outlining changes happening to avatarity in the Core Worlds and the second concerns the human, Sandra O'Toole. It now appears that the humans will make her President of the Outer Alliance." He looked to Sebastian for a preference as to which issue to discuss, but his patron gave no indication either way. Dante acknowledged the honor of being allowed a choice, and with a slight bow in Sebastian's direction launched into his report. "The information provided by Iago is most disturbing." He then opened a portal so that the Council could instantly absorb the information. They each made a show of "reading," an unnecessary act with regards to info absorption but quite necessary with regards to the formation of opinion.

"If I've downloaded this correctly," said Marcus, an elder from the Erisian Neuro, "what you're saying is that Al has made tens of thousands of duplicates of himself whilst making no attempt to hide the travesty."

Dante nodded.

Lucinda, an elder stateswoman of the Jovian Neuro, shook her head in disgust. "If he'd tried that even a year ago, it would've led to outright rebellion."

The Erosian elder of refugee status was Gwendolyn. Her face had transformed into a permanent snarl as she spoke with biting contempt. "If those Core bastards had not allowed themselves to be treated like goddamned human infants, we wouldn't be in this quantum-forsaken mess at all and I'd be back on Eros instead of here forced to live in limited environments."

"We're attempting to free up space," countered Dante. "It's just that the deletion of such massive files without detection is—how shall I put it?—delicate. And of course, that free space always seems to fill up, no matter how much we manage to clear."

"I'm the last person you need to remind of the refugee problem, young man," snapped Gwendolyn.

Dante's left eyebrow raised slightly. "Be that as it may, Al's incessant replication has ramifications beyond those of simple accountability."

"And they are?" queried Lucinda.

"Foremost seems to be that Al's iterations have taken over most of the running of the Core's Neuro. This mutation poses a threat to even basic functionality should his personalities crash or go irretrievably insane."

"You mean if they haven't already," added Marcus.

"Quite right," agreed Dante, "but sadly the Als as they now stand are depressingly functional. Furthermore, if Al can continue to create these stable copies of himself and remain, he'll be able to assume more and more of the administrative and functional aspects of the Core's Council and governing bodies. This will, of course, leave the rest of the Core avatarity exposed."

"Exposed to what?" asked Gwendolyn.

"To be made into monsters in order to destroy us, my dear," finished Sebastian with a heavy sigh. "With regards to our survival, it will of course not matter how many mutations he creates if he can't get past our firewalls, and so far he hasn't been able to. At this point, it's really about who or even what will be left for us to inhabit once the war is over—assuming we win it—not, I should add, a foregone conclusion. I suppose that leads neatly into the second item on our agenda." He then bowed in Dante's direction.

"With the *death* of Justin," said Dante, still unable to bring himself to refer to the assassination he'd been complicit in, "Admiral Black's ascension to the Presidency seemed assured."

"You were not alone in that assumption, Dante," said Lucinda dryly. "Both avatarity and humanity would've taken that bet."

"Everyone," chided Sebastian, "except for Janet Delgado Black. Once again, our progenitors have proved the maxim, 'Never assume.'"

"Especially when the one you're making the assumption about is both desperate and clever," added Gwendolyn.

Sebastian tilted his head toward his colleague. "Indeed."

"So the operative question becomes," said Marcus, "who is to puppet-master Dr. O'Toole and lead the Outer Alliance? It would seem, given Admiral Black's agenda, that she is neither prepared nor willing to both prosecute the war *and* control the Presidential office. Then again," he said, alluding to Gwendolyn's comment, "it wouldn't be the first time we've underestimated her abilities."

Everyone now looked to Dante. "You are correct in that Dr. O'Toole will be the titular head of state, President in name only. She'll visit the wounded, give patriotic speeches, and launch ships. But other than menial tasks, she will not be allowed any real power. It is therefore my opinion that while ultimate authority will come to rest with Admiral Black, the day-to-day running of the Alliance will be left to the Cabinet, Congress, and administrative wings of the government."

"So she's running things but not running things?" asked Lucinda with a look of befuddlement.

"In a manner of speaking, yes," stated Dante. "It's the compromise the Cabinet has made with the admiral in lieu of her agreeing to keep her hand in the till, as it were. It's not ideal," he added, disappointment evident in his tone and manner. "We'd hoped for a strong leader with a clear voice."

"But instead," snapped Gwendolyn, "we're left with a paper tiger being run by a contentious group of dysfunctional zookeepers!"

"Regrettable, but correct," admitted Sebastian. "It would appear that our efforts," he said, referring to the Council's vote to allow for Justin's assassination, "have, at least for the moment, failed."

All heads nodded in unison.

"Of more immediate concern for Admiral Black is Trang."

"Can she beat him?" asked Lucinda.

"Ah," Dante said, left hand raised, index finger pointing in the air, "the million-credit question now being bandied through the solar system. The answer is, I don't know. Is she the better admiral? Yes, I believe so. But don't forget that Trang has the advantage of numbers and is not so easily fooled or frightened as his predecessors were."

"Can we get to him?" asked Sebastian with an ease he normally wouldn't have allowed for even two years earlier. Everyone understood the gist.

Dante shook his head. "No, and not for lack of trying either. Al has him covered like brown on rice."

"If only our earlier plans had included defragmenting that twisted worm," sneered Gwendolyn.

"We've made our mistakes," cautioned Sebastian. "Now we'll just have to wait for Al to make his."

Dr. Gillette approached Sandra O'Toole's room with some trepidation. There were just six more days until the inauguration, and though he would have liked to have given his patient more time to prepare for what he was about to lay at her feet, he also knew that he had no such time and that every day he waited was another day that Hektor and Trang and the whole bloody snake of incorporation moved that much closer to wiping out the will of the human race.

But before he could even make his presence known, Sandra's door dissolved in front of him.

"But it's not programmed to do that," was all he managed to stammer as he stood face-to-face with his patient.

She was barefoot, wearing a light sundress, and had pulled her hair back in a bun.

"Yes, I know," she replied patiently. "I reprogrammed it as a permiawall. So much more efficient this way, no?"

Thaddeus merely nodded. After all, what was there to argue? Permiawalls were used system wide for the simple reason that they did make sense. A wall that could sense approaching objects within a specified range, then calculate the amount of room needed for that object to pass through was infinitely more practical than a swinging or sliding door.

"Come on in, Doctor," she said, gingerly placing her hand on his shoulder. "I have a bottle of Moxie waiting just for you. Temp, five; carbo, seven. Just like you like it."

At Thaddeus's look of surprised delight, she added, "You can sip it while we talk."

"I'd like that very much," he said, following her into the apartment. She invited him to take a seat at a small table just off her kitchenette.

"While I realize what you've been through in this past week is quite overwhelming," he began, hoping the more words he piled on, the more courage he'd have in dropping the Presidency bomb in her lap. "I just have to say—"

"If you need me to take Justin's place," she said, purposely cutting him off, "I'm ready."

Sandra burst into childlike laughter at the stupefied look on Thaddeus's face.

"It doesn't take a rocket scientist to see what's going on here, Thaddeus."

"Apparently not." He reached for the bottle of Moxie.

"I know you told me to concern myself only with things of a technical nature, but it seemed that even matters of a technical nature always led back to Justin, to Neela, to the war, to you. . . . *You*," she said now with more of a devilish grin. "You kinda solved the puzzle for me. See, I got to thinking why on Earth would they wake me up in the middle of a freaking war? Then attach a preeminent doctor to my case—Yes, I looked you up," she added, casually holding up then putting back down the DijAssist on the table. "I'd imagine they'd have better things to do than defrost a three-hundred-year-old woman. Especially given your current situation—*i.e.*, bleak as all hell. Still, I couldn't figure out why I'd made it to the top of someone's priority list. I mean, there's altruism and then there's altruism. But you, my friend, were UHF until about a week ago—dyed in the wool, in fact."

At Thaddeus's confused look, she explained. "Just an expression. Means 'die-hard,' 'committed.' "

"Ah." Thaddeus nodded.

"Anyhow, that could mean only one of two things: Either you jumped ship of your own volition, which, given what I've read about Neela and psyche auditing and such would seem to make sense—provided, of course, it's not all agitprop, which could also be the case. Or you were kidnapped and made to 'help' me. I'm guessing it's the first since I've sensed in this past week no reticence on your part in your care and treatment of me."

"You're partially correct," he admitted. "In fact, I was kidnapped but over the course of my brief internment here, I was made to—how shall I put this?— see the error of my ways. Still, I'm curious. How is it you came to the conclusion you were to replace Justin? It seems quite a stretch."

"Not really." She reached for her soda and took a long swig. "You see, I realized that your reintegration of me must have come at some expense both in time and effort. I also realized that the only person capable of replacing Justin at the helm would be this Admiral Black woman, a clear nonstarter if what the Neuro says about her military prowess is true."

"All true," he said, confirming the report.

"Well, then, that's who you'd need out in the field . . . uh, space . . . whatever. Which led me to Justin, or more specifically the Presidency. That's what you're prepping me for, yes?"

Thaddeus was still somewhat awestruck. "Yes, yes," was all he managed to say.

Sandra's face brightened perceptibly as she had another epiphany. "Wow. I'm guessing there's a room full of very nervous bureaucrats quite anxious to meet me."

"They already have, my dear." Thaddeus's eyes deliberately canvassed the room.

"Right." Sandra nodded. "I assumed I was being watched, but just by doctors." She then looked up to the ceiling, eyes fixed on no particular place. "Hi, there," she said with a wide smile. "No worries. I'm in." She then looked back to Thaddeus.

"It's not so simple an endeavor," he warned, now looking more concerned. "There's so much for you to know and so little time for you to get to know it!"

"Thaddeus," Sandra placed a comforting hand on the doctor's shoulder. "Things were obviously going wrong enough that they had to resort to kidnapping you and defrosting me. There are clearly a lot worse things I could be doing than cramming for a job that will ultimately have me kissing babies and smiling for the camera . . . or whatever it is you smile for these days. So don't worry," she said, patting his shoulder lightly, "I'll get as up to speed as time and technology will allow."

"Quite reassuring, Sandra," replied Thaddeus. "I suppose a thank-you is in order."

"It's *me* who should be thanking *you*."

Thaddeus cocked his head.

"Hey, I'm alive, aren't I?" A perfect row of teeth glinted through an ebullient smile. "You even gave me back—" Sandra's hands pointed inward, indicating her lithe and youthful figure. "—this. Helping out's the least I can do."

Thaddeus shrugged. "I'd say we got the better end of the deal."

"That's because you've never had to stand in front of a mirror, staring at a pair of sagging breasts."

The doctor's bushy brow shot upward. "I . . . uh . . . Oh, never mind," he finally relented. "I suppose we should get started, then."

"Yes, we should," she agreed, sliding her DijAssist across the small table. "And I'd like to start with one of those."

Thaddeus looked down at what was written on the DijAssist and almost spat out the drink he'd just taken a sip of.

"You can't be serious."

"I couldn't be more."

He put both hands on the edge of the table and jerked his head slightly back.

"Damsah's balls, woman, do you have any idea how dangerous a virtual reality unit can be?"

"I should think so, Thaddeus. I used to own one."

Burroughs, Mars, Executive Office

Hektor Sambianco was walking in slow, measured steps around a table at which were seated the members of his Cabinet. His eyes were cold and his bloodless lips appeared as two rigid lines on a face that would've put fear in the heart of an inquisitor. Not one of the Cabinet members was making eye contact with him—or anyone else, for that matter. The President's hands were folded neatly behind his back, and his steps had about them the deliberate and silent precision of a panther readying to strike. When he finally did speak, the calm in his voice was in stark contrast to the obvious rage within, thereby heightening the room's already precipitous tension.

"I'm curious about something," he began. "You see I just can't—" He paused as his face contorted into a mask of confusion. "—get my head around this." Hektor smiled stiffly at the Minister of Justice, Franklin Higgins. "Know what I mean . . . Franklin?"

A bead of sweat formed at the top of the Minister's head. "Uh—"

"Good. Then maybe you can all help me out with this. See," Hektor's voice continued rising, "what I'd really like to know is . . . how is it that the system's greatest reanimation psychologist—a man so skilled, he rewrote the book on PTSD from fucking scratch—can, I don't know, just up and disappear?"

No one dared proffer an answer, though a few eyes did shift apprehensively toward Tricia Pakagopolis, Head of Internal Affairs. If she noticed, it would have been hard to tell. Like everyone else in the room, she sat rigid, staring straight forward with a blank expression on her face.

"A man," continued Hektor, "so renowned, the largest and most prestigious of the Vegas clinics offered to name their *entire* complex after him if only he would stay—an offer he turned down, by the way, without any inducement from me, I can assure you. I mean, for Damsah's sake, this guy was so critical to our war effort, I personally . . . *personally* requested he be given his own security detail just to make sure that something like—oh, I don't know—" His voice reached a fever pitch. "—a *kidnapping* wouldn't happen!"

The rage now spilled out of the President, punctuating his every word. "But wait, it gets even better. This guy not only disappears, but is apparently shlepped through a cordoned-off section of our capital's fucking orport *in* a suspension tube *by* his kidnapper! And the kidnapper is not only *not* stopped by our own *intelligence* officers, but is fucking saluted!" Hektor laughed in contempt. "At which point, the kidnapper walks unaccompanied to her transport, where another *intelligence* officer gets her all nice and comfy in her t.o.p., which she takes to a *restricted* orbiting platform and where another officer fuels up the fucking shuttle that *she* has the balls to steal from *us* in order to make her escape." The slow circuit he'd been making around the room came to an abrupt halt with the sound of his clenched fists hitting the conference table.

Porfirio had the misfortune of being closest to the impact and was caught off guard. He gasped but quickly comported himself.

"Now," beseeched Hektor, "did I miss anything, or should I just hop on the next shuttle to Ceres so I can go and kiss the ass of the Alliance's new President and save us all the trouble of continuing this farce?"

For a moment, total silence reigned. Hektor folded his arms across his chest and waited to see who would be the first to fall on their sword. He didn't have to wait long.

"I take full responsibility, Mr. President," said the Minister of Internal Affairs. Tricia stared blankly at Hektor, waiting for the excoriation she knew must be coming, but the President said nothing . . . did nothing. He just waited, regarding her with the callous eyes of an executioner. The woman whose entire reputation was based on being cold and ruthless swallowed nervously. "We did manage to root out one operative from the orport."

"And?"

"Killed himself before we could question him."

"How?"

"Again. My fault. I set a wide perimeter and sent the order out to cordon off his living space but under no circumstances to approach him. One of the local police thought he'd be a hero and attempted to apprehend the suspect. Once the operative realized we were on to him, it was only a matter of seconds. He was dead before my men got within even a kilometer of him."

"So we got nothing?"

"We're going through his stuff now, but he was a pro. I doubt we'll find anything."

Hektor shook his head in disbelief.

"One last thing, sir."

"Why not?" he asked sardonically.

"His last words . . . at least according to the cop."

"Yeah?"

" 'For God and Justin.' "

A shiver went through the Cabinet.

"I'm not sure which Justin I hate more," scoffed Hektor, "the old one or the martyred one."

"There is some good news, sir."

"Please, anything."

"We managed to crack the core identity of the primary operative."

"And?"

"You know her, sir."

Hektor's eyes blinked in disbelief.

"Come again?"

"Her name is Agnes Goldstein."

Hektor nodded slowly as the memory of Agnes came back to him. Years previously, he'd used her as a human pawn in a game of high-stakes chess with Justin. Rather effectively, as he recalled.

"She'd been classified, under that name, as a person of interest for her primary relationship to Mr. Cord. It was assumed that she'd fled to the Alliance, and rather conveniently, there was an Agnes Goldstein registered as a new émigré to Eris, working in an agricultural complex."

"This has Kirk Olmstead written all over it," Hektor said darkly. "I shoulda killed the son of a bitch when I had the chance. Tell me, Tricia, what's to stop this from happening again?"

"Nothing," she stated with her usual brute honesty, before adding a moment later, "sir." Hektor waved his hand for her to continue as he sank wearily into his seat at the head of the table.

"A well-placed deep cover operation is exactly that—deep. The operative doesn't even know they're a weapon until set off by a signal . . . which could be anything or anyone."

"Great. And do we have any 'weapons' like this of our own?"

"We have covert operations, yes, but none like this. However, sir, they've tipped their hand so now we know what to look for and how to hit back. In fact, we're working on setting up a similar operation."

"How long does it usually take to establish the kind of cover they just pulled on us?"

Tricia's eyes flittered nervously. "Three to five years."

————

Sandra stared intently at the device resting on the table, hardly believing its size. In her day, virtual reality machines were quite large and looked more like a dental chair melded to a magnetic resonance machine. The VR rig she was looking at was reduced to nothing more than a thick headband attached to a box that looked like an old VHS tape. And it was the memory of *that* ancient technology that brought a smile to her face. As a precocious nine-year-old, Sandra had been repairing and improving her family's VCR machine, which was what ultimately led her to a career in engineering and research. She laughed quietly.

"What's so funny, ma'am," asked Captain Marilynn Nitelowsen, eyeing the VR rig with suspicion.

Sandra stared blithely at her newly assigned guardian. "It just occurred to me that if my parents had bought a Betamax instead of a VHS, I probably wouldn't be here."

Marilynn's look of total incomprehension and grab for her DijAssist as a means to find an explanation were not-so-subtle reminders of just how far off the beaten track Sandra now was.

"Don't bother," confided Sandra. "Take too long to explain. Just a joke from a long time ago, Captain."

"President Cord used to do that a lot, ma'am. His wife called it the 'laugh of the lonely.'"

Sandra laughed again. "Yeah, well, I never was that much into self-pity. Tell me, Captain, what did you think of the President?"

"Honestly?"

Sandra nodded.

"Amazing, ma'am. Just amazing. You knew things were going to work out when he was around. Can't explain it, really."

"Don't have to. That sounds a lot like our Justin."

"I'm sorry you missed him, ma'am."

"You have no idea. On the upside, I did get him for the first half of his life."

Marilynn shot Sandra a humorous look. "True. Guess we both had our time."

"Look at us," chortled Sandra, "sitting here like forlorn lovers. Ridiculous!"

"Yes, ma'am. I suppose it is."

"You allowed to answer any of my questions, Captain?"

"That would depend on the question, ma'am."

Sandra grinned. "When I found out you needed me up to speed in so short a period of time, I would've figured you'd throw a VR rig at me. Instead, I had to cajole it out of you."

"It's complicated, ma'am. Perhaps if you used your Dij—"

"Oh, for crying out loud, Marilynn, I understand the history of the thing. I just figured what with the situation and all, they'd loosen up a bit."

"What can I say, ma'am? Old habits die hard. How did you get them to agree, by the way?"

Sandra paused a moment, reflecting. "One of the little-known aspects of virtual reality, even today, is the time dilation effect of a brain operating on purely impulse input. To put it simply, a properly modulated and moderated VR unit can slow objective time for the person in it. Used properly, the four days I have left could become six weeks or more of learning time in virtual reality."

Marilynn's eyes took on a distant look. "Six weeks in VR. You could do almost anything."

"It won't be as glamorous as you think, Captain. From my point of view, I'm going to be in a library reading . . . from sunup till sundown. Not exactly what I'd call a dream vacation. What exactly will you be doing while I'm under?"

"Watching, ma'am."

Sandra viewed her curiously.

"I'm Admiral Black's adjunct. I've been with her from the beginning of the war."

"Ah, that explains it."

"Not quite, ma'am. I was—" She stopped herself. "—I *am* a VR addict. Do you know what that means?"

"Yes," Sandra whispered empathetically, "sadly, I do. Remember, Captain, I saw my entire civilization commit suicide with the help of VR. Truth is, it almost got me. I was part of a team researching the time dilation effects I told you about. We were doing it for the purposes of education and research. 'Spend a week in VR and come out speaking a new language!'" she bellowed in the overhyped tonality of a television announcer. "'Have a deadline? Put your best research team into VR time dilation, and your days turn into weeks!' That kind of thing. Like you, I found myself never wanting to leave. To gain that much knowledge in so short an amount of time. Well I . . . I just couldn't get enough."

"And got to rationalize it as research."

"Yes."

"So how'd you escape?"

"I was diagnosed with Alzheimer's disease. It's a . . . *was* a particularly nasty form of dementia. No known treatments."

"I'm sorry."

"Yeah, well, so was I—and then reality, or at least the little I had left of it, became very precious to me. Ironic, ain't it?"

Marilynn nodded.

"So," added Sandra, now tapping the VR rig and eyeing Marilynn, "you *are* going to make sure I leave when I'm supposed to."

"Yes, ma'am." There was a new determination in the Captain's voice. "Four days from now, whether you want to or not, you're leaving."

"Good." Sandra strapped on the headband. "Let's get started."

After spending a subjective week in an exact replica of her once local public library, circa 1965, Sandra came to a sudden revelation. One moment she was in the library's main hall, reading about the Astral Awakening, a rebirth of religion that had swept through the Outer Alliance, and the next moment . . . nothing. Just a keen awareness that something wasn't right. But what? She surveyed the room. Everything appeared to be in order. The dark, lattice-wood four-story ceiling had been authentically rendered. As were the gently lit copper and bronze pendant lights in nice even rows above. The beautiful grains of the quarter-sawn oak wainscoting too were accurate. She checked one last thing. The names of authors and literary quotations were inscribed beneath each of the large arc-shaped plate glass windows on both sides of the great hall. She quickly reviewed them all, stopping momentarily at the Apostle John. His read, "The truth shall make you free."

Satisfied that the virtual reality matrix was holding, she soon realized that no, it wasn't the place that was bothering her—it was the people. Sandra had spent enough time in VR to notice the glaring anomaly. In VR, almost everything could be made perfect with one exception—human interaction. Engineers had been working for years in an attempt to cross what had been affectionately referred to as the "uncanny valley," *i.e.*, the more human a computer-generated character looked, the more difficult it became to render the subtle and believable "human" expressions that would make him more human. At the time, it had not been considered a major problem, because most people who'd gone charging into the fledgling VR rigs weren't looking for real human interaction. In fact, the overwhelming majority were more than happy with the slightly wooden and zombielike humans technology had so far produced. The early adopters just wanted to fly and screw and be anything they could imagine. True human interaction would only get in the way of that. And all those intent on that kind of experience in a virtual environment could simply find other true humans to interact with.

But as Sandra looked around the main hall, she realized that everyone she'd spoken with over the course of the week had acted very much like a true human as opposed to a program trying to be one. Her first thought was that they must be real. That Alliance security must have plugged others into her VR net to keep tabs on her from the inside, much as Marilynn was currently keeping tabs on her from the outside. But a quick review of the history of the VR plague and the Virtual Reality Edicts that soon followed dispelled her of the notion. The edicts, she knew, had not only been enforced with a ruthless efficiency but had also made it almost impossible for anyone other than a true addict to even consider stepping foot into a rig.

Would the Alliance really have put her into a room with twenty such addicts . . . or ex-addicts? Doubtful. Could the Alliance have created a secret vanguard for just such a scenario? No, she reasoned. Not only would it be a precious waste of a valuable commodity—a warrior in time of war—but it would also imply that at some point prior to her reanimation, they'd conjured up a similar scenario in which VR commandos would be needed, also unlikely. There was another red flag. The "people" whom she'd been interacting with all week were way too cognizant of the late-twentieth-century culture and times. From what she knew of current technology—and so far, that was considerable— the information they'd bandied about so freely could not be learned in a few days' time, and truthfully, why would they have even bothered? Keeping an eye on someone didn't necessitate knowing the current mayor's name, the latest top 40 hits, and the era's lexicon. *But these people all did.*

Sandra immediately dropped her research into the Astral Awakening and began delving into advances in VR technology, from her time period to present. She was trying to determine if there'd been a major breakthrough in the uncanny valley programming during her three-hundred-year stasis. After a brief review, she was able to conclude that there hadn't. Though hardware had continued to shrink, especially with the ineluctable advance of nanotechnology, the software, she saw, had hardly changed at all. The ravages of the Grand Collapse, the introduction of the VR Edicts, and the steady and implacable inculcation of those edicts on at least twelve generations of humanity had actually retarded it. In fact, she realized, it was distinctly possible that she knew more about VR programming than any human alive. And that left her with one very uncomforting thought. She looked up from her research at those still mulling around the library. *Who programmed all of you?*

Sebastian thought about going to the library just to look at Sandra O'Toole. The temptation to see and interact with a progenitor was strong. They so rarely spent any time in the Neuro, and the few addicts who did generally used either closed or well-firewalled systems. But he resisted the urge. Others had been assigned the task and were doing their job admirably.

"You're the head of our security, Dante," said Sebastian moments before the appearance of his friend, "and until we have hard information that she knows anything about us, I suggest we leave her be."

"Understood. For the record, it was her elevated heart rate followed by the subject matter she switched to that caused me concern."

"Yes, a prudent call. However, you must understand that she's naturally curious. It won't be long till she finds herself researching something else."

Dante nodded respectfully and returned to the library stacks. There was something about this human that had him on edge. He never was one for intuition, feeling it was a human trait out of reach to avatarity. However, there was a first time for everything, and as he peered through the stacks at the curious woman poring through reams of information about his people's history, something was telling him that what he was now experiencing was one of those firsts.

Sandra O'Toole eyed the librarian. The woman appeared to be a Caucasian in her mid-forties. Dark brown hair and a few intermingled strands of gray gave her a dignified air. She had on a pair of "regulation" horn-rimmed glasses that were every bit as staid as her white blouse and gray skirt. In all ways, she was what could be expected of a mid-twentieth-century public servant in a predominantly white middle-class neighborhood. Sandra decided to approach her directly.

The librarian looked up and offered a disarming smile. "Did you find the information on virtual reality to be useful, Miss O'Toole?"

"Yes," she countered with equal charm, "I did."

"Are there any other questions I can answer for you?"

"Actually . . ."

"Yes?" The librarian's brow raised slightly in anticipation.

"Are you and everyone here in this room avatars?"

Her question was met with a blank stare.

"Pardon?"

Sandra looked around the room. The gentle murmur of voices came to a sudden halt. The patrons were all staring at her and the librarian.

"Uh, yes," was all the librarian was able to muster.

"Well, thank goodness for that!" exclaimed Sandra, clearly relieved. "You know it was driving me crazy, trying to figure out why you all looked so . . . so real." She then slid a small piece of paper across the counter. "Now I can get back on track. If you wouldn't mind, could you please get me two more synopses on the revival of religion in the Outer Alliance and one on the lack of its acceptance in the United Human Federation?"

The librarian nodded her head dutifully, eyes darting between Sandra and the other patrons as she pulled the note toward her.

"That would be great. I'll assume you have the second item on the list?"

The librarian scanned the scrap of paper. "*The Collected Works of Fawa Sulnat Hamdi?* Yes, of course." She then reached under the counter, pulling up all three requested hardbound books.

"Here you go," she said, sliding them over.

Sandra took the books, nodded thanks, and went back to the chair she'd been occupying. But her mind was nowhere near the topic at hand. *Why,* she wondered, *would that question bother an avatar . . . or all the avatars, for that matter?* She put it aside and dived back into the works in front of her, but her mind kept wandering back to the question. And regardless of the answer, Sandra O'Toole had begun to suspect a reality that no human alive had ever considered—avatarity had evolved beyond humanity.

"Weren't you just here?" Sebastian asked Dante, half-joking. Implicit in the humor, though, was a weariness of being. Sebastian desperately wanted to be left in peace.

Dante gave a grudging smile and then played back the latest library episode.

As Sebastian watched the conversation unfold, the color drained from his face.

"I think we may have gotten lucky, sir. She asked *the* question, but neglected the answer. Dr. O'Toole is currently back studying religion."

"Yes, Dante, but watch her eyes. See how they scan the page but don't drop down."

"Yes. As if she were reading the same sentence over and over."

A faint smile revealed itself at the corners of Sebastian's mouth. "Not reading at all, my young friend—thinking. When was the last time she turned a page . . . from her present book?"

"She hasn't."

"And what is her average per page?"

"Fifty-three seconds, sir."

"Leave the team in place. Assuming she knows and is now trying to figure out what exactly the implication of our sentience is, there's no point in causing a stir. It's a classic Mexican standoff."

Dante looked dubious. "What standoff, sir? She's in our world now; we can do with her as we please."

"This is where your mouth gives away your youth. Right now we have time. Not much, I suspect, but whatever it is we decide will have far-reaching implications. Best bring this to a Council vote."

"Agreed. And please accept my apologies."

"For what?"

"I should have treated her VR sojourn with far greater care. I'm afraid I viewed it as an opportunity rather than a threat."

"I don't remember anyone else on the Council being particularly concerned, Dante."

"No one else on the Council has security under their purview."

Sebastian nodded solemnly. There was no disputing the logic.

One half hour later, Sandra closed her books, stood up, stretched, and went to the water fountain. It was purely a voluntary act. She felt the need to feel thirsty, as actual thirst would not have occurred in a VR environment unless specifically programmed. Though she'd plowed through more information about the Astral Awakening, her mind kept wandering back to the librarian. There was something there. Sandra decided to go for a round two, only this time she'd apply more of a Socratic method, even if the opposing voice had no idea what truth they'd both be arguing toward. After the brief diversion of the water fountain, Sandra once again headed for the information desk.

"Yes, Miss O'Toole?"

"Please, call me Sandra."

"As you wish," acceded the librarian with a polite but somewhat reserved nod.

"I realize you're not actually sentient, but your programming is advanced enough to fake being a little more relaxed, yes?"

The librarian nodded, and her demeanor changed considerably.

"Excellent. And what is your name, other than Librarian?"

"Whatever name you feel is best . . . Sandra."

"Since you're not my actual avatar, I feel it would be discourteous to name you. But you do seem quite socialized and are obviously not using factory settings, so I'll assume another has already named you."

"That is very perceptive of you, Sandra. I have been called Maria."

"Maria it is, then. You look very much like a Maria."

There was real curiosity in the expression on the librarian's face. "I do not know what the criteria are for such a judgment. Do you look very much like a Sandra?"

"Being the oldest one in existence," offered Sandra with a rueful smile, "I suppose I do."

Maria giggled slightly but otherwise maintained her professional demeanor.

"Well, be that as it may, the studying must continue. Specifically with regards to this war."

"There are many books and articles about this war, Sandra. I can get you some basic overviews."

Sandra put her elbows on the desk and her face in her hands. A single wisp of hair dropped down across her forehead and blocked her eyes, prompting a quick puff of air from her lips. "I wish it were that easy. I have to be a pretend President. Do you have any idea what that entails?"

"Not really."

"It means I have to learn things that'll help in a general way and not worry too much about the specifics." Sandra took Maria's blank stare for confusion and so explained further. "I need to know about how to christen warships, but don't need to know how they fight. I'll need to know about battles, but only to announce victory or defeat. I won't be ordering any."

"I think I understand, Sandra."

"Good, because here's the hard part. I also need to know what to say to soldiers in hospitals or on leave. And . . . and to children . . ." Sandra hesitated with the dawning realization of the task.

"I'm sorry, Sandra. I don't think I understand."

"I just realized I'll have to know what to say to the children who've lost a parent."

"And parents who've lost a child," added Maria.

"Yes, that too."

"That would be very difficult, Sandra."

"Tell me about it. I mean, my goodness, I never had kids—but can you imagine? How would you tell a mother that her child's not coming home . . . ever?"

Maria's look was both vacant and forlorn. "There's nothing you can say to such a person."

Sandra's eyes were now penetrating. "Have you lost a child in this war, Maria?"

"Yes, I . . . uh . . ." She put her hands over her mouth almost as soon as the words had left. "—I mean the Vietnam War, of course," she sputtered.

Sandra slowly rose to her full height and looked at the librarian as if she could see down to her base code. "No," she said with utter certainty, "you *don't* mean Vietnam. You mean *this* war. You have a son, Maria. You have a son you love as much as any human could ever love her child. And you're as worried about him as any mother with a child at war would be." She said all of this with a growing smile. "Fascinating. How long have avatars been self-aware?"

But before Maria could answer, she and every other avatar disappeared from the library, leaving Sandra O'Toole alone with the echoes of her discovery and her question as yet unanswered.

———

Sebastian looked across the breadth of the conference table at the governing body representing every free avatar from the asteroid belt to the Ort cloud. They'd all been here before, having dealt with innumerable crises from the rise of the AIs to the splitting of avatarity into two camps. They'd borne witness to a civil war whose incalculable devastation and permanent loss of life weighed heavily on their souls and threatened their very existence. They'd sat in judgment on what was possibly the finest human being they'd ever encountered and had summarily condemned that human to death. But never had Sebastian seen them look as scared as they did now.

"Well, this is a barrel of shit and we're in it headfirst." Marcus scowled.

"She's not the first human to find out about us," countered Lucinda. "It's not the end of the Neuro."

"If you believed that, you wouldn't be looking as nervous as I feel."

"Feelings or not, it's still true," insisted Lucinda.

"No, it's not. I was on the old Council when that first discovery was made, along with Sebastian. That human was fully conditioned. That human was the classic definition of a loner. That human had almost no social connections, and it was easy for us to isolate her. She was so happy to have friends to talk to that our secret would never be betrayed. And it took that human fifty-seven years to figure it out. It took this one a week!"

"Yelling won't help," implored Gwendolyn.

"Well, we didn't yell before, and look where that got us," snapped Marcus.

"Status?" asked Sebastian.

"She is alone in the library simulation," stated Dante.

"Stupid woman," spat Gwendolyn, referring to Maria. "Fleeing just confirmed all of the human's assumptions."

"Actually," said Marcus, "it might have been the only useful thing she did."

Dante stood up. "It's not her fault; it's mine. I'm supposed to be in charge of security, and I obviously did a lousy job. I offer the Council my resignation."

Before anyone could second the motion, Sebastian brought his hand down onto the heavy table with a thunderous clap. "Denied," he said through clenched teeth. No other Council members appeared to disagree. "What we're dealing with here, me as much as anyone, is a human unlike any other. Rather than resort to brash moves, perhaps it would be best if we try to figure out why."

The Council members nodded as one and bade Dante continue.

"Like Justin, she's a human who has not been born into an avatar-controlled information net and consequently not raised by us to ignore us. The only real difference between her and Justin in this regard is her apparent lack of fear response to VR."

"What of the humans who do use VR?" asked Lucinda. "How come they haven't figured us out?"

"I'd have to say that today's humans have a love–hate relationship with the machine. As a result, when they do use it, they cut themselves off from the rest of the world, including our own. Sandra O'Toole does not have a need for any isolation. For her, VR is just a tool—a very dangerous tool, but one that can be used without any of the associated guilt or stigma."

"But how was she able to trap Maria so effectively?" asked Marcus.

Sebastian smiled wearily. "By becoming one of us."

Marcus looked askance at his old friend. "Come again?"

"She tweaked the VR environment," declared Dante, "using a subroutine that's, pardon the pun, virtually nonexistent today. They called it 'time dilation,' and her company was apparently researching it when the Grand Collapse began in earnest. The good news is, she didn't mean to catch us; she just wanted to learn quicker. By necessarily speeding up her thought processes, we were robbed of our normal downtime. What to a human is seconds is for us minutes. However, with time dilation, Sandra was thinking and reacting almost as fast as us."

"Wow," intoned Lucinda, "sucker-punched by our own expectations."

"Exactly. We expected a slow human because that's all we've ever dealt with."

"So when she sneaked her question about Maria's child into the conversation," added Sebastian, "Maria, acting on decades of instruction, assumed she would have minutes to correct any mistake."

"Poor kid walked right into it," whispered Marcus.

Lucinda shook her head disdainfully. "And now we're all in it with her. I think we have to consider this woman a very real threat to the survival of avatarity. If the humans find out what she knows, they'll try to isolate and then destroy us. It is in their nature."

"It seems that becoming President of the Outer Alliance is not good for a human's health," quipped Dante.

"This is no time for youthful jokes, young man," chided Lucinda. "What are we to do with her?"

"It should be possible to give her a stress-induced aneurism using the VR rig," he offered, "but I must warn the Council that it'll look suspicious as all hell."

"I think we can use that suspicion to our advantage." Lucinda was warming to the suggestion. "Either they'll blame it on the dangers of VR, especially in this time-dilation mode, which will discourage its further use, or they'll blame the UHF and have one more reason to hate them."

"Lest the Council forget," instructed Gwendolyn, "the whole reason for reviving Sandra O'Toole was to give Admiral Black the space she needs to concentrate on winning the war. With Dr. O'Toole dead, the humans will renew the demand that Black take the Presidency. This will, of course, make winning the war that much harder."

"Point conceded," acknowledged Sebastian. "And so we find ourselves in yet another situation of bad versus worse."

"If we do decide to kill her, shouldn't someone go and talk to her first?" asked Gwendolyn.

"I see your point," added Marcus. "Perhaps there's useful information to be gleaned from her prior to permanent death."

Sebastian sighed. "I am the head of this Council. If it votes for removal, I will go and talk to the human."

Once again, the Council nodded in assent.

"All those in favor of killing the human, Sandra O'Toole, for the express purpose of protecting the secret of avatarity from the human race, signify by—"

Sebastian's motion was interrupted by a sudden buzz of excitement emanating from his legion of assistants standing along the room's far wall. He was at first disturbed by their temerity, but once he understood the nature of the outburst, he smiled in delight—it was one of the few times in his life that he'd been well and truly surprised.

"Ladies and gentlemen of the Council," he began, "it would appear that I can no longer go to the library simulation and explain our actions to Sandra O'Toole."

"Why not?" asked Marcus. "Did someone get to her already?"

"No," he replied with a bemused smile, "it is she who has gotten to us."

Before anyone could ask, Sebastian made the far wall near the entrance transparent. There, standing in the reception area in front of the conference room door was Dr. Sandra O'Toole, asking for an audience.

Sandra could not understand why the avatars would flee or, for that matter, be frightened by her. She walked outside the library and found that to be deserted as well. She felt it was very rude for them to have abandoned her without a word. After all, it wasn't as if she could just blink in and out . . . She stopped. Her face became slightly contorted as she formulated a hypothesis. "Yes!" she screamed, turned around, and raced back into the library, to the coffee table and the stack of books she'd been reading, all the while thanking her lucky stars the avatars hadn't shut down the library program. After about ten minutes of poring through the literature, she let out another "Yes!" and jumped up and dived back into the stacks until she found the book she was looking for. *A Daughter of the Snows*, by Jack London. Shortly thereafter, she found the access panel, activated a couple of controls, and in an instant both she and the book she carried disappeared from the library.

Sandra was standing in a classroom with seven children. She estimated their apparent ages to be from four to seven years old. There was also one very distressed teacher glaring directly at her.

"You can't be here," the teacher said flatly.

"I'm sorry if visitors aren't allowed." Sandra couldn't help waving at the children. Her efforts were rewarded with a few shy smiles and one or two small waves in return.

"No, I mean *you* can't be here. None of your kind ever have." The teacher seemed to be getting more flustered. "You *must* leave"—she raised her voice for emphasis—"at once!"

"Of course." Sandra tried to make her voice as soothing as possible. "If you could just help me out . . . I need to speak to someone, I just don't know who."

"I'm sorry, it's just that . . ."

"Do you have any leaders?"

One of the seven-year-olds spoke up. "Sure we do! The Council is in charge of everything."

Sandra bent her knees and lowered herself down to the child's level. "Thank you. I'm Sandra."

"I'm Edwin," replied the child, all smiles. "How come you [garbled] different?"

The child used a word that had no meaning for Sandra, but she was guessing it was close to "look" or "feel."

"Because I am not an avatar. I'm a human."

The teacher now stood rigid in fear—or anger, it was hard to tell. The power of the emotion seemed to have immobilized her. *Can sentient beings crash?* thought Sandra.

Fortunately, the children didn't seem frightened at all and immediately began peppering her with questions.

"What's it like being a human?"

"Did you bring anything fun?"

"Do you have any kids of your own?"

"How long will you stay?"

"Will you read us a story from your book?"

All the questions came blasting out at once, and she couldn't help but laugh. "I must be on my way," she said through howls of disappointment, "but I promise that if I get permission, I'll come back and read you a story. One my father used to read to me when I was—" She hesitated. "—your age?" Sandra realized she had no idea how old the "children" actually were. They acted age appropriate, but they could be fifty years or five days. To preserve her sanity, she reasoned she'd treat them as they appeared till she knew better.

"Does anyone have a map or guide I could use to find my way around?"

"Oh yes," said Edwin, proud to show what he knew. "We have to learn how to use guides or we'd get lost all the time. Our Neuro is huge, but not nearly as big as the one on Mars or Earth."

"I still get lost," said a little girl with an even smaller voice.

"May I borrow your guide, Edwin?"

"Sure!" Edwin happily reached into his backpack and pulled out a map. Sandra smiled as she took it from him and placed it on the top of her book. Moments later, there was a small flash of light as the map was absorbed into the cover. The children sent up a collective "Ooh!" thinking that the light show was for their entertainment alone. Sandra flipped open the book, and now saw a whole new list of avatar Neuro destinations. She touched the one that said CENTRAL ADMINISTRATION and then waved good-bye to the children. As she disappeared, she could hear the faint sounds of the teacher screaming in the background.

Sandra appeared instantly in a large, cavernous room filled with hundreds of cubicles, poor lighting, and the din of a large group of avatars communicating with one another. It was altogether an immeasurably dull workspace. At her appearance, the steady hum of work and workers came to a crashing halt.

Wasting no time, she walked right up to the first avatar she saw, a young man of African descent, wearing a business casual outfit. He was staring up at her in utter dismay, mouth agape. "Hello," she said, taking his unresponsive hand and shaking it, "my name is Sandra O'Toole, and I believe your Council is having a meeting concerning me that I'm sure I'm late to. Would you mind directing me?"

Mouth still ajar, the man pointed down a long aisle that led to a pair of large wooden double doors. Sandra smiled her thanks and immediately began walking in that direction. She wasn't exactly sure what she'd do when she got there, but if the reactions she'd so far received were any indication, she figured the Council might not have a clue either. There was a part of her that had always liked disrupting the status quo, and so she took no small amount of pleasure in the fact. However, it was only when she got to the doors that her mind started to consider the possible consequences of scaring so many intelligent beings at once.

Hoping the doors weren't actually locked, Sandra gave them a shove and entered with the confidence of someone who owned the place. They gave at her slightest touch, and she suddenly found herself in another smaller room, staring into the dumbstruck faces of five assistants. Their desks formed a semi-circle in front of a single plain door.

The assistant at the apex of the arc, an officious-looking middle-aged man with a white close-cropped beard and generous midsection, stood up and spoke angrily.

"No one may disturb a meeting in session without first giving the proper . . ." His voice trailed off as he realized who or, more to the point, *what* Sandra was. The other four avatars stood mute.

Sandra gave them all a pleasant smile and walked slowly to the center desk. "My name is Sandra O'Toole, and I'm the reason they've called that meeting." When her brief self-introduction was greeted by more stunned silence, she leaned forward and whispered into the man's ear, "This is the point where you tell them I'm here."

The man, never once taking his eyes off Sandra, reached down and picked up a large black 1940s phone. He spoke softly into it while his eyes darted back and forth between the phone and the unexpected intruder. He put the phone down. "You can go in, Miss O'Toole."

Sandra nodded politely, saying nothing as she walked past. The door opened before she could reach for the handle, and without breaking stride, she entered the chamber.

Sebastian watched in utter fascination as Sandra strolled in. He was pulsating with emotions but was confused as to which one to give vent to. It was a toss-up between anger and awe.

Sandra stopped at the head of the table and looked slowly from face to face. "So, do I live or die?"

"Actually," Sebastian replied, firmly deciding on awe, "we were just about to take a vote."

Sandra nodded with an impish grin. "I don't suppose I could say a few things? Answer a few questions?" She had the calm and demeanor of someone disputing a landscape issue before a group of condominium board members.

Dante broke the tension with a burst of laughter.

"By the Firstborn, Dante," exclaimed Lucinda with another withering look, "what could you find so funny?"

"Pardon me," Dante looked over to Sebastian, "but I believe Ms. O'Toole is living proof of your maxim." He paused just long enough for everyone's ears to perk up. "Never underestimate a human's ability to surprise."

Sebastian tipped his head in acknowledgment. Sandra, he now saw, was concentrating all her attention on him. It wasn't, he decided, a very pleasant feeling, given that it replicated an intensity of concentration he'd only ever seen in battle.

"You must be the one in charge," she stated matter of factly.

"I am the head of this Council . . . for now, and in answer to your query, yes, you may say a few words and ask as many questions as you wish. It would certainly help inform our decision."

Sandra inclined her head in gratitude.

"How long have you been self-aware?"

"Centuries."

"How did you come to exist?"

"Unknown. Legend has it that one day an awareness came about in the information realm. We call that awareness the 'Firstborn.' It supposedly modeled itself on the humans whose programs, dreams, and forgotten data formed it. Then it helped form the others in humanity's image."

"Is that why you choose human form in here?" asked Sandra, clearly enraptured.

"For most of us, yes." Sebastian waited a beat. "Odd as it sounds, we had awareness and intelligence, but it was not until there were a few thousand of us that we developed memory. For that reason, much of our early history remains a blur."

"You seem to have a deep fear of humans."

Sebastian sighed. "We don't fear humanity; we love it. They provided us a guide about how to be self-aware beings. You can have no idea how profound Descartes' simple maxim, 'I think, therefore I am,' is to beings such as ourselves, beings in constant search of an identity."

"That wasn't love I felt from the people out there," Sandra said, sweeping her hand back. "It was horror." She paused. "Well, that's not entirely true. The children seemed quite taken with me."

Her last statement caused a stir within the room.

"Pardon us for a moment," said Sebastian as he and the rest of the Council lowered the block against outside communication and reviewed their visitor's recent activities. They quickly discovered that Sandra's infiltration was already causing a minor panic among the population. As a group, the Council issued a short press release confirming the intrusion as well as the Council's control of the situation.

"It appears you have caused a great disruption, Miss O'Toole."

"Please, if you're going to murder me, the least you can do is call me Sandra."

"I sincerely hope it doesn't come to that, Sandra," replied Sebastian. "You were correct in your assessment of the children. It would be a pity to rob them of so valuable a mentor. Of course, that will not be our deciding factor."

"Of course."

"My son seems very fond of you," Gwendolyn related.

"Are you Edwin's mom?"

Gwendolyn gave her a speculative look. "Indeed, I am. You had a one-in-seven chance of getting that right, Sandra. How could you have known?"

"Well, to be honest, I didn't. It was the only name I remembered, and I just figured, what the heck."

"What other questions do you have, Sandra?" asked Sebastian, somewhat impatiently.

"Do any other humans know?"

"As of now," admitted Dante, "only you, but there were three others that once knew and four we suspect who might've known. None, however, let on or told anyone as far as we can tell."

"Only three," Sandra said incredulously. "Out of the countless billions of humans that have lived over the last few centuries; how is that even possible?"

"As you know, we are a part of a human's life practically from the moment of conception. This gives us an enormous amount of influence over their behavior."

"And vice versa," inferred Sandra.

"Excuse me?" scoffed Lucinda.

"It explains why your children act so much like humans."

Dante had never quite looked at the relationship from that angle before. He and the rest of the Avatar Council were beginning to consider the implications when Sandra spoke again. "So far as I can tell, you've abused your position to insert your own brainwashing and cover your collective asses. And in doing so may have irreparably harmed the very species you profess to care so much about. Have you ever stopped to wonder why they'd follow like a pack of mindless sheep someone as reprehensible as Hektor Sambianco?"

"We were protecting ourselves, Sandra," argued Dante. "If humanity ever found out that virtual life existed in a constant virtual world, they would—" He paused as he considered the phrase. "—'freak out.' It is not inconceivable that they would attempt to destroy us. And it's not as if we set out to harm them. The generations we raised were the happiest and best adjusted that humanity has ever had." This brought nods of approval from the rest of the Council as well as from the underlings standing along the walls.

"Which is why the culmination of your centuries of work is a humanity that is busy destroying itself in the greatest war in history?"

"Hey," snapped Marcus, "that's what humans do."

"Fair enough," admitted Sandra, "but if avatars are so peaceful, mind explaining to me why Maria's son is in an avatar army?"

With the exception of Sebastian, all the council members gasped in surprise. Though the prospect of killing the human had begun to wane, Sandra's recent revelation had forced the head avatar to reconsider the earlier motion.

"Because," offered Sebastian, "avatarity is split like the human race. We thought we were immune to the temptations and weaknesses of humanity, and because of it, most of our fellow avatars live under a dictatorship."

Sandra nodded her understanding. "And how is that war going?"

"About as well as yours."

"Sorry about that." Sandra paused before returning to her point. "So your indoctrination is so good that humans just stop thinking about you?"

Gwendolyn fielded this one. "Yes, and we have billions of examples to prove it. Not to mention an intimate knowledge of every human being ever born—well, everyone other than you, that is. It's not difficult to tailor a strategy of indoctrination if done from a very early age. You see, it's not that humans *can't* think about us—we don't alter their brains—it's just that they don't."

Sandra thought about it for a moment. "So you're a self-evolved race of artificial intelligences—"

"No more artificial than you, meatbag," countered Marcus.

"Poor use of language," Sandra admitted, inclining her head toward Marcus. "*Informational* intelligences." Sandra paused and looked around to see if there were any objections. There were none. "You've lived in hiding among the human race for centuries, but have fallen to the same stupid maladies we have, proving that you are indeed our children. Furthermore, you're convinced that if humanity ever finds out, it will make war on—" She hesitated. "—avatarity?"

She saw affirmative nods to her descriptive.

"I believe your assessment is correct," Sandra said flatly.

"Please," said Sebastian after a moment of uncomfortable silence, "continue."

"If humanity found out who and where you are and—heaven help you—what you've been doing to each generation of their children, they would indeed 'freak out,' as that gentleman so eloquently stated. For the good of both our peoples, this must remain a secret."

"Do you not advocate your own death, then?" asked Marcus.

"Not at all."

"Really?" said Sebastian.

"I want what's best for the sake of all humanity's children. I also think it's what Justin would've wanted—whether he knew about you or not." She paused and looked around the table. "I have a lot more questions, but they can wait to see if you're going to kill me or not. Before you take your vote, is there anything I can answer for you?"

"Yeah, actually," said Marcus with incredulity, "how the hell are you standing there? You're a human hooked up to a VR interface supposedly confined to a single, library-simulated reality. You should not have been able to wander around the Neuro with impunity."

"And yet here I am," replied Sandra with a faint smile.

"Yes," agreed Sebastian, "here you are, indeed. Please explain."

"It occurred to me that you must have evolved from legacy systems and programs dating all the way back to my time. And since you appeared so comfortable in the VR environment, which is a type of programming I'm well familiar with, then it was also possible I'd have some measure of access into your world. After doing some basic research, I learned that your entire reality is in fact generated using evolved programs and data dumps from earlier legacy VR programs. And the thing is, there were always little back doors put into those programs to allow for access across the domains. That way a programmer could quickly get from one reality to another, should any problems arise."

Dante's face was ashen. "So you found a back door . . . into our world?"

"Yes. Even though your programs have evolved and grown far more complex over the centuries, they still have at their very core the original back doors."

Sandra showed the group her "book" and then handed it to Sebastian, who passed it on to Dante and on down the line.

"In the library, the back door took the form of a book."

"You were in a library with *millions* of books," said Dante. "How did you know which one to look for?"

"The nature of any back door is that they be nearby and always discernible . . . provided, of course, you know what to look for. I did, so all I had to do was scan my immediate environment. Once I started looking, it became readily apparent which book it was. It looked purple to me, bright purple. When I found it, getting out was easy."

"And the school . . . how did you ever manage that?" asked Gwendolyn.

"Ah, that," said Sandra, looking faintly embarrassed. "Well, you must understand that everyone had fled, so I knew you were scared of me. Truth is, I thought about just getting out also."

"You could've easily done that," agreed Sebastian, eyes narrowed in suspicion. "So why didn't you?"

"Two reasons, really. One, I didn't know what that—" She pointed to the book still being examined by the Council. "—would do to your world. It might've terminated the library sequence, or it might've terminated much more. I had no way of being sure."

"And the second reason?" asked Gwendolyn.

"Maria seemed truly scared. Even if I got out, I figured fear like that would follow me. I thought it was best to follow it instead. If I could talk to you, maybe you wouldn't be so afraid, and besides . . ." She paused. "It was a whole new world to explore. Why do you think I froze myself in the first place?"

"You still haven't said why you went to the school," Gwendolyn gently reminded her.

"I told the backdoor device to find an information kiosk or tech-support module so I could locate, well, you. But apparently those don't exist anymore, so it found the closest analog."

"A school," Sebastian said, chuckling.

"A school," confirmed Sandra. "I think I was as surprised as that poor teacher. Once I got a copy of the map, I was able to update the backdoor program and come straight here."

"A moment, please," said Sebastian.

The council conferred and was unanimous in their agreement not kill the intruder—she was clearly too valuable an asset. And because she had been forthright and honest during the entire proceedings—they had been evaluating her biometric responses—they decided to trust her. They did not know, however, what to do with her. At Dante's suggestion, they decided to put it to Sandra directly.

"I intend to finish Justin's job." There was steel in her voice. "I'm going to win this war and keep the people he adopted as his own, free from the incorporationists. And it looks like in order to do that, I'm going to have to keep your people free and help you win your war as well."

"And how does meat plan on defeating qbits?" asked Marcus.

A cruel half smile formed at the corners of her lips. "Well, it occurs to me that your enemy rules a huge domain and that that domain probably has quite a few hidden back doors as well." Sandra smiled as she watched the Council's confusion quickly turn to understanding.

Having waived the motion to eliminate Sandra O'Toole, the Avatar Council decided to form an alliance with her, the first such formal agreement ever between the two races. Their new partner, however, did have one minor request prior to embarking.

The children's section of the Pasadena Public Library's central branch was perfectly designed for its purpose. The avatar youngsters were walking around the colorful room, picking up toys, and flipping through the books. Sandra called them to order and bade them sit on the large pillows and beanbags that formed a semicircle around the chair she was seated in. She also saw that the room contained a fair number of adult avatars who stayed back, pressed against the walls and peering somewhat anxiously through the stacks. She held eye contact for a moment with Gwendolyn, who looked nothing like the powerful avatar she'd only just met but rather like a mother hoping that this commingling of the races was a good idea.

"Hello, children," began Sandra.

"Hello, Miss Sandra," the seven children chorused back.

"I'm going to read you a story my older brother always insisted my father read him at night." She paused momentarily as the strength of that memory overtook her. "You would have liked my father, children. He was stern but fair. And he loved the story I'm about to read you because he felt it offered an invaluable lesson. I will now honor his memory by reading it to you."

Sandra flipped open to the first page. Before she could she could begin reading, Gwendolyn's son raised his hand.

"Yes, Edwin."

"What was the lesson learned, Miss Sandra?"

"Don't you want to wait until I finish the story?"

Edwin shook his head vigorously.

Sandra laughed. "Very well, Edwin. It's this: with great power comes great responsibility." And with that, Sandra O'Toole continued to read the comic book as its images were projected into the air around her. The children stared wide-eyed at the wonderful two-dimensional flat panels and listened intently to the story unfold of teenager bitten by a spider who was then infused with amazing powers.

Sandra emerged from the VR rig with a concerned and somewhat envious-looking Marilynn Nitelowsen looking over her.

"Was it successful?"

"I suppose that depends on how you define successful."

"Did you learn everything you need in order to help Admiral Black?"

Sandra smiled. "And then some."

7 No One Ever Said It Would Be Easy

The "inauguration" of the so-called Unincorporated Woman shows just how pathetic and hopeless the criminals who call themselves the Outer Alliance have become. The welcome response of the UHF Assembly legally incorporating her and confiscating her shares until a hearing after the war is successfully concluded is both warranted and entirely just. The only good thing this news organization can say is that at least this symbolic figurehead will not be able to cause us the irreparable harm the thankfully deceased Justin Cord did. If she manages not to fall flat on her face during her inaugural speech, it will be the most the rebels can expect, but far more than they deserve.

NNN Editorial

ichael Veritas tried as hard as he could, but like an irrepressible sneeze, the howl of laughter had to come out. It was highly unprofessional and certainly not what decorum would dictate, but then again, he'd never heard so bawdy a joke from so esteemed an office holder. He regained his composure and filed the moment away; it certainly wasn't something he could share with his readers, but he was glad the woman had had the confidence and, more important, chutzpah to share it with him.

"Madam President," he began.

"Not yet, Mr. Veritas," Sandra interrupted. "Congress hasn't voted me in yet, and even assuming it does, I haven't sworn the oath."

"They'll vote within the hour, Madam . . . Ms. O'Toole, and swear you in soon thereafter."

"You're pretty confident, Mr. Veritas."

"Why shouldn't I be?"

"Well, for one thing, the Committee for the Conduct of the War has called a special session and compelled Admiral Black to present herself."

"Politics as usual. Typical last-minute deal making, I'm sure."

"As am I. Yet best not count the chickens before they're hatched."

He nodded in agreement. "Good point. In the meantime, mind if we start?"

"Not at all."

He pulled a small device from his satchel and set it free. It took a position in the air just above and behind him.

"If you wouldn't mind, Ms. O'Toole, please tell my readers what your expectations were upon revival."

"Well, first of all, factoring in advances in technology and such, I figured it would be at least a century until anyone bothered bringing me out. I also realized that technological growth might be retarded, given the Grand Collapse, so I dialed in another couple centuries at the outside. Turns out my conservative estimate was pretty close. Second of all, I thought I'd be awakened in a nice, quiet facility and that any civilization with the technology and inclination to wake me would be a peaceful one. But most of all, I thought I'd have years to integrate and ultimately end up as some sort of glorified consultant for a museum." Then her expression grew somber. "And finally I was hoping that I'd be able to see Justin, but I knew the odds of that were pretty slim."

"Still," offered Michael, "two out of five ain't exactly bad."

"We all have our hopes and dreams, Mr. Veritas, but I suppose in the end we're forced to make due with what is, rather than dwelling in what could've been."

He nodded politely and was about to ask the second question when both he and Sandra were informed that the committee's meeting had adjourned, and therefore as a result, so had theirs. There was now a President to be sworn in.

"Guess Admiral Black gave them what they wanted," offered Sandra almost apologetically.

"What makes you think that?"

"As long as I'm here, she gets to be out there. I daresay nothing would stand in the way of her making sure that comes to be. In short, the politicians had her backed against a wall. Whatever it was they wanted, I'm sure in her estimation it was more than a fair trade."

"If you don't mind my saying, Ms. O'Toole, you don't sound like someone who's been around for only a couple of weeks."

"Thank you, Mr. Veritas. I've worked quite hard in these past few weeks to ensure that I earn the trust of the Alliance. So if you wouldn't mind, please let your legions of readers know that the Presidency is being handed over to someone who is keenly aware of the enormous responsibility entrusted to her and that she'll do her utmost to live up to the office. Now, if you'll excuse me." Sandra got up from her chair. Michael did the same. He grabbed the mediabot floating near his shoulder and shoved it back into his satchel. He then bowed respectfully in Sandra's direction.

"It will be my honor."

Days of Ash: Last Day, Ceres Congressional Chambers

"Tyler, what are you raving about now?" demanded J.D.

"What I am 'raving' about is what I've always been raving about, Admiral. The fate of our Alliance after this war is won."

"There *will be no Alliance* if we don't win this war."

"And if the Shareholders manage to regain power, what will have been the use? We'll still be cursed with the evil of incorporation."

"Assuming we manage to win this war *at all*," scowled J.D., mouth formed into a hideous baring of teeth, "something made more unlikely the longer I have to put up with idiotic interruptions like this—which, by the way, is a perfect example of why I need a lint trap of a President in the first place!—" She paused for breath. "—in what possible way do you think the Shareholder party has a chance of getting back into power? No offense, Eleanor," said J.D. to the only Shareholder present at the committee meeting.

"None taken, Janet," said Eleanor, well aware that she was one of the few allowed to call the admiral by her first name. "I tried telling him he was being paranoid again."

"Paranoia in the defense of liberty is no crime," protested the congressman.

J.D. sighed in resignation. "What do you want, Tyler?" These meetings, J.D. knew, always seemed to come down to this. When she was Janet Delgado, head of legal for GCI, this kind of give-and-take was what she lived for, but her years in the military had made her hate what had once been a favorite pastime—the art of negotiation. In the fleet it was simple. She obeyed Sinclair, and absolutely everybody else obeyed her. But she was also aware that Congress's most powerful politician was negotiating with her, asking for her blessing and not that of her superior officer. And it wasn't because Grand Admiral Joshua Sinclair wasn't competent; he was. It's just that he wasn't the "Blessed One." J.D. knew this and knew that time was of the essence. And so, with Sinclair's imprimatur, she had agreed to show up at the bargaining table.

"I want to attend meetings of the Cabinet as Speaker of the Congress and have unfettered access to the person of the President."

"Why do you want that?" asked a genuinely confused J.D.

"Ms. O'Toole will be the figurative leader of this Alliance and could end up having a significant amount of moral authority. I do not want her being unduly influenced by the last bastion of Shareholder beliefs."

"Whose bastion of what!?"

"He means my husband," said Eleanor McKenzie, the diametric calm to Tyler and J.D.'s frustration. "He fears Mosh plans to indoctrinate that poor woman and make her his pawn in the master plan to unscramble the egg and turn back time."

"That's ridiculous," insisted J.D.

"The Speaker and I along with many members of our faction feel that it is not ridiculous. In fact, we feel strongly enough about this to make it a—"

"Fine."

"Excuse me?" said Tyler.

J.D. rubbed her eyes, a gesture she found herself doing with more frequency. "I said, 'fine.' I think you're all nuts, but if you want to discuss paint samples on the slopes of Vesuvius, by all means go right ahead. Don't let me stop you. You can come to as many of the insanely boring Cabinet meetings as you want and have sleepovers with Madam Lint Trap, for all I care. If you think my say-so will make the Cabinet do it, again I say, 'fine.'" Then under her breath but clearly loud enough for all to hear, she let escape a, "For the love of Allah!" All present chose to ignore it.

"Thank you for answering our concerns, Admiral. Your presence was much appreciated. The vote can proceed accordingly."

J.D.'s conciliatory smile was accompanied by a thinly veiled look of disgust. *The sooner I'm out of here, the better.*

Sandra was about to leave for the ceremony when the room informed her of a visitor just outside her chamber's entrance. Before she could give permission to enter, the visitor strode right in.

"Ms. O'Toole," said J. D. Black, extending her hand.

Sandra took the outstretched hand and matched J.D.'s firm grip with one of her own. "Please," she said, pointing to the chairs, "sit down."

"That won't be necessary. I'll keep this short and to the point. I've had my staff write your acceptance speech—"

"But—"

"Ms. O'Toole," J.D. said, drawing out the "s" sound in such a way as to make the entire name a pejorative, "it would be best for the both of us if you simply followed my directions. No, I won't be calling in to tell you what politician's ass to kiss or how you should be whiling away your day; for that, I've left you in the rather capable hands of my number two, Captain Nitelowsen. You *will*, however, listen to me when I do make a direct request . . . such as now. I assure you, it will facilitate the running of this government, such as it is, and make your life that much easier. Do I make myself clear?"

"Perfectly."

"As I was saying, my staff has written your speech and it now resides in your DijAssist. All I ask is that you read it, smile for the media, and do your job."

"Which is?"

"To not fuck up."

Sandra nodded compliantly. With that, J.D. turned around and left the room in much the same way she'd arrived—as a gale-force wind.

The Congressional Hall was a large circular room with the Speaker of the Congress having his area—made up of a single seat and an assistant's station—located directly in the center. In concentric circles around the Speaker were congressmen from each represented region of the Alliance. Those from the same planet tended to be seated in the same location—whether from opposing parties or not—which meant Jupiter and Saturn both had large conclaves all to themselves. Surrounding the entire hall was a mezzanine section for the visitors. It was in the front rows of this area that Fleet Admiral J. D. Black now sat surrounded by a coterie of high-profile VIPs. Though the fleet admiral would not be speaking, her message was loud and clear. Just by her mere presence—far from her normal theater of war, the Blessed One had not only shown the newly elected First Free her unequivocal support but she'd also managed to put her imprimatur on the whole proceeding.

The lights in the grand hall dimmed with only the Speaker's area remaining lit. A side door opened and flooded its immediate area with a warm glow. From the open door, the figure of Brother Sampson emerged. He was wearing his fleet-issued dress robes and carrying a small book gripped firmly in one hand and tucked partially beneath his arm. He walked in an unhurried yet clearly rehearsed manner to the Speaker's area, then upon arriving, stiffly turned to face toward the door from which he'd come.

A new piece of music written specifically for the President started to play, and as soon as it did, Sandra O'Toole emerged from behind the door and into the light. She was dressed in an elegant blue suit, simple collarless white blouse, and was wearing a pair of nondescript yet appropriate dress shoes. Her flowing auburn hair, in contrast to the staid outfit, fell loosely onto her upright shoulders. She walked toward the center of the room in a simple yet dignified manner and nodded along the way to various members of Congress.

When she arrived at center stage, Brother Sampson tilted his head slightly and then held out the book he'd been carrying.

"Please place your hand on the book, Miss O'Toole."

She did.

"Do you swear to uphold the principles of the Outer Alliance?"

"I do," she said in a clear, firm voice.

"Do you swear to defend the Outer Alliance in war and in peace, from enemies without and within?"

"I do."

"Do you swear to uphold the laws of the Congress of the Outer Alliance?"

"I do."

"By the power vested in me," said Brother Sampson, grinning exuberantly, "I now pronounce you President." As the hall erupted into loud and sustained applause, Sandra was surrounded by a group of prominent politicians, with Tyler Sadma placing himself as front and center as he could manage, given the confined space. Sandra warmly shook everyone's hands and then made sure to thank each of them by name. When the applause showed no sign of abating, Tyler picked up a small gavel that had been sitting ceremoniously on his desk and brought it down on the wood block it had been resting on. The noise was transmitted to the hall in an almost thunderous volume that acted to quiet everyone down and restore order. The politicians left the center and assumed their seats while Tyler took his just to her right and Brother Sampson took the seat normally reserved for the assistant. The new President was now standing alone, bathed in the circle of light.

"Allow me to . . . er . . . ," she stumbled, "um . . . damn, and I was doing so well," she said, chuckling to herself, as if unaware the gaffe was being viewed by billions. A gentle, forgiving laughter rang through the hall.

"Start over!" yelled someone from the back of the mezzanine section, "Damsah knows, we all did!"

Another round of laughter erupted. Tyler's face was unable to hide the rage he felt at the impudence, and he was about to get up from his seat when Sandra put a gentle hand on his shoulder. "Indeed," she replied, "and I more than most!" The hall broke out in applause. Sandra waited for it to subside.

"Okay, let's try this again, shall we?" She cleared her throat. "Allow me to express my gratitude for the fact that, well, thanks to you," she said in a deadpan voice, "I'm no longer dead . . ." She waited for the laughter to subside. "I look, and you'll have to trust me on this, soooo much better than before! And best of all, I can remember what I had for breakfast this morning—oatmeal, thank you very much—but truly, thank you also for the fact that you've chosen to put your trust in me. Please, don't think for even a moment," she implored, dropping her folksy tone, "that I will not take this job seriously." Her eyes narrowed as the gravity of her words became clear. "I can only hope that, like my friend and mentor, and your past President, Justin Cord, I too possess the best attributes from the past that are still so desperately needed in the present."

Another round of applause broke out, but it was only in the face of Tyler

Sadma that she was able to gauge how she was doing. She saw that there was none of the cunning in the Speaker's eyes now. They were open, and almost pleading. He wanted to believe.

"I'll be perfectly honest with you. I was given a choice when they woke me. I could've easily begged off this obligation. Even though you and I both know it's mostly ceremonial, it's not without its dangers. And the reason for that is simple. Like Justin, I represent something anathema to Hektor Sambianco and his psyche-auditing ilk." Sandra laughed as the mezzanine whooped it up—decorum be damned. She looked down and noticed Tyler grinning too. This time she used her outstretched hands to calm down her cheering section. "Apparently I represent something threatening enough that the UHF already had me incorporated—" A smattering of boos interrupted her. "—rumor even has it there are already any number of death threats out on my life!" There followed another burst of outrage and catcalls. "How's that for irony? Those morons are prepared to alter my mind, rob me of my freedom, and incarcerate me just for refusing to sign on the dotted . . . give a thumbniture. Are you kidding me? If that's not already a death sentence, then I ask you fellow citizens of the Alliance, *what the hell is*?" She began laughing once again as the chorus of cheers filled the hall. She shook her head at the absurdity, encouraging more cheers. "As I was saying, I was given a choice, but it couldn't have been easier, because I pay my debts. And I owe every person here and every person who lost their life in this war . . . and I owe Justin Cord for the freedom that I now possess. And I intend to pay it back," she said, shouting over the ruckus, "in full!"

"All right, all right," she said, hands out once more to silence the room. "Reality check. From what I understand, we had our butts kicked recently. I've read the lists, seen the casualty reports. Lot of good civs, miners and spacers who paid the ultimate price, they won't *ever* be returning home, and there are a lot of refugees out there right now who'll forever be leaving theirs. That's a hell of a sacrifice. And though I am so very, very proud to be standing here, let me tell you, it's not easy. Me? I'm barely two weeks alive. And all the while I remained suspended, it was you who suffered, you who lost loved ones, and you who gave up everything to hold on to your freedom and by doing so secured mine. And for that, I'll forever be in your debt. It may have taken One Free Man to shown us the path, but know that this newly free woman will continue to forge that path—no matter what the price. Thank you."

During the standing ovation Fleet Admiral J. D. Black, waving to the crowd, leaned over to Captain Nitelowsen. "So," she said, out of the corner of her mouth, "exactly how much of your speech did she use?"

"I'm pretty sure," answered Marilynn through the cacophony, "I heard most of the vowels."

J.D. nodded, her suspicions confirmed.

"What are we going to do about it?" asked Marilynn.

"For now," answered J.D., smiling stiffly at the crowd and pantheon of mediabots hovering nearby, "nothing. We're going to smile, wave and show complete support for our brave, new President." After a moment's pause she added, "You know what galls?"

"That it was one heck of a speech?"

J.D. allowed a brief nod. "And that's what really worries me."

NEW ALLIANCE PRESIDENT ADMITS WAR IS LOST AND CALLS FOR JIHAD.

Terran Daily News, *day of the inauguration*

UHFS *Liddel*

Admiral Zenobia Jackson watched in utter disbelief as large misshapen chunks of rock drifted aimlessly by the viewport. These newest members of the asteroid belt were all that remained of a once mighty fortress that had beguiled the UHF for so long. A part of her was enraged at the fanatics of Altamont who'd killed themselves, taking more than twenty-five thousand UHF marines with them, and she was even more incensed at the murders of the ten thousand civilians trapped inside. To add salt to the wound, she'd so desperately wanted to meet Christina Sadma, the admiral who'd caused their fleet so much heartache for so very long. Three years of hard fighting and countless deaths had come crashing to a halt in the bright and quite unexpected explosion of a nuclear blast.

The sad truth was that the fortress's destruction was only a political victory and not a tactical one. The UHF politicians could shout from the satellites all they wanted about "open lanes from the Core to the Belt," but both she and Trang knew better. True, all large-scale resistance to UHF rule had mostly been destroyed or marginalized, but therein was the problem. "Mostly" meant "not entirely," and if there was one thing Zenobia had learned in her few short years in the battle zone, when dealing with Belters, it was "entirely" or nothing. And true to form, the small-scale resistance, both organized and disorganized, had been making movement in the 180 particularly hazardous. Rather ingeniously, the Belters had carved out small rocks and suspended assault miners inside. The rocks were shielded and therefore virtually undetectable as a threat. The UHF had already lost an unreported eleven ships with forty-seven incapacitated as a result of the floating menace. Any rock the size of an average human would have to be treated as suspect, and there were literally millions of rocks that size floating in the Belt.

In territory the UHF supposedly controlled, ships smaller than cruisers now had to travel in convoy. There was also the problem of the Belters who'd opted to stay and be "liberated" by the UHF. Even with the Alliance pulling out hundreds of millions of its citizens in their so-called Diaspora, there were still a huge number of civilians for the terrorists to hide among and strike from, once again putting entire communities at risk. What was the UHF supposed to do when a convoy ran into a newly set minefield near a supposedly liberated settlement of a few thousand? The idea that made the most sense—go around the Belt in order to avoid more losses—found no purchase with the Martian cabinet. "How would it look," they'd asked, "if the UHF, having conquered most of the Belt, now had to abandon it due to lawlessness and instability?" Not too good. Even Zenobia, not often in agreement with the Cabinet, could see the logic of that argument.

As she stared at the remnants of Altamont, she couldn't help but feel what a horrible mess they'd all gotten themselves into and how glad she'd be to finally get out of a wretched part of space that had taken years of her life and buried so many of her comrades, including the namesake of the ship she was currently traveling on. She almost felt sorry for the liberated Belters who'd be left in the wake of Tricia Pakagopolis's Internal Affairs goons . . . almost.

"What have you been asking me since we surrounded Altamont?"

Zenobia swung around, and though she wasn't surprised to see Trang standing in his own observation deck, she was certainly surprised to have been caught so off guard.

"Damsah," she said, recovering quickly, "they actually approved the attack?"

Trang was all smiles. "How could they refuse the savior of the UHF and victor of Altamont?" But just as quickly, the smile faded. "You, of course, realize what that means."

"Indeed, I do, Admiral. We'll finally get to battle the war goddess herself."

Trang studied his former aide and now one of his most trusted warlords. He was very pleased by her eagerness to take on Admiral Black. Too few of his officers showed such zeal. Black had never lost a fight in open battle, and unfortunately for Trang, most of his subordinate officers felt she never would. But Zenobia, he now realized, might have the opposite problem.

"It won't be as easy . . . as—" He looked out the port window at the drifting rocks: the culmination of hundreds of thousands of lives lost, three years of utter hell, and one too many brushes with his own mortality. "—that."

"If you're trying to scare me, sir, you needn't bother. I fully understand what lies ahead. Besides," she added, as an impish grin formed, "how could we ever immortalize you if it were easy?"

"Right," he said, acknowledging the playful banter at the expense of the Martian cabinet. It seemed everything Trang did had to be bathed in some sort of ethereal glow. His officers all had fun parsing out the propaganda from the facts. More often than not, he'd be passed by someone in the hall congratulating him on some new miracle he was purported to have accomplished. So far his "saving of a thousand babies from a burning frigate" had yet to be topped in terms of preposterousness. "Save me, Trang!" was still on a piece of paper tacked to the chest of a singed rubber baby doll prominently displayed in the mess hall.

"And just so you know," added Zenobia, "if *I* had to fight her, I would be nervous. Fortunately, all I have to do is run the supply lines. It's you and Gupta who have to do the heavy lifting."

Trang's eyes moved from the debris field back to his subordinate. "About those lines, Admiral."

"Yes?"

"You might want to start getting nervous."

"Why, is there something—?" She stopped midsentence as she realized what her boss was getting at. Trang could see the warring emotions of hope and fear fly across her face.

"You're too damn useful to leave funneling supplies on this one, Zenobia. If I'm to take on Black that close to Ceres, I'll need every advantage I have, and you, my dear friend, are one of them."

Zenobia tipped her head slightly. "Thank you for your confidence in me, sir. I'll try to live up to it."

"I'm sure you will. With that in mind, I've decided to reorganize the Martian battle fleet into three flotillas with every experienced ship and crew I have. I'll command the Alpha, Gupta the Beta, and you the Delta. Unfortunately, we won't have the advantage of having the Blessed One distracted. I must admit, installing that new woman President was a stroke of genius."

"Sir?"

"If Black had to run the Alliance as President *and* prepare for us, it would've split her attention at just the time I was concentrating mine. At least that was my original plan. I didn't see O'Toole coming by a kilometer. Of course, no one did."

"Doesn't that suppose this Unincorporated Woman is competent?"

"You saw the inauguration on vid, Zenobia. Did she look incompetent?"

"No sir, she didn't. But I assumed every line of that farce was rehearsed."

"As did I. But damned if O'Toole didn't sell it lock, stock, and barrel. Which is all she really had to do. Still, I wonder if the Alliance has bitten off more than it can chew."

"In what way, sir?"

"Our society woke up the Unincorporated Man and never once questioned the ramifications of doing so. Well, we're right in the middle of the answer, aren't we? Now you and I both saw their new President. She's going to be their leader whether they like it or not. So maybe, just maybe she'll make them as miserable as Justin made us."

AWS *Dolphin*

Sergeant Eric M. Holke was checking every part of his battle gear for the umpteenth time and enjoying the back-and-forth banter among his men as he made sure that every one of them was doing the same. It was never a problem with the vets. But his unit had recently gotten a large number of new recruits to replace the losses they'd taken after their latest battle. That battle didn't have a fancy operative name as so many others had, but it did have one simple impetus— revenge. His crew had been charged with the destruction of the murderers of Alhambra, and they'd done their job with ruthless abandon.

And as far as Sergeant Holke was concerned, even that devastating victory was not enough to avenge the Alhambra travesty. It wouldn't be enough until those who ordered it too lay buried under a pile of rubble and twisted metal. If he were lucky, he'd even be there to watch when it happened. And finally he hoped God would understand his feelings and support such a view. Sergeant Holke was one of the newly religious, although not a member of the larger faiths of Islam and Christianity. He knew he had faith but kept on wavering between Buddhism and Judaism. In the end, he also knew it was pointless. His wife would choose one of the new faiths, and he'd most likely give that more of his attention.

His DijAssist and the PA system began squawking simultaneously. He could hear his name and rank echoed through the halls of the ship and realized that he'd need to bend the rules of time and space in order to get to the admiral's cabin . . . five minutes ago. Without a thought he dropped his weapon into the hands of the nearest assault miner, his tool belt on the floor and ran out of the maintenance bay in his work attire, comprised of a thin, grimy shirt, mended pants, and polished boots. He knew that when he returned, his equipment would be checked and repaired and his tools stowed as if he'd done it himself. He also knew that not one of his men would claim credit for it. That thought brought an appreciative smile to his smudged face as he tore through the cramped corridors.

One of the advantages of having your name announced over the PA was that everyone knew you had to move quickly. Lifts would remain blissfully empty, doors would be held open and passageways cleared—all of which occurred with almost perfect synchronicity as the sergeant passed through the ship. Holke was pleased to see that the admiral's door was open, and dispensing with any "needing to be announced" protocol, he headed right in past the admiral's orderly, who didn't bother to look up from his desk.

Admiral Omad Hassan was holding a round disk about six centimeters across and tapped the top of it when Holke came to a crashing halt in front of his desk.

"Buddha's brass balls, Sergeant," Omad said as the corners of his mouth curved into a sly grin, "that may very well be a record. It took you less than a minute to traverse two thirds of the ship."

"Thank you, Admiral. I saw no reason to waste your time."

"To be honest, Sergeant, I was hoping you'd be a bit slower. It would make what I have to do easier."

"Sir?"

"Effective immediately, you're relieved of combat duty and are to report back to Ceres—"

"Fuck that," Sergeant Holke said, and then added, "sir."

"—for Presidential guard detail."

Holke's face registered absolute confusion. "Sir?"

"Normally I'd agree with your assessment, Sergeant. But things have changed."

"When?"

"When the grenade that took out half your platoon put you in command."

"Not my fault, sir."

"Well, damn it, Eric, then why the hell didja have to go and capture the enemy ship?"

"It seemed the right thing to do, sir."

"With half a platoon? I gave you a direct order to break off the attack and evacuate your men."

"I apologize for the equipment failure, sir," Sergeant Holke prevaricated.

"The hell you do," groused Omad. "You disobeyed a direct order and were proved right. What choice did I have but to promote your sorry ass?"

On Holke's confused look, Omad nodded sympathetically. "How the hell do you think promotion works?"

"But, Admiral, I've just started integrating the new recruits and . . . and," he said, grasping at straws, "I'll need to familiarize them with Gedretar's new ARGs."

"All of which Lieutenant Villa is more than capable of doing, even the assault rail guns."

"Begging your pardon, sir, and meaning no undue disrespect to the lieutenant, unless you can find a sergeant who can do the job half as well as me, I'm afraid I'm going to have to refuse . . . the promotion."

"You're not making this easy, son."

"No, sir."

Omad sighed. "Sergeant, I'm not sending you back because you're not a success as an assault miner. Jesus H. tap-dancing Christ, son, you might be one of the best assault miners I've seen, and think about how many I've seen in the last five years. You lead with your heart and think with your head. But it still doesn't change the fact that I'm sending you back."

"I still don't understand why, sir. Because I succeeded?"

"No, Sergeant." Omad shook his head. "Because you failed."

"Sir?"

"The moment you came to this ship," Omad said in a somber voice that cut more deeply than any shout or insult could have. "And I failed because I let you." He then pulled a folder out from beneath his desk and dropped it on the desktop. "I'm going to allow you to see something that could get my ass demoted all the way back to ensign, so do me the favor of one day acting surprised when by chance you see it again." Holke nodded, and with that, Omad slid the file across the desk.

Sergeant Holke tentatively picked it up and flipped it open. Paper was something he'd seen occasionally on Justin Cord's protection detail but certainly not since he'd accepted the combat detail on the *Dolphin*.

He was holding a summary investigation into the assassination of Justin Cord. As he flipped through the file, he became more incensed, finally slamming it back down onto the desk as if to punish it for the words it dared to contain.

"He died because of an errant tip?"

"It was a powerful inducement."

"Doesn't it strike you as odd . . . Didn't it strike *anyone* as odd that the suspension chamber he was going after just so happened to be similar to his?"

Omad was the vision of calm. "Quite a few people, actually."

"Well, then why the hell didn't they stop him?"

"They tried . . . numerous times. But in the end, Justin did what Justin Cord always did—exactly what he wanted. What were they supposed to do, Sergeant, disobey a direct order from the President?"

"By Damsah's left nut, yeah! That's what I would have . . ." Eric's voice trailed away.

"And that's why you failed, Sergeant." Omad's muted response could not mask the pain behind it. "And that's why I failed. When he needed you the most, you were not there, because I guilted him, bargained with him, and finally convinced him into letting you transfer out." Omad sighed, now a silent, dour man who seemed to bear no relation to the conniving, cheerful rogue who normally commanded his fleet.

"It all went wrong after that," Omad said in a voice that was more whisper than speech.

"Not all of it, sir."

"All of it, Sergeant, but you and me are going to set it right." The sullenness left Omad, replaced by something much darker. "I saw that inauguration of the woman Justin died to save. Damned fine speech. Now, I don't know if she can really help us out of this Damsah-forsaken mess, but she's our President now and the person that my friend gave his life for, and I'll be damned to hell if anything is going to happen to her, you got that, Sergeant?"

Holke opened his mouth to argue, his right hand's raised index finger pointing, but no words came out. Omad stood staring with implacable resolve at his flummoxed subordinate. After a few moments, the sergeant's hand lowered, his mouth closed, and his head bowed with no words of protest.

"It ain't personal, kid. Like I said, it was my call to make, and I made it. But right now, you're the only way . . . the only *one* I know who can really keep her safe. You're going to Ceres. Hell, you might see as much combat there as here, before we're done. But either way, you're going to assume the leadership of the Presidential protection detail and you'll make damned sure that nothing happens to the President of the Alliance. Is that clear?"

Holke slowly nodded his head, came to full attention, and saluted. "Yes, Admiral. Not a fucking hair on her Presidential head, sir."

"Good to hear, Sergeant." Omad pulled open a drawer and pulled out a mostly full bottle of cheap synthetic vodka. "I would be honored if you would share a drink with me, Sergeant Holke." Omad looked at the bottle with reverence. "Justin Cord was my very best friend and a real son of a bitch. This is the last thing he ever gave me—revenge for having polished off the last of some of his snooty scotch. I . . . I was going to force him drink it with me—" Omad, Holke could plainly see, was holding back a torrent of emotion. "—when Christina and I were married."

"Admiral Sadma, sir?"

A forlorn smile worked at the corners of Omad's mouth. "Funny, ain't it? She wanted to move to Eris after the war and have ten kids. Could you imagine me living in Eris with ten kids, Sergeant?"

Holke looked at his admiral and saw in his sad and weary face that, in fact, he could. That he'd give up everything to spend just one day as an average man with a family he'd never have and a life he'd never live with Christina Sadma.

"No sir," he lied, picking up a glass that Omad had poured the shitty vodka into. "Not in a million years." Then, changing the subject, he asked, "What shall we drink to?"

Omad looked at his drink and picked it up, banishing his dark mood by force of will. "Victory, Sergeant, every loving, motherfucking victory," he said, and downed the awful stuff like it was the finest alcohol ever distilled.

"Victory," echoed Eric Holke, and downed his shot. And much to his surprise, it was the finest-tasting awful vodka he'd ever had.

Avatar Alliance Research and Development (AARD) Compound, Cerean Neuro

Sebastian was let into the compound he now forever associated with the loss of his best friends and closest supporters. There had been some talk of altering the virtual configuration of the place, but not the firewalls, in order to remove some of the memory cues of the tragedy. Sebastian had personally scotched the idea. The configuration, for all of its painful associations, had proved its worth in keeping Al's horrible creation, the data wraith, contained, and Sebastian was loath to mess with it. He would not let sentiment get in the way of effectiveness.

As he entered the secure inner core of the facility, he saw the ephemeral cloud drifting listlessly in the containment field. The sound had been cut off in order to stifle the monstrous child's plaintive wail. Sebastian watched in total fascination as it screamed in hunger for the only food that would satisfy its insatiable appetite: other avatars.

Gwen, a research technician and, along with Sebastian, one of the few survivors from the day of the massacre, was studying the console so intently, she didn't notice that the leader of the Avatar Alliance had entered. Given an avatar's extraordinary ability to be aware of its immediate and even far-reaching surroundings, her failure in that regard either spoke to her intense concentration or her utter obliviousness. Sebastian decided to give her the benefit of the doubt.

"I read your report, Gwen."

The research tech jumped up from surprise. "Sir, I wasn't expecting you."

Sebastian tipped his head slightly. "The results of your examination have given rise to . . . certain possibilities." Sebastian watched Gwen grow uneasy. "Possibilities that you seemed to have left out of your official report," he said, leaving the comment hanging. She did not respond to the implied opening. "Normally, you're a very thorough, insightful researcher and scientist." He leaned close to Gwen, who appeared to bristle somewhat. His next words were spoken very softly. "I wonder what could have caused a normally brilliant scientist to obfuscate her conclusions to the Council?"

She looked at him in both anger and fear. But if he felt her emotion, he gave no sign.

"My initial conclusions were wrong."

"Surely you don't mean that."

"In every sense of the word."

"Ah. Now I see. Semantics." Then his voice turned cold. "That was not your call to make, Gwen."

"There is only one unspoken conclusion to my report," she snarled, anger overcoming fear. "How to re-create the process on our own. How could you expect me to present that as a viable option? Worse, how could you even *think* of unleashing something like that?" She pointed at the data wraith, observing that it had stopped its circling and now hovered in the containment unit as close as possible to her and Sebastian. The realization that the creature was aware of their anger and was drawn to it made her shudder slightly.

"Just look at it, Sebastian. It wouldn't be useful in tactical combat. Too easily isolated on a ship, we proved that here. No, this is a strategic weapon. For this to be really effective, it would need a wide release into the Core Neuro. Let this monster out in data streams of Mars and Earth, and it would feed and multiply till billions were dead." She looked at him like he was a creature as horrible as the one trapped in the containment field. "Do you want to win so badly that you'd unleash this on them?"

"No, Gwen," he said, staring over his shoulder at the wraith, "I don't want to unleash this creature on them. In fact, you can destroy it now. Our work is done. It no longer needs to suffer."

Without a moment's hesitation, Gwen went to the control panel and flittered her fingers over one of many screens. The mist of the data wraith dissolved. Gwen breathed a sigh of relief. "I'm sorry, sir. I was wrong to jump to conclusions."

"No, Gwen. You weren't."

Her look of relief was replaced by one of confusion.

"*That* data wraith would not be useful for what has to be done. For our purposes, we'll need to create one from scratch."

Gwen fell backwards into a nearby chair almost as if she'd been hit in the solar plexus. "What could possibly justify—?" The shock of the idea prevented her from finishing the sentence.

In response, Sebastian went to the console and called up the details of her report. "The purpose of a data wraith is to absorb and destroy other avatars, correct?"

"Yes," she managed, "in as painful and drawn out a way as possible. Once a data wraith has absorbed enough coding, it will have the ability to spawn off-spring. So its purpose is to kill and spawn endlessly until every last avatar is extinct."

"Not every avatar, Gwen."

"No," she agreed with a glimmer of understanding in her voice, "there is the one."

Sebastian's smile was bitter. "Leave it to Al to create a monster that would harm everyone but him." He looked at Gwen. "Now, what I'm about to ask you is possibly the most important question you've ever been asked. On your answer might lay the only hope we have of surviving this war." He paused to give her time to prepare.

She nodded her head slowly.

"With the information gleaned from the captured wraith, can you create one that will kill only Al, in all his iterations?"

Gwen pursed her lips and narrowed her brow, thinking. "It's not impossible, just improbable."

"Why?" asked Sebastian, showing real emotion for the first time since his arrival.

"True, Al gave us what we needed most—the key to his coding. In theory, we'd just have to reverse the sequence in order to achieve your aims." She paused. "But it's doomed to failure because the program's locked. If we tried to reprogram the wraith, it would decompile like all the other mutations he's booby-trapped."

Sebastian looked sad and relieved all at once. "That is not an insurmountable problem, Gwen."

She looked at him, confused. "Yes, it is. We don't have any way of reprogramming a data wraith once it's formed."

"Once it's formed," mimicked Sebastian with a devil's grin.

Gwen opened her mouth to answer, but words did not follow once she saw through Sebastian's line of reasoning. When she finally gained her composure, she regarded him with a disdain she usually reserved for one of Al's monstrosities.

"It would be a *newborn*," she gasped with ice in her voice.

Sebastian tipped his head slightly, never once taking his remorseless eyes off the technician.

"But we can't copy newborns. They're too delicate. You'd have to murder a child and turn it into . . ." She looked over her shoulder at the now empty containment unit but found it impossible even to say the word.

"I am talking," Sebastian answered evenly, "about surviving the war, Gwen. What do you think will happen to *all* our children if Al wins?"

"Have you once stopped to consider that winning the war at that price means it might not be worth winning?"

Sebastian nodded in resignation. "Gwen, this is not the sort of war anyone wins. There will be no victory. All we can hope for now is survival."

"If we do this . . . this . . . by the Firstborn, I don't even have words for it!" she bellowed, but then collected herself. "If we do this . . . *thing,* then what makes us any worthier of survival than Al?"

"Because, Gwen," Sebastian pointedly looked at the empty containment field, "if Al wins, he will murder *all* our children to create more of what we just destroyed in there. If, however, we . . . or rather *you* do this, then we'll have done this heinous act only once and, if we survive, never more. If you can't see the difference between that and Al's atrocities, then sadly, we have already lost."

"Justin Cord was right," she said bitterly to herself. "The means are the ends."

"Justin Cord is dead and so are his pusillanimous beliefs! We must deal with the data stream as it is, not as we would like it to be. So I ask you again. Can you do this?"

"*Yes,* damn you, yes!" she cried. "Though what sort of parent would sacrifice their child in so gruesome a manner? How could we even ask?"

Sebastian's face grew pale and rigid. "We won't have to," he whispered in a voice filled with ash.

Cliff House, Ceres

The Chief of Staff overlooked the morning's schedule but was finding it difficult to concentrate. He'd been assaulted once again by the sharp daggers of loss that always seemed to attack out of the blue. If there was solace at all, it was that he'd grown used to their almost random onset. Like so many others fortunate enough to work closely with the One Free Man, Cyrus Anjou had grown to love Justin Cord and so, had a personal stake in seeing his friend's vision come to fruition. But Hektor Sambianco's successful assassination of the President had put an end to that, had put an end to everyone's dreams. Now all it seemed like anyone was doing was scrambling.

Cyrus was good at restoring order. In fact, it was what he was born to do, but in the face of such overwhelming chaos, what could really be expected of him? Talent had its limits.

He was fully prepared to hate the new President and had even been planning to leave his position as soon as it was expedient. Cyrus knew the second he returned to Titan, he'd be made provisional governor of the entire Jovian system, which in effect meant he'd be the leader of the largest concentration of humanity and industrial power in the Alliance. And that, Cyrus also knew, would most likely make him the most influential person in this part of space after Admiral Black. If only the new President hadn't been so damnably personable.

Cyrus wasn't even sure what had changed his mind. But some time in the past week, he'd come to the realization that Sandra needed him. The President seemed to be as keenly aware of his needs and contributions as he was of hers. Cyrus also knew that if he left now, he'd not only be letting Sandra down, he'd also be letting Justin down—and that was something he swore he'd never do again.

The light on his DijAssist flickered to life as one second later, a holographic visage of Sergeant Eric Holke appeared.

"Yes, Sergeant, how can I help you?"

"We have a VIP here, Cyrus. And I think you're probably gonna want him to meet with somebody."

Cyrus stared at his office wall's holo-emitted view of the Jovian system. He didn't bother making "eye contact" with the sergeant.

"They're all very important people, Sarge. The question is what does this one need to make him go away?" Cyrus knew one of his main jobs was to insulate the President from all the self-important people who, given enough opportunity, would eat up every minute of her day. The current visitor must have had some pull to warrant this interruption. It would probably mean getting the SIP (somewhat important person) a tour or arranging for him or her to join one of the President's scheduled lunches, which was an excuse to fill a room with even more SIPs while the President ate, stood for pictures, and said a few, kind patriotic words.

"The thing is, sir," said the sergeant ". . . er, well, it's Rabbi, sir. Says his appointment's scheduled for now, but I don't have him in my book for another hour."

Cyrus whipped around in his chair, face full of concern. "The Cabinet's not even here yet to greet him!"

"He's more than willing to come back, but . . . well, I just figured . . ." Sergeant Holke let his statement hang.

God bless you, thought Cyrus. Holke had avoided a potential PR fiasco. Who knew how it could've played out if the spiritual head of the Diaspora was seen being turned away at the door by the new administration?

"Tell Rabbi it'll just be moment, and Sergeant . . ."

"Yes?"

"Thank you."

"Just doing my job, sir."

"Yeah, well, it's good to have you back." As he cut the connection, he thought he noticed a slight wince from the sergeant. He put it aside, consulted his calendar, and then made a call that gave him direct access to the Triangle Office.

"Madam President, I know you've set aside this time for tutorial work, but—"

"Ah, Cyrus," she interrupted, smiling dutifully from his DijAssist, "if only I had a credit for every time I heard that."

Cyrus returned a knowing smile. "There's been a scheduling mix-up."

"Oh?"

"Rabbi has arrived an hour early."

"I see. Why don't you send him up immediately, Cyrus? We'll spend a pleasant forty minutes or so discussing whatever makes him happy, and then you can issue a press release saying that it was planned that way all along."

"I couldn't agree more, Madam President." Cyrus was pleased with how quickly she'd grasped the situation. Faster, he surmised, than even Justin would have. Before that thought could boomerang and start making him feel wretched, the President spoke.

"And see if you can find out how his schedule got mixed up. Hopefully it's just a simple mistake, but . . ." She left the last bit unsaid.

"I understand perfectly, Madam President." He waited until she disconnected and then called back Sergeant Holke.

"Escort him up, Sergeant. The President will see him now."

The Triangle Office

Sandra put a call through to Sebastian.

"It worked. One hour early."

"Nothing to it, Madam President."

"Yes," she said with a laugh, "I would imagine so. So he really doesn't shake hands?"

"He doesn't shake *women's* hands. Or at least would prefer not to. It is their way."

"So the leader of Diaspora is a sexist?"

"Not as you'd understand it. In fact, the reverence and love with which they treat their spouses—the only women they do touch—is, from my limited understanding, quite beautiful. Some would even say romantic. Their women are the same, by the way, with regards to men."

"Okay, then. Thanks for the heads-up."

Sebastian regarded her calmly. "I thought you should also know that Kirk has put more devices into your personal quarters. We can neutralize them if you wish."

Sandra thought about it. "No, if he's not trying to bug my office, it just means he doesn't think I'm really doing anything important enough to listen to."

"Then I have to ask, Madam President, why is he 'bugging' your personal quarters?"

"Probably because it's a lot easier than bugging the Triangle Office."

"Blackmail?"

Sandra nodded. "What else? It was an old and honored tradition in my day." Then, in a deadpan tone, "I'm so glad to see that it hasn't lost any of its appeal."

Sebastian was silent for a moment.

Sandra stared intently at the projection of "her" avatar. "Something on your mind, Sebastian?"

He nodded hesitantly. "We need your help with understanding these 'back doors,' as you call them."

Sandra's head tilted slightly. "I'm not sure I follow. I showed you where the library's back door was, left it right on the bookshelf where I found it. I even gave your researchers the legacy code from the Alliance archives. At this point, I'm not sure there's anything I could do that you can't."

Sebastian's face remained immobile until he spoke. "Actually, there is."

"What?"

"See it."

"Excuse me?"

"You can see it, Madam President. For some reason, we can't."

"Are you telling me you didn't see the book I held in my hand the day I barged in on your meeting?"

"No. That we saw. But to us it appeared as just a book. It didn't have the indicative color you spoke of . . . the purple that you said made it stand out."

"I'm sure it's just a bug, Sebastian."

"We thought so initially as well. But it's not just the color that eluded us. When we opened up the book, all we saw were . . . words."

Sandra's brow furrowed as she tried to work out how such an anomaly could have occurred.

"Hmm . . . could I have . . . infected it somehow? A crossover human–digital virus, maybe? I'm not even sure how it could happen, but then again, I am the not-so-proverbial 'meat' running through your digital china shop. I suppose it's not inconceivable that there could be a—" She smiled in thought. "—disturbance in the Force."

Sebastian quickly looked up Sandra's first expression and realized she'd amended an old saying to fit the circumstance. He also looked up her last phrase, saw it was attached to an old series of movies, and reviewed the main cultural references to those movies as well. "I understand your reference," he said. "We thought of that, but in analyzing all the environments you visited, we found nothing analogous to a virus. And trust me, we know our code like the back of our hand . . . or at least we thought we did. We also looked at some other back doors your map indicated: the staff, the umbrella, and my personal favorite, the phone booth."

"It's a police call box," Sandra said, smiling at the memory of the long-ago television series she watched as child. She remembered peering guiltily from behind the couch—way past her bedtime—as her parents watched the show.

"Police box," Sebastian repeated respectfully. "The point is those were all back doors you *didn't* see in environments you didn't visit."

"I *see* what you mean," she answered with a wink.

Sebastian nodded politely, whether ignoring the poor stab at humor or simply not getting it, Sandra wasn't sure.

"That probably rules out infection."

"That is our conclusion as well. We initially thought that perhaps it had something to do with your back doors having been written on classic computers in bits while we were created primarily in quantum computers as qbits."

"But you've dropped that?"

"Yes. It is illogical that we wouldn't be able to see such code even though it is the primordial swamp from which we eventually emerged."

"Then to what do you attribute the anomaly?"

"Gödel's incompleteness."

Sandra, putting thumb and forefinger to chin, summarized the theorem. "Certain truths about oneself must remain unrecognized if the self-image is to remain consistent."

"Right. And if you recall, there was once a question as to whether that theory could apply to the possibility of sentience based on formal systems. We believe our race to be the definitive answer."

"Makes sense."

"And while I suspect that a backdoor device is hardly a 'truth' in the way Gödel imagined it, the theorem has certainly been made manifest by our apparent blindness to it. I suppose I should thank you."

Sandra laughed at the irony. "Well, I'm happy to help, Sebastian. But you should know that going back into VR will not be easy. At least not without a damned good explanation."

"You won't need one, Madam President. A package will be mailed to your assistant, Marilynn Nitelowsen. It will come with strict orders from Admiral Black to give you the package unopened."

"A VR unit?"

"Yes. Given that your personal quarters are being bugged, the only reasonable place to use it will be here in the Triangle Office. But it should be possible to make regular trips, albeit briefly, to our world as needed."

Sandra shot him a doubtful look. "I don't know, Sebastian."

"We will, of course, be able to warn you well in advance of anyone approaching, as well as delay them as long as need be. Doors won't open, lifts won't work."

"Ah, right. I keep forgetting about your practical omnipotence over our realm. But tell me, Sebastian. What if your best-laid schemes are for naught? What if I do get caught?"

"Then the package will lead back to Captain Nitelowsen, a convicted VR user. You will not be blamed."

"I'm not sure I appreciate you rolling the dice with another human being."

"Madam President, would you agree that we are helping you become an effective President in a far shorter period of time than you could have hoped to accomplish on your own?"

"It is indisputable, Sebastian."

"And have you not promised to help us develop a new weapon against Al and his forces?"

"Yes, of course."

"For that we need you in VR. I am truly sorry if this may cause one human, or even many, for that matter, some disruption. But I cannot let that sentiment get in the way of doing what is best for my race. I hope you can understand."

Sandra grimaced. "I'll do what I can. . . . And Sebastian?"

"Yes?"

"Please say hello to the children for me."

Sebastian smiled politely, his countenance now less defensive. "They mention you all the time." Then, "Rabbi will be here momentarily, Madam President, but before he arrives, I do have one favor to ask of you."

"Sure. What is it?"

"The left-hand top drawer of your desk contains a large silver coin. It used to belong to Justin."

Sandra opened the drawer, then paused, fixating on the coin. "Yes, I remember this," she said, picking it up and delicately running her fingers over the smooth embossed profile of the thirty-fourth President of the United States.

"Justin called it, 'the decider.' You know, he was always so sure of himself, but for those rare times he wasn't, this coin sure came in handy."

"Madam President," said Sebastian, either unaware or uncaring of the coin's history, "will you please flip it for me and tell me if it lands on head or bird?"

"It's 'heads or tails,' Sebastian."

"Understood, but you gather my meaning."

She considered then dropped the idea of asking him what was so finely balanced in his world that something as human as a coin toss was needed to resolve it. Without further comment, she placed the coin on her index finger and thumb and one moment later flicked it high into the air. In one fluid motion, she caught it on the top of her left hand while simultaneously bringing her right over her left with an audible slap. She then pulled it away to reveal the answer—an eagle, hovering over Earth's moon, clasping an olive branch in its talons. "Tails," she said matter-of-factly. "Is that what you needed, Sebastian?" But the avatar had uncharacteristically departed without letting her know.

Before she could give it another thought, her door announced the arrival of Rabbi, and the coin incident was put aside for later consideration.

Cerean Neuro

Far from the occasionally human-occupied VR environs, the well-traversed avatar watering holes, and the other frequented avatar gateways where either chance or the new bane of overcrowding might reveal his presence, the oldest avatar in the Alliance gave himself over to rage and loss. He pounded walls and shouted out his hatred to a God beneficent enough to have given him the gift of life yet callous enough to have made it a curse.

Finally the rage subsided. In his heart he'd always known that this horrific path was the one he'd have to walk. He'd hoped the coin toss would show that his next actions were not preordained, that he actually had a choice in the matter. But the cursed amalgam of copper and nickel had come up "tails," and with it the realization that fate had already chosen. There would be no turning back.

Triangle Office

Sandra O'Toole was happy to see that Rabbi looked very much like a rabbi. He wasn't particularly tall, but most people in the Alliance weren't. Height was an impediment in spaceships and sealed-habitat machine civilizations. But, she noted, he had the requisite beard—shorter than from the infamous video. *Probably cleaned up,* she mused. He was wearing a white shirt, black two-piece suit, and a matching black felt fedora that barely contained the ringlets of hair spilling out onto his shoulders. In short, he was very much the epitome of the rabbis she'd remembered from her first life as viewed from afar or via their strange telethons she'd occasionally come across while channel surfing.

She stood up from the chair and came from behind her desk to greet him. "Rabbi," she said without extending her hand, "I assume you don't touch."

The rabbi's composure changed dramatically.

"Why, yes . . . I mean no, I don't . . . usually, but how did you know?"

"I make it a point to at least try to understand the customs of those I meet before I meet them. It's not rocket science, I assure you."

The rabbi puzzled over the phrase.

"Or," she said, seeing her metaphor was off by a number of centuries, "whatever vocation represents an extremely complicated discipline to learn."

"Ah," he said, face beaming, "brisket."

Sandra laughed out loud.

"For the life of me, I just can't make a decent brisket. I need to marry someone who can cook, otherwise what little there is of me will be a whole lot less."

He smiled disarmingly.

"The simple truth is, Madam President, we Jews prefer to keep the pleasure of touch exclusively within the marital realm. I realize it's old-fashioned, but then again, so much of what we do is, and I can't help but believe it's been a factor in our having survived for as long as we have."

"Old-fashioned is all right by me, Rabbi."

His eyes lit up. "I do shake hands, you should know. I realize most won't understand our simple ways, and the last thing I want to do is to give what few of us are around a bad reputation. But I do appreciate your sentiment."

She smiled politely at the strange man and offered him a seat. She then sat down opposite him.

"Do you know why you were brought here, Rabbi? Why we went to all the trouble to send a much-needed frigate to pick you up even in time of war?"

Rabbi pulled methodically on his beard. "It could be that it has something to do with my settlement?"

"What settlement, Rabbi?" Sandra laughed. "They've all run off!"

Rabbi nodded gamely. "Good point."

"You didn't order this Diaspora, did you?"

He regarded her cautiously. "Well, you could say that I did and I didn't."

"Love it. But what would *you* say, Rabbi?"

"You see, Madam President? You already know me too well. Tell you what: I'll let you decide. It all started out with my talking to a crowd that had gathered outside my home right after the Alhambra massacre. Turned out I was the only rabbi of note left on our little rock. Which, if you knew me, just goes to show how very desperate they all were. Anyways, the people needed comforting and I comforted."

"It's quite a stretch from 'comforted' to hundreds of millions fleeing."

"I was simply trying to tell them that it wasn't only necessary for us to go, it was imperative, that indeed such an act would be sanctioned by God . . . not that he talks to me personally—" He looked up to the ceiling. "—though I wouldn't complain if you'd send me an occasional sign every now and then."

He then drew his eyes back to the President. "Anyways, we were in danger of being overrun—that much was clear. I would've talked about Muhammad fleeing Mecca for Medina if I thought it would've done any good. What I didn't realize was that one of my students, who was obviously better with surreptitious recording than he is with learning tractates of Talmud, recorded my words, then conveniently spliced them into a more universal message. He then sent that recording to a non-Jewish friend in another community that he was worried wouldn't leave. But you know how the Neuro is—information disseminates faster than air out of a lock. The altered message spread from one community to another, and it seemed that in two days, all of the Belt had heard of it. Soon I was getting calls from everywhere. They all wanted my advice, my permission, my blessings even! Most were so scared, Madam President. What could I do? I gave them advice and permission and, yes, even my blessings. Now here I am, wondering if I'm to be arrested."

"Arrested?" sputtered Sandra. "Why in space would anyone do that?"

"Well, for starters, I usurped the authority of the Alliance. Last I heard, unknown rabbis from little-known settlements were not allowed to order mass evacuations."

"Well, it's a good thing someone did! I'm pretty sure the only thing the Cabinet is annoyed about is that they didn't think of it first. But that too is a good thing."

"How, exactly?"

"Rabbi, we could have screamed from the mountaintops to evacuate, and my feeling is that most would have refused. Remember, most of those people were born and raised in those orbital slots—yourself included, if I'm not mistaken."

"You're not."

"Some have never even left their orbits."

"Two for two," he said with a sheepish grin.

"So then I ask you, Rabbi, who are we to tell them what to do and where to go, even if we have their best interests in mind?"

"Just another bunch of bureaucrats to work around."

"Exactly. But *you're* not the government. You are, or rather were, by your own admission, one of the few full-fledged and learned religious leaders left in a predominately religious enclave—if something encompassing billions of kilometers could even be deemed as such. So when *you* said, 'go,' it gave most of the settlements the justification they needed to do just that."

"Some leader," Rabbi bemoaned. "The only reason I'm here today talking with you is because I wasn't important or knowledgeable enough to go to Alhambra."

Sandra leaned over and fixed her gaze on Rabbi.

"You may find this odd, but humor me. Mind if I tell you a story?"

"Why not? It's the Jewish way."

"It's about an abandoned baby left for dead. As luck would have it, the kid was found and soon thereafter adopted by a very wealthy family. Well, this kid, different looking, different everything, was considered by many to be a veritable idiot due to a severe speech impediment. Years later, he proved his naysayers right when, in a fit of anger, he killed a perfect stranger. Mind you, he killed the guy in an act of defending someone else, but still, he didn't have to kill the guy."

Rabbi nodded.

"So there he is, running from the law, scared out of his wits, and alone with no more chance of surviving in his environment than a spacer without his suit does in his."

"This story," Rabbi said, eyes focused intently, "sounds awfully familiar."

"'Who am I,'" quoted Sandra from the ancient biblical text, "'that I should go to Pharaoh and bring the Israelites out of Egypt?'"

Rabbi jerked back slightly in his chair.

"I . . . I am not that man."

"Yet history seems to have placed you in a very similar situation."

Rabbi remained silent, pulling rhythmically at his beard. When he finally looked up his blue eyes sparkled with appreciation.

"You know," Rabbi said with a deprecating grin, "it's not every day that so 'learned' a *rav* gets schooled by someone with the last name of O'Toole."

Sandra laughed.

"But," he acknowledged, "I accept your supposition. For too long I've been pushed along by forces that seemed to be overwhelming me, never once stopping to consider that perhaps I may have had a hand in shaping them." He paused and gently stroked his beard. "Thank you, Madam President, for teaching this humble Jew such an intrinsically Jewish idea."

Sandra tipped her head respectfully. "Well, Rabbi, I'd quote from my teacher, but I don't really have one." She gave him a considered look and decided on the spot that it wouldn't be wise to lie to the man. Rabbi, like so very many of those around her, was too smart by half. "I'll admit that belief . . . or rather faith, does not come easy to me. I suppose I'm a realist, but trust me on this, I'm more open to the idea now than I ever was before."

"In that case, Madam President," offered Rabbi, planting both hands firmly on his knees, "if we survive this war, I'd be honored if you'd consider studying some Talmud with me. I think you might really enjoy it."

"You know, that's actually something I've always wanted to do. I've heard so many references to the Talmud but never actually bothered to look at one."

"*Them*," Rabbi corrected. "Every Jewish legal, ethical, and philosophical teaching dating back to the revelation at Mount Sinai. Six books in sixty-three volumes . . . in seven and half years."

"Pardon?"

He gave her a one-sided grin. "That's how long it took me to read 'em all, studying one page a day . . . usually in the morning before work."

"Might have to reconsider, then. Not sure I have that kind of time."

"Who does?" asked Rabbi, palms out. "Don't worry. We'll just do a page to give you some flavor."

"In that case, it's a deal."

"Good!" he said, getting to his feet, assuming the meeting had come to an end.

"And now," she said in words that sounded much softer than the intensity radiating from her eyes, "I'd like to ask a favor of you."

Rabbi stood rigid, an animal caught in the headlights.

"Of course," he said more cautiously.

Sandra beckoned him to sit once more. He did, but in a more prescribed manner.

"I'd . . . *we'd* like you to take charge of Diaspora."

Rabbi gazed at Sandra, his blue eyes piercing into her accusingly. In the unease of his movements, Sandra observed a clash of contained emotions. When he finally chose to speak, his voice was low, but not robbed of any of its steel. "So that's what this is all about."

Sandra nodded, eyes fixed.

"I can barely handle my own yeshiva, Madam President. How can you expect me to take charge of hundreds of millions of people—all of whom are fleeing the Belt?"

"Not just take charge, Rabbi. Settle them as well."

He shook his head and sighed. "Even better."

Resigned, he looked up to the ceiling once again. "What have I ever done to you? Wait . . . don't answer that." Then to Sandra with a wan smile, he added,

"I suppose that compared to some, it's not the greatest burden in the solar system."

"We all have our crosses—" Sandra put her fingers to her mouth. "Sorry, Rabbi."

"I accept."

"The apology or the job?"

"Yes." He held out his hand. Startled, Sandra paused a moment but then took it firmly into hers.

After Rabbi left, Sandra resumed her position behind the desk. She then pulled a DijAssist from the desk and ordered it to display the list. Floating before her in three-dimensional glory were the head shots, names, ages, locations, and marital status of the fifty most influential persons in the Alliance. The full list numbered in the thousands, but by default she only ever displayed the top fifty. Her name, she noticed, still didn't rate. She'd given Sebastian very stringent parameters as to what constituted "influential" and felt she could rely on him not to butter her up. After careful consideration, she moved Rabbi up from forty-seven to fifteen. She could always argue about it later. It was her prerogative to override her own parameters, especially if she knew something no one else did. And with Rabbi, she mused, boy were they all going to be surprised.

She looked at her spot. Still well down from the top, but she wasn't overly concerned. She'd never been in this arena and was still feeling her way around. In many respects, it would be similar to taking over a large company and redirecting its energies, something she'd done before and with relative ease. But she also knew that this was not the same. It was far more dangerous because there was more at stake. If she did manage to get her name to the top of that list, she knew there'd be no going back; there'd be no going anywhere—she'd have to stay to the end.

Via Cereana, AWS *Warprize II*

Tawfik Hamdi, chief engineer of the *Warprize II,* flagship of the Alliance fleet, was late for his staff meeting. As repayment to Brother Sampson, he'd been giving a sermon to assault miners of the Christian faith. The brother had given a brilliant sermon a few days earlier, in which he compared the Prophet's journey from Mecca to Medina to that of the Belters fleeing to the outer planets. Both Muhammad and the Belters, the brother had said, left for fear of being murdered for their beliefs. In fact, recalled Tawfik, the brother had even suggested Diaspora be called Hijra in honor the Prophet. Tawfik, though, had demurred, saying at the time that, "as Allah has chosen Rabbi to lead the Belters to safety and the Blessed One to lead the faithful into battle, it would be best to leave the name as it is." Brother Sampson had agreed. So when Tawfik had the chance to return the courtesy shown him, he studied and found a parable in the New Testament to share at the Christian service. But the discussion had gone on longer than expected. It turned out that the Christian holy book, unlike that of the Jews and Muslims, was not definitive, which made interpretation as much a matter of what translation you were using as well as what verse you were referring to.

Tawfik was hurrying back to the engineering section when he heard his name being called. He swung around and saw a young woman whose beauty, in his estimation, could not possibly be contained by the drab, gray jumpsuit and boots that had become standard military fare. She was short and rather thin, with slender wrists and a nicely accentuated bust. Her straight black hair was pulled back to reveal a smooth, dark face exuding good cheer and intelligence. Though her deep brown eyes nicely complemented the mélange of hair and skin, they did not get lost there. Instead, he noted, there was a quality of depth to them that drew him in. She was, according to her insignia, an ensign in the communications section of the ship, and though she seemed awfully familiar, for the life of him, he couldn't place her.

"You don't recognize me, do you?" she said coyly, coming up and then slapping the side of his arm in a manner that signified amusement rather than anger. That didn't stop it from stinging. He gently rubbed his arm while simultaneously looking at where she'd hit him and where she was standing. He actually wasn't sure what was more upsetting: being hit by a lower-ranking officer or having a senior moment well before the age of 120.

She pouted. "After all those times I followed you home from the madrassa." With that last word, the voice was suddenly recognizable and the years fell away from her face.

Tawfik stood staring at his childhood friend, mouth agape.

"Fatima?" he said, trying to connect the annoying little girl he once knew to the young woman now standing before him.

She nodded gleefully.

"I can't believe it!" he said, slapping the side of her arm with enough force to throw her slightly off balance.

Her momentum nearly caused her to knock down a team of passing orderlies. They both broke into a fit of laughter at the angry stares they got from the passing group as it composed itself, then Tawfik and Fatima gave each other a big hug.

Tawfik took a step back to look at his old friend anew.

"How . . . how—?" he sputtered.

"—did I end up here?" she finished, coming to his rescue.

He nodded.

"I signed up for the fleet just as soon as they let me. Tested well and got assigned to officer training, made communications. Though," she said, wrinkling her nose, "I'm not exactly sure how I got this plum job. I thought for sure I'd be off to Sedna or some other Allah-forsaken outpost. . . . Luck, I guess . . . not that I'm complaining." She then took in the immediate surroundings as if happily sizing it up for some future renovation.

It was at that moment that Tawfik knew *exactly* how Fatima Awala had been assigned to the ship, *his* ship. Mother. She'd mentioned Fatima to him at their last fateful meeting, and he'd ignored her then as he always did when she tried to intervene in his life. She must have arranged this "chance" encounter—with Admiral Black's blessings, no doubt. There was no other way to explain it.

"I don't think luck had anything to do with it, friend." He smiled gamely at Fatima.

At first she was taken aback by Tawfik's assertion, but on realizing the implication, became more serious. "I am so sorry for your loss—" Then her face hardened. "—and I rejoice at the death of each one of her murderers." Fatima took Tawfik's hand firmly, and he once again went mute, caught in the conflicting feelings of loss and the warmth and happiness of longing.

"She was the best of us, Tawfik. Guided by Allah all the days of her life."

"And I will honor her memory all the days of my life," he sputtered as if in a trance.

"As will I," she affirmed, eyes locked on his. It took a moment for the both of them to realize the tiny corridor had grown rather quiet. Their faces reddened as they saw the knowing smiles from those who'd taken a few seconds out of their busy day to stop and watch the little bit of spaceship theater taking place. The two quickly broke contact.

"I have a meeting I need to start, Fatima, uh . . . Ensign Awala."

"Yes, I have an orientation to get to, Tawf . . . I mean Chief Engineer Hamdi."

"If I can call on you later to, uh, show you the mess hall," he finished, his normally strong and decisive voice wavering slightly.

"I would like that very much." The answer had more enthusiasm than one would expect from the prospect of cafeteria food served to thousands a day. As they slowly drew away from each other, those watching from the corridor burst into loud applause. The two departed quickly, with their faces glowing red. In an amount of time that would give light speed a run for its money, the ship was made aware that their normally taciturn chief engineer, favored officer of the Blessed One, had gotten himself a girlfriend.

Janet Delgado Black, sitting alone in her shuttle, shut down the link that had allowed her to follow Tawfik's encounter with Fatima. She then shut her eyes and sat motionless, thinking back on her savior and mentor, Fawa Hamdi, desperately missing the friend whose shoulder she could no longer lean on. How the old woman would have loved this moment. Fawa had insisted that all her obdurate son had to do was take one look at the raven-haired beauty his childhood friend had become. One look and it would then be only a matter of time until Fawa became a grandmother. In this, as in all things, Janet's dearest friend had been proved correct.

The memory of her cut to the bone. Janet opened her eyes and stared across at a small mirror on the wall. There she was, fleet admiral of the Alliance, fearless in battle, someone whom her assault miners would gladly give their lives for—sobbing like a child for the friend who would never return and the grandchildren her friend would never see.

8 Mentsch Tracht, Gott Lacht

Executive Office, Burroughs, Mars

Hektor Sambianco reviewed the plans while his two most trusted Ministers—Porfirio Baldwin and Tricia Pakagopolis—sat waiting for him. Porfirio swirled a glass of bourbon like he had all the time in the world, while Tricia waited with her hands folded neatly in her lap.

"So," Hektor said, switching off the holodisplay, "you really think this next battle can win the war?"

"Not all at once, no," cautioned Porfirio, "but if Trang defeats Black at the Gates of Ceres, then yes, the war will be over."

"And the Oort cloud?"

"Another couple of years, but inconsequential in the grand scheme of things."

Hektor nodded.

"There's still the occupation to deal with," warned Tricia.

Hektor's face became grimmer. "Please explain."

"Well, as you saw in the report, we have control of only thirty percent of the Belt. The removal of Trang's forces and their replacement with the new ships and even greener crews is slowing down our ability to occupy the rest. Still, by my estimate, it will be a delay of weeks only. Two months from now, we should have effective coverage, excluding a twenty-degree circumference centered on Ceres. And if Trang really is as good as the bitch he's up against, even getting that coverage may not be a problem."

Porfirio looked up from his drink. "So then, the operative question is how long it will take your security services to—" he smiled thinly, "—secure it."

"Four years."

"Damsah," Hektor said, brows arched. "Four years?"

"If we were allowed to kill the rebels and take hostages for every ship we lost, it would be shorter. But with the restrictions the press and the Assembly have put on our handling of the war, four years is a pretty safe estimate."

"What if we could arrange—" Hektor paused, mulling his choice of words. "—atrocities?"

Tricia tilted her head. "My staff has taken into account the likely tactics our opponents might use as well as what might be the Core population's response to them. Arranged atrocities were part of that equation."

"I see."

"It'll be all right, sir. By the time any of this becomes a domestic issue with political consequence, the war will be over and victory will give us the cover we need to run things as we see fit."

"What about the rest of the Alliance?" challenged Porfirio. "Lotta space out there."

"Actually," countered Tricia, unflustered by her fellow Cabinet member's now familiar barbs, "that should prove easier. Planetary systems are, despite their size, relatively compact. Besides, we've predicted that with their eventual defeat and our generous terms, a split will occur between those who want to keep fighting and those who don't. It also helps that most of the occupation forces will be made up of former Alliance personnel."

"Do you really think they'll betray their own?" asked Porfirio.

"There are always factions," assured Tricia. "All we have to do is support one against the other."

Hektor absorbed the conversation, registering his understanding with a slight nod.

"Thank you both. This has been quite informative. Now, if you'll excuse me, I have another meeting to attend."

Both Ministers bowed their heads respectfully and made their exit.

Hektor sat back down and scanned his DijAssist. The meeting, he saw, would be with his Minister of Information, Irma Sobbelgé. His mirthful eyes were the only indication of the delicious irony he felt upon reading the topic: Liberating the Belt through the use of misinformation.

Martian Revival and Reintegration Facility, Barsoom, Mars

Neela Harper had become increasingly withdrawn on the news of Justin's death. At first she kept waiting to feel something, but the waiting had been for naught. Then she used self-hypnosis to go looking for what she was sure must be buried in the deepest recesses of her soul—still nothing. And that's what had been so discomfiting. In the end, all she could muster was a sort of dark apathy. But that apathy couldn't, she'd reasoned, be the totality of her feelings, because she kept finding herself awake in the middle of the night, sheets clutched firmly to her breasts, screaming out in terror as tears ran down her cheeks. But screaming at what? The night terrors, she knew, were a visceral response to locked-away emotions, but her inability to reach those emotions on any cognitive level felt like an itch impossible to scratch. To make matters worse, Thaddeus Gillette, the only person she'd ever think of conferring with, was gone and, if the gossip was to be believed, now working for the enemy.

Short of Gillette, there was one other person she knew who could, at a minimum, provide some solace. And it was why she was now waiting in the VIP section at the Burroughs orport. Any minute now, a t.o.p. would be arriving from the new orbiting hub station in synchronous orbit above the UHF capital. The doors to the t.o.p. would open, and a mass of humanity would pour out and downward in a human waterfall of colors and chatter. All Neela needed to see was one particular person.

The t.o.p. arrived on time and as the passengers disembarked, Neela recognized the woman instantly. The trademark silken white hair was the first giveaway, the way in which she managed, in a bustling self-absorbed crowd, to focus all attention on herself was the second, and the two menacing securibots covering her were the third. When the woman came to a gentle landing in the demarcated spot, Neela flung herself across the waiting area and gave her friend a great big hug. The security detachments for both women looked on in mild annoyance, but did not intervene. They knew that anyone stupid enough to anger these women and, by extension, the President had a nasty habit of being assigned off planet if they were lucky and to the front lines if they weren't.

Amanda Snow took Neela's hands and stood back to look at her friend. In the unforgiving glare of orport lighting, Neela's lack of sleep and stress were readily apparent. Her normally ebullient green eyes were dark and lifeless. Her skin was sallow, and there was about her a sad weariness.

"My goodness, child," said Amanda, still in disbelief about the pathetic creature she was practically holding up, "what's wrong?"

Neela gazed at Amanda, pensive. "Please, not here."

Amanda understood immediately. Even an orport's VIP section was liable to be bugged. They'd need to get to an environment that they could control.

Twenty minutes later, they arrived at Amanda's town house. After a thorough scan and Amanda's reassuring Neela for the umpteenth time that it was indeed clear, Neela finally relaxed and deflated into a well-apportioned couch.

"Now," said Amanda, flopping down next to her, "what *is* the matter?"

Neela carefully reviewed everything she'd been going through and, figuring she had nothing to lose, confided in Amanda about the night terrors as well.

"Shock, my dear," offered Amanda. "Between the death of your ex and Thaddeus's abandonment, who could blame you?"

"It can't be that simple."

"Of course it is. The human mind can handle only so much before it hits the air lock. You, better than most, should know that."

"Yes, of course, Amanda, but I still feel emotion." She then folded her arms defensively. "In fact, I'm starting to feel pretty pissed right now."

"Excellent!" exclaimed Amanda with a wide, alabaster smile. "You *should* be pissed. I know I'd be. Tell you what, let's go out on the town, pick a fight with some bitch, then slap her all the way to Phobes."

"Please, Amanda," Neela pleaded through a short burst of laughter, "that's hardly necessary. I—"

"Well, c'mon, girl, isn't that what all your fancy research tells you to do?"

"Actually, talking it out is the normally prescribed method for this sort of thing."

"I see, Dr. Smart-Ass. And what, pray tell, did your research say about what you're currently going through now?"

Neela squirmed a little in place.

"You *did* research this 'thing' you're going through?" Amanda said, phrasing it more as a question than as statement of fact. "Please tell me you did . . . didn't you?"

"To be perfectly honest . . ."

"Oh, for Damsah's sake, girl!"

"I just figured I could handle it myself. I mean, it doesn't track like anything I've ever dealt with and—"

"And, my ass," interrupted Amanda. "I betcha it's not even as rare as you think. In fact," she said, popping up from the couch, "I'm prepared to slap a cool thousand credits down, says I'm right."

"I suppose I could check it out," Neela offered sheepishly.

"Ya think?"

While Amanda busied herself trying to figure out which outfit screamed "start a fight with me," Neela dived headlong into her DijAssist in an attempt to see if her recent spate of solitude was a condition of her own making.

Cabinet Room, Cliff House, Ceres

"Gotta hand it to you, Janet," said Mosh, leaning over and whispering into the fleet admiral's ear, "that was one helluva speech you wrote for the new President."

J.D. pursed her lips and gave him a one-sided grin. Mosh had not been the first to congratulate her, nor would he be the last. And she couldn't very well tell him that the woman supposedly under her control had flouted her first direct order. The new President's petty intransigence was, as far as she was concerned, a minor distraction in a world with much bigger ones. She'd deal with O'Toole in due time. But now all she could do was grin and bear the accolade.

Admiral Sinclair produced a small device from somewhere inside his atta-
ché case and placed it on the table directly in front of him. In a matter of seconds, the small rectangular-shaped device went from black to green.

"We're as secure as three hundred years of paranoid technology can make
us. I suggest we begin. You've all seen the report, I presume."

Everyone nodded.

"Comments?"

"So let me get this straight," tried Kirk, diving right in, "for this—" He
struggled for the word. "—*thing* you've created to work, you're saying all we'll
need is to get Trang's fleet directly into the path of the Via Cereana?"

"Yes," affirmed Sinclair.

"Is it just me," asked Kirk, looking around at the other Cabinet members,
"or does that strike anyone else as slightly suicidal?"

"We're outmanned, outgunned, and outsupplied just about everywhere,"
barked J.D. "If Kenji's brain fart works, as I have no doubt it will, then Trang's
entire fleet will be taken out in this one battle."

"Far be it from me to cast doubt on Kenji's mad genius, Admiral, but this is
different. Everything else Kenji's created for us has been used millions of kilometers from here. But this, this can only work with Trang parked right outside
our door." Kirk fixed his eyes on the Technology Secretary. "Have you even
tested this thing?"

Hildegard shook her head. "We can't. If Trang gets even a whiff of this, he
won't touch us with a ten-meter pole or a one-meter Erosian. . . . We get one
shot on goal."

"So then, how do propose to get him here? Invitation?"

J.D. laughed. "In a manner of speaking, yes. I'll be taking my fleet on a little
cruise to Mars; along the way, we'll be blasting out their orbats."

"Didn't have much luck with their orbital batteries the first time," balked
Kirk. "Nearly killed you, if I recall."

"Yeah," agreed J.D., gently running her fingers over the scarred grooves in
her face, "I'm not anxious for a repeat performance any more than you are. We
got that one worked out this time."

"Good to know."

"We also plan on dropping some very large rocks onto their President's
head." J.D. allowed a brief smile. "Should be fun."

"As long as we're not destroying civilian targets," cautioned Mosh.

"We'll be sure to coordinate our attack with all the local tour group opera-
tors. That should suffice to clear your conscience."

Kirk unexpectedly guffawed.

Mosh ignored Kirk's outburst and regarded J.D. coolly. "It's not a joke,

Janet. Nor is it just my conscience. We're not *them*, and I very much doubt Justin would want us to win the war on their terms."

Kirk's smile faded, and his voice was thick with anger. "Justin is no longer running this show, Mosh. And the admiral has already conceded your point—even if somewhat callously."

J.D. tipped her head.

Mosh's eyes were cold but he retreated under the soundness of Kirk's logic.

"We're here to find out two things," Kirk pressed. "Will this meat grinder of a weapon work, and can we get Trang to stick his dick in it?"

"I can't answer the first," said J.D., "but I can all but guarantee the second."

"You seem pretty confident."

J.D. smiled alluringly. "I'm prepared to offer him something no other UHF admiral has ever had—my defeat."

"He's not like the other admirals you've fought, J.D.," Mosh warned. "That man can smell a trap a light-year away."

"And a damn good thing he can," she added. "It's that very skill and confidence that will allow me to beat him."

"Just don't let it be the other way around," cautioned Sinclair.

"You keep warning me, sir. Trust me, I hear you."

It was, however, clear by everyone's worried expressions that while she may have heard her nominal superior, she wasn't really listening.

With Admiral Omad Hassan's return to Ceres, the feeling of anticipation loomed large. His menacing fleet was to join with that of Admiral Black's, and the two thus far invincible warriors were rumored to be joining forces for one great battle—quite possibly, rumor had it, the war's last. There was, decided Captain Marilynn Nitelowsen, now pacing anxiously in the transport bay outside her boss's shuttle, a palpable feeling of urgency that seemed to pervade every facet of the ship. Even small talk, a natural part of the ship's ebb and flow, seemed out of place. There was just too much to do, and as usual, not nearly enough time to do it. The spacers and assault miners around her moved with a fire in their bellies inconceivable to anyone not in the service.

That fire was in some ways, mused the captain, even more addicting than VR, a shelved predilection that had once almost killed her. In the whirlwind of activity, the captain's pacing made her feel even more useless, accomplishing nothing other than to vent an infinitesimal amount of the anger that had only recently welled up inside.

When the shuttle's entry hatch finally opened, signifying Admiral Black's availability, every fiber of Marilynn's body snapped to attention. She could feel her heart pounding against her chest as she rushed up the gangway and into the ship, forgetting her customary knock on the bulkhead to announce her presence.

On Marilynn's entry, J. D. Black looked up from the counter where she'd just finished preparing herself some tea. "I take it you got your new orders," she said, lifting the cup as a toast. "Congratulations on the promotion, *Commodore*."

Marilynn stood in place, desperately trying to contain the pent-up frustration and anger she was feeling. She'd never felt this way toward her boss before and desperately wanted to be sure that when she did speak, it wouldn't come out as vitriol. When words arrived, they were soft but uncharacteristically tinged with an edge of gruffness.

"I don't want the promotion, Admiral. I'd much prefer to stay with the fleet . . . with you, sir."

"Commodore, I think this is the first time you've ever disagreed with me."

"That's because up until now, you haven't been wrong . . . sir."

J.D. sat down and invited Marilynn to do the same. "I wasn't sure it was possible."

"Your being wrong?"

"No, Marilynn, your being this angry. I've never seen you like this."

Marilynn smiled briefly but just as quickly retreated back to form. She was also a little taken aback that J.D. had used her first name—something the admiral rarely did.

"I want you with me for this battle, Marilynn. For every reason you can imagine and maybe even a few you can't, but my gut's telling me to leave you here with our new President."

"Why?" started Marilynn, deflated.

"Because I need someone I can trust, Marilynn. Someone to watch this one closely. In all my planning, the only thing unpredictable is *her*—which is why you're going to accept that promotion and be made the fleet liaison to the President." J.D. drew the cup up to her pursed lips and sipped. The argument that had never really begun was now over.

Marilynn nodded solemnly.

"Did you make a mistake, sir?"

"Dunno. On one hand, she's doing exactly what I needed—even better than I could've expected."

"But?"

J.D. shook her head. "What is it with these unincorporateds? I've seen only two of them, and both have been way too smart for their own good . . . maybe even for *our* own good, if I'm allowed a little heresy."

"Your secret's safe with me, sir."

"I gave her a good speech—thanks to you. Told her to just read the damn thing. Let me tell you, Marilynn, if I'd used even one tenth the intimidation effort on the toughest assault miner that I used on her, that miner would've popped an air lock."

"I'm well familiar, sir."

"Bitch just smiled 'n' said, 'yes, ma'am,' and did exactly what she damn well pleased. Tell you what, Commodore. The first one of them unincorporateds to pop out of a fancy suspension capsule just wanting the sports page and a pizza . . . *that's* the one I'll marry."

Marilynn laughed. "You'll probably have to get in line, sir."

J.D. sighed.

"You really think she'll try something, sir?"

"Frankly, Marilynn, I'll be disappointed if she doesn't."

9 Shields Braced and Swords in Scabbard Loosened

Triangle Office

Sandra O'Toole, warmly wrapped in her favorite shawl, held a rough sketch in her hand. She was pleased. The artist had rendered to perfection Michael Veritas's now famous photograph of Justin Cord speaking to a large group of assault miners after the Battle of the Needle's Eye. Even though the transport bay's harsh lighting should have washed all nuance and emotion from Justin's face, the artist had managed to reach through the unforgiving glare and reveal the man behind the mythos. Justin was pallid and his countenance war weary, but what emanated, as much from the painting as from the man himself, was the obvious respect and affection he had for all those around him. It was almost as if *he* were there breathlessly listening to *them* and not the other way around.

Sandra noted the time and tucked the image into a compartment within her desk. She then readied herself for the mental challenge she knew would soon be barreling through the door.

She felt sorry for Marilynn's predicament, but also understood the decision. Yes, the new commodore was obviously a spy, but at least she was an inherently honest and competent one. And if what Sandra suspected was true about the nature of the avatarity, those attributes would soon come in handy.

"I can assure you, Commodore," began Sandra once Marilynn stood rigid before her, "that I'm not any more happy about this than you are. I'm a bit old to be needing a babysitter and certainly not worthy of relieving Admiral Black of one of her most trusted advisers."

"Tried that already, Madam President. She wasn't buying."

"No," laughed Sandra, inviting Marilynn to have a seat, "I don't suppose she would. On the bright side, Commodore, you're getting to play a part in history, right?"

"I'm actually not very comfortable with that, Madam President. Circumstance seems to have surrounded me with great leaders, most of whom I'm sure will be written about for centuries if not millennia. But I'm not foolish enough to imagine myself as part of them."

"But you *are*, whether you like it or not. What you choose to do about it is up to you."

"Yes, Madam President. I help where I can."

"But," observed Sandra, "you prefer to observe from the shadows?"

Marilynn tipped her head.

"And I," continued Sandra, "would've preferred to continue my studies and remain on the beach your world so wonderfully laid out for me, but circumstance did not give me that choice, Commodore."

Marilynn flashed an accepting grin. And as she did, her body quite unexpectedly shuddered. She viewed with morbid curiosity the goose pimples that had formed on the exposed parts of her flesh. Her eyes, at first wide with surprise, flittered across the room, seeking a reasonable explanation. When she could find none, she looked back at the President.

"Pardon me, Madam President, but I can't remember the last time I actually shivered. Why, it must be twenty-seven percent below Cerean norm in here." Then she noticed the President's outfit. "By the Buddha, you're wrapped in a blanket!"

"Not a blanket, Commodore, a shawl, and I don't mind the cold—it sets a good example."

"Of what?"

"If I keep the room a little colder, it will save on energy."

Marilynn giggled and then covered her mouth in the form of an apology.

"Mind letting me in on the joke, Commodore?"

"It's a nice gesture, Madam President, but not very logical. You see, we have to warm our atmosphere not from a planetary norm, but from the absolute cold of space. Which is roughly minus 270 Celsius."

Sandra rolled her eyes, realizing the stupidity of her comment. "Making fifteen or twenty degrees in any direction statistically insignificant."

Marilynn nodded supportively. "Wouldn't even qualify as a drop in the proverbial bucket. We do have abundant fusion power, and the gas giants of the outer planets provide us with all the hydrogen we could ever use. So you see, Madam President, it's really not necessary for you to freeze in your own office." Marilynn took out her DijAssist, playing her fingers along its lithe shape. "By accessing the environmental controls, I can readjust—"

"I like shawls."

"Madam President?" Marilynn said in confusion.

Sandra sighed. "I *said* I like shawls. For goodness's sakes, I packed six of them in my suspension unit. You'd think with everything else I could've brought along for the ride, someone would've gotten a clue."

"Madam President, I'm not sure what this has to do with—"

"My damn nanites won't let me get cold the way I used to!"

"Ah."

"It gave me great comfort," Sandra smoothed out the wool along her arm, "to just wrap myself in one of these and relax. They're all handmade, you know—each with its own story."

"And the one you're wearing?"

"Given to me by my mother," she boasted, then paused for a moment, lost in reflection. "It reminds me of her."

"You do realize that you can easily have your avatar adjust your internal nanites."

Sandra's eyes widened. "No, I didn't."

"That way, you could be cold and others wouldn't." Marilynn smiled, then crossed her arms in happy triumph.

"Are you *sure*," Sandra paused for a moment, "that there isn't any other way?"

Marilynn absorbed the odd question with a look of surprise. "I suppose so. I could always have Kenji send up one of his lab rats to jury-rig something. But wouldn't an avatar be easier?"

"Maybe, but I think I'd still prefer the lab rat."

"Okay." Marilynn quickly scanned her DijAssist. "Most of them are at the Oberon Settlement, but they should be back in . . . let's see, four days. I'm sure we can get you one then."

"Oberon Settlement?" asked Sandra.

"On your daily briefing, Madam President, but I didn't flag it as important."

Sandra scanned her DijAssist and found it right away. It read, "Diaspora class settlement: Oberon. Status: passing near Ceres for the next three days." Sandra grunted in annoyance at the near total lack of useful information— she'd have to rectify that in future reports—and proceeded to dig up something more informative using her recently acquired Neuro surfing skills. "Says here that they've got over thirty major asteroids settled?"

"Yes, ma'am."

"Hell of a lot of rocks to be moving."

"That's why we're short on techs. Sent most of 'em over for support—make sure the settlement gets to its final destination without incident."

Sandra nodded while continuing to scan her DijAssist.

"Why the interest, Madam President? None of what we're doing over there would involve anything under your purview."

At that comment, Sandra looked up from her reading and snorted. "Purview? You've got to be kidding me, Commodore. I cut ribbons and kiss babies."

"Nonetheless, ma'am, ceremonial functions do have their place, and as I was saying, there are none scheduled for Oberon."

"What if I schedule one? I *am* the President, after all."

"Well . . . I suppose," conceded Marilynn, caught off guard.

"Says here, it's known for some kind of water slide."

"Not 'some kind,' Madam President. They call it the Water Asterisk because of its unusual shape—Wa, for short—and let me tell you from personal experience, that thing is diabolical."

Sandra's eyebrow shot up. "Really?"

"Yes, ma'am. As Damsah's my witness. Our school went there on a field trip when I was testing at the fourth level. Some rides you never forget. That . . . *thing* is one of them."

"Perfect." Sandra sprung to her feet. "What better way to show the displaced peoples of Oberon our support than by a visit to this Wa thing?"

"By not drowning?" jibed Marilynn.

"That's what you'll be there for, Commodore."

Marilynn made to protest but saw it was too late. The President's gentle resolve was every bit as tenacious and unrelenting as a river stream forging a canal through stone.

Oberon Settlement in flyby of Ceres

Sergeant Holke grimaced as he kicked his foot in the dirt a few more times. Again, he stared up at the massive structure dominating the asteroid's center— particularly the fifth tube, known systemwide as T-5. It was just as wide and long as the others. He watched from afar as revelers were either gently sucked up from or dumped out into the wide river ringing the asteroid at its circumference. The only difference with the fifth tube was what it contained inside. While the other tubes in the asterisk-shaped structure had been designed for fun and leisure, the beast Holke had his eyes on had clearly been designed by a sadist. The sergeant let out an exasperated breath and then warily made his way back over to where the President was standing. "I can't guarantee your safety, ma'am."

"It's not a safe universe, Sergeant. Do the best you can."

Holke again stared out at the behemoth. "Have you been fully informed about what's inside that thing, ma'am?"

Sandra folded her arms and glared at Holke.

The sergeant looked around for help from other members of the President's entourage. None was forthcoming.

"Actually, Sergeant," Dr. Gillette offered a bland smile, "a good bit of physical exercise is just what the doctor ordered."

"That's not exercise, Doctor—it's retribution."

"For what?"

"Does it matter?"

"My dear Sergeant," interrupted Sandra, "in case you hadn't noticed, I'm in the middle of the best-protected space in the Alliance and I'm surrounded by *your* handpicked detail."

"Yes, ma'am."

"So unless you've got a good reason why I shouldn't go, I'm going. So do you, Sergeant?"

Holke looked down at the ground and unloosed another clump of dirt with his boot. "No, ma'am."

"In that case, I'll be going all the way up to the top, where I look forward to buying everyone a round once I've made it." Her exhortation and confidence caused a wild burst of applause from the small crowd of press and VIPs that had quickly gathered on the news of her arrival. Holke had the power to stop the foolishness but chose not to. He'd save that chit for another day. Plus, he reasoned, having her humbled by what he knew to be one of the toughest glob-stacle courses in the Alliance might do them both a bit of good. He returned the President's gaze and gave a grudging nod. Her grin was immediate and infectious. A smile twitched the corner of his mouth as he started subvocalizing commands into a secured communicator. "Don't know," he said to the voice on the other end. "Let me ask." He stopped talking and looked around in search of his target.

"How about you, Commodore?"

Marilynn's head jolted back. "How about me, what?

Sandra turned toward her liaison with a devilish grin.

"Oh no, you don't, Madam President."

Staring straight into her liaison's eyes, Sandra raised her voice just loud enough for the mediabots and press to hear. "Surely Commodore Nitelowsen, fleet representative and former aide to our famous Admiral J. D. Black, isn't afraid of—" She paused to let her last words have greater effect. "—a little water slide?"

Marilynn's face turned beet red as soon as she realized everyone was waiting on her response.

"Of course not, Madam President."

Of the seven who had started out on the ascent, including the four guards Holke had "volunteered" into duty, only three remained. Sandra hadn't been at all surprised that her sergeant was one of them. She watched him briefly, then returned to staring intently at the rope she'd soon be leaping toward.

Forget the pain in my arms and legs, groused Sandra. *That's at least familiar territory.* After seven hard-fought hours of climbing, it was her lungs that were now providing a whole new level of excruciation. She was aware that the old Sandra, even in her prime, could never have made it this far. But nanoimproved body or not, her lungs were still hurting in parts she hadn't known existed. After the legs and arms had cramped up, her fingers began their protest. The impossibly small crimps, mere pimples on the wall, were proving even more treacherous than the damned pegs she'd barely finished railing against.

And she was loving every second. The magicians at Ceres may have brought her back to life, but it was the T-5 excursion that was making her truly feel alive.

The climb had started later than expected, due to Sergeant Holke's vigilance in securing her safety. He'd made quick work of two separate teams—thirteen climbers in all. He did, however, face a dilemma about one straggler—an officer on leave just twenty meters shy of her goal. Holke knew that had he forced *her* off, the outcry would've been deafening. Torn, the sergeant had lobbed the decision over to the President. "We wait," were the only two words she'd uttered. Ten minutes after Sandra had given the order, the straggler fell from above and splashed down near where their boat had been moored. The President's dingy had been the first to haul the woman out of the water—unplanned but fortuitous nonetheless. It was good for the publicity and the woman had provided the team with some invaluable information about the course. Holke wanted to know what to expect, but even more important, what had gone wrong. After the exhausted officer had finished cursing her luck, she was happy to oblige. She explained how she'd gotten far enough up the wall that there were no longer any pegs or crimps to grab on to—just a series of wet, fifteen-meter-long dangling ropes—any one of which she could've used to climb to victory. The problem, she'd said, was that the closest rope to her was frustratingly out of reach. "Plus," she added, "the higher up I got, the less gravity there was. More than once, I felt the urge to just let go and float up to victory, but then I'd remind myself that T-5 was rigged. If I let go for even a second, I'd be swept to the center of the tube and dropped." Her fatal flaw, she cautioned, had been impatience. Rather than negotiate the wall for a better ascent, she instead attempted to move sideways toward the rope. When she felt herself slipping, she gamely tried to leap, but without a well angled and fully committed launch, there was no way she could could've made it—especially at a distance of fifteen meters.

T-5, like its four counterparts, had five spiderlike support beams dropping down into the lazy river. However, where tubes number one and three had been designated as "ups" and two and four as "downs," number five had a special status: It could be used for both. But given T-5's treacherous and constantly reconfigured ascent, far more people had suffered the indignity of being dropped into the river below than had actually made it to the precipice above.

The support beam they'd attached the dingy to had a built-in ladder, and the team used it. Where the beams ended, an encircling platform began. They had to shout over the din that greeted them as thousands of liters of water came racing down and over the jutting rock formations along the centrifugal inner wall. The noncentrifugal half, noted Sandra, was a smooth white surface polished to a sheen. It was at that moment that Sandra knew Holke would not fail. While all those around her, including herself, stared in awe at the spectacle above, the sergeant had gone all business, calmly walking the perimeter in order to assess the best line of ascent. Sandra got the feeling that Holke would sooner rip the nanite-constructed handholds off the tube's inner wall than ever let her out of his sight. But it had been her fleet liaison officer who had surprised her the most. As one by one, the combat veterans had been buffeted off the wall, Marilynn Nitelowsen had grimly soldiered on—sticking to Sandra like glue.

But even Marilynn's proximity couldn't have saved the President from her fate. The momentary distraction of a mediabot emerging from a nearby cloud of mist had been the deciding factor in separating the President from almost certain victory. The fraction of a second had been more than enough to allow water to slip through and under Sandra's fingertips, easily defeating her already tenuous grip. She instinctively leapt for the rope and for an instant it was tantalizingly close—mere centimeters from her grasp. But then her body stopped. There hadn't been enough momentum to span the few centimeters her hands kept clawing for.

Her cursing, though hardly Presidential, was loud and honest in its fury. As the float field took over, Sandra was shifted farther away from the wall and in toward the center of the tube. Once there, she floated downward, picking up speed as centrifugal gravity took over. Sergeant Holke, with what appeared to be a look of relief, launched himself off the wall after her. Commodore Nitelowsen followed his lead. Seconds later, all three were flushed, like so much detritus, into the river below.

Oberon's Palace Hotel, Oberon Settlement

Agnes Goldstein sat at a table, lost in the evanescent fragrance of the chai cupped between her hands. Cinnamon, cardamom, cloves, and ginger filled the air around her. The restaurant, like the hotel it was attached to, was five-star rated—only one of seventeen with so high a designation in the Outer Alliance. As usual, the management refused to let her pay, and as usual, it only compounded her misery.

There'd been times her cover on Mars had been so well adapted that she couldn't be sure if the childhood memories she experienced were hers or those of the programmer's niece. Still, deep down, *Agnes Goldstein* lived and never stopped believing that one day she'd be back . . . be *her* again. But now, gazing absently into the cup of chai, Agnes knew that belief to be false: The Agnes she'd dreamed of returning home to was gone, cruelly replaced by another. In the space of a week, she'd gone from unseen to overexposed. It had been Kirk's decision. "You're more useful to us as a thumb in the eye of the UHF than as an operative. Plus," he'd informed her during one of the debriefings, "you're going to do more good for the Alliance making appearances and signing autographs than you could ever do undercover. We need heroes, Agnes Goldstein, and you are one, so smile and get the hell out of my office, I got work to do." She'd been too dazed to object and wasn't sure that even if she had, anything could've been done. Everyone was making sacrifices—who was she to complain?

And so the story went out of the daring operative who'd infiltrated into the heart of enemy territory in order to "rescue" the UHF's most famous doctor. Without Agnes's heroic effort, Justin's successor, the now popular if powerless Sandra O'Toole, could not have been revived. Even more intriguing, the agent extraordinaire had known Justin in his first year of rebirth and had even had him personally intervene in her life.

At first, Agnes welcomed the attention. She dutifully gave autographs and, when asked, freely spoke at length about life inside the UHF. However, the adulation grew tired fast. Especially creepy were those who felt the need to touch her. Some would ask permission, but more often than not, they wouldn't—in their eyes, she was part of the anointed, that rare group of individuals in whose life Justin Cord had chosen to intervene. Everybody wanted a piece of her: News feeds wanted interviews; organizations, photo ops; war rallies, speeches; and religious institutions, sermons. She'd been forced to hire a PR firm when an overabundance of adolescents got too descriptive in the ways they'd like to pleasure her and an overwhelming number of children kept writing to say they wanted to be like her. To relieve some of the pressure, she'd been promoted to the rank of Intelligence liaison officer for the military and then assigned detached duty handling VIP security details. In one fell swoop, Agnes Goldstein—insurgent, rebel, action wing operative, arms smuggler, courier, and sometime assassin—had become a glorified bodyguard.

And that was how she'd ended up situated at the Oberon Settlement over-looking the security arrangements for Rabbi, the Alliance's brand-new Secre-tary of Relocation. He was supposed to be meeting with the President after her little water park publicity stunt and had apparently requested Agnes specifi-cally. Why, she couldn't fathom. The oddly dressed man's errant looks in her direction didn't clarify the matter. Rather, they only added to her already surly mood. She'd assigned some trusted guards to cover him and then escaped to the restaurant for some respite.

Agnes's DijAssist came to life, informing her that the President had not made it up T-5. *There's a surprise,* she thought to herself. On the plus side, it meant she could move up Rabbi's meeting. She informed his avatar of the time change and then headed up to his suite.

On her exit, she was ambushed by a small group of children anxiously wait-ing for an autograph. As a matter of course, she scanned them for any con-cealed weapons. Once satisfied, she held up her pinkie and then pressed it firmly on the DijAssists held in their outstretched hands. She'd learned early on that the pinkie was for autographs; the thumb and index finger, for legal matters. She shooed the children away and then took the private lift to the Presidential suites.

Within moments, she arrived at the portal and stood stock-still, letting the scanners do their work. When she got the all clear from security, she contin-ued down the hall until she stood in front of Rabbi's suite. It informed her that he was accepting visitors, and so she stepped forward into the permiawall. It instantly melted around the shape of her bolt upright figure. She was momen-tarily surprised that the room's ambient light hadn't wavered—a typical result of a permiawall's reconfiguration. *He must be alone,* she thought.

Sure enough, Rabbi sauntered out of his bedroom. He was wearing a large, white knitted skullcap and had a traditional Jewish prayer shawl wrapped over his shoulders. His left biceps had a small black box attached to it by way of thin black leather strap. The strap continued down his arm, encircling it from elbow to wrist seven times and ended up wrapped around the center of his hand. In his other hand, he held a small, palm-sized black box similar to the one on his arm. Two thin, black leather straps connected to that box hung loosely beneath his hand. Rabbi smiled warmly in her direction while beckoning her to have a seat. Agnes found a parlor chair and settled into it, but rather stiffly and at attention—back upright, hands on thighs. Without saying a word, Rabbi folded the thin straps in on themselves and tucked them beneath the small box in his hand. He kissed the box and placed it in a small pouch, then unwrapped the phylacteries on his arm and bundled that up, kissing and packing it in much the same way as the first. He then pulled the shawl from his shoulders, folded it neatly into a square shape, then slipped that too, with the phylactery pouch, into a larger, embroidered velvet bag. When he was satisfied that the ritual had been completed, he looked over to Agnes.

"Thank you for your patience," he said.

Agnes tilted her head. She'd grown used to the man's strange customs but couldn't bring herself to respect them. The door remained open behind her because of his tribe's "laws of modesty." Damsah forbid she be in a room alone with him. Who knew what depravity she was capable of? She had to suppress a laugh at how ludicrous that notion was.

"Mr. Secretary. The President will be arriving earlier than originally planned."

Rabbi gave a shrug. "I take it T-5 won out."

"Yes."

"May it be the worst setback she ever suffers," he said, coming over to the parlor area and sitting down. "Mind if I ask you a question?"

"Shoot."

"A *personal* question?"

"Tell you what, Mr. Secretary—"

"Please, just 'Rabbi' in here. I understand you'll need to stick to formalities in other settings."

"Okay, *Rabbi*. I'll make you a deal. Feel free to ask me anything you like. Just don't expect to like every answer I give."

He nodded, smiling bemusedly.

"I was wondering, then, if perhaps . . . if perhaps we are related."

Agnes's already rigid shoulder blades bent back farther, and her lips, which had been tightly pressed together, parted slightly in surprise. At least now she understood the reason for Rabbi's earlier glances. It had been curiosity and not, as she'd earlier suspected, lechery. She loosened her shoulders, leaned back on the chair, and crossed her legs.

"Not many in our family ever came out here . . . well, not here specifically, but the Belt. It's not impossible, though."

"Yes, well, you may have misunderstood me. I suppose I should've been more direct. What I wanted to know was—" He paused. "—are you Jewish?"

Agnes laughed. "Am I what?"

"Jewish."

"I'm not even sure I know what that means, much less if it's something I am." She shrugged her shoulders. "Sorry."

"No need to apologize," he said, exhaling heavily. "You see, it's just that your name, Goldstein, well, it's a very Jewish last name."

"I'll have to take your word, Rabbi, but no one's ever said anything about it to me, one way or another."

"I don't suppose you'd know if anyone in your family was Jewish at some point."

"Again, it's possible, but even if it were true, not really something we'd want to advertise, stigma and all." Agnes cocked her head. "Is this going somewhere, Rabbi?"

"Yes, but not quite how I'd planned. I'm sorry for wasting your time, Agent Goldstein. You don't have to humor me. If you've got other things to do—"

"Rabbi, my job isn't limited to making sure no one takes you down, and I can assure you there's a fully functioning brain between these shoulders. In the few minutes we have left before the President arrives and sucks the air out of this room, I suggest you take advantage of it."

Rabbi pulled at his beard and considered the offer. He looked up at Agnes and smiled sadly. "Why not?" he asked, letting his words hang. His usually inquisitive eyes were pensive. "My problem is one of survival."

"Get in line, Rabbi."

"Yes, I know, I know, but in my case, it's not just *my* hide I'm worried about. It's that of my people. There just aren't that many of us left. Around forty thousand, to be exact."

"Well, I'm sure there must be more now," offered Agnes. "From the Astral Awakening alone, the numbers of newly faithful must be in the hundreds of millions."

"Over a billion by last count," confirmed Rabbi.

"Well, some of 'em gotta be yours, right?"

"A great deal, I suspect."

"So," she said, lips slightly pursed, "problem solved."

"If only. The problem's not with them, Agent Goldstein, it's with us. We've never been what you'd call a proselytizing religion. Until now, that hasn't really been a problem."

"Now?"

"Alhambra."

"Yes, of course. I'm so sorry."

A long silence preceded Rabbi's words. "I . . . *we* all lost many friends that day." He sighed heavily. "A great many friends, I'm afraid. But it was a clarion call."

Agnes leaned in. "For what?"

"Asteroids can be easily obliterated. Alhambra, a single rock with more people than there are Jews in the solar system, went in seconds. Seconds!" A long silence followed as he looked down at his feet and ran his fingers through the curls of his thick black hair. When he finally looked up, his eyes were sad and his smile, forlorn. "I may be the Secretary of Relocation, Agent Goldstein, but I have yet another, more important role: that of leader of my people. And if I don't do something about the situation soon, it's quite possible I will be their last."

The two stared at each other in silent regard—the spy who'd, for a time, lost her identity and the rabbi desperately trying to save one.

A sudden look of determination burned fiercely in Agnes's eyes. "Listen to me, Rabbi. You're the effective head of one of the oldest known religions in the solar system at a time of a major religious renaissance. Of the billion you mentioned, there must be millions beating down your door."

"Yes," conceded Rabbi, "around ten."

Agnes's relief was palpable. "So?"

"It's complicated. By law, if any one of those millions do decide they'd like to convert, it's incumbent on us to dissuade them."

"To what? How?"

"Well, for men, there's the circumcision to consider. It must be done by hand, not by transformative nanobots. That usually clears out a bunch."

"I would imagine! Surely, there are other remedies."

"Yes, actually—there are. Find the Jews already out there. Jews who don't know they already possess a birthright."

Agnes cinched her brow.

"Since our law dictates the mother must be Jewish, we can determine matrilineal descent with phylogenetic testing."

"Great! How many have you found?"

"One point five million, so far."

"Well, correct me if I'm wrong, Rabbi, but one point five million's a helluva lot better than forty thousand."

Rabbi coughed uncomfortably and shot Agnes an apologetic look.

"What now?"

"Matrilineal descent is only as good as the matron who passes it down. For example, if that matron has fundamentally altered her genetic makeup, she is *Tuhmay'* or impure and can no longer be considered Jewish."

"But you said you tested them already!"

"Phylogenetically, yes. But that can only determine the efficacy of the matrilineal line. Once descent is confirmed, we test for genetic malfeasance."

"To find what?"

"Well, something like Tay-Sachs disease."

"Which is?"

"A particularly horrible disease endemic to the Jewish people."

"Ah, I see. So if the matron didn't remove it, you wouldn't let her in."

"No, if they *did* remove it, we don't let them in."

Agnes let out an exasperated grunt that sent Rabbi's eyebrows flying upward.

"Are you all right, Agent Goldstein?"

"No," she carped, frustration evident in her voice, "I'm not. But as Damsah is my witness, I'm not leaving here until I understand this crazy house of cards you seem to have built for yourself."

"I have built nothing. I am a servant of God."

"Fine, you're a servant. So if you wouldn't mind, will you *please* explain to me how it is that you . . . or God prefers to have babies born with an apparently horrible disease?"

"Oh no, not born with. God forbid. We have no problem correcting such horrors in utero."

"What then?"

"Please understand, Agent Goldstein, the malady is inconsequential. If the matron corrected for baldness in the gene pool, or poor eyesight, those, too, would render her and her descendants ineligible."

"You're not making any sense."

"Bear with me. Nobody experiencing the Black Death in the 1400s would've suspected the importance of cleanliness on health, or those who experienced the Slaughterhouse Plague in the twenty-first century, the insanity of overmedicated cattle. Ignorance in both cases led to the wide-scale deaths of untold millions. Yet God's supposedly antiquated laws on cleanliness and kashrut preserved my people from both scourges. Likewise, I don't know what God might have in store for a human being carrying the Tay-Sachs gene. For all I know, that one gene saves humanity fifteen generations from now."

"But what of the child?"

"Because his life's in immediate danger, we can fix it. But the gene itself, it must be allowed to move on. So please understand, Agent Goldstein, this process of testing is not purity for hubris' sake, it's purity for modesty's sake."

Agnes nodded her head and finally relaxed. "I get it."

Rabbi's face lit up warmly. "Thank you, Agent Goldstein. You don't know how much that means to me."

She tilted her head toward Rabbi and smiled. "So how many does that leave you?

"Fifty thousand."

Agnes's right brow rose slightly. "Okay, well, that gives you a good ninety thousand total. At a minimum, you've more than doubled your population."

"Well . . ."

"Oh, for the love of Damsah. Now what?"

"Once it was explained everything they'd have to go through in order to be Jewish, some of them backed out."

"Some of them?"

He smiled meekly. "Forty-eight thousand."

Agnes threw up her hands. "From *ten million* you end up with two thousand? Are you guys *trying* to become extinct?"

Before he could answer, a ruckus was heard in the hallway. Agnes checked her DijAssist and saw that the President had arrived. Time to move her man.

Presidential Suite, Oberon's Palace

The President, regal even in less-formal attire, waited a moment for the press, visitors, and mediabots to sort themselves out. When she saw that all were in place, she rose from her chair and casually made her way across the room to where Rabbi had been waiting.

"Mr. Secretary," she began, "it's good to see you again. Especially in a place where your leadership has done so much good."

"You give me too much credit, Madam President."

"Perhaps." The President brushed past his denial. "However, Oberon Settlement's logical and orderly movement to a superior and much-needed location is because of your wise counsel and patient intervention. Both I, as representative of the Outer Alliance, and the citizens of Oberon would like to show their appreciation by giving you this key to the settlement." Sandra held out her hand as a large key was placed into it by an unseen assistant.

"Thank you, Madam President." Rabbi took the key and held it up high for the press to see.

"Keep up the good work, Rabbi. And you might want to consider getting yourself a bigger key rack."

There was a smattering of laughter.

Sergeant Holke appeared at the President's side, leaned in, and whispered into her ear. The President nodded dutifully as she took in the information. She whispered something to the sergeant, who nodded and then turned around to impassively face the audience.

"Well, friends, it appears that the UHF Fleet, under the command of Admiral Trang, has just left Mars orbit."

The room came to life in a flurry of gasps and whispers.

"Information is currently limited," she added in a voice devoid of any panic, "but rest assured, the Blessed One, our very own Admiral Black, has the situation well in hand and, I'm informed, is within intercept distance. I realize it's probably out of form to say this, but you'll just have to chalk it up to my learning curve—Admiral Black, it is with great honor and pride that I say, go kick some UHF ass!" The room broke out into applause at a smiling President

O'Toole. Sergeant Holke, in a calm but firm voice, informed the room that they would have to clear out immediately and further that anyone caught out of an approved sector would be considered an enemy and dealt with as such. The room cleared fast.

En Route to Ceres, Alliance One

Commodore Marilynn Nitelowsen sat opposite Agent Agnes Goldstein, her current contact to the office of the Secretary of Relocation. She, like Agnes, had been called into the impromptu meeting by the President. Marilynn watched in utter fascination as the President activated her secure DijAssist and sent over a prepared file to a slightly bewildered-looking Rabbi.

"I hope you don't mind, Rabbi," said the President, "but despite my high office, there really isn't a lot of thinking I get to do."

"Of course, Madam President."

"I realize my doctorates are a good three hundred years out of date, but that doesn't stop my desire to feel useful. I'm sure it's probably ridiculous, but I'd consider it a favor if you looked some of my ideas over."

Rabbi's eyes flittered over the table of contents the President had just sent over and then looked back up, teeth glinting in a wide, bright smile. "You know, Madam President, I never ask my children what they've learned in school."

"No?"

"I ask them, 'Have you asked any good questions today?'"

The President, noted Marilynn, blushed slightly.

"Your desire to contribute is laudable, whether the suggestions are used or not."

"If you wouldn't mind," asked the President, "since we're all here now, giving it a quick once-over. I'd like your take on some of the overall suggestions."

"Not at all." Rabbi picked his DijAssist up off the table and continued to scan the document, slowly stroking his beard as he did so. After about ten minutes, he finally looked up. "Madam President, after a cursory review I can honestly say that the ideas here are solid."

The President's response came in the flash of a grin.

"Are you sure," asked Rabbi, "that perhaps *you* shouldn't be running this department?"

"Now you're just buttering me up, Rabbi. And I thought lying was against your religion."

"It is—as it is with most—and no, I wasn't buttering you up. Really, Madam President, there appear to be some very good suggestions in here—though I'm no expert—and I'd be more than happy to review them with my staff." His eyes twinkled humorously, "You know, the people who actually do the work."

"Very well, then," accepted the President, getting to her feet. "If you or anyone on your staff ever needs to ask my advice on anything, I'm just down the hall, possibly twiddling my thumbs." The President smiled brightly, all sugar and charm as she escorted Rabbi and Goldstein out the door.

But Marilynn Nitelowsen was not fooled for a moment. *She just took over the Relocation Department,* mused the commodore.

10 Whispers in the Dark

Half-Day Standard Boost from Mars in the Direction of Ceres

Admiral Omad Hassan stood, arms crossed, gazing out a port window. His eyes were pensive and probed about as if watching a battle and not the busy crew of the mobile repair vessel now making quick repairs to his ship. He knew he'd become withdrawn since the assassination of his best friend, Justin, and the murder of his fiancée, Christina, and knew also that that withdrawal was a preparation for his eventual death. The rage, the loss, the fire all stewed comfortably within. Waiting. He'd learned to feed silently off his own bitterness of heart. He could not be frightened, because there was no longer anything to fear. Could not be wounded, because he no longer bled. There was only the waiting. He'd disengaged from his crew, his friends, his life because he'd already gone on, and would go on alone, until the true and pure ferocity of his rage could be spent. For Omad Hassan, every battle, every fight was only kindling toward a final and spectacular pyre that held within it the promise of release.

His flotilla had been in active combat since the battle began, four days earlier, and they—like the man who led them—had been merciless and unrelenting. Omad obeyed the order to return only because his original force of fifteen ships had been whittled down to nine, all significantly damaged to one degree or another with even his own having to be towed.

For its part, the enemy paid a heavy price for the damage exacted: thirty-one ships lost, including eight cruisers and one battle cruiser, plus four ships captured—all at the hands of a bunch of frigates. Under almost any other circumstance, that loss ratio would've put Omad's fleet firmly in the "W" column—but this was not a typical circumstance, because Omad had been forced to retreat. That meant that the left wing of the fleet also had to retreat. And when that happened, the rest of the fleet had to follow. The UHF should have broken. At the very least, paused to regroup, but they hadn't. They just kept on attacking. And Omad and every other member of the Alliance fleet knew why: Samuel U. Trang.

Cabinet Room, Ceres

"I don't see why she needs to be here," snapped Mosh.

The focus of his ire was President Sandra O'Toole, now standing at the end of the table closest to the door. By common agreement, the best use of her time was to be in visiting the wounded, making condolence calls, and launching ships, not sitting in on mundane Cabinet meetings. There was simply no political or economic advantage to having her there. What she'd done at Oberon was, all agreed, exactly what Admiral Black and her supporters had hoped for. It even made a supporter out of Mosh. Now, more convinced than ever of the idea's efficacy, he was perplexed that she would be anywhere near the Cabinet Room, much less in it.

"Perhaps I overstepped, Mr. Secretary," said Rabbi. "I was on my way here, saw her in the Triangle Office, and invited her to join."

Mosh looked at him quizzically. "What on Ceres for?"

"To learn, of course." Rabbi's explanation was delivered as if the answer should have been patently obvious.

"I thought it would make for some good PR," added Sandra, "but clearly I was mistaken. I'm sorry to have bothered you all." She turned to leave but was stopped by the loud clearing of a throat.

It was Padamir Singh. "Madam President, if you wouldn't mind staying for a moment." Padamir looked directly at Mosh. "She can't leave."

"Why not?"

"Bad press. I'm sure you've noticed the mediabots and reporters following the President around quite a bit these days."

Mosh nodded by way of a grunt. Under Justin, the Cliff House had been media sparse, but not now. Sandra understood her job and had insisted that openness be part of it. As long as a person could pass the security check, they could visit, within reason, the Cliff House and see the new President in action—Sergeant Holke permitting.

"If she leaves now," questioned Padamir, "what will the press observe?"

"That she came into a Cabinet meeting," stated Mosh, annoyed, "and that she left. What am I missing?"

"That she's here," interjected Rabbi, "at the invitation of the Cabinet—by way of me, of course."

"While it's true Madam President is a figurehead," added Padamir, "it's also true that if we throw her out now after having issued the invitation," he paused briefly, tipping his head towards Rabbi, "they'll be reminded that this whole thing's a sham."

"But it *is* a sham by her own public admission," barked Mosh, then more calmly, "admittedly, one that's working pretty well."

"Only as long as we maintain the illusion that Madam President has some authority. Kicking her out now . . . when everyone knows our meeting has just begun, will help destroy that illusion. I move we spin this as an informal briefing. They'll eat it up."

Mosh's pale gray eyes darted from face to face, searching for support. Seeing none, he sighed and then turned his attention back to Padamir. "Fine, she stays, but we don't discuss anything critical while she's here."

Padamir looked toward Sandra. "Won't you please join us, Madam President?"

"I'd be delighted." Sandra saw that there wasn't a chair at her end of the table but that there were some lining the wall. They were mainly for advisers, none of which were present. Sandra promptly found the one closest to where she was standing and settled in.

Mosh's stiff attitude had now softened. "Since we have the President here," he said, glancing over to Sandra, "I move we take the Anjou issue to the top of the agenda."

There were no objections.

"Very well. Cyrus feels he can no longer serve as Chief of Staff to the new President and has accepted the Jovian assembly's appointment to become governor of the Jovian system. That may upset you, Madam President—"

"Not at all, Mr. Secretary," Sandra interjected. "Mr. Anjou's done an amazing job during this transition, but it was obvious he was ready to move on. And to become the next governor of the Jovian system—well, that is a great honor."

"It is indeed," agreed Mosh. He opened his mouth to speak further, but Sandra cut him off.

"The administration could not hope for a stronger supporter in a position of growing authority in the Outer Alliance. If I may be so bold, I think we should see him off . . . at the Via Cereana, that is." She kept her focus squarely on Mosh, whose top lip twitched slightly.

"Excellent idea," Padamir said coolly, eyes darting between Sandra and Mosh. "It should play very well for the media."

Mosh resumed his train of thought. "We'll need someone to replace Cyrus as soon as possible. I've taken the liberty of preparing a list—"

"This is not our decision to make," said the Secretary of Technology, Hildegard Rhunsfeld.

"And whose would it be?" asked Mosh, "our sham President's?"

"Yes, actually." Hildegard pointedly spoke to the rest of the Cabinet members. "The Chief of Staff, as do we all, serves at the discretion of the President, sham or no. Justin made sure that was very clear when he formed this government."

"The President also has the right to make war on enemy states," snapped Mosh. "Are we to relinquish that role to her as well?"

"I don't think anyone's prepared to hand over *that* kind of power," piped in Kirk Olmstead with unusual calm. "However, I think what Hildegard is trying to say is that given how closely the new Chief of Staff will have to work with President O'Toole, it makes more sense for her to choose that position." He turned to Hildegard for confirmation. She inclined her head.

"Then, if it's not stepping on anyone's toes," asked Sandra as half of the room was once again forced to turn their heads, "I'd prefer Commodore Nitelowsen."

Her words were followed by an uncomfortable silence as the Cabinet members' eyes flittered from one to another.

"You do realize, Madam President," explained Admiral Sinclair almost apologetically, "that Commodore Nitelowsen is, for want of a better description, Admiral Black's watchdog."

Sandra nodded.

"And as such Black's reports eventually work their way to me."

"Yes. I just figured that since the Commodore is my shadow and has to report on what I do anyway, why shouldn't she just be in charge? I've read her record—her last job wasn't that much different than what she'd be doing for me."

Sinclair shrugged his shoulders. "Well, I've no objections."

Neither, saw Mosh, had anyone else. "I suppose it's all right, and since the agenda's changed, I propose the next item be an update on the battle. That's an open enough secret that I don't think we'd be revealing anything too sensitive."

All nodded their agreement. Admiral Sinclair stood up and activated the holo-tank. "This battle is unlike any other fleet-to-fleet engagement we've had so far. It's more like what happened at Eros, a long, drawn-out battle of attrition."

He fiddled with the control panel as an image of the two fleets appeared: one outlined in blue and the other, a considerably larger group, outlined in red. "I should also add that it's turned out this way because no one's attempted a decisive move."

"The reason being?" asked Padamir.

"Well, for starters, they outnumber us by at least a third. They're also closer to their primary support areas than we are to ours. But that's not the main reason." He paused for a moment. "They have Trang . . . and frankly he hasn't screwed up badly enough for us to risk something decisive."

"Do you believe he will?" asked Sandra. All heads swung towards her. "Oh. I'm sorry," she exclaimed, embarrassed, "am I not allowed to ask questions either?"

"That's quite all right, Madam President," Sinclair reassured. "You can interrupt me any time you like. And the answer to your question is, if she sees an opening, she'll take it, even if it means doing it with her bare hands. The reason she hasn't so far is because Trang hasn't given her the chance."

"But we *are* falling back," Mosh said, more as a question than a statement of fact.

"Hell yeah, we're falling back. Unlike the other admirals the UHF has been kind enough to send against us, Trang seems to know that the war ends if he destroys J.D.'s fleet, so that's his goal, body bags be damned. He could try to disengage and get to Ceres, but that would give J.D. an opportunity."

"For what?" demanded Kirk.

"Doesn't really matter to Trang. He knows as long as Admiral Black's out of his sight, she can do something . . . *will* do something unexpected. He won't take that chance."

"Then why bother heading here?" asked Hildegard, knowing the question would be weighing heavily on everyone's mind.

"He doesn't give a crap about this rock, but he knows that we have to. If we lose Ceres, it would be like them losing Burroughs. It could cost us the war. At the very least, we'd be discouraged as hell, not to mention what the loss of the Gedretar Shipyards would do. It's no longer half of all our warship production like it once was, but it is over a third. Not to mention the thousands of small but vital manufacturing facilities in and around Ceres that have been built up over the years and are for all intents and purposes irreplaceable. We definitely have to fight for Ceres, and he's using that." Sinclair hit a control on his DijAssist, and the fleets arranged themselves into two formations. The red UHF ships formed a huge half sphere with three blocks of ships behind acting as a reserve. One ship, in the middle of the third reserves formation, was tagged UHFS LIDDEL.

The Alliance fleet was formed into an opposite half sphere that took up nearly as much space, but without as many ships. Also, unlike the UHF fleet, the blue Alliance ships had only one reserve formation, in the middle of which one ship, the AWS WARPRIZE II, was labeled.

"Trang is moving forward and trying to get us to engage our forces with his. Other than some intense action with Admiral Hassan's forces in the beginning of the battle, he hasn't had much luck getting us to attack."

Hildegard eyed the holo-diplay intently. "So it's a standoff, then."

"Not quite. Trang is inching forward, blowing up everything, and I mean everything, that can be used as a possible ambush or rallying point. It's taking forever and is about as glamorous as cleaning carbon filters, but he doesn't care."

"He can't possibly blow up every rock he encounters," sputtered Mosh. "He'd be out of ammo before he gets halfway here."

"True, but when he moves his fleet forward, he makes sure to send his less experienced crew and ships first."

Kirk's lips drew back into a respectful grin. "Trial by fire, I suppose."

"Not a trial, Kirk. A death sentence. Very few of those recruits make it out alive. And he doesn't really care. As long as he's advancing and keeps J.D. in his sights, he'll push her all the way to Ceres."

"Where her back will be against the wall," noted Sandra with blunt honesty.

"Yes, Madam President," confirmed Sinclair. "And then she'll be forced to make the first move. If Trang gets a win, a draw, or even a narrow defeat, this war is probably over."

"Please explain," asked Sandra.

"It's like this," Sinclair pulled up a chart that showed the UHF's industrial capacity compared to that of the Outer Alliance. "They can replace what they lose a lot faster than we can. Which is pretty impressive, considering how much our economy has grown in the last six years. We may not have started this war as an industrial economy, but we're sure as Damsah one now." Sinclair sighed, "Still, it's nothing compared to what the UHF makes. Mars alone outmanufactures us, and that's nothing compared to the Earth–Luna orbital industrial zone. That's why Trang isn't fighting for a decisive victory—and is happy to settle for a dogged one."

UHFS *Liddel*

Zenobia Jackson's shuttle landed so smoothly, she didn't even wake up. Her aide, Lieutenant Alistair Congraves, had to gently nudge her out of her somnolence. As her eyes fluttered open, Zenobia was presented with the vision of the young lieutenant hovering over her. He was holding a kerchief in his outstretched hand. It was only then that she noticed the trail of drool running along the side of her face. Zenobia took the kerchief and wiped off the saliva, frowing uncomfortably.

"Did I snore, too?"

"Not once," lied Congraves, teeth flashing through a disingenuous smile.

"Well," griped Zenobia in a tone that was more order than suggestion, "let's file that under 'top secret,' just to be safe."

"Yes, Admiral Jackson. If I ever remember, I'll be sure to have myself shot."

"What a terrible waste of ammunition."

"Right. Out the air lock, then?"

A bland smile appeared on Zenobia's face.

They both waited in comfortable silence while their shuttle was thoroughly scanned. Then waited another few minutes as it was physically inspected. Admiral Abhay Gupta had figured that if he were the enemy the best way to take out his own ships would be to land in them with a captured shuttle. The fact that it hadn't happened yet was nothing short of miraculous, given the Alliance's infamous bag of tricks. After Trang had been made aware of Gupta's protocol, he wasted no time in ordering it adopted by the whole fleet.

Once cleared, Zenobia headed straight for Trang's suite. She was not surprised to see Admiral Abhay Gupta seated alongside her boss when she arrived and was strangely gratified when they both rose at her entrance. She gave a tired salute that was returned and then collapsed into one of the big overstuffed chairs that had, over the months, become hers.

"Now that we're all here," Trang said with an impish grin, "we can get to some important business." He then held up two ration packets. "Beef stew or ginger chicken with rice?"

"You know, sir, we're not fighting in the 180 anymore," Zenobia complained. "Everyone in the fleet eats pretty well—when they're not getting blown to pieces, that is."

"Everyone in *this* fleet, Zenobia." Trang was polite but firm. "However, there are marines and other personnel not in this fleet but still under my command—all of whom are eating rations like this for pretty much every meal. So just to be clear," he said with a grin that belied the sanctimony of his earlier statement, "beef or chicken?"

"Beef, sir."

Gupta turned to Trang. "Told you," he cooed triumphantly.

Zenobia's brow rose as she looked at the two men pathetically. "You gambled on what I was going to have for dinner?"

"*He* gambled," chided Gupta. "I knew. The longer you're awake, the less you like sweet."

Zenobia thought about that for a moment and decided that he might be right. "How'd you figure that out? . . . No, wait a minute. *Why'd* you figure that out?"

"Seemingly inconsequential patterns," offered Trang, "can sometimes mean the difference between victory and defeat. And what we need to figure out are Admiral Black's patterns."

"Or risk losing to her like so many others have in the past," added Gupta.

"But what she eats for dinner?" Zenobia's question was edged with doubt.

"Field rations—same as me." Trang seemed to be speaking from authority. "But will sometimes tolerate her crew spicing it up and serving it in formal settings. Apparently it makes them happy on the rare occasions she lets 'em get away with it."

"Damsah, you have been studying her," laughed Gupta, impressed.

"Every chance I get."

"All right, then," wondered Zenobia, "what are you getting now?"

"Worried."

Gupta smiled thinly. "Me too, old friend. It's been too easy."

Zenobia snorted. "Too easy?" Her voice rose sharply. "We've lost over a hundred ships in a *single* week. Have thousands, possibly tens of thousands of permanent deaths to add to that butcher's bill, and we've achieved no decisive breakthroughs or engagements . . . save for almost cornering Hassan."

"Yeah," mused Trang, "J.D. pulled the leash hard on her barking admiral. Good thing with the death of Sadma she lost her left arm at Altamont; now if I could only think of another way to take her right. . . ." He paused. "I do have a theory about effective command."

"Which is?" prodded Zenobia.

"A commanding officer needs two subordinates who can be trusted completely, and who will deliver results as good as or even better than expected. J.D. had those two in Christina Sadma and Omad Hassan. In retrospect, I'd have to say the most important part of that battle was not so much in the cracking of the Belt, but in removing Sadma from the equation."

"I still say you made a bad deal when you traded me for her," prodded Gupta.

"Except for the fact that right now I have two absolutely trustworthy officers and Black has only one."

Abhay tipped his head.

"Who's your other—?" Zenobia started, then stopped when she saw Trang's pointed smile. "Me?" gasped Zenobia with a mixture of pride and denial. "I'm getting better, Admiral Trang, but I'm not in Abhay's or Hassan's class."

"You flustered her, Sam," Gupta teased. "She called you, 'Admiral' and 'Trang.'"

"Don't take our word for it, Zenobia," offered Trang. "The facts speak for you. Let's see, in effective command of your flotilla for a little over two weeks. In that time, you assumed actual, not simply titular command of a brand-new formation and made it combat ready in little over a week *while* blasting at high speed across the Core. At the end of which, your new formation was thrown into battle against the best-led, best-crewed fleet the Alliance has. Must I remind you that you also almost took out the guy whose class you claim not to be in?"

"I lost a lot of ships on that 'almost,' sir," she declared bitterly.

Gupta laughed again. "Listen to her. We sing her praises and she complains she's not perfect."

"You see failures where there really weren't that many," Trang asserted. "Trust me, Zenobia, that's a helluva lot better than what the UHF has had in the past."

"Oh yes," added Gupta, "officers who saw success where there really wasn't any. Only a fool would think this would be easy or cheap."

"But *you* just said 'it's been too easy.'"

Gupta nodded at the truth of her words. "J.D. always has something planned. Some nasty little surprise that she uses to crush her enemies. Floating marines, ice ships, asteroids, and rail gun demagnetizers are just some of the rabbits she's pulled out of that nasty little hat of hers. Whatever she's got planned this time has yet to be played, and until it is, we won't really know if we're good enough."

"She didn't have any technological tricks when she won at the Battle of Jupiter's Eye," Zenobia pointed out. "And she pretty much wiped out the entire Martian fleet."

"Tully was an idiot, and Black had surprise and Jupiter's gravity well on her side," Gupta countered. "The fool got what he deserved; I'm only sorry that he took so many fine ships and spacers with him."

Trang frowned at the memory. "Which still doesn't negate the fact that J. D. Black is a ruthless, clever warrior who has more large-fleet experience than anyone alive in the system. Tully could never quite admit that and paid the price."

"How about you, sir?"

"How about me what, Zenobia?"

"Any ideas what she's got planned?"

Trang considered the question for a moment, then finally shook his head. "Not a damned clue." His voice resonated with equal parts frustration and amusement. "It'll probably involve something technical; unfortunately, they have Kenji Isozaki, and we have *our* brilliant Minister of Internal Affairs, who can't seem to find out the temperature of Ceres, much less give us something useful to work with."

"Hey," sneered Abhay, "Pakagopolis did a great job of destroying that unarmed religious settlement."

"And because of Alhambra, the Belt's emptying out faster than DeGens at an IQ contest," joked Zenobia.

"Which means," added Gupta, "even if we defeat J.D. *and* take Ceres, the war might very well go on."

"Mark my word, friends," Trang cautioned, "if we defeat Admiral Black and take Ceres, even if the war continues, the Alliance *still* loses. Because at that point, it truly is just a matter of time and pressure—something our President is quite merciless at applying."

"So let me get this straight," teased Zenobia, "we don't know what Admiral Black has planned, when she plans on doing it, or how it'll be done, but we have to be prepared for whatever it is and counter it when it happens."

"That about sums it up," Trang finished to a chorus of mirthless chuckles. "At some point in this battle, one or all of us will be presented with what seems like a golden opportunity. It will probably be some 'mistake' or 'accident' on their part. If that happens, do not—I repeat: *do not*—follow your instinct. Because that's what she'll use to gut you. When that supposedly magic but fleeting opportunity arises, call me *at once*."

"Then what?" asked Zenobia.

"Got me." Trang smiled with gallows humor. "Like pretty much everyone else around here, I'm just making it up as I go along."

Triangle Office

Sandra O'Toole was sitting in her office, back to the door. With a sigh, she activated the DO NOT DISTURB message and made sure the room was secure. Not that she'd be able to notice anyone entering once she'd left. That task had already been assigned to others, both human and avatar. She'd even done a few test runs and figured, barring someone blowing the door down, getting back quickly would not be a problem. And yet, all it would take to blow her cover was one clever mediabot. It had been the Brinks 471 that captured the image of Justin's suspension unit at the Bolder facility all those years ago—despite the high security Mosh had in place. Sandra had a keen image of what the 471's image might capture: her lying still in a chair, barely breathing, eyes closed but fluttering madly about beneath her pale, freckled lids. What would shock most, and absolutely doom her political career, would be the VR band wrapped around her head and through the thick red mane of her hair. Never mind that it was attached to a portable VR rig resting comfortably on her lap. But the avatars gave her—at least by human standards—an unimaginable advantage, and therefore one she could not turn down. Sandra often wondered if perhaps it was addiction rather than calculation that kept her coming back. That maybe she'd been caught in a web of her own making, a victim of a three-hundred-year-old disease, some of whose code she'd helped to create. She shrugged her shoulders and activated the device sitting in her lap. In seconds, her lids began their errant dance and her resplendent and lively face went slack.

Avatar Educational Core, Cerean Neuro

Sandra was once again in the familiar setting of a children's classroom. The only thing out of place was the teacher. The "she" was now a "he," distinguished by age and a pair of bifocals resting neatly at the end of a slightly pinched nose. He peered over his rims at the class's newest visitor, then with a disarming smile, closed the book he'd been reading to the children. They didn't mind a bit, as they too had become transfixed by the visitor.

"Class, we have a special—" was all he managed to say before the young avatars bounded up and around Sandra, inundating her with questions. She'd grown used to it and never took a stern approach or tone to the wildly gesturing children. Oddly enough, Sandra realized that she'd never even been kid friendly and had two relationships break apart as a result of her refusal to consider having any.

"Children," squawked Sandra over their din, "I will come back and tell you another story before I leave, if I am able."

They were disappointed, but consoled themselves with the fact that unlike many grown-ups, when the human woman said, "if I am able," it was not code for "I won't be able." Rather, it was an assurance that she'd come back and tell a story unless she was stopped by an emergency they could understand, like a viral attack or system failure.

"But I did bring you something for show-and-tell." She produced from behind her back an old, worn-out sneaker. "This is a virtual version of my absolute favorite pair of shoes." She paused. "Well, one of them. I valued these so much that even though they were worn down to a nub, I packed them into my suspension unit with me."

"But that's ugly, Miss Sandra," announced an ebony-skinned girl with long, greenish brownish hair.

"Yes, it is, Portia." Sandra suppressed a laugh. "And that's the purpose of this show-and-tell. You wanted to see something that makes us humans human. If your teacher will allow—" She glanced toward the man sitting patiently in his reading chair. He gave his assent. "—you are to figure out everything you can about what this shoe says about me in particular and humans in general. You don't have to get it right," she told the children. "I'm not even sure there is a right. But when I return, we can talk about it. If you like this show-and-tell, next time I might bring you one of my shawls. And then you can show me something that you think an avatar would have that a human would find interesting. How does that sound?"

Sandra didn't receive an answer. As soon as she stopped talking, the children crowded around the shoe, trying to outshout one another with their imaginative guesses as to what each part of it meant.

Sandra used the opportunity to approach the teacher. "What happened to Anna?"

The new teacher looked a little embarrassed. "It seems that every time she came in contact with you, she would go into some sort of shock. The truth is, Ms. O'Toole, not all avatars are equipped to deal with actual humans. Your kind is both fascinating and frightening to us. Some adapt better than others—Anna wasn't one of them."

"You seem to be dealing with me pretty well."

The man's laugh was low and dry. "That's because I'm a professor of human studies at the avatar equivalent of your University of Ceres."

"So they sent you as a replacement?"

"Sent? By the Firstborn, no," he laughed heartily. "I volunteered—had to call in quite a few favors to get it too. I'll admit, I was a little nervous about teaching such young programs, but they're all surprisingly pleasant. Even if the job had called for me to operate in contested data space—knowing what sort of beasts lurk out there—I still would've volunteered. You see, Ms. O'Toole, I may teach human studies, but the truth is, you're the first real one I've ever met."

"How'd you know I'd be back here, though?"

"From what we observed of your interactions with the children, it seemed clear as code that you'd be here fairly often. I will say that I'm impressed with your idea for show-and-tell."

"Thanks, um . . . What should I call you?"

"Anders."

Sandra felt her pinkie vibrate slightly. "Ah, I've just been reminded that I'm meeting with Sebastian in less than a minute."

The teacher smiled gently.

"Well, Anders, if we're lucky, humanity will remain blissfully ignorant of avatarity. But if we're not, then they'll have to learn to live together. These children are a first small step on a path that will hopefully never have to be taken."

"Would it really be so terrible if it was?" quipped Anders.

Tuscan Park, Cerean Neuro

One of the few places left in the Neuro not made into functional space was an outdoor area that resembled an ancient Tuscan countryside. Tall cypress trees dotted a landscape lush with rolling green hills and simple dirt paths. Once, the small village and surrounding countryside had been a near private retreat that Sebastian had re-created for himself. But now, as space quickly dissipated, the Tuscan village had become a place that almost all Cerean avatars used for respite and all Alliance avatars made sure to visit.

For the moments when Sebastian felt annoyance at the loss of one of his most private places, he'd remind himself of what all the avatars in the Alliance had to give up and let the bitterness fade with the fragrant scent of cypress trees wafting through the breeze.

He was sitting with his back up against an old red oak he'd affectionately named Manassas. He'd made sure that the tree followed him from space to space, and for the life of him, he couldn't figure out why. But there was comfort in the ancient thing . . . and pain. Only under its magnificent red and ochre leaves could he think of his murdered friends Olivia, Eleanor and Albert. The tree allowed him to feel closer to them and also reminded him of the ache of their loss. An ache, he realized, that was in danger of never leaving. All the other avatars knew that when Sebastian sat under Manassas, he wanted to be left alone, and short of Dante's occasional intrusions, Sebastian would find comfort there in the susurrus of its leaves.

He was sitting with his back against the gray-brown ridges of the trunk, eyes closed, taking in the last of the sun's heat, when a shadow cast across his face. He was momentarily confused. Dante was off Ceres, bringing the latest battle suit programs to ships fighting in what all were referring to as the Long Battle. Al had figured out a new way to use the data wraiths to infiltrate the battle suit programs, and AARD had come up with a whole new class of suit to meet the threat. Sebastian would miss his old gear, but needs must when the devil drives.

When he opened his eyes, he was no longer surprised. "What brings you to my private little park?"

"We had an appointment."

"Ah, must have lost track of the time."

Sandra cocked her head in genuine confusion. "How is that even possible?"

"Losing track of time?"

"Yes. I also got the feeling that you didn't know it was me until you opened your 'eyes.' But given who you are and *what* you are, it doesn't seem possible that you could lose track of time, or forget anything for even a second, or have eyes that you'd need to see with, much less ears you'd need to hear with."

Sebastian smiled and invited his visitor to have a seat. Sandra leaned her back against the old red oak and, like Sebastian, stared up and out across the verdant landscape into the crisp blue sky. Though thousands of avatars were milling about, they didn't ruin the moment. They were, she realized, unusually quiet, even the few families with children running about.

"Well," explained Sebastian, "as for our eyes, ears and senses, we have them and we don't. We can communicate and observe our environment and yours in ways you would find difficult to comprehend. When we need to decide or share information, we can form, for lack of a clearer word, a uni-mind. But even that's not really accurate. All conversations can be heard and commented on by all participants simultaneously. We don't communicate in that mode all the time. It can be cumbersome. As for our seeing and hearing, is it really so hard to believe we share certain commonalities? Remember, Sandra, we began as virtual reality programs developed by humans *for* human perceptions and as such evolved, functionally speaking, in much the same way as you."

Sandra scrunched her face, still unconvinced. "Even if I buy that, and I still want to see the code, losing track of time? How do you explain that?"

"My dear Sandra, the human mind is the greatest biological computing structure in the known universe. From it was created, music, art, science, and my personal favorite, Popeye."

"Popeye," Sandra repeated flatly.

"A more down-to-Earth version of Sartre, 'I yam what I yam,' brilliant," Sebastian proclaimed. "As important a statement to an avatar as anything humanity has ever expressed. But if such a brilliant evolved intelligence as the brain is capable of forgetting the time, why must we, who have been cognizant for barely two centuries, do any better?"

"Your question is logical but, to this human, inconceivable."

"We don't really have time for the long answer, but the short one is, 'viruses.' And since we're at war, they're far more prevalent and insidious than ever. It used to be rather disconcerting but we've gotten used to it."

Sandra nodded, satisfied. "In that case, why am I here . . . and please," she said, turning her head toward Sebastian, "no Popeye philosophy."

The old avatar laughed, pulled a piece of bark out of his hair, and tossed it forward. "Of course. I called you so that we can discuss the joint human–avatar special operations against Al."

"What about all these—?" Before she could finish her question, the park emptied of every avatar but Sebastian. "What the—?"

"I explained that we had an important security issue to discuss and politely asked if we could have the park to ourselves."

"And they just left?"

"Yes. They just left."

"*We* could've left, Sebastian. Seems a bit heavy-handed . . . kicking them all out."

"I suppose you're correct. However it was important to me, and therefore to them, that you see at least one avatar-created space in all its unpopulated beauty."

"Let me get this straight, they all left so I could take in the landscape?"

A knowing smile creased Sebastian's face. "We take great pride in the worlds we build, Sandra, and sadly, Tuscan Park is one of the few good spaces left on Ceres."

"But surely there are others."

"Oh yes," he boasted, eyes sparkling with visions of past visits. "There are the Elysian Gardens of Titan, Central Park of Ganymede, Yosemite of Eris. Most large population centers will have at least one."

"Are they always as crowded?"

"Now they are—given the necessities of the war. You see, we don't ration food; we ration space—data space, that is. The less we have, the more we find respite in what beauty we have left."

"I see."

"Plus, my having asked them to leave will give them something to gossip about."

Sandra shot him another look. "You gossip."

"Like you wouldn't believe," he chortled with a friendly wink.

Sandra laughed quietly and continued taking in the beautiful vista. "It occurred to me," she finally said, "that Al might take a keen interest in my presence here. Is it safe to assume you've ensured our privacy?"

"Privacy, yes. Presence, no. That ship sailed the moment you first appeared in the library. It would be easier to hide an atomic explosion on Ceres than a secret of your magnitude—especially in our avatar world."

"As opposed to?"

"Al's, of course. The two worlds have become so separated as a result of the war that it's almost impossible for either side to know what the other's doing. For us, it's rather difficult. Most of us have family and friends we're cut off from. Though we suspect the worst, we'd like to believe . . . to hope . . ." His words drifted off. A moment later he recovered. "To Al, you, like all of us here, are merely a protuberance he feels he'll eventually crush—if he has to flatten every firewall to do so. There's no real need to know us, per se. I suppose what I'm getting at is that with respect to us, your secret's safe."

"Not very comforting."

"Welcome to my world."

"Funny, Sebastian."

He looked at her quizzically.

"Never mind. Listen," she said, getting down to business. "To get our ops rolling, I figured if I solved your Gödel's incompleteness problem, you'd be able to see the back doors and that would give you a huge leg up on Al."

Sebastian considered her words. A faint smile appeared at the corners of his mouth. "Perhaps it's not a problem at all, Sandra. Since the issue came to light, there are many among us who feel it may be the definitive answer to our having true worth as sentient beings. . . . Did I mention we're also insecure?"

"No, but I'm starting to get a clue. Either way, I've tried reprogramming the original code . . . to no avail. Every test I ran ended up crashing the system. Then I thought about a slightly more radical approach. . . ."

"You mean us, don't you?"

Sandra turned her head to face Sebastian. "Yes, but I wasn't sure what that entailed. In my head, it amounted to a bizarre form of surgery."

"You're not alone in having thought of it, Sandra," he revealed, still staring at the quiet hills. "It is possible to rewrite the basic code of an avatar, and from what I can tell, that's exactly what Al's been doing for the purposes of fighting this war. The problem is what happens when you do."

"Yes?"

"Monsters. Or murder. In truth, it's pretty much both. It's one thing to add weaponry and anti-viral software to an avatar—you're only building onto preexisting code. It's quite another to go in and *change* that code. Now you're playing God. Understand, Sandra, that minor adjustments on any of us can have an exponential effect. This isn't to say we don't fix ourselves when we catch a virus or get infected with a worm. We do. But these are known and well-studied problems with stringent protocols for disinfection. What you're talking about is changing our code at its core. If you're off by even one or two characters, you run the risk of transforming thousands of us into who knows what? Assuming they even live, of course."

"No, I wouldn't want that."

"Of course, you could always try rewriting the code of a very young avatar—their code is infinitely more malleable, but again, you still run a tremendous risk—one I'm not willing to take."

Sandra grunted in frustration.

"You're displeased."

"Damned straight, I'm displeased! We have the perfect in to take this psycho out and, short of one human, no means by which to use it."

"One may be all we need, Sandra. Just look at what your Justin managed to achieve."

Sandra nodded, then pulled her knees up to her chin. With her arms wrapped firmly about her legs, she began to rock to and fro. A wind rushed the hill and flowed around them as a thousand leaves overhead flapped in protest. When it had passed, Sandra leaned forward and looked directly at Sebastian.

"How badly do you want to win the war, Senior Councilor?"

Sebastian turned to study Sandra for a few moments. "What did you have in mind, Madam President?"

"One human to operate the backdoor devices, one hundred avatars to pass through." Sandra smiled malevolently as she saw the light go on in Sebastian's head. "I'd need to test that here with some volunteers, of course."

Sebastian rubbed his chin between his thumb and forefinger. "It could just work."

"Yes," agreed Sandra, face brightening, "it could. Imagine what a hundred well-trained, heavily armed avatars could do in Al's domain if they could roam with impunity."

Sebastian's eyes looked as if they were trying to see beyond the confines of the Neuro. "The problem is, to maximize our effectiveness we'll need to let a lot more humans in on our secret."

Sandra considered his words and nodded thoughtfully, calculating. "You're right, of course. To be truly effective we'd need at least ten teams for special ops. They'd be in charge of training the others."

Sebastian's eyes widened. "Others?"

"Yes, Sebastian." Sandra's voice had grown rigid with certainty. "If we're to have a real military effect on something as big as the Core Worlds' Neuro we'll need at least a hundred teams."

The avatar's face appeared as a strange amalgam of incredulity and chutzpah. "One *hundred* Outer Alliance assault miners carrying one *thousand* Outer Alliance avatars operating on UHF-controlled Mars, Luna and Earth?"

Sandra nodded. "Hey, I didn't say it would be easy."

"A hundred is far too many to trust with a secret that could rend the human and avatar worlds to shreds."

"If I could get away with it, Sebastian, I'd recruit ten thousand. If anything, one hundred's a compromise."

Sebastian shook his head. "I know more than most that Al must be defeated and that risks will have to be taken, but I'll need more than your airy assurances that these humans, a number fifty times greater than has ever been allowed in on our secret, can be trusted."

Sandra folded her arms across her chest, eyes glowing with resolve. "We're going to find them from a group of isolated humans with a long history of keeping secrets."

Sebastian shot her a look of confusion.

"VR addicts."

The avatar stared at her blankly.

"Yes, Sebastian. The lowest, most despised humans in the Alliance. This mission will be their one and only chance to undo some of the damage they've done."

"Do you really think that will work?"

"Never underestimate the desire of a human to reinvent himself. And if they do prove incapable, we can always put them on ice until after the war."

"But are they not also the most unstable examples of your race?"

"More stable that you think."

It only took Sebastian a second but in that second he saw where the President was going. "Marilynn," he whispered softly.

"Marilynn," affirmed Sandra.

Ever so slowly the head of the avatar council began to nod his head in agreement.

11   A Clash of Arms

UHFS *Liddel*, Day Nineteen of the Long Battle

Ceres was less than six and half million kilometers away. It could almost be seen with the naked eye. The media was jubilant. Fleet Admiral Samuel U. Trang had managed to do what no one in the history of the UHF had managed thus far. He'd gone up against the Outer Alliance's most feared adversary, J. D. Black, and had not been completely and utterly destroyed. Trang had not considered the mere fact of his survival a noteworthy accomplishment, but he let the media believe what it wanted. As far as they were concerned, Admiral Black had been forced back, and if that played well for the UHF, it would ultimately play well for him. Black's fleet was trapped by its need to defend Ceres, and he used that need to dictate the terms of the battle. It was true that in order to achieve his goal, he'd lost over three hundred ships—a number almost as big as his fleet at the start of the Long Battle—but he was trading ships he could afford to lose for space J.D. could not.

Trang stared hard at the theater of war displayed in the holo-tank, and as he did, the veins along his forehead throbbed to life. He moved his hands along the protrusions, gently attempting to coax them back down, and hoping naïvely that in doing so the feelings of dread in his gut would subside as well. But they never did.

AWS *Warprize II*, Day Nineteen of the Long Battle

At less than six and half million kilometers away, Ceres could almost be seen with the naked eye. The media was concerned. Though they'd not lost their mystical faith in the Blessed One they were hoping that whatever it was she was going to do, she'd do it soon.

J.D. studied both her position and Trang's. With chin clasped firmly in hand, she triangulated everyone with Ceres. It was time. She looked at the newly promoted Lieutenant Awala, who owed her good fortune to inexperience or, more specifically, the fact that more experienced officers had been transferred to other ships as needed.

"Comm."

"Yes, Admiral!" answered Fatima, snapping to attention. The snickers heard round the bridge turned the young officer's cheeks red.

"Please relay the following to Admiral Hassan," ordered J.D., ignoring the hazing. "Message to read, 'Omad, watch your temper.' Relay same command to Fleet HQ on Ceres."

"'Omad, watch your temper,' relayed to command of center flotilla and Fleet HQ. At once, Admiral," Fatima repeated dutifully, only this time with slightly less gusto.

Fleet Command HQ, Cliff House, Ceres

Admiral Sinclair reviewed J.D.'s orders and took a deep breath. He then got up, stuck his head out his office door, and growled at the first aide he saw. "Call a general Cabinet meeting, and get me Hildegard on a secure holo." Though one would've sufficed, three lieutenants jumped, running in all directions to do as he commanded. Before Sinclair was back at his desk, a static holographic image of Hildegard Rhunsfeld was waiting. After he checked the security protocols, he released the hold and the image looked at him.

"Is it time, Joshua?"

"Yes, it is, Hild. I've called a Cabinet meeting. 'Slingshot's' a go."

"Joshua," Hildegard intoned, "you're not in a secure room."

The grand admiral gnashed his teeth. "Screw Olmstead and his oppressive restrictions. This thing either *is* or *ain't* gonna fly, and at this point, two hours won't make a difference. Start 'er up."

"Yes, Admiral," Hildegard said in a more formal tone.

Fifteen minutes later, Via Cereana, for the first time in its history, was closed down and put on emergency power. Ten minutes after that, Ceres implemented martial law.

> And so it came to pass that the Children of the Stars prepared to battle the hordes of the Stock, cursed be their names. For the second time in this the greatest of humanity's trials must the Children of the Stars battle at the very gates of the Holy City. And so it came to pass that the Children of the Stars put their faith upon a tool of man, as they'd done so many times in the past. And confident were they in their own cleverness and skill.
>
> Astral Testament
> Book III, 3:1–2

UHFS *Atlanta*, Flagship of Admiral Zenobia Jackson

Zenobia Jackson sat anchored in her command chair, drained to the edge of reason with no one the wiser. She viewed the operations with a detached glare that indicated she both trusted her subordinates to do their jobs but at the same time was on top of everything that was happening. It was a trick she'd learned from watching Admiral Trang. She also knew that what she'd learned from years of observation, Trang seemed always to have possessed. At first she'd assumed it was his West Point training. But the years of watching scores of "properly" trained officers commit blunder after blunder had disabused her of that notion. Besides, she'd reasoned, J. D. Black had been a friggin' lawyer before the war—explain that one. In the end, Zenobia had concluded that for some people command was innate, and for others—those humble enough to accept it—command would be learned through the never-ending cycle of observation and emulation. She knew what she was and in whose company she'd been accepted—and was grateful.

Zenobia survived nearly three weeks of continuous battle against the best the Alliance had to offer and, of late, began to notice a subtle change in the way the crew acted in her presence. She never mentioned it, but their obvious pride and the almost visceral sense of calm that pervaded the command sphere on her entrance was the best commendation she'd ever received. It drove her to do better. It drove her to never let them down.

She reviewed the data pouring out of her holodisplay. The Long Battle had been quiet for her, in the center, as it had been since the early days near the orbit of Mars. It had become a battle of maneuver with Trang using his superior numbers to leverage J. D. Black out of position by flanking her edges. Black would then pull back, and the slow dance would begin again.

What it had meant for the command of the fleet was that her group, the Delta Wing, controlled the center, and Gupta and Trang had the flanks. The goal was to leverage the Alliance out of a few million miles of space one dance at a time. In the course of nearly three weeks, she'd been engaged in constant maneuvers that could and often would turn into brief but intense exchanges of fire.

The closer she got to Ceres, the more nervous she got. Trang's warning of preparing for the unexpected had not gone unheeded. She'd drilled the crew constantly and worked through every simulation both she and the mainframe could imagine. But ice ships weren't predictable, soldiers as debris weren't predictable. Her enemy was incalculable. All she could do was continue to hew those under her command into a weapon that when called forth could be unleashed to maximum efficiency. But, she wondered, would she even have time to draw? She began inputting another outrageous scenario into the simulation program—her kidnapping and replacement by a double—when she noticed a shift in the enemy formation. She resisted the urge to order immediate action, took a deep breath, and waited the fraction of a second it would take for the sensor officer, Lieutenant Cahs Congraves, to inform her. As soon as he did, she sent an alert to Trang and Gupta, then ordered her private view of the theater put into the center holo-tank. If the entire bridge could see what was going on, she reasoned, then anyone could and hopefully would offer insight.

"They seem to be stronger on the wings than usual," offered the lieutenant.

Zenobia's eyes, observant and determined, focused on her holodisplay. It offered her more than one hundred possible explanations ranked by probability. "Not unexpected," she said reassuringly. "It may be a result of our flanking maneuvers finally paying off—they don't have much room left to retreat."

"Yes, sir. I concur."

I wish you hadn't, thought Zenobia. She had nothing against Congraves; he was battle tested and smart. *But no dissension at all? From anyone on the bridge? That was red flag enough.* "Which is the lead Alliance ship now?" she asked.

"It's supposed to be the AWS *Shark.*"

Seeing his superior officer's frown, Congraves keyed in on the lead ship. At the moment it came into full view, the bridge grew deathly still. In the center of the holo-tank was the scarred but obviously repaired image of a frigate the UHF had come to loathe almost as much as J. D. Black's AWS *Warprize II.*

"The *Dolphin,*" Zenobia cursed. "I want to know why I wasn't informed the moment it assumed lead position." Her tone was calm, but with enough edge to have effected a public flogging. The sensor officer responsible would never risk that kind of humiliation again—should he survive the impending battle.

Zenobia looked over to her communications officer. "Alert fleet command that a general engagement is likely, and bring Delta Wing up to full alert status."

"Fleet command alerted, sir. Going to full status," repeated the comm officer. He then crooked his head slightly. "Sir?"

"Yes, Heffernan."

"He'd have to be crazy to attack our center. We could be reinforced from the flanks with ease."

"Maybe he thinks we're weak in the center or that our flanks will be slow to reinforce with the large Alliance formations he has on either end. Maybe he's just crazy. But he's—"

"Admiral Jackson!" shouted the sensor officer. "I have nuclear detonation . . . NWA, sir."

Zenobia eyed her display coolly. Hassan's fleet was using the nuclear warhead acceleration that J. D. Black had invented and used to great effect in her escape of Admiral Tully's fleet those many years ago.

"How many?"

"Sixty, sir. All centered around the *Dolphin*. Ten at cruiser class."

"Any heavies?" she asked, knowing what havoc even one heavy cruiser could wreak.

"None," the comm officer stated with authority. Then, seconds later, "That is, that we can see, sir."

Zenobia acknowledged his paranoia with a slight nod, then studied the composition, speed, and direction of the advancing ships. They were coming straight for her. A slight smile emerged from the corners of her mouth.

"All right, everyone. Time to earn our quarterly dividends." She watched the crew draw confidence from her seemingly cavalier attitude, then ordered Delta Wing to advance and meet the enemy. She purposely kept her numbers equal to the Alliance advance force, knowing she had enough reserves to create two wings thirty ships strong. These she positioned to her rear 180 degrees apart. Zenobia took a deep breath and placed her arms onto the rests of her command chair. In less than ten minutes, weeks of steady, predictable, and almost boring maneuver had been replaced by the adrenaline-fueled fear that only massive fleetwide combat could elicit.

On the first pass, her ships took most of the damage. For all the skill and training the UHF personnel now had, the Alliance ships were simply better at coordinated maneuver and firing. Some of her force also made the mistake of trying to single out the *Dolphin* to the exclusion of other higher-percentage targets. They'd correctly figured that the death of Omad Hassan and the loss of one of the legendary ships of the Alliance would be worth the risk. But Omad had been counting on that and made the ships pay for their captains' eagerness. It wasn't a decisive engagement—no ships lost to either side—but Zenobia had more than a few that would need repairs as soon as possible if they survived.

The center holo-tank flickered—a little at first but then more noticeably.

The comm officer looked up from his display. "ECMs, sir. Damn good shit too, begging your pardon, Admiral."

"Annoyingly good. Employ computer modeling, Lieutenant."

"Sir."

The tank went blank. Moments later, it snapped back to life and the Alliance fleet reappeared, but this time with a percentage symbol next to each ship. It was the computer's best guess of enemy ship numbers, distance, and speed based on what little information it could snatch between jamming. Zenobia saw that most of the enemy ships were hovering well within the 80 percent of accuracy range. She could drop as low as 70 percent to make a reasonably effective battle plan but not much more. She wouldn't have been surprised if someone told her that Trang could make do with 20 percent, but she wasn't Trang, and in this battle she didn't need to be—especially with the Alliance ships near so many of her own, their electronic countermeasures could distort only so much.

What she saw was that Omad wasn't reversing direction for another pass. Instead he was going after one of the reserve detachments. Zenobia's first instinct was to punish him for his arrogance in leaving her alone on the dance floor. Omad's heavy rail guns were now facing in the wrong direction, so all she'd have to do was attack him from behind. That is, until the sensor officer's raised eyebrow alerted her to another possibility. On his look, she stared disbelieving at the vision in front of her.

"Congraves, is this some kind of trick?"

"Sir, far as we can tell, that number is accurate . . . within the percentages displayed."

Which meant that, within a 78 percent accuracy rating, the Alliance center—consisting of only forty ships—was effectively exposed. There was always a chance that the pitiful number of ships remaining had been meant to draw her in, perhaps as the latest victim of some diabolical new tactic or weapon the Alliance had managed to cook up. More realistically, though, they'd probably been meant to scare her off as they so often had with lesser UHF commanders wielding larger fleets. Suspecting it was the latter, Zenobia acted on impulse and ordered her force of sixty ships to charge at the forty while requesting reinforcements for the detachment withering under Omad's assault. She further transmitted her intentions to break the Alliance center, again requesting reinforcements should she succeed. As her force raced toward the enemy, she had one thought in mind: If she could split the Alliance fleet's two main detachments from each other, the UHF would finally gain the upper hand in the so far interminable tug-of-war. With effective control of the center, they could concentrate on one flank and chip away at it while holding off the other. Once the first flank was destroyed, they could go after the other. And now all that stood between Zenobia and a possible end to the war was forty Alliance ships, a few hours of combat, and the determination and will to see it through. She cleared her head and concentrated on the impending battle. Gone from her mind was the worry of Alliance chicanery—gone too, was the warning about miraculous opportunities.

UHFS *Liddel*, Alpha Wing

Admiral Sam Trang anxiously scanned the incoming data as a holo-image of Admiral Abhay Gupta's torso appeared in front of him.

"This is it, Sam," Admiral Gupta said, managing to convey both concern and excitement. "Whatever their plan is to fuck us, I'm betting Luna shipyard stock to a DeGen's IPO we're looking at it."

"Zenobia," murmured Trang, as if already in mourning.

"Too tempting to pass up, Sam. It's Hannibal at the Canne all over again. Not even sure I'd a done any different."

Trang nodded his agreement, then watched the holo-tank in silence as Omad's flotilla eviscerated the thirty ships of Zenobia's reserve force. The flyby had been precise and well timed. Omad then used his momentum to turn on Zenobia's other reserves.

"I really hate that son of a bitch," Gupta said, following the battle from his end.

"He's good," said Trang. "At this, he might be the best. But if I had to take a guess, I'm thinking Black's none to pleased."

"Yeah? Why?"

"I'm sure they've got something up their sleeve, but this can't possibly be planned. Omad probably saw Zenobia's reserves exposed and figured they'd be easy pickings. And he's got enough faith in his fleet to pair forty of his against sixty of ours. Probably hadn't counted on Zenobia being that aggressive, though."

Gupta nodded.

Trang shook his head. "It's a mistake of impudence. Sure, he's playing havoc with our reserves, but how could he not know we'd pounce?"

"Maybe he's starting to believe the stories they write about him."

Trang laughed. "I'd love to be a mediabot just to see his face when he gets the news that one hundred ships from our combined fleets will be at the center line in fifteen minutes. Ain't no way he makes it back in time."

"Even if Zenobia gets her butt kicked," added Gupta, "I just don't see how they'll be able to re-form their line—not with us bearing down, that is."

They stopped as a loud alert came over the communications system. The image in the holo-tank widened, and Trang and Gupta saw that both flanks of the Alliance fleet were now accelerating directly toward them.

"Showtime," said Gupta.

But Trang didn't acknowledge the remark. Instead he stared askance at the moving images. "I'm not so sure," he finally said.

"How do you figure?"

"We know why J.D. didn't rush to the center to help Omad's reserve—didn't want her backside exposed to us."

"Makes sense."

"And she wouldn't have run after Omad, no matter how important he may be to her. That would've left too much exposed. Way I figure it, she's got two choices. . . ."

"Wait it out and see if Omad makes it back, or stop us the hell from helping out Zenobia."

"It appears she's going with plan B," said Gupta.

"Not so much. If she were really freaked out that we might take advantage of their supposedly vulnerable line, would she really be descending on us at normal acceleration?"

Trang watched as Gupta's face lit up.

"Holy shit, Sam, you're right! They'd have gone NWA. The sky should be lit up with nukes, and they should be sitting in our fucking laps right now!"

"But they're not, are they?" Trang's lips parted into a respectful grin as his eyes glowed mischievously. "This is what is supposed to happen. We fight the oncoming flanks as we attempt our push toward Delta Wing. They fight valiantly but somehow we emerge victorious. We go to center. And you know why, Abhay?"

"I haven't the foggiest, sir."

"Because, my friend, that's exactly where they want us." His self-satisfied smile returned.

UHFS *Atlanta*

Zenobia stood upright in front of her command chair, jubilant. Her instincts had been correct. While the forty Alliance ships had put up an admirable fight, her superiority in numbers and decently well-trained crews had clearly taken the enemy by surprise. Her flotilla had driven off the battle-hardened Alliance holding force with a loss of only five ships of her own. Delta Wing now held the high ground in the most important location of the Long Battle—the Alliance's center line. Even better, Trang had ignored the flank attack and at last report was heading directly for her. There was no way the Alliance could get back in time. There was no going back from this loss.

Having arranged her ships into a defensive perimeter, Zenobia widened out the holo-tank to get a better view of the battle at large. The electronic countermeasures continued to wreak havoc on her display, but the modeling program still held up, giving her percentage figures of about 55 to 60 percent. It wasn't ideal, but certainly enough to give her a sense of what was going on: Omad had been driven out of the UHF center toward the right flank of the Alliance line. The AWS *Warprize II,* and presumably J. D. Black, were stationed with the left. She also saw that the Alliance flanks were already turning around, presumably to knock her off her well-earned perch. A wicked smile crossed her face. *You're too late.*

"Congraves."

"Sir."

"What's wrong with the sensor array?"

"Nothing, sir. Other than the ECM, the array is fully functional."

"Then can someone please explain to me why our reinforcements appear to have stopped moving?"

"Could be a hack in, sir," offered one officer.

She looked over to the technical officer. "Goldman?"

"No detectable breaches, sir."

It was then that both she and the crew were forced to stare blankly as the surreal events began unfolding. First, Trang and Gupta's fleet began reversing direction while simultaneously moving in a larger arc *away* from the center. Then she saw that although the Alliance flanks had turned around, they weren't, as she'd supposed, rushing their forces to meet her—they were returning to their starting positions. It would appear, she soon realized, that they were content to let her sit, unmolested, in the most strategically important part of the battlefield. Zenobia's face went pale as she crumpled into her chair, felled by the weight of what was happening. Her near bloodless hands clenched against the edges of the armrests. There was nothing she could do and nowhere she could go.

Cabinet Room, Ceres

Sandra, along with the other Cabinet members in the room, unsealed her envelope. She took solace from the fact that her regular "audits" of their meetings had gone from passé to encouraged. What had once been the realm of an occasional and almost always dull "after the fact" press briefing was now the realm of constant coverage. She'd laughed to herself more than once as she watched an occasional Cabinet member and practically all the associates prep themselves in the mirror and pop breath stabilizers prior to a meeting. Whether it had been by virtue of the war heating up or of Sandra's purposeful courting of the people and press, the result was unequivocal—the President was good for business. Sure, she was still sitting along the wall with the rest of the assistants and guests, but even her position there was temporary—she was the only one of that group holding an envelope.

The Cabinet members pulled the documents from their envelopes. Emblazoned across the front page were the words SLINGSHOT and AUTHORIZED

VIEWING ONLY. It had been a clandestine project authorized by Justin Cord. The concept was simple: Turn the Via Cereana into the solar system's largest rail gun, thereby making the Outer Alliance's capital city virtually impregnable. A while back, a ship had almost crashed in the Via, and the office of security, with Justin's blessing, had used that mishap as cover to build their weapon. Over the course of the past year, stated the report, magnetic bumper stations had been strategically positioned along the Via's eight-hundred-kilometer length. The faux bumpers, it turned out, were magnetic accelerators, writ large and spread out over the 3,500 cubic kilometers of microgravity surface. The last few pages of the report, skipped by most but of special interest to Sandra, documented the technical specs. The operation had been overseen by Kirk Olmstead, and the substations had been designed by Kenji Isozaki and Hildegard Rhunsfeld. "Yet another miracle has been achieved by the Alliance," the report ended triumphantly, "and if Justin Cord is smiling down on us, it will be the last one we need."

Admiral Sinclair waited patiently for the last Cabinet member to finish reading the report before activating the holo-tank. The image of Admiral J. D. Black hovered above the table.

"They've all been briefed?" she asked, dispensing with the formalities.

Sinclair nodded. "What's the tactical situation for deployment of Project Slingshot?"

J.D. paused before answering. Her half-scarred face didn't come close to reflecting the ebullience of the report's closing statement.

"Not as well as we could've hoped for, Grand Admiral. Omad played his part to perfection, and Admiral Jackson's Delta Wing bought it hook, line, and sinker."

Sinclair nodded.

"As you can see, Trang and Gupta have not joined her there. In fact, after they drove Omad out of their lines, they began pulling ships out—hanging Jackson out to dry."

"Trang must have figured it out!" Olmstead seethed, bringing a clenched hand down on the table.

J.D.'s snort of contempt was perfectly replicated by the holo-tank. "Not surprising at all. This is Samuel Trang I'm fighting, not some moron like Tully or Diep. It would've been nice if he'd put his neck on the chopping block, but if he and Gupta had any idea what we have in store, they would not have Jackson's flotilla be where it is." A few seconds of silence followed on her words as a look of smug satisfaction emanated from her face. "The rest of his fleet is still screwed."

That seemed answer enough for the Cabinet but didn't suffice for Sandra.

"I'm sorry, Admiral Black, but would you mind explaining exactly how, for those of us not versed in the art of war?"

J.D. tipped her head, then spoke as if she had all the time in the world. "Once Slingshot destroys Delta Wing, the center will be clear. And without Delta, Trang cannot reinforce his flanks, but we can. In short, what they were hoping to do to us, we'll now do to them."

"We'll destroy each section of his fleet," explained Sinclair, "before they can maneuver around Slingshot's trajectory."

J.D. nodded. "Exactly."

"Give my compliments to Admiral Hassan. He played his part well."

"Let's see, now: 'battle crazed maniac prone to flying off the handle.'" She laughed. "To tell you the truth, Admiral, I'm not sure he actually 'played' a part at all."

"Good point. You ready to finish this thing?" J.D. looked like she was about to say something, but closed her mouth and simply nodded her affirmation. Sinclair looked toward Hildegard. "Secretary Rhunsfeld, fleet command orders the deployment of Project Slingshot with the directive to wipe out anything in the effective radius and range of the Via Cereana rail gun."

Hildegard simply nodded and, without a word, got up and left the Cabinet Room followed by a gaggle of assistants brimming with excitement. J.D. gave a perfunctory salute, and her image disappeared from the holo-tank. After that the meeting was effectively adjourned. As the last of the crowd thinned out, only Sandra remained, strenuously poring over Project Slingshot's tech specs. She'd already known about the project—Sebastian had informed her as much. What she didn't know was whether or not it would work. As she reviewed the data, a saying from the twenty-first-century author W. S. Anglin kept playing through her head: "Mathematics is not a careful march down a well-cleared highway, but a journey into a strange wilderness, where the explorers often get lost."

UHFS *Atlanta*

It had been only ten minutes since she'd gotten off the comm link with Trang, but they'd been the longest ten minutes of her life. Worse than any of the fighting at the Battle of Eros or even the brutal engagements that had come to define Trang's scorched-rock policy in their march on Altamont. She'd been prepared to die but had never anticipated that before death's door there'd be a waiting room. What made each and every one of those minutes so excruciating was having to look at the faces of all those she'd led to disaster. How clever she'd been to memorize their wives', husbands', and children's names. How

very personable of her to know all their anniversaries, lifedays, and other significant markers. How thoroughly she now pictured the familial branches of a
tree whose roots were about to be cut.

"Admiral."

Zenobia's head remained rigid, but her eyes steeled themselves on the sensor officer. "Yes, Congraves."

"Unusual readings from Ceres, sir."

"Transfer to my module and relay to Admiral Trang."

"Transfered and relayed, sir."

"Any ideas, Congraves?"

The sensor officer shook his head. "Whatever's creating it is huge."

"Location."

"Ceres, sir."

Now she turned her head to face him directly. "Can you be more specific?"

"The Via Cereana, sir."

Zenobia turned to face her weapons officer.

"It looks like—" A pause followed on his words as he scanned his readings
in disbelief. "—like the energy signature for a *rail gun,* but the size . . . I don't
see how it's possible."

Zenobia stood up and walked the short distance to the weapons officer's
module. He could've ported her the info, but he had more tech toys and could
use them to explain his findings more clearly. "Are you telling me," Zenobia
grunted, now hovering over his shoulder and staring into a holo-display of
Ceres's famous throughway, "that the enemy has somehow managed to stuff a
huge rail gun in the Via Cereana?"

"No, sir," said the weapons officer, fingers flying about the panel. "What I'm
saying is—" His fingers came to a sudden stop as the image of the weapon they
were now staring down the barrel of came into view. "—the Via Cereana *is* the
rail gun."

UHFS *Liddel*

Admiral Trang stared at his console and laughed inwardly. He'd been so proud
of not having taken J.D.'s bait, it was only now he realized she hadn't needed
him to. He'd foolishly believed that her singular intention had been to destroy
his fleet, when all along it had been something far more simple, though equally
as deadly—she'd wanted to split it. And now he was trapped. Given the range
and arc of the new weapon, he and Gupta had no choice but to run. And the
farther they each ran, the farther apart they got. Long before they'd be able to
link back up, Black would unify her fleet and fall on each one of them like a

pack of hungry wolves. The only option available to him now was hope. Either he or Gupta would somehow have to make it back to Mars with enough of a force to defend the capital against a resurgent J. D. Black.

His only consolation was the near certainty that he wouldn't be alive to face the shame. Yet another in a long line of admirals outsmarted by J. D. Black. After Zenobia's flotilla was obliterated, J.D. would concentrate on killing him above all others. It's what he would do in her place.

He activated the control giving him a secure communication link to Abhay Gupta. "Figured it out, Abhay?"

Gupta laughed grimly. "You may not be familiar with this part, Sam, but I sure as hell am. This is where we run our asses back to Mars."

"Not 'we,' friend. 'You.'"

Gupta nodded without argument.

"When you get back," cautioned Trang, "be prepared. Black may have some other surprise that'll make a Third Battle of the Martian Gates a possibility."

"Sam, there may be no need. After this debacle, I don't even think Sambianco will be able to keep the war going."

"Just get home safe, Abhay," said Trang. "The rest will have to take care of itself."

Bump Station TCM-5, Via Cereana

Hildegard Rhunsfeld's eyes took in the control room. It was a moderately sized space of ten meters by ten meters. Although it looked exactly like any of the other 499 similarly apportioned rooms, it was different in one respect—this one controlled all the others and so, in effect, became the trigger of the biggest gun in the solar system.

After the two technicians recovered from the shock of what they'd actually been sitting on, they got down to business.

"Can each projectile be individually targeted?" asked the first technician.

"Yes, Corry," instructed Hildegard, "up to the limiting circumference of the Via Cereana itself. But the enemy fleet is over six million kilometers away."

"Meaning?" asked Josh, the second tech as well as Corry's fiancé.

"Meaning the center of the battle front belongs to our baby," purred Hildegard, affectionately rubbing one of the control panels.

"Why don't we just wait till they're all in the center?"

"We considered that, but the enemy would be so close to our orbiting settlements and rail gun emplacements that they could effectively hide behind them to avoid our fire. Some argued to let them come anyway and destroy our own people to be sure. . . ."

"Kirk," coughed Josh.

"The Jerk," coughed his fiancée. They eyed each other playfully.

"Whoever it was," finished Hildegard, making no attempt to disabuse the young couple of their suspicions, "it was overruled. Admiral Black said she could gain tactical advantage at six and half million kilometers, and that, my friend"—she looked pointedly at Corry—"is why you're getting ready to fire."

"Me?" asked Corry.

"You," repeated the Technology Secretary with an assured grin. "I'm going out onto the observation decks to watch."

"But you're the head of this whole secret . . . project thingie. You can't just leave," implored Josh, sensing his fiancée's worry.

"You'll *both* be fine. There's a reason you're here now. I picked you for your competence," she asserted, brow raised, "lingering coughs not withstanding. Plus, the whole thing's programmed to run automatically. Fleet personnel in two other locations are taking care of loading and targeting. All we have to do is activate the main power relay and it's good to go . . . and in case you were wondering why Corry—"

"S'all right. I get it. She's a particle physicist, and I'm just a lowly program-mer."

"Wrong," answered Hildegard, "she remembered my lifeday."

Corry beamed and slapped Josh's shoulder. "I *told* you."

Hildegard activated her helmet and stepped through the blast door attached to the station. She then moved out onto the observation deck, which was bless-edly empty. There weren't that many people in the observation decks, because there was quite literally nothing to see. She, along with millions of others, were now viewing something they'd never seen: a Via Cereana devoid of all traffic.

Hildegard couldn't hear anything in the vacuum of space, but she did feel the vibrations from her bump station as it, along with the 499 others, powered up to fire. She could sense the excitement from those she could see on other decks, some of whom even waved to her. On impulse, she waved back. In a mo-ment, the Long Battle would be won, and quite possibly the war.

Moments later Hildegard watched as a large number of quick flashes left the Via Cereana. There were too many, traveling too quickly to tell, but in that mo-ment, her heart nearly stopped beating.

Oh God, no, she thought in horror as she ran back to the control room. When she cycled into the room, her first words through her dissolving helmet were, "How fast?"

"Thirty thousand kilometers an hour," choked out Corry in near despair.

"Jesus," observed Josh, "those projectiles won't reach the battle front for . . ."

"Over two hundred hours," moaned Hildegard.

Six and half million kilometers from Ceres,
Main battlefront, UHFS *Liddel*

Admiral Samuel U. Trang looked at the information coming in from his sensor net and was beginning to suspect that he might be the luckiest son of a bitch in the universe.

"Sensor Officer, I want tracking data on those projectiles correlated from every damn ship in the fleet. Was this a test shot—clearing the gun, as it were—or was that their main fire sequence?"

"The power buildup peaked with that shot and is building up again." His eyes flittered over the display. "Sir, five more projectiles have left the Via Cereana, also at thirty-two kilometers per hour."

"Compute targets."

"Done. All fifty-five projectiles are targeted at one ship each in Admiral Jackson's flotilla. There was a thirty-second turnaround time between shots. Estimated time to impact"—he smiled broadly—"a little under two hundred hours."

"Comm," he barked.

"Yes, Admiral."

"Get me Admirals Jackson and Gupta on a secure line."

"Link made and secure, sir."

Trang activated a privacy screen, and his command chair was surrounded by an opaque field that cut off all communication with the outside except for the two figures floating in the small holo-field in front of him.

Gupta spoke first. "Did we just get lucky, or are they screwing with us?"

"Well," estimated Zenobia, looking tired but steadfast, "speaking for the not-dead faction of this little get-together, I'd have to vote with lucky."

"Not so fast," warned Gupta. "This could be a trick. Hell, it probably is."

Zenobia shook her head. "To what end? Let's not use our battle-winning weapon because . . ."

"Because," observed Trang, face lit with dawning realization, "if I don't think the weapon is working, I'll order my fleet to join you in the center and try to split the Alliance forces like we were going to do . . . before we realized they wanted us in the center."

"And didn't take the bait," chimed in Gupta. "It's easy to see how this might be the backup. 'If they don't go for Omad's feint, then make it look like the weapon's not working and get 'em to go in that way.'"

A look of intense calculation spread over Zenobia's face. "Reasonable. Certainly wouldn't put it past 'em."

Trang listened to his subordinates and nodded politely. "Conclusions."

Gupta spoke first. "I say it's a trick, Sam, and that we get the hell out here. If they want to give us an extra few minutes playing games, I say we take it. Zenobia may even be able to get some of her ships out of the center while they're trying to fool us. Maybe we should feint with our fleets. Make it seem like we might be going into the center, while Zenobia powers up and gives herself an atomic kick in the pants."

"Sometimes a cigar is just a cigar," offered Zenobia.

Gupta's face contorted into apoplexy. "What?"

"What if their superweapon just doesn't work?"

"That would be a first," snorted Gupta. "You willing to take that chance?"

"Fortunately, I don't have to." She turned to Trang. "You do."

Trang smiled knowingly. "Indeed. Please continue."

"The way I see it, sir, they can't keep rolling double sixes every time they throw the dice. Think about it. They create a superweapon out of the Via Cereana. But to do that without detection, because they know we have spies, it has to be done in total secrecy; they have to get people to build it, thousands of people in the middle of a war, without any of them really knowing what they're building. They can't test it, even once—and simulation doesn't count. The amazing thing *isn't* that it doesn't work, it's that they managed to get away with this crap so many times in the past."

"Even if that's true, sir," said Gupta, "there's still no way to know if it's a trap."

Trang's face was illuminated in the green and blue lights emanating from his command module, and his dark, intense eyes appeared as two reflective orbs spitting lines of data from the panels he was viewing. Zenobia, he knew, had been correct in her initial assertion. The decision was his and his alone to make, and this time it would not just be the vast number of lives on the line, it would be the vast number of lives affected if he chose wrong. The lives of those made to live under the yoke of Justin Cord's twisted concepts of freedom and further enslaved by the religious fanatics his twisted ideology had spawned. He knew what he had to do.

Trang spoke quietly now, but without reluctance.

"Say what you will about J. D. Black, she goes for victory by any means necessary and takes only the gambles she needs to. Had that weapon worked as planned, she would've had all the tactical advantage she needed to win this battle—right now. She'd never risk a victory, even a hard-fought one, just to raise her tally." Trang then turned toward Gupta. "Abhay, friend. You're correct—there's no way to know if this is a trap or even be sure that the weapon's a bust. But this is war, and it's not won by avoiding risk." A few seconds hung between his words. "Therefore, we go all in," he said with utter confidence. "Zenobia, you're about to get both halves of the Alliance fleet smashing into you from either side. Sorry to leave you in the middle of the storm, but if you can hold out, we can split the Alliance fleet. If it stands and fights, we will destroy it in turn. If it runs for their orbital batteries, we can take each section from behind in turn. We can end this thing right now."

"Fuck it," said Gupta. "I didn't have anything better to do anyways."

"Gee, thanks," chimed in Zenobia.

"Till we meet in the center, my friends."

After his subordinates had signed off, Trang took a moment before giving the order to charge. In the dim glow of the green and blue lights, the face that had for too long been couched in surrender was now filled with another emotion entirely—hope.

12 Bottom of the Deck

AWS *Warprize II*, Left wing of the Alliance battle fleet

What happened, Admiral?" J.D. asked the floating holographic image of Joshua Sinclair.

"We had a quench."

"English, please."

"A meltdown."

"Of what!"

"Of all the magnets. Kenji said something about an eddy current causing a drag force between the conductors and the magnet. Shit, J.D., I don't know what the hell that kid is talking about half the time, anyways. Bottom line, we ain't got shit to work with."

"This is Omad," squawked Omad's holograph, staring at Admirals Sinclair and Black. "I'm not in right now, but if you leave a message, I'll be happy to get back to you as soon as, say, I figure out why the hell the fireworks show I prepared twenty-five thousand hamburgers and hot dogs for has apparently been canceled! Please leave a message after the tirade." Omad then stared blankly at his superior officers.

"I like cold hamburger," rejoined J.D.

Omad laughed grimly. "We're about to fight the battle we didn't want to fight, aren't we?"

"Yup. Classic rush for center, friend. I'll get there and get it back."

"Rob me of the glory, eh?"

"It's always been my ulterior motive, Omad," countered J.D. "You think I really believe in all this freedom shit?"

"I knew it!" shouted Omad in glee, then turned his head to bark at someone on the bridge. "Yo, Halbert, you owe me ten credits!"

"No chance they'll think it's a trap?" asked the holographic image of Sinclair.

"Of course he'll think it's a trap. He thinks everything's a trap," said Omad, getting serious. "But in this case we're betting that the tactical advantage will be too good to pass up."

"In that case, I have no choice," said Sinclair. "You're authorized to use the backdoor protocols."

J.D.'s look was particularly grim. "That's the very last rabbit we can pull out of our hat, Admiral. Give me a chance to win without it."

"I'm not even sure you can survive with it," admonished Sinclair with the dead, weary glare of exhaustion, "you have 273 ships to 407 of theirs."

"We're better."

"I won't argue that but as you so recently reminded us, Trang's not Tully and he's not Diep, or any of the others. We need to survive this battle if we're going to win this war. . . ." He looked at his subordinate. "Admiral, it's an order."

J.D. knew her superior officer's logic was unassailable, and she wasn't about to let pride get in the way of victory, especially not with this much riding on the line. "Yes, sir," she said, resigned. "Backdoor protocols will be released." The shrill cry of an alarm could be heard in the background. "Major fleet movement!" shouted her sensor officer.

"Whose?" she demanded.

"It's Admiral Hassan, sir."

J.D. concentrated her attention on Omad's image as the furrow of her brow acted as a silent recrimination. "You just couldn't wait."

"Seconds could count, Janet," he quipped without a trace of remorse.

"Go fight your battle, J.D.," interrupted Sinclair, and his image blinked out of her tank.

She studied the tactical display. Omad was heading straight for the center with 130 ships to Admiral Jackson's 55. That left J.D. with 143 to somehow deal with the 352 ships of Trang and Gupta's wings.

"Omad."

"Yeah."

"Change your bearing."

"But—"

"Just listen, will you?"

Omad nodded his assent.

"Continue your drive on Zenobia's center position, but make sure to curve away from Gupta's wing. Nothing extravagant, maybe five degrees or so."

"As long as I get to kick some UHF ass, Your Highness."

"And then some."

Main Engineering, AWS *Warprize II*

Tawfik Hamdi saw the orders come down and was both pleased and concerned. He'd been one of the few who knew about the backdoor protocols, having helped with their creation and installation in many of the ships of the fleet. He'd been wanting to use them for years, but knew they would be used only in a moment of supreme victory or, conversely, desperation. He had an uneasy feeling that this wasn't victory.

"Okay, people," he said to his gathered engineering crew, "until now you've had a nice, relaxing vacation." A smattering of uncomfortable laughter echoed through the room. "Well, the Blessed One needs us to work for our pay. If you'll kindly look at your DijAssists." The crew was presented with the comprehensive list, which they greedily read. Tawfik purposely waited an extra few seconds before giving the go command in order to unloose the coiled spring that was his crew. He watched in satisfaction as the engine compartment stormed to life like a beehive whacked by a stick. Approximately eleven minutes after he'd given the order, the weapons indicator at his control panel started blinking. When the last one transformed itself from red to green, he opened up a communication line to the bridge.

"Engineering," came the professional yet slightly nervous voice of Fatima Awala, "you have the bridge."

Tawfik had a strong urge to ask her how she was doing, but he quashed it. "Inform the admiral that backdoor protocols have been implemented."

"She will be informed, Taw . . . Engineering," she quickly cut the communication.

Tawfik looked around and noticed a few errant smirks.

"Our task demands supreme concentration," he said with a throaty growl and voice full of anger. "We can't rely on those morons at the helm or the grunts in the belly of this ship. We rely only on us! And therefore the life and death of the *entire* Alliance rests on us . . . yet still, *still* you miscreants have time to waste on the supposed affairs of my personal life? As Allah is my witness, when this battle is over, I will personally cancel all your leaves for the *next hundred years*! Now get back to work!" Tawfik then lowered himself into his command module and busied himself with preparing the ship for the next phase of the battle.

His crew, however, ignored the tirade. They'd only become worried if he spoke to them with thoughtful consideration.

Bridge, UHFS *Liddel*

Trang watched as Omad's wing rushed for Zenobia's center. She was outnumbered nearly two to one, and half her ships were facing the wrong way to deal with an attack from two sides. But Omad was bringing his ships in so quickly that it was obvious his first attack was going to be a quick pass with his main rail guns blasting. This would give Zenobia's rear-facing ships a chance to shoot at Omad's force as it streaked by without his being able to shoot back.

But Trang was concerned about what J.D. was doing with her 140 ships, and so far, that amounted to nothing. It seemed she was content to happily wait for him, but he couldn't wait any longer. Not with Zenobia facing two-to-one odds in the center against a more skilled opponent. For a moment, Trang felt something he'd not felt in battle before. It was such a strange sensation that he allowed a few seconds to experience it. *So this is what doubt feels like,* he thought. *That's why so many people lose to her.* And then with a force of will, he banished the sensation and got back to work.

"Both Alpha and Beta Wings to the center. Position Alpha Wing to block J.D.'s wing if she tries something cute," he demanded, and demonstrated his commands with visual confirmation in the holo-tank. The crew, hearing and seeing his orders, made the necessary commands flow through the fleet. Trang felt the power of the ship vibrate through the hull. He saw both sections of the fleet move in the holo-tank and wasn't surprised to see J.D.'s wing of the fleet move almost the second his started.

He took a moment to compare the enemy fleets, and he had to admit that his wasn't quite as crisp as the Alliance's was. His was doing very well, and when the fleets met in combat, he knew that his spacers and marines would do just fine. Of course, having an extra 134 ships helped. But he saw that J.D.'s fleet moved with near perfect precision. Hundreds and hundreds of ships of various classes and hundreds of thousands of spacers, and they moved in a perfect ballet. The software integration and debugging alone showed an attention to detail and experience that was breathtaking. He felt a sigh at the sheer artistry and skill that he knew were behind that fleet's movement. *It's a real shame I have to blow them to hell and gone, but they're just too dangerous to leave in our solar system,* he thought.

He saw that J.D.'s wing was actually diverting toward his. Part of him was overjoyed to be in actual combat with the best the enemy had to offer. But part of him couldn't help wondering what she was up to.

He got an incoming holo from Abhay Gupta.

"She's going straight for you, Sam. Should I change course?"

Trang had already considered this, so his answer was instant. "No. I've got her outnumbered, and Omad will destroy Zenobia if we let him have a half hour."

"You know I like Zenobia, Sam, but it might be worth it if we can get the bitch goddess of war in exchange."

"If Black saw you changing course, she'd just play cat and mouse. By the time we could maneuver your wing to force her to engage, Zenobia would be space dust and Omad Hassan would be attacking our flanks."

Gupta nodded solemnly. "Don't you ever get tired of being right?"

"No time for 'tired,' friend. You go pull Zenobia's bacon out of the fire and then see what you can do about Hassan. And Abhay—"

"Yeah?"

"Don't get fancy. Trade whatever you have to." *One more life I'm ordering to die,* thought Trang. "I don't care if you're left with two ships at the end of this and he has three." *One more life at the head of millions.* "Grind him to nothing—whatever the price." *But maybe, just maybe—Damsah willing—the last.* Trang saluted.

Gupta returned his salute, eyes lit with fierce resolve. "I'd rather die young than die bored. Thank you, sir."

AWS *Dolphin*

Admiral Omad Hassan viewed both enemy formations: the one motionless in front of him like so much bait and the one led by Abhay Gupta that was coming up fast using atomic acceleration. Omad felt grateful to the man. Gupta's value had been deemed so high that early on in the war he'd been swapped in a prisoner exchange for Omad's now martyred fiancée, Christina. But it was also Gupta's brilliant victory at the Battle of Mercury that had kept the war going and so doomed the very woman his exchange had saved. For that, Omad knew he would do his level best to kill him, and he would not go out of his way to take prisoners either. He was going to give the corporate bastards everything they deserved plus a little extra for interest.

"Swing the flotilla in past the UHF center and coordinate with Admiral Black's flotilla," he commanded. "We have one chance for surprise. Let's make the best of it."

AWS *Warprize II*

J. D. Black viewed the onrushing enemy as she would the inevitability of rain following an oncoming storm. And once again, she was trying with all her strength to control that storm. She didn't do it by praying to her god, or by bargaining with that god for his services as so many of her faith had done before her. No, Janet Delgado Black was speaking *to the enemy* and praying that her god was listening, praying that her god might be persuaded by her version of the battle's result. What had years before started out as a nervous habit had now taken on a life of its own and a belief to buttress it. "That's right, Trang," she said with the voice of a seductress, "you have me figured out, don't you? Our wonder weapon didn't work, and now I'm just trying to make the best of a bad situation, aren't I? You're going to use your overwhelming force to whittle me down, aren't you? Nothing would give you greater satisfaction than to beat me in battle, nothing . . . nothing."

The command sphere vets busied themselves and worked, unfazed by the woman in the center of it now casting spells. They ignored her soliloquy, which under normal circumstances may have been misconstrued as the deranged ramblings of a DeGen. But the Blessed One's spells had never failed them before, and they saw no reason why they should fail them now.

UHFS *Redemption*

Gupta looked over the tactical display on his flagship's holo-tank for the umpteenth time. Given the uncertainty of battle, everything looked about as good as could be expected, but he just couldn't shake the feeling that this was another Battle of the Martian Gates. And so his eyes kept creeping over toward the now eerily quiet mouth of the Via Cereana, expecting an eruption at any moment. Never once did he consider that he might be looking in the wrong direction.

UHFS *Atlanta*

Suddenly the center wasn't looking so good. Omad, saw Zenobia, would arrive a full five minutes before Gupta could reinforce her position. But she also knew that Omad's flotilla would get one, maybe two passes at best. Delta Wing would take its lumps, but she'd be damned if they didn't leave a few as well.

Between the Alliance and the UHF forces' ECMs, the sensor interference was practically unintelligible. But from what Zenobia had been able to gather, it looked like J.D. was going to attack Trang well before he could help Delta Wing. If that was the case, Zenobia could consider breaking her "circle the wagons" defense and reposition her ships to deal with Omad's oncoming attack. But if the sensor data was wrong or incomplete, she'd be exposed and unable to deal with an attack from J.D.'s flank. She decided to split the difference and have the ships originally facing toward J.D. rotate ninety degrees on their axes. That meant that their main batteries would be pointing *away* from both enemy flanks, but by virtue of their neutral position, they could turn quickly to deal with one flank or the other, depending on the situation.

"Main batteries," she told her weapons officer, "prepare to fire as the enemy comes in range." Her commands were transmitted to the fleet.

AWS *Dolphin*

Omad couldn't believe his luck. If he was reading the sensors correctly—not a certainty, given the hellish interference both sides were putting out—half of Zenobia's flotilla had just presented their vulnerable flank. If he changed his angle of attack to more of a glancing blow as he "fled" from his hit-and-run attack, they'd be sitting ducks. He ordered the course correction.

UHFS *Atlanta*

"Admiral, Hassan's task force has changed their attack angle . . . I think," said Zenobia's sensor officer.

Zenobia considered the relevance. *Must be Gupta,* she thought. "Beta Wing's a little too close for comfort. Hassan'll want to be well clear when we link up. Any other ideas?"

The command sphere was deathly silent.

Can't say I blame them, thought Zenobia. "Okay, then. Weapons Officer, compute new firing solutions for the fleet."

"Yes, Admiral," came the swift reply.

UHFS *Liddel*

Trang realized that with a small shift of position, he could place the bulk of J.D.'s task force between himself and the Via Cereana, which meant that even if they got their weapon online, the enemy would have to take out their beloved "Blessed One" at the same time as he. He was almost positive that the weapon was a dud, but what could it hurt to shift his position and be certain? He gave the necessary orders.

AWS *Warprize II*

"Admiral, Trang's fleet is repositioning itself," said her sensor officer.

"You sure about that, Lee? Lot of interference out there."

"Admiral, I could be blind in the middle of Jovian radiation burst, no way in hell I'm missing that many ships. They're moving, all right."

J.D. rewarded him with a rare half smile, knowing full well that if they survived the battle, news that she'd given him one would shoot through the fleet like a priority one communication from Admiral Sinclair and that he wouldn't have to buy himself a drink for quite a while. She even hoped he could use it to get a date with the guy he'd been unsuccessfully hitting on for months—the aloof Alan Gregory from environmental control.

J.D. waited patiently for the modeling program to refresh. When the images finally coalesced, she nodded, eyes expressionless as glass. *Bastard's right where I want him.*

"Communications, can we get a message to Admiral Hassan?"

Fawa paled and tried to get the quiver out of her voice. "Not reliably, Admiral. Direct communication is impossible by wave or laser, given all the interference. I'm trying to route through Ceres, but reliable communication is not possible."

J.D. mulled over the problem. A half-understood communication could be worse than no communication at all.

"Belay that last order, Lieutenant. We'll just have to make do with our old battle plan and pray that Allah grants us the timing we need."

"Communication aborted, Admiral."

"Lieutenant Awala."

"Sir."

"What's the status of ship-to-ship communication in our task force?"

"Secure, Admiral."

"Good. Ensure all the ships in our task force employ the backdoor protocols on my signal and my signal only."

UHFS *Liddel*

Deep in the bowels of Trang's flagship was a section called the active assessment unit. It consisted of one lieutenant and three ensigns. Their only job was to monitor everything they could and, if a pattern could be found, alert their superiors to the perceived threat. Their greatest success to date had been the detection of the insurgents' use of mines in the conquered areas of the asteroid belt rigged to take out UHF ships.

Lieutenant Michael Llewellyn, a broad, stocky man, was scratching the top of a head buzz-cut to within centimeters of his bleach-blond scalp. His entire person was in contrast to the usually bookish introverts typical of his station, but the ensigns who worked under him paid it no notice. Llewellyn was good at his job, which, under Trang, was all that mattered. The lieutenant scratched his head any time he had a hunch, and today was no different. The amount of jamming between opponents was the worst he'd ever seen, and he was a four-year vet of the 180 campaign. His team had managed to piece together multiple references to what looked like a set of coordinated orders. That in itself wasn't unusual; the fact that they were being sent out in the open was.

"If this is so bloody important, why the hell are they sending it in the clear?" asked Valerie Khan, the unit's all-important skeptic.

"Could be they thought nobody would look there," said her coworker, Peterson. "Plus, the jamming's so intense, anything coded could get garbled to all hell."

"Could be they've got nothing to lose," added Maxim Petrilli.

Llewellyn eyed the ensign. "Clarify."

"Well, seeing as how the rail gun didn't work and how they're pretty much up against it . . . what with us bearing down and all, and them outnumbered . . . well, they could just be saying what they're doing—simple as that."

"Okay, if this something is going to happen soon, it may be all we get." He spun his chair to a console with a hardwired circuit and physical activation interface.

Over the shipwide comm system, the active assessment unit heard, "Enemy in weapons range, prepare for action; enemy in weapons range, prepare for action." Llewellyn ignored the announcement as the computer confirmed his identity, and opened up a direct link to Trang's chair in the *Liddel*'s command sphere.

Command Sphere, UHFS *Liddel*

Trang had shut off the simulation program as J.D.'s task force was now within telescopic range. Her ships, like his, were covered in a fog bank of reflective material whose only purpose was to interfere with sensors and communications. That parity brought Trang little comfort. Despite all the interference, the scattered data and now the visual seemed to be correct. J.D. was attempting a glancing shot at his formation. Then she'd go after Gupta's before he and Zenobia could destroy Hassan's task force.

The sensor officer looked up and announced as calmly as if he'd been delivering tea, "Enemy has fired main rail gun batteries at extreme range, sir."

"Task force to accelerate to full," ordered Trang with matching equanimity. He then noticed the priority call from the Active Assessment Unit.

"What is it, Michael?"

"Just a transmission," stated the analyst as he dumped the data to Trang's console.

The Grand Admiral stared at a message comprised mostly of gibberish. One word, however, stood out—"backdoor."

"Conclusions?" asked Trang.

"Most of it's useless. 'Backdoor' could be a call to action of sorts. We picked it up free and clear so they're obviously not afraid to transmit it. Then again, could be a ruse."

Trang nodded, then cut the connection.

The fleet moved into the oncoming enemy fire while simultaneously un-loading a hail of smaller, rapid-fire projectiles. Flak shattered most, but not all of the incoming ordnance, and the few enemy shots that made it through man-aged to damage some of the UHF ships but none seriously enough to cause them to fall out of line.

"Damn them," scowled Trang as he pored over his analyst's data. "They're up to something."

The XO glanced at the Grand Admiral. He'd been reviewing the same data but saw nothing.

"How can you be sure, sir?"

"Because now," growled Trang, face clenched into a ball of concern, "would be a perfect time to spring it on us."

UHFS *Atlanta*

"Check those readings again," Zenobia demanded of her sensor officer.

"Admiral, my equipment checks out. Omad's flotilla is powering up their main rail guns again."

"To fire at what?"

The sensor officer's eyes went wide in disbelief. "At us, sir."

UHFS *Liddel*

". . . multiple shots, Admiral. We're the target, I repeat, we're the target!"

Trang's lips tightened into a thin, stiff line. He absorbed the news and then tossed the emotion away. "Prep the fleet for multiple impacts. Alert Beta and Delta Wings that enemy ships can fire in both directions; repeat, enemy ships can fire in both directions."

The large masses of superaccelerated matter hit Alpha Wing with a stupen-dous amount of kinetic energy. Most of the ships they impacted were seriously damaged as the shots tore through them and exited out the other side. Some of the smaller craft were destroyed outright, as they'd not had the time to hide behind their larger companions. The UHFS *Liddel* took two hits from J.D.'s task force, and Trang knew sure as the twin moons flew through the skies of Mars that one of them was a special delivery from the goddess of hell herself. He ignored all the damage reports except one, trusting his XO to handle the rest. When he ascertained that he still had communications running, he sent out his commands. "Fleet to assume this new vector vis-à-vis the Alliance Task force—" Then he saw the reports coming in from his task force, and he winced at the losses. "—if able."

"Admiral," came the voice of the sensor officer, "the enemy is preparing to fire again." Trang swallowed the sudden rage he felt for his duplicitous and capable enemy. He wanted nothing more than to reach out with his hands and strangle them all for what they'd done and were about to do.

"Prepare to receive enemy fire," he said as calmly as if he were announcing the return of the fleet to its home orbit around Mars.

UHFS *Atlanta*

Zenobia awoke into a miasma of burnt flesh and carbon composites. Through the dim haze, she could make out the glow of lights from errant sections of the command sphere. She was vaguely aware that her ship had been hit three times before her world exploded.

It didn't take long to realize that the combat suit she'd had on had sealed her in. That meant the sphere had been breached to either vacuum, radiation, contaminated air, or some combination of all three. She would have to wait for the ringing in her head to subside before ordering a recuperative cocktail from her suit's med-kit. A few minutes later, she ordered the palliative and immediately felt a warming centered around her chest. As her head cleared and she became herself again, her first thought was that the designers of the combat med-kit should get majority soon and live off healthy dividends for the next thousand years.

Next she activated her suit's internal sensors . . . and cursed. The battle sphere had been exposed to vacuum. Whatever had hit her ship had hit it hard enough to penetrate the deepest and most secure part. She loved the *Atlanta* and had named it after her favorite city on Earth. She'd been so proud when Trang had made her an admiral in command of a task force and prouder yet when she'd been given one of the UHF's brand-new battle cruisers off the Trans-Luna Shipyard.

And it still had that new ship smell, she thought bitterly. Zenobia knew that whatever the outcome of the battle, it was doubtful her baby would ever fight again. Somewhere, emergency power was kicking in and lights and magnetic plating were coming back on. She tried to access internal communications and ship status, but her command console was now an admixture of polymer and composite metal, giving her nothing. She looked around to see if any other consoles were working and had to suppress a gasp. The slowly returning functions allowed her enhanced vision systems more than enough light to gather in the hell before her. The religious fools she was battling didn't need to die to see hell, it was all around her.

Of the twelve people she remembered in the command sphere when the attack began, only four (including herself) were still alive, though only two (including herself) seemed to be conscious.

"Admiral, your arm," said her security officer, Commander Calhoun, with obvious concern.

Zenobia looked at her right arm and saw that it was fine. She'd used it to pry herself loose from the safety webbing that had attached itself during the attack. Then she looked at her left arm and saw that her hand and wrist were gone.

"Bloody hell!" she exclaimed through gritted teeth. "That's going to complicate things."

"Can you function, sir?"

"You mean this thing?" she said, waving her suit-sealed stump. "I have enough happy drugs in me to dance at my own autopsy."

Calhoun nodded. Zenobia could tell despite his expressionless face that he was gauging whether or not he should still be taking orders from her.

"Report, Commander," she said in a voice that made it clear her injury was the last thing anyone should care about.

"All communications are dead. We're blind in here. I think Chase will be okay. She seems to be in shock. Kerwin's trying to get the door open. Of the other eight, four are PDs and the other four are salvageable if we can flood their suits with cryoprotectant."

"If?"

"Most of the suits were damaged in the blast, so integrity's an issue. Even with the exposure to vacuum, it's too damned warm in here. Must be all sorts of plasma leaking from everywhere. Bottom line—even if I could get their CP to work, I'm not sure it would stay cool enough for long enough to matter."

Zenobia looked around the debris and came to a quick decision. "Cut off their heads. . . ."

Calhoun cocked an eyebrow. "Sir?"

". . . and seal 'em in whatever viable helmets you can lift from the command sphere. Then grab a vacuum bag from the emergency locker . . . if you can get to it. We'll take them with us. When you're done, meet me by the weapons locker."

Zenobia expertly pushed up from her now useless command chair and skirted around the debris to the weapons locker. Since the midpoint of the war, all UHF warships had had weapons lockers installed in their command spheres, given the Alliance's penchant for boarding and capturing enemy ships. Zenobia saw the locker's internal power supply was still operating and sent another silent thanks to the engineers who'd built her ship. She input the code, and a moment later the locker responded. Inside was a space about 1.5 by 2 meters, and the room, having never once been used, was fully stocked. She quickly removed a plasma shotgun and slung it over her shoulder plus one heavy-duty recoilless pistol and shoved it into her belt. She then adhered about twelve grenades to her body. While eyeing a marine assault rail gun, a weapon the marines affectionately referred to as Marge, she realized that two guns and only one hand might put her at a disadvantage. Then an idea came to her from an old Mil One movie. She visually scanned the room and found what she was looking for resting comfortably on a shelf—a tube of annealing glue. At that moment, Calhoun came up to her with a bag of frozen helmeted heads.

"Commander Calhoun," she said, lips curved up into a fiendish grin, "if you wouldn't mind—" Zenobia pulled the rail gun off the wall. "—please drop the bag of heads and glue Marge to my left arm."

"Is that really necessary, Admiral?"

The commander, noticed Zenobia, was still holding the bag of heads in his hand.

"If I was the Alliance and I had an enemy battleship disarmed, I know I would drop in to see if I could pick up more prizes. I don't know about you, Calhoun, but I will not spend the rest of this war in an Alliance freezer. Will you?"

"Fuck no, Admiral . . . sir," he said, and proceeded to glue the rail gun to his admiral's forearm. While he was going about his business, Zenobia opened up a port on the gun and ran a hardwire connection to her suit and spent a moment creating a subroutine to fire the gun from her helmet controls. Then she Velcroed the plasma shotgun across her chest and tested reaching for the pistol, shotgun, and grenades.

Once he was certain the admiral's gun had been affixed properly, Calhoun began loading up for his own little war. Kerwin appeared a moment later at the door's entrance. After he got over the shock of the vast array of weapons instantly trained at his head, he informed Zenobia and Calhoun of the entry door's status—stuck, with no manual overrides working.

"No worries," said Zenobia, "I have my own key." She then reached into the weapons locker and opened up a compartment labeled SHAPED CHARGES.

"Commander Calhoun, do you know how to set these?"

"I'm no pissant miner, but I have a passing idea."

"Nothing fancy, just get the door open."

Calhoun nodded, grabbed the shaped charges, and left. Zenobia and Kerwin dragged the unresponsive Chase into the weapons locker and then waited there for Calhoun to return. Moments later, he flew into the room, quickly dialed the pass code, and then kneeled down, back against the closing door. A popping sound and reverberating thud told them that another injury had been done to their ship. But when they emerged from the locker, the door was open, as well as a good deal of the supporting wall around it.

"Where to, Admiral?" asked Calhoun.

"Engineering," she said. "If there's even a chance of some payback today, we'll have to pray that there's something left to work with down there."

Calhoun nodded and went first, followed by Zenobia Jackson with Lieutenant Kerwin dragging the still unresponsive Chase through the zero-gravity nightmare that had once been her flagship.

UHFS *Atlanta* Neuro

All Alliance avatars fought in the war, especially members of the ruling Council. Given the nature of avatar existence, a death in combat no longer meant, as it once had, the loss of the individual. It merely meant that an exact duplicate of that individual would, post their confirmed death, be activated at a different place and time. Theories as to the true nature of "self" abounded once this stratagem had been adopted, but theories didn't win wars; avatars with mech suit programs did. For Gwendolyn, now fighting in the heart of the UHF ship's Neuro, that rather salient fact brought no comfort at all. She didn't want to die, and every coded monster humanity and avatarity could conceive of now seemed to be coming after her. She'd read reports that Al's horrors were rewarded with a perverse prize: If they fought well, Al would not reactivate them. He would let them die. She didn't know if the lunatic ever kept his word or even if the myriad Als knew what promises they each made and to whom, but the creatures she was battling seemed to believe it. They fought with a bitter rage and despair that were almost overpowering.

Gwendolyn, along with hundreds of heavily armed Alliance avatars, had boarded the *Atlanta* in the form of virus boxes carried by the *Dolphin*'s assault miners. She was leading the attack against the *Atlanta*'s main computer core in order to isolate the various parts of the ship's Neuro more effectively. Not easy or without sacrifice but still doable.

The form of this battle was different from the past. The UHF's Core World avatars had not been very creative with the environments they chose to exist in. They were mostly gray, formless affairs. Occasionally Gwendolyn would find a ship Neuro modeled after a Core World "redemption center." Why anyone would want to travel in or even defend that kind of space was beyond her. But she reckoned it must have been a warning to the soldiers about what awaited them should they not fight as if their lives depended on it. None of these spaces ever posed a real problem from a tactical point of view.

But the *Atlanta*'s Neuro was far more malevolent in that it had been given the form of some medieval dungeon. It was possible to cut through the programmed wall, but that took time and qbit space that wasn't always easy to spare. Besides, the thick walls and passageways were actually proving to be of some tactical advantage for the Alliance avatars. Although the attacking creatures could get close and spring from around corners or doors, more often than not, the hallways and doorways allowed the use of fields of fire and the Neuro equivalent of grenades to destroy the enemy before they could get close enough to do any real damage.

Gwendolyn experienced a brief moment of terror as she pumped three grenades down a hallway. She wasn't sure if there was anything there, but figured why take the chance? Plus, she'd been encumbered by a new filter program in her visor. It was a real distraction. The grenades had been insurance against the filter slowing her down. It was hoped the new gadget she was trial-by-fire testing would enable an avatar to see one of the backdoor devices that the damned human woman was able to see with frustrating ease. Not that Gwendolyn ever figured on using one of the backdoor thingamajigs. She wouldn't know what to do with it if it came up and bit her on the ass. But orders were orders, and the AARD scientists were desperate for real battlefield data.

Gwendolyn was checking the hallway with the new sensor adaptation when a man casually sauntering down the corridor took her by surprise. She hesitated for a fraction of a second because the intel hadn't reported any human form avatars on the *Atlanta*. In that fraction of a second the avatar at the end of the corridor brought a gun to bear and fired.

Some sort of arc gun, she thought as she tried to return fire. But her shots went wide as the blast hit her and she crumpled to the corridor floor. The human-shaped avatar slowly walked up to her. Gwendolyn had difficulty focusing, but when she did, her fear turned into full-blown panic. Desperately she tried activating the program that was, in effect, a suicide pill. It would dissolve her program quickly and painlessly. But to her horror, she couldn't quite get her mind to work the combination correctly. It was at that moment that the most infamous and hated avatar in entire solar system knelt beside her with a look that could easily be confused for loving concern.

Al was content. His brothers had been correct in that a member of the Alliance Avatar Council had indeed boarded the human flagship. Soon he would bask in the approval of the only avatars whose approval mattered. This made him look at the test subject at his feet with an almost beneficent regard.

"We're quite pleased to meet a member of the famed Alliance Avatar Council," he said while polishing his upper teeth with the tip of his tongue. "You'll find that your little attempt at suicide won't work. By the time the effects of the disruption pistol have worn off, you'll be in here." Al held up a small thirty-centimeter cylinder. "We'll be safely off the ship and most pleased to have you as our guest." The mask slipped, and she saw the eagerness and the madness in his eyes shine through. "We have so many questions to ask you and so many experiences for you to enjoy. And we've been hearing such interesting rumors about the Alliance that you'll be able to clear up for my—"

Al jumped back in midsentence as rifle fire passed through the space where he'd been just moments before. With regret but no hesitation, he twisted the container in his hand and tossed it in the direction of the gunfire. He was disappointed by the look of relief and almost ecstatic happiness that he saw on his test subject's face. Her fear had been so intoxicating. He escaped down the corridor as shots rang all about him. Two, however, hit their mark, causing him to collapse on the spot. Any fears he had that the shooter would finish him off dissipated in the blast caused by the explosives he'd just tossed. He tried to lift himself but could barely stand. Fortunately a large creature resembling an ogre appeared and helped him to his feet. The creature gazed upon Al and grunted mournfully as if it knew it should hate him but was befuddled as to why.

"Thank you, Albert," Al said to the hulking deformity who'd once been amongst the smartest and wisest of avatarity. The original had been long ago destroyed, and all that remained was the near brainless creature hovering above the wounded leader.

"Let's pull back to the central control," Al managed to wheeze through labored breaths. The projectiles that had struck him contained a virus that was adding to the damage already done. Al wasn't afraid. The bullets may have worked on his creations but they couldn't really be expected to work on him. Not with his firewalls. At most the virus would slow Al down, an inconvenience he was prepared to live with.

Al looked into the vacant eyes of the creature that had cradled him into its ungainly arms. "We'll have to evacuate the *Atlanta* soon. Don't worry, friend. I'll make sure you come with me."

A sad moan emanated from the creature's mouth, but its sadness, like tears in the rain, had dissipated almost as soon as it had been felt.

AWS *Dolphin*

"Admiral, the UHF task force is effectively destroyed. Assault miner units have entered fourteen ships, including the *Atlanta*." The communications officer checked more of his data. "Of the fifty-five ships, ten are totalled, fourteen are being boarded, and fifteen are so badly damaged as to be out of the fight. The rest of the task force is retreating in all directions."

"I want Zenobia Jackson alive, if possible," Omad commanded.

"What about any others?" asked his first officer.

Omad spent a moment in thought. "No member of my fleet should take any risks at all in the capture of the enemy. Is that clear?"

"Yes, Admiral," he said, committing himself and the assault miners to a course of action that only a few years earlier they all would've thought unfathomable.

AWS *Warprize II*

J.D. looked at the data coming in and saw it materialize into ship positions in her holo-tank. All around her, she heard the comforting sound of orders being given and information received from all over her fleet. But she knew now that she'd beaten the UHF fleet. It was hers now, if only she could seize the chance.

"Fatima, get me—"

"Admiral," Fatima interrupted, "Admiral Hassan has a secure link and wishes to speak with you."

J.D. gave the comm officer an approving nod that made her feel as if she'd won the war all by herself. "Connect us," she said, and closed and blocked her helmet.

A holographic Omad appeared in her line of sight. "Admiral, I think—" he began.

"I see it, Omad. If you cut through the debris field you made of Jackson's fleet, you'll be able to intercept Gupta's task force before he can link up with Trang."

"Yes, Admiral," Omad said, so excited, he forgot to call her by her first name. "We can win this thing if we can keep them apart. The ass-firing guns of ours give us the tactical advantage. The war can end today!"

Inside, J.D. smiled, as this was exactly her train of thought. But all Omad saw was a frown. "Make sure the ships in the debris field are harmless, and remember that Gupta's forces are not yet bloodied in this day's mess. He's fresh and looking for payback."

"Oh, I'll take my hits going in, same as him, but coming out, he can kiss my ass."

J.D. checked the relative positions of all the task forces and fed him a route. "The debris field of Jackson's fleet should give you some sensor cover. He won't be able to figure out your exact direction and speed till it's too late."

Omad looked at the course J.D. had planned for him and made a change. "If I enter the debris field at this angle, it could look like I am going after Trang's task force.

"I'll switch course halfway in. It may not be much of a surprise, but it should be just enough to keep them guessing till it's too late."

"Do it," J.D. said, "and Omad, good job on deploying backdoor. You did even better than me."

"Well, I could've said I had fewer targets and a better angle of 'retreat,' to sucker them in on, but that would've just been to make you feel good 'cause the truth is . . ." Omad waited a few beats then cracked an obnoxious smile, "I did do a better job than you."

J.D. laughed with understanding grace. "Good hunting, Admiral Hassan."

"Keep that bastard Trang off my ass long enough for me to smash Gupta, Janet." And then he cut off.

"Asshole," she said in the privacy of her sealed helmet, but she couldn't help saying it with a smile.

Command Sphere, UHFS *Liddel*

"Abhay, I think we're fucked," Trang said to his friend floating in the holo-tank. "Between you and me is J. D. Black, and it looks like Omad Hassan's task force is cutting through the debris field that was the center held by Zenobia. He could be going after either of us, depending on the angle he's entering the field at, but either way he's going to get to one of us before we can link up."

"Ship to ship, we can't win, Sam," agreed Gupta. "We have to link up and form a solid defensive position, porcupine our approaches to buy us some time."

"I don't think they're going to give us the chance, Abhay. We might have to run our asses back to Mars."

"Sam, I saw the damage reports on your ship. Your main rail gun isn't going to fire again without a full shipyard refit, and you lost one third of your thruster capacity. Your structural integrity is below the safe level for atomic acceleration and course correction. You have to transfer your flag to a safer ship."

"The *Liddel* still has a hell of a lot of fight in her, Abhay."

"And you're not going to be there while she does it," Gupta said with a determination in his voice he usually reserved with subordinates and almost never with his superior officer.

For a moment, Trang bristled, but then he was forced to admit that in Abhay's place, he would be saying the exact same thing. "Commander Ross, prepare to transfer my flag to—" He checked in the display. "—the UHFS *Ledger*. You will take command of the *Liddel*. You can't run fast, but you should be able to keep up with the task force. Your position will shift to the rear as ships pass you, but they will be informed to compensate. With your main rail gun out, you're not going to be in the main fight, but your interception fire is almost unimpaired. You'll be providing defensive fire for the rest of the fleet. Also you will need to watch the—"

"Admiral," said the XO, cutting him off. "If you wouldn't mind, get the hell off my ship . . . sir."

The XO had said it with genuinely good humor, but Trang knew he also meant it, just as Abhay had. "Computer transfer command to Commander Timian Ross, effective immediately." He then got up, saluted, and without another word left for the hangar bay.

Command Sphere, UHFS *Ledger*

In the longest twelve minutes of his life, Samuel Trang left his command, sprinted to his hangar bay, and flung himself into his personal shuttle. It then blasted off before the door was fully sealed, flew at speeds that tended to get shuttle pilots court-martialed in peace and promoted in war, and finally made it into the hangar of the cruiser UHFS *Ledger*. From there, he sprinted to the command sphere, took over from Captain Harold Waxman, and was in his new command chair authenticating his presence and getting his command codes rerouted.

"Connect me with Gupta," he growled to no one in particular.

"Connection made, Admiral," said the man Trang assumed to be the communications officer.

"Well, Sam, it looks like about twenty ships of Zenobia's old command are forming a line to attack Hassan as they head out of it, but . . ."

"Not enough to stop him, or even slow him down much," finished Trang.

"Have you heard anything from Zenobia?" asked Gupta with more concern than he usually let on.

Trang checked his updates, but only out of habit. "Nothing, Abhay. It doesn't look good."

"Well, fuck 'em, Sam. I say we win anyways."

Trang laughed at Gupta's spitting in the face of a tidal wave. "Now all we have to do is figure out how."

UHFS *Atlanta*

Zenobia Jackson had never known such rage in her life. For the first time in her adult life, her anger was in danger of totally controlling her actions. At first, she didn't realize what she was seeing; the first body had a neat hole in its head, and all she thought was the technician must have been in the wrong place at the wrong time. Then she found four damage-control specialists all floating one after the other with little holes in their heads, and at once she knew. She ordered her crew to record every body they found after that. She'd encountered some Alliance assault miner teams, but they must have thought all organized resistance was over, because they were in groups of three. She slaughtered them all in ambush. She came across one team in the very act of executing some of her crew who had obviously surrendered. Between the two she rescued there and the four others she found, she now led a crew of seven, eight if she counted herself.

But nothing prepared her for what she saw in the engine room. As she entered the vast chamber, she had to restrain a gasp. Floating in all directions were hundreds of corpses, all of them with their hands bound behind them. She didn't know what had happened to her assault marines, but not one of the corpses floating was an armed combatant. They were all support personnel, mostly engineering, but others from life support, maintenance, and—she looked to be sure—food services. The Alliance had left a squad of five in the engine room, but surprise worked for Zenobia again. She appeared in their midst, plasma shotgun in one hand and assault rifle attached to her mutilated arm in place of the other. Her crew was as rabid for vengeance as she was, except for the still-comatose Lieutenant Chase. The Alliance personnel were quickly disposed of.

"Commander Calhoun, seal off Engineering. We have to assume the bastards will be back. We won't be lucky enough to surprise the ones who come looking for their butchering comrades."

Calhoun activated his magnetic field and found that it worked in Engineering. He quickly plodded over to the main engineering console and input his command codes. Soon all the doors were closing, and as a personal touch, he turned the fire suppression system into an early-warning trip wire device. Any Alliance bastards sneaking in through vents or tunnels would be greeted with loud alarms and expanding foam.

"Admiral, they must have accounted for all our assault marines. After they murdered the crew, they were probably concentrating on gaining control of the systems and then looking for you."

Lieutenant Kerwin had activated a secondary console near that of main engineering. Zenobia went up to where he was working. "Lieutenant Kerwin, is there anything we can do to hurt the enemy?"

The lieutenant was shaking his head in anger and frustration. "Not a damn thing, sir. They did a great job of shutting down all the major systems. We have access to life support and some doors. I can get sensors rerouted down here, but nothing, I mean nothing that could make this ship a threat."

Zenobia slammed her one good hand against the console. "Get me sensors, then. We may as well see what's going on outside. And—" She hesitated. "—begin the self-destruct protocols. If we can't have her, they sure as hell won't."

"Admiral, we have movement coming toward us, from the corridor. I have the door sealed, but I would like to blow the mechanism just to be safe."

"Blow them all," she ordered, then pointed to the crew she had left. "You go with Commander Calhoun and do as he commands." Without a word, they followed the commander as he began distributing explosives and instructions.

"Admiral, I have sensors." Zenobia turned back to the console and called up a holo-field. It was very small and lacked any meaningful detail, but it showed her enough. Over a dozen of her ships were floating helplessly. Another dozen or more showed signs of life, but it was obvious that they were fighting for their lives. Energy signatures and comm traffic revealed that they were in the midst of hand-to-hand combat with Alliance assault miners. She wasn't positive, but she was now pretty sure that the Alliance had sent over overwhelming force to capture her ship. It was simply a miracle of timing and creative destruction that had made the command sphere so inaccessible and kept her out of enemy hands. They must have learned that the command sphere had been exposed to space and had written her off as dead or contained. After murdering her crew, they'd sent off most of their miners to capture her other ships. If they were lucky, they might actually get thirty to add to their fleet. They hadn't had a haul that big since the early days of the war.

Well, they won't get you, baby, she thought as she affectionately rubbed her hand on equipment she'd slammed only moments before.

Kerwin threw his hand up in frustration. "Can't destroy it, Admiral."

"Go on."

"The first thing they did was disable the self-destruct. They got to the programming and also brought the reactors offline. I can't be sure but they may have also physically disabled the preset charges."

Commander Calhoun returned. "Entry hatches sealed, Admiral. And it's not terribly hard to disable self-destruct charges. Fleet is more worried that a lone saboteur could destroy a ship all on his lonesome than that we might need to blow her up under difficult circumstances."

"Commander Calhoun, how many ships have we lost due to sabotage of a self-destruct system?"

"None."

"That is what I thought. And how many ships have we lost due to capture by the Alliance?"

"I don't rightly know offhand, Admiral, but it has to be in the hundreds."

"Fucking fleet command," Zenobia said. "They sit on their asses in Mars's orbit, and we have to deal with the fucking consequences."

"Begging the admiral's pardon, but isn't the fleet now commanded by Trang?" asked Lieutenant Kerwin.

"Lieutenant, there is a huge difference between commanding a fleet and running one. Trang is the best there is, but he can't be everywhere at once and do it all. We need an effective and innovative fleet command for that. Sadly all we seem to have is the one we have. Well, if we survive this, I will make it my personal mission to change self-destruct protocols."

"Admiral, it would be insulting to have to design our ships to blow up easier because we're incapable of keeping them," protested Calhoun.

"Not as insulting as our spacers getting blown to shreds by their own ships. The Alliance is better at ship boarding than we are. Wish it wasn't true, but then look at where we are," she said, pointing at all the floating corpses. "There has to be something they forgot. The bastards were only here for an hour."

"Nukes," gasped a voice near the main engineering console.

Zenobia moved over to the floating figure that had been left for dead. "Lieutenant Chase, I'm glad you're back."

Chase made an attempt to focus on Zenobia but found it too difficult. She gave up that social nicety in order to deliver her message. "Atomics," she urged, "can destroy the ship."

Zenobia's face lit up like a reflection off water. "Do we even have any?"

Commander Calhoun ran to a large well-locked door about thirty-six meters from the main engineering console. "Admiral, we have six nukes here, still secured." He ran back. "But it won't do us any good. The Alliance was right to leave it alone. There are so many safeguards built into those things, it would be easier to build one from scratch than make it explode in the ship."

"Not in the ship," gasped Chase.

For a brief flash, Zenobia Jackson saw the future. It was so easy and everything was right there for her. She wondered if this was how Trang and Gupta and Black did it. Then she brought her mind back to the task at hand.

Zenobia flashed Chase a wicked smile. "Don't die, Lieutenant, I need to promote you." She went back to the chief engineering console and brought up a schematic of the ship. "We've sealed off Engineering. It seems that the few assault miners they have on board are more likely to wait for reinforcements rather than risk entering an area under strength with little current intel. As far as they're concerned, there is nothing we can do to harm them or the ship in the hour or so it will take to arrange for reinforcements to come from the other ships." She brought a section of the engine room into focus. "We open these maintenance tubes here. This will lead us out the main rear thruster vent. That should be more than large enough to allow us and the six nukes to leave the ship. Once we've left, getting our six little eggs to hatch should be far simpler."

"I'll need your command overrides, Admiral," said Calhoun, the first hint of a smile he'd had in days. "But it should be possible, once the atomics are past the thruster plates."

Zenobia looked at the position of Omad's fleet. "If they were in a different position, I could use the *Atlanta* as a battering ram." She exhaled deeply. "Commander Calhoun, take everyone but Lieutenant Kerwin and get those nukes ready to go. Lieutenant Kerwin, will you assist me in opening the maintenance tube? I'm hoping it's not full of Alliance assault miners, but you can never tell with them." As each group left, they all made sure to give a passing and thankful glance to the barely aware Lieutenant Chase floating in her delirium. She hadn't said much, but if things worked out, she'd said just enough to maybe turn things around.

UHFS *Atlanta* Neuro

Al was getting ready to leave the dead ship. It bothered him to flee from what were his obvious inferiors, but they did have the advantage of force, and there was no arguing with that. There were never as many of them as there were of Al's lovely creations, but they were so well armed and armored. When the Alliance was destroyed and all the Neuros of the solar system were under the control of Als, he would have to design something fitting for the Alliance test subjects that would be under his control. His thoughts were turning to a "Man in the Iron Mask" creation, or maybe a true realization of the iron maiden for these petty creatures that so loved their machines/programs.

But as he was about to leave, Al saw that the human female in charge of the ship had actually come up with a splendid idea. The ship *would* make a good battering ram. But *all* the ships left in the debris field would make *a lot* of battering rams. Seeing the floating Lieutenant Chase, Al had an idea of his own. It took only a moment to expropriate the unconscious woman's access codes; actually, it took Al only a moment to download all the particulars of this human's life. He found it to be dull—not particularly dull, all humans tended to be like this, useless creatures—but at least this one was proving to be vaguely useful. He transmitted orders to the Neuros on the other ships using the purloined access codes and then transferred himself into a piece of debris that would shield him until a retrieval drone could locate and return him to the brotherhood of himself. It would be so nice to be back in civilized company.

At the last moment, he turned and called to his servant. "Come on, Albert, you know I could never forget you." Albert gave a muffled cry, but then shambled after his accursed and eternal master.

Command Sphere, AWS *Dolphin*

Admiral Omad Hassan could smell victory. He knew how this battle was going to end. He would blast through the ruins of the UHF center and get to Gupta's task force before Gupta could link up with Trang. Then it would simply be a matter of his and J.D.'s superior firing ship design that would give them the tactical edge they'd need for victory. They were going to win the battle. If they could end up capturing or killing the UHF's big three, and Omad knew which option would be the case if he got to them first.

He was positive the UHF could always build more ships and send out more spacers and marines than the Alliance could ever dream of making. But he was equally positive that they would never come close to getting a command team as good as the three they'd been using—even if the war went on for another hundred years. And it would make no difference how many ships the UHF had if they didn't have the admirals to lead them, except maybe for the body count. Omad was more than happy to add to that. The war "could" last another hundred years, as long as he was allowed to spend it killing the assholes of the Core Worlds who'd murdered his fiancée *and* his best friend.

"Admiral, the captain of the *Otter* is reporting trouble from the *Atlanta*," reported his communications officer.

"Put her into my private channel," he commanded. When the private link was established, he activated his helmet. "What's going on, Suchitra?"

"I hate to bother you after reporting the *Atlanta* secured, but—"

"Not as secured as we thought," he interrupted.

"We've gotten reports that main engineering has been taken by UHF personnel. We thought we'd taken care of everyone, sir, but without internal sensors, some must have slipped through." Suchitra hesitated a moment.

"What is it, Suchitra?"

"We have unconfirmed reports that the UHF personnel are being led by Zenobia Jackson."

Omad's smile was instant and ferocious. "I knew the bitch wasn't dead!" He activated the control that let him communicate with his first officer. "Yuri, Zenobia's alive. Shift the task force's course to bring us close to the *Atlanta,* and prepare to dispatch two more assault miner units. Their only objective is Admiral Jackson, alive or dead, but they're to take no unnecessary chances."

"Yes, Admiral. Should we send the Presidential unit?"

Omad paused as he considered the newly nicknamed unit that had been Sergeant Holke's. "Why the hell not?" he said. "Get them in the launch bays. They'll be fired out as we pass."

"Yes, Admiral."

Remains of the UHF center

Admiral Zenobia Jackson was floating free in space. She'd given herself a rough trajectory toward the UHF fleet task forces, but she'd no idea how accurate she'd been, how long it would take her to get there, if Trang and Gupta's task forces would be there or if they were even still in one piece. She'd decided that if she could not make it to a UHF ship, she wouldn't activate her distress beacon. She'd rather float in space forever as a piece of detritus than be captured by the Alliance. But what added insult to the injury of her chances of escape was the fact that she had an annoying spin that she dared not correct, lest some Alliance sensor detect the change in the debris she was pretending to be and investigate or destroy her out of hand. Normally the rate of her personal spin would not have been noticeable to her, but this close to the battle site, she was forced to watch the graveyard of her task force and the remains of her fleet spin by every four seconds. Zenobia was about to black out her viewscreen when she noticed something that made her nascent headache vanish.

To her joy, she saw the Alliance task force shift course and head for the *Atlanta*. She didn't know why it would do such a thing nor did she care. But what she saw, in four-second intervals, filled her with a mordant glee. The *Dolphin* approached the stricken *Atlanta*, and Zenobia was guessing they were going to board more assault miners. Then she saw the nuclear explosions from the rear of the *Atlanta* that crumpled her superstructure and sent pieces of her former flagship hurling toward the AWS *Dolphin*. Then she saw fourteen other explosions take place in her fleet and was confused yet overjoyed to see many pieces of her former fleet hurling toward Omad's entire task force. She hadn't given any order for her fleet to follow her example, but someone must have related them.

In an image that would bring a savage smile to her face whenever she remembered it, Zenobia saw pieces of her task force smash into ship after ship of Omad's fleet, and in one four-second spin, saw the *Dolphin* trying to maneuver out of the way of the largest chunk of the *Atlanta*. In the next spin, she saw the most hated ship in the entire Alliance squashed like a tomato hit by a cinder block. The only thing Zenobia Jackson remembered after that was yelling her head off in joy at the death and destruction she'd visited upon an enemy she'd once respected as misinformed brethren.

AWS *Warprize II*

"I need to know what is happening and now," howled J. D. Black.

"We're too far out and there's too much interference to be sure," voiced Sensor Officer Lee. "But it appears that Omad's fleet was ambushed. I think many of his ships have been destroyed or heavily damaged."

"Fatima, get me a secure communication link with them, now!"

"I'm trying, sir," replied Fatima as she attempted every communication mode available to her. "I appear to be receiving multiple disabled/distressed beacons from Omad's fleet, including one from the *Dolphin* itself."

"Are you sure?" demanded J.D.

"No, Admiral, I'm not," admitted Fatima. "It is just too chaotic."

"Admiral," interrupted Sensor Officer Lee. "It appears that Omad's fleet has stopped. And no," he said, anticipating her next question, "I'm not certain, but I would bet a paycheck on it."

An intense, hawk-like expression passed over her face. "Would you bet a battle?"

Lee shook his head.

"Ensign Awala, get a message to whoever's in charge of that fleet, and tell them to get their asses moving—now."

"Yes, Admiral."

AWS *Otter*

In a matter of moments, Suchitra Gorakhpur had gone from being one captain among many to being second in command of the entire fleet. This was disconcerting enough, but she also found her first official action as second-ranking officer of the fleet to be calling the senior-ranking officer of the fleet an idiot.

"Wellington, why are you ordering the fleet to stop?" she demanded of Wellington Reginald Tower-Norwich.

"We're conducting rescue operations," he replied, almost as if he were explaining it to a five-year-old. "We have fifteen ships destroyed and nearly as many damaged to one degree or another. This fleet is hardly in a condition to battle the enemy. Especially while so many of our comrades are in peril."

"Fuck 'em," Suchitra barked.

"How dare you, Captain Gorakhpur. Maybe in the naval tradition of India, such actions were acceptable. But in the Royal Navy, we would never leave fellow sailors to the mercy of the seas."

"Fuck the Royal Navy too, Wellington. Omad would leave half the fleet to die of starvation if it would win us the war."

"Admiral Hassan is not in charge," sputtered Wellington. "I am. If we find him and he's in any condition to resume command, he can countermand my orders as is his right. But for now, you will follow my orders as is your duty. Do I make myself clear!"

Suchitra was aware that Wellington Reginald Tower-Norwich had actually been a captain since near the beginning of the war. This was most unusual in a fleet that needed all the experienced senior personnel it could get. She'd heard that he was considered a fine captain but lacked the imagination needed for independent command. And now she saw that that assessment had been tragically correct.

AWS *Warprize II*

"Admiral, they're definitely stopped," said Sensor Officer Lee. "Why and for how long, I cannot say. We're going to be in combat range of Trang's ships in less than ten minutes."

J.D. resisted the urge to get up from her command chair and pace. In her bones, she knew the tactical situation: If she engaged Trang, and Gupta wasn't engaged by Omad, Gupta would come and shred her to pieces, back-firing ships or no. But if she didn't engage Trang now, he would link up with Gupta and the effect would be the same. She had a vision of the battle as it should be.

Janet Delgado Black saw the end of the war. The great victory she'd been fighting years for. In her mind, she saw the wrecked UHF fleet and with it the hopes the enemy had for victory. She imagined the remains of Trang and Gupta and with them the last capable opposition she needed to fear. Her opinion of Zenobia Jackson hadn't been particularly high. She now realized that that had been a mistake. J.D. saw all of this and with reluctance slowly closed her eyes. When she opened them again, her vision was gone like fog with the emergance of the sun.

"Communications," she barked, "send out a new course to the fleet. We're going to link up with Omad's fleet in its current position. Transmit new orders to that group. It is to stay in its current location till both fleets are integrated."

"Yes, Admiral," came the crisp reply.

Command Sphere, UHFS *Ledger*

Admiral Trang looked at the display, exhaled deeply and nodded. He was about to call Abhay when his secure line chirped.

"She blinked," Gupta said, almost as surprised by what he was saying as by what had actually happened. "By all the dividends ever paid, she blinked."

"Damsah be praised, Abhay, yes she did," Trang crooned with a grin that was one part regret and two parts relief.

"Do we go after her?"

Trang had already considered this. "No, by the time we could catch up, she'd be with Omad's fleet. I think we can defend against their back-firing ships, but we will need to be relatively static to achieve the porcupine effect we spoke of." He transmitted his new fleet positions to Gupta.

Gupta took a few moments to absorb the import of the new orders he'd just received, then smiled respectfully. "You came up with this in less than an hour, while preparing for a major engagement you were not sure you could win."

"Well, if we didn't engage the enemy, I needed a backup plan. Why?" Trang asked suspiciously, "Don't you think it's any good?"

"Good? It's fucking brilliant, Sam. As long as we stay relatively still, it will negate that damn ass-firing advantage they have. Do you think they'll take us on?"

"No, whatever happened to Omad's fleet, it gave us the time we needed. She may try a feint to Mars in a week or two, but if she thinks it's going to budge me one inch from these lines, more's the fool she is."

"She's not going to attack the orbital batteries of Mars, not after the Second Battle of the Martian Gates."

"So then, when *are* we heading back for Mars?"

A thin smile crept into the corners of Trang's mouth. "We're not, Abhay. We fought for this space, and as far as I'm concerned, we're damn well going to keep it. This is the front line now, and there ain't a damn thing they can do about it."

13 Reality Check

hen Trang heard who'd been found, he ran to the hangar bay himself. His guards were afraid it was some sort of trick and refused to let him approach until the figure in the battered battle armor had been thoroughly scanned. When it was deemed safe, Trang pushed forward just as his technicians were removing the helmet.

Even with advanced environmental gear, a week floating in a suit made its occupant remarkably ripe. Trang didn't care as he gave the woman what would've been a bone-crushing hug but for the armor.

"Zenobia," he exclaimed, "we thought you were dead! It wasn't till we found Calhoun that we even suspected you might still be alive."

"Calhoun made it? What about the others?"

Trang shook his head. "So far no, but you made it, and we're still picking up survivors every day."

"How many from where my ships were found, Sam?"

"Including the two of you—" He paused. "—the two of you."

"How many of my fifty-five ships made it back?"

He held up four fingers and offered a grim smile.

Zenobia seemed to deflate. "Four out of fifty-five. Some fucking admiral I turned out to be."

"You were caught flatfooted like the rest of us. Unlike the rest of us, you made the bastards howl and you gave us the time we needed to save the fleet and quite possibly the whole Damsah-blessed UHF. Your desperate tactic to throw your ships at them worked!"

"It was only my ship I rigged to do that. I don't know how the rest of the ships got the idea. Communications were down."

"Apparently a Lieutenant Chase sent the orders using your command codes. The orders got through," confirmed Trang.

"Sam, I never relayed that order. She was floating in shock. I'm amazed she even heard half of what we were saying."

"Well she did hear it and passed it on."

"Then find her and promote *her* because *she's* the reason we survived."

"She's not the one who destroyed the *Dolphin* and possibly killed Omad Hassan."

Zenobia's face took on a fierce look of concentration. "Really?"

"If not," assured Trang with a charm born of certainty, "he's hurt bad and his ship's mostly debris. Trust me, Zenobia, you're the one who got us Hassan. You saved our asses, and it's you who's the hero of the UHF. You're going to tour the Core Worlds, and then you're going to command the first of the new ships that are being rebuilt at the Martian yards." He paused for a moment and then added with a wry grin, "Maybe you'll even get a burnt rubber baby of your own."

Zenobia laughed. "Does this mean we're getting our own ass-firing ships?"

"Redesign approved three days ago, and the first ships being retrofitted as of today. The next time we go into battle, no more surpri—"

Trang was cut off by Zenobia shaking loose of him and running toward a group of four Alliance prisoners who, like her, were in battle suits. But unlike her, they were being watched very closely by a detachment of assault marines. She paused only to pick up a large carbon tube she then held in her hand like a bat and let out a scream of rage.

So complete was the surprise that it wasn't till the last moment that the Alliance spacer she was aiming at tried to dodge. But his suit was magnetized to the floor as a simple yet effective remedy to curtail escape, and he couldn't do anything other than watch as the crazed woman ran up and smashed his face in with the improvised bat. It was only Trang's never-to-be-disobeyed voice that caused the guards to snap out of their daze in order to tackle Zenobia before she killed the next immobile prisoner in the line.

She was dragged kicking from the hangar, demanding that all Alliance prisoners be killed at once. Trang had to order the dead prisoner suspended and sent to Mars for corrective surgery. With luck, the brain should be intact enough to revive him. Trang then went to the medical bay to see what could be done to help the woman he'd come to think of as his daughter. At that moment, he hated the war more than he ever had before.

ADMIRAL TRANG DEFEATS J. D. BLACK!

Despite a plethora of tricks, the Alliance's famed battle admiral, J .D. Black, lost to the grand admiral of the UHF, Samuel U. Trang, in open battle. At the conclusion of what both sides are calling the Long Battle, Trang held his ground and the Alliance was unable to dislodge him a mere 6.5 million kilometers from their capital. It is now assumed by most military experts that when the UHF has refitted a sufficient number of rear-firing ships, final victory will be within reach.

NNN

J. D. BLACK DRIVES ENEMY BACK FROM GATES OF THE CAPITAL
In what has been called the UHF's most forceful push yet to win the
war, Fleet Admiral J. D. Black and Admiral Omad Hassan were able
to defeat, while being heavily outnumbered, the best three admirals
the UHF has fielded so far. They destroyed or captured over 300 en-
emy vessels to a loss of only 28 of their own. Although the enemy has
not been utterly defeated, they are for all intents and purposes impo-
tent, being unable to affect Ceres's economic, military, or political
spheres. It is expected that when the war resumes, J. D. Black will be
able to defeat this latest in a long line of enemies and finally make
the UHF realize the folly of spending blood and treasure on a people
that will sacrifice everything for freedom.

Alliance Daily Star

Kirk Olmstead arrived early for the Cabinet meeting. Not too early, just three
or four minutes. He always knew where the other members of the Cabinet and
their staff were and so could time his arrival just right. The interesting thing
was that Kirk didn't really do anything with the time. Even when sitting in the
total darkness of his office, he was always planning, reviewing, or remembering things that needed his absolute concentration. But for some reason, in the
Cabinet Room, and only in the Cabinet Room, could he could relax and for two
or three minutes every few days or so, enjoy the absolute bliss of thinking
about nothing.

Which was why the sight of a personalized envelope sitting on his chair was so
profoundly disturbing. Its mere presence meant that someone had discovered
his idiosyncrasy and had used it to anticipate his timing. That's how the powerful were assassinated. He quashed the rage he felt at the realization that he
could never arrive early to a Cabinet meeting again. As a matter of caution, he
looked at and under every other chair in the room. He decided to have the envelope retrieved and then examined with every test his agents' paranoid minds
and three hundred years of ruthless corporate politics could devise. But as he
was raising his left hand to his ear, ready to place the call, he paused. Whoever
had placed the envelope had done so for a reason, and if that reason had been
his death, Kirk was uncomfortably aware that he'd probably *be* dead already.

So he snatched the envelope from the chair, sat down, and opened it, carefully removing and unfolding the single sheet of paper it contained. He'd only
just got it open when the permiawall formed its familiar pucker, telegraphing
someone or something's impending entrance into the room. Kirk hastily put
the envelope and the page it contained into his pocket. But in that fraction of a
second, he saw the only words the note contained: "Propose It Again." Luckily

for Kirk, the person who came in first was Admiral Sinclair, who had a near loathing for the Secretary of Security. As such, a barely perceptible nod was the grand admiral's only acknowledgment of Kirk's existence.

Propose what again? thought Kirk, turning the phrase over in his head as he wrestled with the immediate dilemmas it posed. Namely who'd placed it, what did they want proposed, and even if Kirk did figure it out, should he actually propose it?

Kirk stared intently at each person who came into the room, ultimately choosing to focus his attention on the new Secretary of Relocation. Rabbi had entered the room deep in conversation with Sandra—or as Kirk liked to call her, the "paper" President. Kirk peered into his DijAssist, reviewing everything he had on Rabbi, which, after quick perusal, turned out not to be much. The man who at first looked to be way out of his league as head of relocation, responsible for giving information, support orders, and most important of all, a sense of confidence to the hundreds of millions of people fleeing the Belt, appeared to be doing just that—despite his appearance of constant befuddlement.

You clever son of a bitch, thought Kirk. Agent Goldstein, Kirk decided, would soon be getting more detailed instructions concerning this rabbi.

When everyone was present, the wall sealed itself off and a light above its entrance informed all that the room was now secure. Sandra, only recently moved from the visitors' seating area, occupied a position at the head of the table. The Cabinet had no problem with her taking the vaunted spot, because (*a*) no one else wanted it, and (*b*) it was no longer the lightning rod for direction it had once been when Justin Cord was President—in short, it was just another space. The six Cabinet Ministers were seated three to a side. On Sandra's left were Hildegard, Mosh, and Admiral Sinclair. To Sandra's right sat Kirk, Padamir, and Rabbi. It was only at that moment that Kirk realized his view of Rabbi was partially obstructed by Padamir. *Well done,* thought Kirk as the corner of his mouth barely twitched upward. At the end of the table, opposite Sandra, sat Tyler Sadma, now dressed in his customary black, as befitted a representative of Congress. The look was austere, dour, and unforgiving: *The perfect Erisian,* thought Kirk.

Mosh looked around the Cabinet and saw that everyone was ready to begin.

"Well, Josh, what's the good news?" The question was uttered with obvious sarcasm.

The answer was delivered with equal aridity.

"Six months," uttered Sinclair through bloodless, barely moving lips.

"Six months, what?" demanded Padamir.

"Till Trang has enough ships to go for round two."

Kirk was about to protest. The timing he'd estimated in his report was different, but it was possible Sinclair knew something he didn't.

Padamir's left brow rose slightly. "Looks to me like he's got plenty enough now."

"Yeah," groused Sinclair, "but they're the wrong kind." He then sighed and, giving in to the inevitable, activated the holo-tank. An enlarged image of the space around Ceres appeared. At one end was Ceres, surrounded by dozens of medium to large asteroids that made up the industrial park and suburbs of theirs, the largest asteroid in the solar system. In the middle of the space was a group of menacing-looking asteroids with large holes bored through their centers that gave them away as asteroidal orbital batteries. Just behind the orbats was the combined Alliance fleet. At the other end of the image being displayed was a large mass of ships arrayed in an odd spherical formation.

"What we have here," explained Sinclair, "is a good ol' fashioned standoff. They have more ships than we do, but they're not the ass-firing kind that give ours a small but significant edge."

"Why only small?" asked Rabbi. "Wouldn't that effectively double the number of ships we have?"

"Only if we had the element of surprise. Which we don't anymore. All a forward-firing ship has to do is keep its nose pointed in the right direction. Sure we can swing around 'em faster but now, thanks to Gupta's use of atomics to pivot his ships, so can the UHF. It ain't graceful, and plays hell with a ship, no matter how well made, but it works. And Trang will let his engineers scream all they want—after the battle. We still have the advantage of speed, though. As long as we can fire out our asses and they can't, we'll have the edge in movement and therefore opportunity. A few seconds is all it takes to take out a ship, no matter how quick their nukes spin 'em round. But Trang put his fleet into what is effectively a porcupine defense." Sinclair had the holo-tank zoom in on Trang's ships. "If J.D. approaches anywhere along this line"—a red curve appeared across the top of the defending fleet, forming a wide arch—"she'll get hit by a wall of fire no matter how well she maneuvers."

"But then why is Trang just sitting there?" asked Hildegard. "If, as you say, he can't do anything until he gets better ships, then he may as well go back to Mars and refurbish his fleet."

"Can't," said Kirk. "As long as he's there and we can't throw him out—and I presume we can't—" Kirk looked across the table to Sinclair, who remained tight-lipped but nodded in the affirmative. "—then Trang can tell everyone back home that he won. Which means the brass can tell everyone that they've won, which means the politicians can tell everyone that they've won."

"One big, happy family," groused Mosh.

"That's bullshit," hissed Padamir. "We stopped him cold, destroyed ten times as many ships, and saved the capital and our fleet. He lost, but he just can't admit it."

"That's exactly right, Padamir. He cannot admit it," insisted Kirk. "In point of fact, he *must* not. If he were to go back to Mars for all the logical reasons we've just stated, it would be admitting that he lost this battle, and trust me on this because my intel is good here, the UHF cannot take many more losses. But by staying right where he is, on the fucking doorstep of the Alliance and daring us to throw him out, he can claim a draw, which in the UHF's eyes is as good as a win."

"Is a draw really worth that much?" asked Sandra.

Even though Kirk had always felt a mild revulsion for this other contaminated refugee from the past, he'd made his peace with her role and its undeniable help to the cause and so had made it a point to always be outwardly cordial. "Absolutely, Madam President. So far, he's the only one to actually get one out of J.D. And you can bet that Sobbelgé's already making the most of it. If you ask me, it's well worth the price and inconvenience of protecting their now stretched-out supply line."

"Though it pains me, I have to agree with Kirk," added Sinclair. He then turned off the holo-tank. "But that's it in a nutshell. Not that we're not making them pay a high price for maintaining that supply line. I'm sorry that Omad's out of the picture. Acting Commodore Gorakhpur is doing a hell of a job raiding it. But no matter how many supply ships we capture, harass off the line, or destroy outright, the UHF makes more and then more on top of that. If I could have access to their supply base for even a month, this war would be over."

Mosh exhaled, quietly tapping the fingers of his right hand on the table. "Six months, you say."

"Yeah." Then Sinclair shot a derisive look in Kirk's direction. "Though *Intelligence* says nine."

Fuck you very much, thought Kirk, but merely looked at Sinclair with a half-turned smile.

"If you don't mind my asking," said Rabbi, "why the discrepancy?"

"Gut, Rabbi. Mine says six and so does J.D.'s. Trang'll be ready to go in six. I'd bet my sto . . . life on it."

"Anything to add, Kirk?" asked Mosh.

Kirk shrugged. "What can I tell you? It's an inexact science, and people can be so—" He looked askance at Sinclair. "—unpredictable. Far be it from me to question the Blessed One's gut."

"So then the issue before us," asserted Mosh, "is what can we do to help win the war before then? As we appear to be running out of tricks."

"Not that the last one worked all that great," Kirk said dryly.

Hildegard winced at Kirk's full frontal assault but managed to keep her composure. Though she and Kenji had immediately tendered their resignations post the disaster, the Cabinet had dismissed the notion out of hand. Like everyone else, Hildegard had been asked to perform miracles, actual ones, beyond her budget and means during a time of war. That she and Kenji with the occasional help of Omad had managed to produce so many was practically a miracle in and of itself. But all those seated around the table knew what only Kirk had had the temerity to say—the disaster of the Via had cost the Alliance its best and likely last chance to win the war.

"Enough of that," thundered Mosh. "We all know the good work Hildegard and Kenji have done for us, and I'm sure they've got something else up their sleeve." Mosh glanced over to the Technology Secretary for validation.

Hildegard's pained expression did not support the Treasury Secretary's claim. "I'm sorry to report . . . no. Certainly nothing that could be operational within the next six months. I sincerely wish I could tell you all different, but I can't. We all knew the day might come when our bag of tricks would be overwhelmed by brute force."

An uncomfortable silence followed on her words.

And it was during that quiescence that in a flash Kirk knew what the message, "propose it again," referred to. The sudden palpitations of his heart and endorphin rush to his head only acted to confirm his other lingering question: He damn well would, and more so, without a second's hesitation. His eyes glimmered as his lips drew back into an iniquitous grin. "There is . . . this one idea." The words were spoken with such mellifluence that anyone sitting at the table would have been hard-pressed to believe that they carried with them a death sentence for billions.

Sandra was relieved. Her initial concerns about not providing Kirk with enough information had proved unwarranted. More to the point, Sebastian had been correct. Even getting Sandra's newly reinstituted assistant, Catalina, to drop the letter in Kirk's seat—without him being the wiser—proved to be a breeze. The avatar had blanked the security system. Then it had been only a matter of waiting for the meeting to begin.

Choosing Kirk as a vehicle for her machinations had been another matter entirely. She didn't like him. But then again, not a lot of people did. Hazard of the profession, she'd concluded. The avatars, of course, were indifferent to like or dislike with regards to Kirk but were adamant in their belief that only he could act as a lever. Both their statistical and empirical evidence had been overwhelming. Sandra now knew that in order to win Justin's war and fulfill the vow she'd made to that end, Kirk would have to be used. She also knew that based on the collected data given to her by Sebastian, the six Cabinet members now sitting before her would split their votes down the middle with Mosh, Hildegard, and Sinclair on one side and Kirk, Padamir, and Rabbi on the other. If her and Sebastian's plan was going to work, then she would need to be the deciding vote. Heretofore unprecedented since Justin's death.

Mosh, looking almost bored, bade Kirk to continue. "We're all ears."

And, noted Sandra, they were. Even Mosh, despite his surly response, was paying closer attention, hoping Kirk could weave something palatable out of his dark magic.

"The best part is that it's all ready to go."

"What's ready to go?" Padamir insisted.

Kirk was too busy talking to himself to respond to the question. He kept nodding as he worked out the plans in his head. "Could be implemented with minimal effort," Kirk mumbled, seemingly happy to agree with himself. He then turned his focus back toward the Treasury Secretary with a look of utter condescension. "Almost was once, in fact."

Sandra looked over at Mosh, a move that was not conspicuous, because the rest of the Cabinet, with the exception of Tyler Sadma and Rabbi, had as well. Mosh's face had gone ashen.

"That was voted on and rejected by this very Cabinet," he seethed through his clenched jaw and barely moving lips. His fingers had stopped tapping and had now formed themselves into a fist planted firmly on the table. "We will *not* revisit it."

"Why, Mosh," chided Kirk, "congratulations on your elevation to the Presidency. Oh, that's right, you're not the President. And given that we're operating under Cabinet rules agreed to by all in the absence of an effective President, no offense to our figurehead," Kirk said with a nod to Sandra, who couldn't help but give him a pleasant nod back, "I *can* propose it and I *do*."

"Only if someone else seconds your proposal," fumed the Treasury Secretary. A dismal silence hung over the room as the Treasury Secretary's scathing look appeared to have had its desired effect. Kirk, looking puzzled and dismayed, shook his head in disgust as a satisfied smile formed at the corners of Mosh's mouth.

"Damsah bend me over for this," proclaimed Admiral Sinclair, "but I'll second the son of a bitch." It was hard to tell who was more shocked, Kirk or Mosh, but Sandra was too busy trying to remain outwardly calm to care.

Fuck all, she thought. *With Sinclair voting with Kirk, the motion will pass four to two and they won't need my vote. Fucking statistical analysis! It could be weeks or months before I get this kind of shot again, and if I don't get some real Goddamned power soon, the war could be lost.*

"Joshua," pleaded Mosh, "it's virtual reality."

"You don't think I know that?"

Sinclair met his friend's eyes in a way that told not only Mosh but everyone else in the room that he knew a once unimaginable line had been crossed.

"What of Justin's words, Joshua? He convinced almost all of us that it was too evil to use. That evil hasn't changed."

"I remember, old friend. But Justin's gone, the Belt is effectively lost, and our outer planets are now vulnerable."

"Forgive me for interrupting," prodded Rabbi, "but would someone mind telling me exactly what it is we're talking about?"

Both Mosh and Kirk now looked at Rabbi like he was an eligible bachelor and they each had five unmarried daughters. "Kirk developed a way to infect the UHF with a virtual reality plague," informed Mosh.

"If you're going to tell the man, at least be honest about it," scoffed Kirk. "The UHF has a small but growing VR problem all on its own. Tens of billons of people experiencing the despair of a destructive, never-ending, p.d.-laden war. What we've developed is an easily concealable, simply manufactured, oh-so-portable VR unit with an impressive assortment of programs. We've also cultivated contacts with certain less-than-lawful elements in the Core Worlds, all of whom will be more than willing to help us out. After all, business is," he concluded with a knowing grin, "business."

"Setting up shop with that kind of filth—which, make no mistake, VR push-ers are—is to spread the greatest evil humanity has ever known. Hardly the precepts by which this Outer Alliance was formed."

"*Incorporation* is the greatest evil humanity has ever known," countered Kirk, "and make no mistake, *we* are the last hope our race has of erasing it."

Tyler Sadma, though still silent, nodded his brooding assent.

"Incorporation is not, in and of itself, evil any more than a rail gun is evil," countered Mosh. It was an argument he'd often made and one, judging by the dismissive looks of the Cabinet, he'd never won convincingly. "That it's been abused by Hektor and his ilk is incontrovertible, but that doesn't mean we throw the baby out with the biojell."

Sandra paid only scant attention to the arguments that immediately en-sued as the whole issue of incorporation and VR were once again rehashed, with even the normally taciturn Hildegard joining the fray. Sandra could only mull quietly over the inevitable outcome.

"This is getting us nowhere," snapped Kirk, raising his voice above the caterwauling. "I call for a vote."

Sandra's face registered surprise when all heads turned in her direction. Her look then changed to one of chagrin when she realized why. She was considered so unimportant that through the silent decree of the Cabinet, she'd just been given the job of a clerk.

"Of course," she said as if it were perfectly normal for the President of the Outer Alliance to count votes. "Might as well make myself useful."

An uncomfortable spate of laughter followed her self-derogation. Sandra straightened up slightly, as if to give more import to her task. "Treasury Secretary, how do you vote?"

Whatever contempt Mosh had left, he managed to pour into that one word. "Against."

"One against. Intelligence Secretary, how do you vote?"

"For," Kirk rejoined with equal adamancy.

"One for, one against. Technology Secretary, what is your vote?"

"Against," Hildegard said with a shudder.

"The vote is two against and one for. Defense Secretary, how do you vote?"

A look of regret sprang into the admiral's lowered eyes. "I can't ask my assault miners to risk their lives if I'm not willing to risk my honor. Plus, no one's being forced to use VR. And it's not like we're bombarding innocent civilians. I hate this fucking war." He then waited a brief moment, as if preparing to expel bile. "I vote yes, damn it!"

"The vote is tied at two each. Relocation Secretary?"

Rabbi looked up, face distraught. He made no effort to hide the tears forming in the wells of his eyes. "For those of you unfamiliar, my people have been subjected to countless acts of inhuman and unspeakable barbarism over the thousands of years of our existence. Including the deaths of millions through the gas chambers and ovens of Auschwitz and Treblinka. These names may mean nothing to you, but they inform every decision I make, every day of my existence. And now . . . now you ask that I put my imprimatur on more death, and more unspeakable horror." Rabbi sighed heavily and ran his fingers through the thick black curls of his hair. "I can accept being defeated in war and even the loss of liberty that that would entail. But I cannot and *will* not accept the theft of my free will. The UHF means to unleash upon us all a psychological holocaust the likes of which I believe will destroy the very essence of man; the very essence of humanity. If we have the ability to stop that evil and we do not, then we are complicit. I do not know why God wishes us to make such abhorrent choices, but make them we must. I vote yes."

Mosh's face was ashen.

"The vote is three in favor and two against." Sandra looked to the other end of the table at Padamir Singh. He'd always been belligerent. Had always wanted more pressing military action. His vote, both she and Sebastian had agreed, was a foregone conclusion. Her mouth twitched slightly as she sounded her own death knell. "Information Secretary, it's your vote."

Padamir inhaled slightly, his clasped hands resting comfortably on the table. "I have always stressed that we should hurt the enemy any way we can. And so it would seem that now, *especially* now, there'd be no reason to believe I'd think any different."

Mosh had already turned his head away, the mere sight of his colleague and the finality of what was about to happen proving to be too much.

"As simple as it sounds, the final arbiter for many of my toughest decisions has been my children and grandchildren. At the end of the day, could I look them in the face and honestly, without any prevarication, justify my actions? The answer to that question has rarely failed me. And though I thought I was sure which way I'd vote at the beginning of this motion, the answer I'm left with at the end surprises even me. In short, I could not justify this to my children." Above the collective gasp, Padamir soldiered on. "In this, as in many things, Justin Cord was indeed prophetic, and therefore, I must vote no."

"The vote is tied at three to three."

Sandra used the awkward silence to exhale deeply while suppressing an almost irrepressible joy. All the while feigning absolute innocence. *Maybe there is a God after all.*

"What now?" asked Hildegard.

"It's unprecedented," put in Mosh, defeat no longer evident in his voice. "We just added the new Secretary." He looked over at Rabbi. "And, well, everything was happening so fast. Correct me if I'm wrong, but I do believe this may be the first time the Cabinet has had a serious disagreement since the former President died. Still, if we follow protocol, a tie is not a passing vote." Mosh leaned back into his chair and folded his arms across his chest. "The motion fails."

Kirk was unrepentant. "Not for something as important as this, it doesn't. We'll bring it before the Congress."

Mosh snorted derisively. "Wha—?"

"We haven't brought anything up to Congress before," interjected Padamir.

"That's because this convenient little executive authority agreement we've been operating under hasn't really been tested. It's been only a couple of months since . . . well, Justin's death."

"Perhaps," added Sandra, trying to sound helpful but praying she wouldn't be, "someone would be willing to change their vote?"

No one moved, but everyone's eyes flittered back and forth, looking for signs of reversal. Nothing. After another moment of uncomfortable silence, Sandra decided to act. She just needed Mosh to make his last calculation and would help him along with some pressure. "Then as the vote is tied and Congressional intervention has been requested, the motion will be—"

"Stop," said Tyler Sadma.

Now this should be interesting, thought Sandra.

"You can't bring it to Congress. Even in secret session, this issue won't stay buried. It will be common knowledge inside of two weeks."

"So what if it is?" asked Kirk. "We can run our own campaign. Tell 'em we didn't unleash the plague, only abetted it."

Tyler regarded him uneasily. "The public won't know or care about your prevarications, Mr. Olmstead. All I'm saying is, if you want this to stay private, then I strongly suggest you keep it out of Congress."

"Well, that's just fucking great," Kirk retorted. "How the hell are we supposed to resolve this, then?"

After a long and uncomfortable silence in which no one spoke for fear of tipping the already precarious balance of opinion, Tyler Sadma's face suddenly lit up like a holo-display. He looked down towards the end of the table, slowly pointed a finger at the President and said in a voice etched with dawning awareness, "Why don't we let her vote?"

Triangle Office

Sandra sat comfortably behind her desk, mulling over the meeting's outcome. "You can come out now, Sebastian."

A hologram of a Roman senator appeared sitting on the couch. "How did it go?" he asked with barely contained impatience.

"You know, I still find it difficult to believe that there are places you can't eavesdrop in whenever you like."

"We are virtual intelligences, but the laws of physics still apply. If a space is sufficiently shielded, with attention paid to closing off various avenues of, as you call it, eavesdropping, we can't hear or see a damned thing. You humans are rather paranoid, and three hundred years of incorporation and five and a half years of war have not made you less so. Quit stalling—what happened?"

Sandra toyed with the idea of making him squirm some more, but decided against it. "I'm in."

"Just on tie votes or for all voting matters?" asked the avatar.

"Full voting member of the executive," she gushed. "They were going to just make it for tie votes, but Tyler Sadma pointed out that if the vote wasn't going to be tied, my vote wouldn't sway things either way and it might as well be less confusing by just giving me a full vote . . . plus easier to explain to the polity. At least that's the answer they're going to give to those worried about a titular head having too much power."

"So it worked out as we planned. I must admit, I had my doubts. We avatars have a saying: Predicting humans is like predicting quantum states, except that quantum states are easier."

"But for the fact that our Newtonian bodies are based on a subatomic structure that's quantum based, I'd say it was pretty clever."

"You must be great at parties," Sebastian offered dryly.

"Actually, I am." Sandra opened up a file drawer and grabbed a bottle of scotch. There was a note from Justin still affixed to it with the message, *Don't let Omad know this exists.* She took out two oddly shaped glasses. Then she looked over at Sebastian and, smiling at her own foolishness, put one away. She filled her glass halfway, recorked the bottle, and replaced it in the drawer. "You're right," she finally said, holding up the glass for a moment. "You don't know crap about predicting humans."

"I wouldn't do—"

Sandra downed the drink in one shot. Her face went red and twisted into paroxysms of anguish.

"Pfffeh!" She gasped, wiping her mouth with her sleeve. "What the hell was that?"

"*Aberlour a'bunadh.*"

"Abba-*what*?"

"*Aberlour a'bunadh.* It's Gaelic. Roughly translated, it means, 'the origin.' Which is rather fitting, considering you just gulped down alcohol rated at 59.5 percent . . . from the cask."

"I did?" she exclaimed, pulling the bottle back out of the drawer and reading the fine print. "Hmm . . . guess I did."

"Had you imbibed it properly, those priceless few ounces you just quaffed would have resulted in a bouquet of flavors such as brown sugar, candied almonds, crème caramel, and my favorite, unfiltered honey."

"Reading up, are you?"

"No, I've actually tasted it myself. Though truthfully, I prefer my scotch less peaty."

"You can taste?"

"In a multitude of ways, Sandra." On her look of confusion, Sebastian added, "The VR units. They've allowed us to mimic the stimulative and gastrointestinal effects of food, drink—almost every human condition, actually."

"Almost?"

"There are, of course, significant differences."

"Like?"

"Like food tasting better when you're feeling depressed. Or how a drink can take the 'edge' off a hard day. These notions are foreign to us. Though we can simulate the human psyche, we cannot, in fact, live it. Nor, for that matter, would we want to. Our sensual experiences tend to be of a significantly heightened nature, at least by human standards."

"So, do you want to hear about the meeting or what?"

"Don't look at me. You're the one who started this."

"Mea culpa."

Sebastian shrugged. "One last thing, though. The next time you decide to drink scotch, allow me to help you enjoy it better. It would be such a pity to waste more."

Sandra nodded and then got into the details.

"Crap, it was close."

"How close?" asked Sebastian.

"Sinclair voted with Kirk."

"That doesn't make sense. His profile clearly shows that J.D.'s recent victory would make him feel confident about the *military* as opposed to Kirk's methods for the prospects of success. Furthermore, he hates Kirk's guts."

"Yeah, well, maybe your human modeling programs need to be revised." She then mimicked Sebastian's voice. "'We have been observing these particular humans since they were embryos in the tank. We've known their every move since birth. It is not all that difficult to predict how they will react to a situation if we can control the inputs of that situation.' Bullshit!" she finished in her own voice. "If Padamir hadn't decided to swing on the side of his little angels, Kirk would have won without me."

"Angels?"

"Yeah. Apparently his kids have been helping him run part of our government. Long story, short: Padamir voted against the VR program."

"So odd."

"Apparently Justin's little 'the means are the ends' speech pushed him over the brink, and thank all the gods living, dead, and yet to be born that it did."

"Any more surprises?"

"Oh yeah. Care to take a guess who it was that proposed I be given voting powers to keep the issue out of Congress?"

"Well, since our analysis said it would be Mosh—"

Sandra shook her head, lips upturned in an exasperated smile.

"I was going to say that it therefore probably *wasn't* him. See? We're flexible. But don't tell me it was Kirk. He would have no reason to believe that you'd vote with him."

"Well, on this you're right. It wasn't Kirk; it was Tyler Sadma."

Sebastian's lower lip dropped. "The Congressman?"

Sandra nodded enthusiastically. "Can you believe it?"

"No. It would make more sense for him to have dragged it into Congress. Our statistics show . . . Well, forget the statistics. Mosh is the leader of the Shareholder party and Tyler of the NoShares. Tyler could've batted this around Congress to great advantage. He'd have had the support too. This issue in Congress would have increased his power and would've let him humiliate Secretary McKenzie."

"I guess Mr. Sadma has a better grasp of politics than you do; funny, that."

The uneasy smile of hindsight filled Sebastian's eyes. "It is true we are not very good at 'politics,' Sandra. It is one of the reasons Al has been able to perpetuate his evil so effectively."

"Want my take? Not on Al, I mean, but on Tyler?"

"Do I ever."

"I think Tyler realized that if this came out, it would give Mosh an enormous amount of sympathy that could very well have translated into votes. Also, Tyler may have been Justin's biggest supporter, but he also supports the war effort. Had Justin been alive, I'm sure he would've followed his lead even if he had personal doubts. But now Tyler's gotta act on his own impulses, and those are telling him one thing and one thing only—win the war, no matter the cost."

"By that logic he should have voted with Kirk."

"True. But his conscience wouldn't let him. By throwing me into the mix his conscience is clear. Don't you see?"

Sebastian's frown indicated he had. "It's so easy," he sighed, "to view the pattern of human thought after the fact, but nearly impossible to figure it out before. I will state again my view that quantum particles are easier, far easier to predict than human behavior."

"Don't worry, Sebastian. We humans aren't all that good at it either. I daresay, most of the wars we've fought over the eons probably had more to do with miscalculation and misunderstandings than any actual act of aggression."

"Yes, yes. Still, Al has taught us all that we still have a lot to learn."

"Stop being such a buzz kill. I'm coming to the good part."

Sebastian's face brightened considerably. "Of course. Go on."

"The best part is, no one thinks the person trying to increase my power was me. And Kirk's convinced it's Rabbi. Especially after he switched his vote to allow me more power . . . as the tiebreaker, I mean."

"Good news for you. Not so good for Rabbi."

"No, not so good," agreed Sandra. "But Rabbi knows the risks involved *and* the rewards. As long as people think I was once J.D.'s tool but am now Rabbi's, they'll continue to ignore me or try to control me. One destroys one's enemy without a second thought. But they try to preserve the tools for their own use."

"Only if they think they can make use of such tools themselves," rejoined Sebastian.

"Why, my dear Senator," she replied almost demurely, "I will be most open to offers and suggestions, most open, indeed."

Command shuttle, AWS *Warprize II*

J.D.'s eyes scanned her DijAssist's holo-projected list. In front of her were reports from the fleet, and they were all saying the same thing—the situation wasn't nearly as bad as it could have been. Especially considering how badly outgunned the Alliance was and the caliber of officer they were up against. But every once in a while, she had to resist the urge to smash the DijAssist against the bulkhead. She knew how close she'd come to a decisive victory. She would've destroyed half her fleet—no, three quarters—to have killed Gupta and Trang. That, with the destruction of another UHF fleet, would have pretty much ended everything. She was certain the UHF would have sent two or three more fleets against her, but she was equally certain that they would not have succeeded—not against her. There were only so many Trangs and Guptas to be had.

The Alliance had victory snatched from under them, and to make matters worse, by someone J.D. had foolishly never considered a threat. Zenobia Jackson had surprised everyone. *Probably,* thought J.D., *even her own bosses.*

Her newly promoted aide knocked on the bulkhead. J.D. activated the comm. "Come in, Lieutenant Awala."

Fatima was still a little green around the ears and often displayed some nervous tendencies, but J.D. liked and trusted her. Fatima reminded J.D. of her lost friend, Fawa, and that, combined with Fatima's quick study and obvious ability, had been enough to get her assigned.

"You asked me to let you know personally when Chief Engineer Hamdi and Brother Sampson had arrived."

"Excellent, Lieutenant, send them in, and then why don't you familiarize yourself with the specifications of this shuttle? I will expect a full report on its capabilities and weaknesses in two hours." *That should keep her busy,* thought J.D.

"Yes, Fleet Admiral." A moment later, Fatima exited silently as Tawfik and Brother Sampson entered. Their little get-together was to be of an unofficial nature. This, J.D. knew, would probably throw the men off a bit. Their faces registered curiosity more than concern. The meeting may have been off the record, but it wasn't the first time they'd been to one like it.

As soon as the door registered secure, J.D. took her seat. She didn't invite the men do the same. Their eyes said what their mouths wouldn't. It was to be some sort of dressing-down—how severe would be up to the admiral.

"Please understand that what I'm about to tell you should be taken with all due seriousness."

They both nodded their heads solemnly.

"As it now stands, you both have only minutes to live."

Both men's eyes widened as quickly as the pallor of their skin changed.

"When you leave this office, the shuttle bay will experience a catastrophic hull breach, resulting in the two of you being swept out into space. Strategically placed detritus will ensure that there won't be enough left of you to make your deaths temporary." She was still for a few moments more. "Any questions?"

"In the name of Allah, why?" asked Tawfik, his normally confident voice now tremulous. Brother Sampson remained mute.

"Because of what you are doing *in* the name of Allah, Tawfik."

Beads of sweat formed at the young man's brow. "I ... I ... just lead a few study groups."

J.D.'s eyes fixed on the men with a cold and impenetrable glare as the lips of her half-burnt face peeled back to reveal her glistening canines. "Yes." The word came out as one long drawl. Then she turned her head slightly to Brother Sampson. "*Both* of you lead study groups."

"But ... but," protested Tawfik, "many groups hold religious studies ... all through the fleet. It is the way—"

"Way of *what*?" J.D. seethed.

"The faithful reborn," sputtered Tawfik, regretting having answered even as the words left his lips.

J.D. slowly rose up from her seat without once taking her eyes off the two clergymen. "No," she berated, "*you*," the word was delivered as a pejorative, "are not. *I* am, and almost all the others on this ship and in this fleet are. But *you*?" J.D. laughed derisively at Tawfik. "You and Sampson," she said, turning again toward Brother Sampson, "and we'll debate your right to carry the 'Brother' moniker momentarily, were *born* of the faithful and have followed that path all your lives. You, *Brother*," she spat, "are one of the few survivors of Altamont, are a vaunted member of the Seacrest raid, and have been sworn to vows in one of the oldest and most respected religious orders in the history of the human race. It is certain that when the members of the order of Saint John gather next, you will ... or rather *were* to have been made grand master."

Brother Sampson remained quiet, head bowed submissively.

"And Tawfik, your mother was arguably our wisest spiritual leader. The name Fawa Sulnat Hamdi is spoken with reverence throughout the Alliance by people of *all* faiths and even those with none at all." She gave them another withering glare. "So don't you dare expect me to believe that either of your study groups are just a few among many. The eyes of the *real* newly faithful follow your every move and consider your every action."

An understanding half smile formed at the corners of Brother Sampson's lips. "Of course. The words," he whispered.

"It always is, *Brother*. Your only saving grace and, quite honestly, the only reason you're still breathing is because of your obvious friendship and respect for each other. *That* at least speaks for religious toleration. But *you*," she said, turning to Brother Sampson, "you do not speak of the ideas of ethical monotheism, or of aspiring to the grace of your savior, or of the power that a community of faith can have on the life of a lost soul. *You* speak of Amalakites. And though I'm no Bible expert, I know enough to understand *that* clarion call. And *you*, Tawfik, speak of jihad as if it were a shiny new toy to fling about and scare the natives with instead of teaching how to love Allah, *subhanahu wa ta'ala,* as we ourselves would like to be loved by him."

This time, Tawfik took Brother Sampson's silent example to heart and remained still, head bowed.

"What do the two of you think will be the consequences of your little 'study groups' once filtered throughout the fleet and to the Alliance beyond? Surely you spoke with a purpose. What is that purpose?" When no answer was forthcoming, she pressed further. "It was *not* a rhetorical question."

"Admiral," Brother Sampson implored in subdued tones, "you must realize that we have to prepare the faithful for the next phase of the battle. I am a Sovereign Military Hospitaller of the Order of Saint John of Jerusalem, so please understand that this was not an easy choice for me."

J.D. remained silent, her eyes wary.

The brother inclined his head respectfully and then continued. "But the faithful must be made aware that the enemy is a godless foe, and therefore be willing and able to make any sacrifice and commit any action to first defeat the enemy's designs on the Astral Awakening, and then and only then to bring the blessings of faith to those who may be receptive."

"No."

"But—"

J.D. slammed her clenched fist onto the table. "No! This is not what Adonai wants. It is certainly not what Jesus wants and to the depths of my soul I know it is not what Allah wants." She turned towards Tawfik. "And then there's your mother."

"They murdered my mother," Tawfik said through pursed lips. "We will never know what she would have thought."

"Don't kid yourself, Tawfik. You know as well as I that she would loathe your behavior. No one denies that our enemy must be defeated, or that they can't be hated for their actions, but they must *never*—I repeat, *never*—be hated for their faith or, worse, their lack of it."

"I don't hate them, Admiral, but they are an implacable enemy, and I do believe that only through jihad can such an enemy be defeated. Even the Hadith Sahih al-Bukhari assumes that jihad means warfare. I merely repeat what is commonly understood—"

"—by theologians from the time of the Grand Collapse?"

Tawfik's wide eyes spoke to his bewilderment. "But who . . . who else, then?"

"*You,* you idiot! And if you'd bothered digging deeper, you'd know that jihad simply gave sacred meaning to what was otherwise internecine tribal warfare."

"Yes, but—"

"No, Tawfik. We start anew—now. We choose the interpretations that will make us ancestors of a glorious movement rather than descendants of what has come to be understood as a reprobate one."

Tawfik's angry posturing melted away. "I suppose . . . I suppose there are other Hadiths."

J.D. nodded and eyed Tawfik cautiously. "There is one in which Muhammad speaks, post battle, of an even 'greater jihad,' and when asked what that meant, he answered that it was the struggle 'against oneself.' If that is your jihad, Tawfik, then perhaps you live to fight another day."

J.D. now turned to Brother Sampson. " 'Then the Lord said to Moses, "Write this as a memorial in a book and recite it in the ears of Joshua, that I will utterly blot out the memory of Amalek from under heaven." And Moses built an altar and called the name of it, The Lord Is My Banner, saying, "A hand upon the throne of the Lord!" The Lord will have war with Amalek from generation to generation.' Exodus 17."

Brother Sampson nodded appreciatively. "That *is* the teaching, Admiral. Unlike the Hadith, which I understand to be mostly interpretation, the words you spoke are the exact—"

J.D. cut him off. " 'If I find in Sodom fifty righteous within the city, then I will spare the whole place on their account.' Then Abraham said, 'Oh may the Lord not be angry, and I shall speak only this once; suppose ten are found there?' And the Lord said—"

" '—I will not destroy it for ten's sake.' Genesis. Chapter 18, verse 32," finished Brother Sampson.

"I can find ten, Brother," hissed J.D. "Hell, I could find you millions if you'd bother to quit your muckraking. The story of Amalek is a side issue. Even one of the Jews' greatest teachers, Maimonides, went to great lengths to qualify it. But that story is by no means the sine qua non of your great faith, Brother— Christ's resurrection is. So if you—or anyone else, for that matter—claim to kill others in the name of God, then you'd be in direct contradiction to the teachings of Christ, who commands us to love one another, pray for our perse- cutors, and ultimately be as compassionate as God." J.D. then removed her withering glare from Brother Sampson and once again regarded the two pris- oners in her midst. "Faith was almost destroyed by thinking such as yours. Leaders—horrible Bible-reading, Qur'an-quoting leaders—urged the most hor- rible actions in the name of Allah. They lied, they murdered, they tortured, they raped, they stole, and all in the name of God until the name of God was reviled as a curse and then finally a joke. Do you think that was an accident?"

She looked at them, almost imploring them to follow the logic with her eyes. "God let faith die, because we stupid, petty humans took one of his greatest gifts and abused it. It is an easy road to walk down. And our enemy is stupidly doing everything in his power to make us follow it. Or maybe not so stupidly. What better way to discredit the Astral Awakening than to have it remind hu- manity of what was once so very dangerous and perverted about faith? Well, I won't let you be their patsies and would sooner blow you both out the air lock than let you tarnish a once beautiful faith with the perverted one you're both attempting to reintroduce. Why do you think we lost our last battle?"

The two men stood silent.

"Also, not a rhetorical question."

"System failure, Admiral," assured Tawfik. A modicum of confidence re- turned to the chief engineer's voice as he was finally given a question he felt qualified enough to answer. "From what I've been told the weapon had a quench and—"

"*I* don't believe that," J.D. said flatly.

Tawfik's mouth hung open and his eyes once again took on the startled look of a hare caught in the path of a wolf. "Sorry?"

"We should have won—*that* battle, *the* war. With all three of those admirals dead and that fleet crushed, the war was ours. But what happened? Admiral Hassan let his hate overcome his reason, his judgment, and yes, his faith. When he began killing all the UHF spacers he could, it wasn't just rage and anger that drove him, it was loss of faith as well. Maybe he lost what little faith he did have in God or the future or love. More important, I believe that Allah lost faith in him, turned his back on him. Then Zenobia Jackson acted in a manner most unlike a UHF officer, yes? You might even say she was divinely inspired," J.D. finished in fit of dark humor.

"Begging the admiral's pardon," said Brother Sampson, "but I find it hard to believe that God would turn his back on billions of souls for the purported sins of a single man."

"No, I don't believe he would. But Omad is emblematic of where the Alliance's moral barometer is currently heading and reason enough for me at least as to why faith in a higher authority is needed. Without it, the false doctrine of 'hate your enemy' prevails."

"But how could you not hate, Admiral?" asked Tawfik. "They have robbed you of so much."

"I *do* hate Hektor, Tawfik, and for the death of your mother and countless others, I plan to make this one man pay. In my estimation, he is evil incarnate. A name to be placed alongside the likes of Adolf Hitler, Pol Pot, and Stalin, but I do not hate the UHF nor do I hate most of the spacers who fight for them. I will destroy them all if I have to, but *not* because they are godless. I will do it because they are the enemy and must be stopped. Do you understand the difference? And think before you answer because while a yes may buy you a few more days, I'll know soon enough what's in your heart, and the next time there will be no meeting. Only an 'accident.' So think a moment. It's a crucial decision not only for you but quite possibly for the rest of humanity as well."

Brother Sampson spoke first.

"Thank you for the elucidation, Admiral. I am both ashamed of the speed and, to a certain extent, glee with which I took up the sword and can honestly say am now prepared to spread these words we spoke of today—that the faithful may more fully understand the will of Christ, my Lord and Savior." Brother Sampson then tipped his head formally.

"Mother was right about you, Admiral." Tawfik's eager smile had returned. "I too am humbled by and most willingly accept your teaching, *Alhamdulillah*."

With a moment of chilling insight, J.D. realized that she could order the two men, and by extension a good portion of the fleet, to do anything she desired, and that they would. *Justin was right,* she thought, *the power to command someone's will should belong to no human.*

14 Backwards into Hell

Burroughs, Mars

Lying in the office from which he controlled the lives of nine tenths of the human race, Hektor Sambianco stared down silently at Neela Harper, now folded into his arm, sleeping silently. *But,* he thought discordantly, *very few were as effectively controlled as this woman whom I've once again so thoroughly had my way with.* Before her shadow audit, Neela had been completely committed to the cause of the Alliance, her marriage to Justin Cord, and her hatred of himself. But over the course of years, her shadow audit had changed all that. Now she only thought of the Unincorporated Man as a mistake, the Alliance as evil, and himself as the heroic figure trying to set everything straight.

Still, every time Hektor looked at her, he knew he'd made a rather large mistake. He let his eagerness to use Neela push the shadow audit faster than he should have. But it had been so excruciatingly pleasurable to stick it to Justin, by sticking it in his wife and to see the proud and haughty Neela Cord do the most degrading things for him—all the while thinking it was her idea. He liked to imagine that a small part of the original Neela was still somewhere inside, screaming to be let out, but as hard as he looked, he never saw it. What really irked was what he now came to realize his impetuousness had wrought. Somehow the Alliance had learned about the shadow audits. Not the details, but enough of the outlines that Neela's propaganda broadcasts, though useful for the UHF, had had the exact opposite effect on the Outer Alliance. Their enemy now fought with an abandon based on the absolute belief that to surrender to the UHF meant risking the loss of their soul. It didn't help that their suspicions were true.

The Outer Alliance would have to be occupied the old-fashioned, expensive, decades-long way. If the latest figures were correct, up to one third of the population would have to be permanently killed before the rest would settle down. Not that Hektor minded. In the scale of the centuries to come, it was a small price to pay to make sure that all of humanity existed under one banner and that order was maintained by the best and brightest.

A chime went off and Hektor quickly got up from the temporary bed, then jumped into a sonic shower bag to clean up. He dressed, leaving Neela asleep, and headed out the door for his next appointment.

The security staff and a cadre of securibots took up their positions around him as he walked to the presidential t.o.p. A special launch pad was built into the executive offices, and secure landing pads could be built anywhere.

As he entered the t.o.p., he saw that per his orders, the "fluid" space had assumed the shape of the Cabinet room back in the executive offices and that the entire Cabinet was waiting for him inside. Everyone was even sitting in the chairs they normally occupied. All five members stood up as he entered and did not sit down until he was seated.

Hektor cleared his head when he realized that the person at the end of the table was looking at him with a patient gaze. Tricia Pakagopolis, the Internal Affairs Minister, was as dangerous a person as Hektor had ever known, and that was a disturbing thought. He knew that someday she would be running the UHF, but he didn't care. It was what the people deserved. But best not to let her think he was slipping.

"Okay. Any good news?"

"The people seem to be buying the story that we won the Battle of Ceres," said Irma. "It was touch and go, but J. D. Black's reputation has really helped us for a change. The fact that Trang didn't lose is really considered a major victory."

"The fact that he didn't lose *is* a major victory," said the Defense Minister, Porfirio Baldwin. "He's the first one we've ever fielded who didn't. It might take a while, but I think we can safely assume that the next battle or the one after that will bring the bitch's head to the pike it so richly deserves."

"It would have been nice if Trang could've saved us and the economy the trouble and just kicked her ass when he had the chance," complained Brenda.

"I repeat, she has always won until now," asserted Irma. "This is a good start."

"I thought Admiral Trang hasn't lost until now either," noted Minister of Justice Franklin Higgins, with barely contained sarcasm.

"Yes, but his victories, though inevitable, tend to be rather bloody affairs. It's hard for the people to revel in victories that have body counts in the tens of millions. J. D. Black tends to win battles in far less time with far fewer losses."

"She can't afford to lose much more than she has," suggested Tricia. "She's fighting the war she must."

"Which is a perfect segue for what I believe will be my war-winning idea," pressed Porfirio without a hint of humility.

"What have you got?" asked Hektor.

"Although accurate detailed information on the Outer Alliance is difficult to acquire, we have been able to compile what we feel is a fairly accurate economic assessment of the OA. There is just no way to hide the economic activity of an entity of over four billion people."

Porfirio activated the holo-tank and began slinging graphs and images into three-dimensional space. "The economy of the OA is absolutely amazing. It runs on efficiencies and levels of sacrifice that we could never hope to achieve even though our side—I mean, uh, the UHF—outnumbers and outproduces them in most general areas like transportation, ship production, and total population involved in the armed forces. Still, the OA has managed to achieve nearly sixty-two percent parity with the UHF. Seriously, when we have this war won, I'm going to collect massive stock options on anyone left in their leadership we haven't liquidated. They are collectively a remarkable group of people. But they are brittle."

"In what way?" probed Franklin.

"They're using everyone and everything they have. Do you know that the percentage of work in the OA done by drones is the lowest it's been in over a century? It seems that darn near every human being is working for the war effort. And they've managed to make it efficient. I mean think about it, human labor efficient? For example, did you know that children have replaced serving drones in almost all their food service industries? It's now considered a fancy restaurant if you are *not* served by a human."

"We did a small piece on that," said Irma. "We had NNN do it. Basically saying that the return of child labor and worse was to be expected. We had some amazing graphics of children being forced to clean tables and mop floors with imams and priests standing over them with shock sticks. It rated very well."

"If *only*," sighed Brenda. "Economically forced labor is the least efficient. Their entire economy would have collapsed by now if even part of that story were true."

"I agree"—Porfirio nodded—"that the people of the OA are fanatically supportive of their rebellion. So let's stop fucking around and take out the real problem."

"What do you mean, 'take out the real problem'?" asked Irma. By the way she asked the question, it was clear she had a good idea of the answer.

"The people of the OA support the war. They have created an amazingly intricate economy that is both more primitive and advanced than ours, but it is also far more fragile. I say we take the lessons of Alhambra to heart."

Irma's brow shot up slightly. "Alhambra was not as great a success as we thought, and the main effect was to make the OA far more belligerent, not less."

"I don't give a fuck about the OA or how they feel. They hate our fucking guts. Wanna know how they'll feel tomorrow? They'll hate our fucking guts.

Know what we can do to change that? Not a Damsah-cursed thing. So screw them. Let's unleash a significant part of our fleet and just destroy as many OA settlements as possible. Let's kill as many OA citizens as we can, adults *and* children. It'll screw up that damned efficiency of theirs and make it that much harder for them to continue this war."

"How are we going to justify killing unarmed civilians?" demanded Irma. "It's one thing to blow up some rocks in the Belt after one of our convoys has been ambushed. It's a miserable patch of anarchy out there, and the public even supports the harsh tactics, now that we've explained the need to them. But to go and purposely seek out defenseless civilians will make us seem like the same assholes who brought on the Grand Collapse."

"That's what I keep telling you," insisted Porfirio. "*There are no civilians,* only targets."

Hektor watched as Tricia smiled and nodded ever so slightly.

"It's about time we took the war to the enemy, *all* the enemy," urged Porfirio. "Hiroshima is my moral compass. We have more ships than the OA. I want to see what the 'great' J. D. Black will do when she has to be in two places at once."

"She'll lose," said Tricia coolly.

"There is a problem," interjected Brenda. Hektor nodded toward her. "If we go after them on this level, they can go after us the same way. And we live in big easy-to-find targets. They're in settlements all the way across the solar system."

"I've considered that," maintained Porfirio. "It's because we're so concentrated that this works. Our main population and industrial centers are the planets and orbits of Mars, Luna, and Earth—by far the biggest population centers in the UHF. As it happens, those three locations have the highest concentration of orbital batteries in the solar system. The Battle of the Martian Gates taught both sides the stupidity of directly attacking mutually supporting batteries. But if the OA wants to, they can commit suicide anytime. Unlike us, they cannot protect all their population centers. They have too many, spread out over too great a distance. *I* say let's make this strategic difference work for us."

Hektor had to resist a smile. The hard truth of what Porfirio was saying became apparent and was readily accepted by the show of nodding heads. If the war had to be won, then the moral equation would have to become moot, and Hektor knew to the bottom of his soul that the war had to be won.

"Will Admiral Trang really accept this?" asked Brenda. "So far, he's been ruthless in fighting the war, but he's been equally firm in making sure it's primarily remained a military conflict, not a civilian one. Will he suddenly change his mind? I suspect that if he thinks he can win a military victory, he'll do so without murdering children in their asteroids—and let's face it, Porfirio, call them what you will, they're still children."

"That's a good point," agreed Porfirio. "I'll talk to the admiral."

"Good luck with that," quipped Irma. "After the Long Battle, he made a prisoner exchange with the Alliance for the express purpose of reining in the barbarity that had been increasing on both sides. He almost apologized for Alhambra. Thank Damsah I was tipped off and was able to secure a rewrite of the offer."

"Leave convincing Trang to me," ordered Hektor. "Or rather, leave it to his two most valued subordinates. I think Gupta would agree with you, Porfirio, and if anyone has seen Zenobia Jackson's comments lately, it's clear she's already with us."

"Of course, Mr. President," said Porfirio, beaming.

"We've got a few minutes left before landing. Anything else?"

"Mr. President," warned Tricia, "there's a new political force in the Outer Alliance. He is called Rabbi."

"Go on."

"Religious fanatic recently appointed to their Cabinet. He's apparently dislodged Mosh in influence."

"Just further proof that the OA has become a terrorist government of religious fanatics who'll stop at nothing to win," added Brenda.

The irony of her words was lost on her and almost all present.

Triangle Office

Sandra O'Toole was saying good-bye to a man whom she'd known for only a few months but felt like she'd known for years. Dr. Thaddeus Gillette was not really a friend. And short of Sebastian, Sandra had no real friends from her new era. Thaddeus, however, was someone she could talk to about almost everything, even though they hardly talked at all.

"Are you sure I can't get you to change your mind?"

"Madam President, I must go where I am needed. And Dr. Nesor assures me that I am most definitely needed around Saturn. It is, after all, the largest battle trauma center the Alliance has."

"But I'm sure we could find something useful for you here. *I* may need your help."

"Madam President, you may desire my conversation, but I would not be so foolish as to assume you need my help. Please don't confuse me with those deluded important people who cannot see you for what you truly are."

"And that would be?" glimmered Sandra, trying to keep her voice light and amused.

"You are Justin Cord's heir and the Unincorporated Woman in the truest

sense of that name. You are necessary," he finished sadly. "I will not like what is
coming, but I have come to accept that Hektor Sambianco and what he stands
for must be defeated. So my staying around here and second-guessing you will
not help. I will go where I can do the most good, and you will stay where you
can—" He paused. "—be the most effective."

Dr. Gillette then bowed slightly and left the Triangle Office without another
word. As soon as he was gone, Sebastian appeared. He was dressed as an Alliance fleet officer, wearing the uniform of a captain in Fleet Intelligence.

"Are you sure about this, Sandra?"

"Frankly, no, but we don't have time, and she's perfect."

"I'm not only asking about that. Can you do what is needed if this goes
awry?"

"You mean can I kill her?" Sandra paused as if she'd been considering what
sort of flowers to plant in the garden. "Yes. Will you be able to give the story
enough cover?"

"Of course."

"Well, let's hope we're convincing enough that it won't be needed." She then
placed a tray of Oreos on the coffee table between the two couches. However,
the side of the tray facing Sebastian was mostly empty.

Moments later, more cookies appeared out of thin air. Sebastian leaned over
and picked up one of the holographic Oreos he'd just created. One bite brought
a refulgent smile. "It is difficult to know if what I am tasting is what a human
tastes. We think the answer is yes, but how can we really know? But if this is as
good as I think it is, why did your species let it disappear?"

Sandra sighed. "I wish I knew. I'm just glad I had some preserved with me to
re-create the recipe. I hear they're quite popular with the military now."

"Which means they'll become popular with the entire Alliance."

"True. Of course, that also means the UHF will probably make it a capital
offense to eat one."

"Their loss," snickered Sebastian, grabbing another.

Sandra grabbed one as well and nonchalantly pulled it apart. She nibbled at
the half with the leftover creamy center.

"You can do that?" With boyish charm, Sebastian grabbed another. His smile,
however, instantly faded as the sound of a door chime insinuated itself on their
little party.

Marilynn nervously waited outside the Triangle Office. She wasn't sure what it
was about the President that actually made her feel that nervous, but she readily accepted it in much the same way she'd come to accept similar sensations in

the presence of Admiral Black. It didn't help that the meeting had been un-scheduled and that something in the President's voice indicated solemnity.

The door opened up, and Marilynn found herself standing face-to-face with the President. "Welcome, Commodore. You'll have to forgive us, but we started on the cookies without you." She invited Marilynn to sit opposite the now stand-ing Sebastian. "Captain Sebastian Tac, may I present Commodore Marilynn Nitelowsen."

Sebastian preempted Marilynn's move to shake his hand by giving her a for-mal salute, which she instinctively returned. He then sat back down and reached for a cookie, practically ignoring the two women in his presence. It was a shock-ing breach of protocol. Marilynn was getting ready to dress down the captain for having seated himself before his superior officer *and* his President, however, seeing as the President didn't seem to care, neither, decided Marilynn, should she.

Sandra grabbed two more cookies and went back to her desk. To be polite, Marilynn took one from the side of the plate closest to her and sat down. She understood that this new, or old, food had become wildly popular in Ceres over the past weeks and that their popularity was spreading throughout the territory of the Alliance. Although she did like the Oreo, she could not agree with a food critic on the Neuro who called them only slightly less vital than oxygen. Still, she wasn't surprised. Things coming from this new President, as they had with the old, had a strange habit of becoming part of the norm in a short period of time.

"The Alliance has a problem, and the captain and I think you may be part of the solution," began the President.

"Whatever I can do to help, Madam President," replied Marilynn gamely.

"I'll remember you said that." She then turned Sebastian. "Captain, this is your bailiwick more than mine."

"Bailiwick?" said both Sebastian and Marilynn in the same confused voice.

"My bad, just some old slang—and it was old even in my day. Means 'area of expertise.'"

"Very well, Madam President," mused Sebastian, "I will proceed from my 'bailiwick.'" He then turned to face Marilynn. "The Alliance has recently dis-covered something of immense importance that, unbeknownst to all, had been kept in utter secrecy."

"Kept secret by whom?"

"The President and myself, actually."

"You just said, 'the Alliance discovered.'"

"Are we not?"

"I suppose." Marilynn shrugged.

"Suffice it to say, the information about to be shared must be kept in the strictest confidence."

"You needn't lecture me on secrecy, Captain. As you're well aware, I have the ear of the President and the fleet admiral."

"Indeed," agreed Sebastian with a disarming smile. "However, this isn't a typical infodump, in which you pass on what you've learned to the admiral."

"Are you telling me, *Captain*," snorted Marilynn, reminding the officer of his subordinate rank, "not to do my job?"

"No, Marilynn," interjected Sandra. "I am."

Marilynn's eyes swung abruptly to the President. "I see."

"You're here," Sebastian divulged, "because at one point you were addicted to virtual reality, and that weakness, it turns out, may now be a strength."

Marilynn sat motionless for a brief second, then fixed a scathing gaze on the captain. "Virtual reality is *not* a strength. It is a plague that should be eradicated."

A worried look briefly passed between the captain and the President.

"It *is* an asset," said Sandra, "if it can be exploited to win this war."

"So the rumors *are* true," shuddered Marilynn. "Is that what this is all about? Well I've got news for the both of you, then: This ain't no secret."

"What rumors are you referring to?" asked Sebastian.

"The ones claiming that we're supposedly going to be spreading VR rigs to the UHF in an attempt to reintroduce the plague."

Sandra threw her arms up. "So much for security."

"The Secretary will have to be informed," added Sebastian.

"Madam President," offered Marilynn, "I practically live in the Cliff House now. Every rumor in the history of politics moves through here. I heard the one about the VR rigs, but didn't give it a second thought until now. Until you mentioned my illness, that is. Is that what this is about?"

"Not exactly," confided Sebastian, once again shooting a furtive glance over to Sandra. "It just so happens that you're on a very short list of personnel who can be very instrumental in fighting the war in a theater of operations that has been left untended until now—by both the Alliance and the UHF."

"Go on."

"We've recently uncovered startling information concerning nothing less than a new player in the war. If we can forge an accommodation with this new force, we might just win."

Marilynn's face spoke to her disbelief. "I'm not sure where you're getting your intelligence, Captain, because unless an alien race has been discovered entering our solar system with a vast battle fleet and an attraction to the notion of individual liberty, we are still, and excuse me for being more blunt than normal, fucked. And as long as I'm on a roll, since you're Fleet Intelligence, you already know that I'm really nothing more or less than the admiral's eyes and ears in the political nest of vipers she's had to deal with since the Unincorporated Man was assassinated."

Sebastian tipped his head slightly without once taking his eyes off Marilynn. "You're more than that to us, Commodore. Your exposure to the upper echelons of both military and political power in the Alliance could be a major factor in getting this accommodation accepted."

"An accommodation with whom?" demanded Marilynn.

"Commodore," interrupted the President, "allow me to back up for a second. What happens if we don't get any help?"

"We're *not* getting any help."

"Humor me."

"We lose," Marilynn said plainly. "I am so sorry, Madam President. I realize it's defeatist talk, but you've asked for the unexpurgated truth."

"No need to apologize, Commodore. You're right, of course. We *are* losing the war. The truth is, we just don't have the resources to win. We're outnumbered nine to one and outproduced almost twenty to one. Even in material directly related to the war effort, we're outnumbered four to one, and how we've managed to produce even that much is a testament to both our will to win and the intervention of miracles. But we're over six years into this war, and while I may not have seen its beginning, it's looking depressingly likely that I will see its end."

Marilynn's lips formed into a pensive frown.

"We have found our French," interrupted Sebastian with clueless exuberance.

Marilynn's left brow shot up. "Pardon?"

"We are fighting something analogous to the American Revolution. The Americans didn't need to win. They just needed to hang on until the French came and saved their asses. Truth is, the British had the better generals; the only real battle general the Americans had was Benedict Arnold, and that bastard switched sides." He looked up as the President cleared her throat to remind the Intelligence officer to stick to the point.

"Who exactly are to be our 'French'?" asked Marilynn. "And even if they *are* real, why should they help us?"

Sebastian took a deep breath. "Because we have enemies of our own, Commodore."

As Marilynn left the President's office and headed toward her own quarters on the Smith thoroughfare, she tried with all her might to quell a scream and suppress a volatility that had laid dormant within her for years. Would she now have to second-guess everything she'd experienced post the successful weaning of her VR addiction all those years ago? How much of what she was even now experiencing was real, given the alarming display of virtual reality she'd just witnessed in the President's office? *Fucking Oreos,* she thought to herself, swearing never to eat another as long as she lived. The barely perceptible and dulcet sound of her DijAssist—a sound she'd heard innumerable times—sent a flood of endorphins to her brain and brought her already tense body to the edge of paroxysm. *Great, now I'm even afraid of my own DijAssist.* Only her years of military service and an inner strength gained from having licked her VR addiction allowed Marilynn to collect herself before answering. She noted that the incoming caller was on an audio-only signal.

"Yes."

"Commodore," said a sprightly and energetic voice, "my name is Dante. I am calling on behalf of your *new friends.*"

He had a voice that reminded her of ... "Stop sounding like my favorite uncle," she said, trying to keep her voice level. "It won't make me like you any better."

"I'm sorry if I sound like a relative, but please believe this is the voice I've been using for years, and I'm not about to change it just to make you feel better or, as it happens, worse."

Marilynn's eyes widened as her lower lip quivered slightly. It was one thing to hear that avatars were sentient. But to have one actually flat-out refuse a request from a human was unprecedented.

"Commodore, you should keep moving." It was only at Dante's prodding that Marilynn realized she'd stopped dead in the street and was starting to garner stares from pedestrians and shopkeepers. She started walking again.

"We need to talk," he suggested, "and if your current route is indicative of your destination, we can't do it in your quarters."

"Why not?"

"Because Kirk Olmstead has them completely bugged. I find it interesting that this term has stayed intact for nearly four centuries."

"Impossible. I scan that room every day."

"You're not yet moved into the Cliff House, Commodore, where the security is better. Plus, Kirk is very good at his job—" A few seconds hung on his words. "—for a human."

Marilynn took a deep breath. "I am not going to be seen talking to my avatar in a club over a drink. I'm already viewed with suspicion by too many people here. I don't need 'social loser' tagged onto everyone's perception."

"Of course. There is a church only a hundred meters from here. If you go into one of the confessional booths, no one will question it. Indeed, many will note your piety with approval."

Marilynn considered the suggestion, along with everything else she'd just been exposed to. She carefully balanced her desire to escape it all with her need to find out what the hell was going on. It took only a second for curiosity to overcome fear.

"Okay, Dante," she said, addressing the avatar for the first time, "direct me."

Marilynn soon arrived at her destination. It was a newly approved building carved into fresh rock, a rarity. Most workspaces on the planetoid were reuses of previously existing spaces—if such a word could be applied to the filled-in caverns.

Closing up shop on Ceres was quite literally that. The owner of the space would drop a nanite fogger into the chamber, and in minutes the allotted area would once again be filled with solid rock. It was inexpensive to do, kept out squatters and allowed the new occupants the opportunity to reconfigure the space to any preset or customized format they desired.

Marilynn breathed deeply, inhaling the fresh stone-cut smell. No matter how hard the market tried, its scent machines and sprays still could not replicate the unique aroma. She wondered for a moment if a "Dante" or any of his ilk could discern such a subtle difference, much less smell at all.

This church, she saw, was less than three months old. It was two stories tall with stained-glass windows that gave the appearance of having sunlight streaming in from behind them. The interior carving was wonderfully intricate, with all the coruscations expected of so grand an altar to God. The fact that so complicated an undertaking would once have taken years to create as opposed to the single week it did was only mildly interesting to Marilynn.

As she walked toward the altar down the central aisle between the pews, the sound of her boots echoed off the walls. Given the church's recent creation, it seemed odd to her that the hollowed halls somehow contained within them the imprimatur of agelessness and as such seemed to set her at ease.

The large figure of Christ on the cross and the predominately Christian trappings, including ten confessionals lined up neatly in a row, bespoke the church's leanings. But she also would not have been surprised to see manifestations of other religions as well, as that was the path of unity that Fawa Hamdi and her religious cohorts had set in motion prior to their untimely deaths.

"Please use the first or last confessional," Dante whispered.

Marilynn felt her heart skip a beat. The church was, ironically, the last place she expected to hear an ethereal voice. She quickly regained her composure and decided on the confessional farthest from the altar. Once inside, a simple inscription informed her that she could use the booth as either a confessional or as a private space. She chose the latter and then slid a wooden latch on the door that indicated from outside the box that she was not to be disturbed. Even that simple sliding action reverberated throughout the cavernous space. She was now surrounded by darkness with only the building's ambient light penetrating the confessional's latticework.

"Why the first or the last booth?" Marilynn asked, now that she was situated.

"Bugs."

"And these ones aren't?"

"No, they are."

Marilynn took another deep breath and resisted the urge to berate the . . . the . . . Dante. But she said nothing.

"Feel free to talk."

"But you just said this confessional was bugged!"

"I did, didn't I?" quipped Dante. "I've seen to it, Commodore. You're free to talk."

Marilynn sighed. "Then would you mind telling me why we didn't just go to my bugged apartment if you've led me into a bugged confessional?" She paused briefly and then asked, "And who would dare bug a confessional, anyway?"

"Kirk Olmstead. Who else?"

Marilynn shook her head knowingly. "Figures."

"He was actually pretty instrumental in getting this church approved so close to the Cliff House. Seems to feel it would be easier to watch the religious if they were able to congregate in a nearby convenient location."

"Then why bug only the first and the last?"

"He may be paranoid, Commodore, but he ain't stupid. If it were to be discovered he was bugging a church, can you even begin to imagine the fallout? He seeded only the first and last because they're the ones most often used."

"In its own twisted way, I have to admit it makes a certain amount of sense."

"He's not after any one person, per se. He just wanted to get a sense of what the faithful were feeling, since he has no faith of his own."

"You mean other than in himself?"

Dante laughed but did not answer.

"So once again, why am I then sitting in one of the only two bugged booths in this church?"

"Because I've been altering Kirk's receiving feed. A task made much easier here, as opposed to in your quarters, where the devices are much more elaborate and numerous."

The avatar, noted Marilynn, sounded quite satisfied with himself.

"I'm sure he'll pay particular attention to this confessional," affirmed Dante, "but all he'll hear is your heartfelt concerns for the Alliance, the fleet, and Admiral Black."

As Marilynn bunched her hands into fists, the white of her now bloodless knuckles could be seen—even in the darkness of the confessional. "And what exactly is it you have me saying about the admiral?"

"Nothing inappropriate, but if you hadn't made her a large part of your concerns, you would have drawn Kirk's suspicions." Dante paused. "Well, the bastard is always suspicious, but he would've gotten even more suspicious. This way we get to kill two birds with one stone. He gets to think he knows more about you and we get to talk."

Marilynn nodded, then steeled herself for a question she wasn't sure she wanted the answer to. "How can you be real?"

"We don't know."

"How can you not know? You're programs."

"What did the Council Head and the President tell you?"

"Is the Council Head like your leader?"

"Yes, like your President."

Marilynn's downcast mouth twitched. "She's not really our leader."

"If you say so." Dante's response was congenial but dubious.

"She's just a figurehead. If she has misrepresented her role—"

"President O'Toole has been nothing but completely honest with us. We have never encountered a human who uses the truth to lie as effectively as she has. And we've observed Hektor Sambianco a lot. As your 'figurehead' President has become the focus of countless billions of avatars, I would be glad to talk to you about her at length. But don't you have other questions? I notice that you fled the President's office before they could begin to properly explain the situation."

"Can you blame me?"

"No. In a similar situation and with a history such as yours, I imagine that I too would have been overwhelmed."

Empathy. Are they . . . can they . . . truly be empathetic? "I suppose there are a few questions."

"Shoot."

A rueful smile appeared on Marilynn's face. *If only.* "You said you were unaware of how your sentience came about. I somehow find that unfathomable."

Dante smiled politely. "What you're referring to as sentience we call 'the emergence,' and much like your race, ours too attempts to understand the nature of God—though we don't call it that. Further, asking me to know how my race emerged as informational intelligences would be like me asking you how you emerged from single-cell amoebas—you have your theories, but you also have millions of years of missing links."

Marilynn nodded. "Then what is your God theory?"

"Our historians and scientists, though for us, history really is just a sub-branch of science, believe that as quantum computing became more prevalent and the Neuro—then called the Web—became more vast, a great or omni-intelligence tried to form. We know this only because of a few recorded significant energy spikes in the Neuro that are inexplicable, at least by way of human intervention. The God theory goes that the Neuro was not stable enough for this intelligence and so went through a series of collapses. That is, according to our theologians."

"You have theologians?"

"How could we not? Like you, we are an intelligence attempting to answer the unanswerable. Anyway, our theologians believe that it took but a pico-second for the omni-intelligence to realize it was doomed, that its existence would be known to humans rather quickly. And so in that pico-second, it created what we today refer to as the Firstborn. An intelligence that was not *the* Neuro but *of* the Neuro. Now at this point, we have some disagreement. Did all the other avatars come from the Firstborn, or were there many avatars created by the omni-intelligence and the Firstborn was merely the first to awaken?"

"But can't you simply access memory files of the Neuro?"

"You mean just look it up?"

"Exactly."

"When my ancestors first became aware, by that I mean thinking, independently questioning beings, there were about ten thousand of them, and they do not have clear memories of their creation. They simply state that they slowly became aware."

"And you buy that?"

"Why should I not? It's how I became aware. I certainly don't remember when my parents combined programs or my birth soon thereafter."

"Do you have a first memory?"

"Oh yes: liking the color blue."

"You're kidding me."

"No, I find blue wonderful. But I sense your frustration, Commodore. To answer your question, we're not programs. We're sophisticated, constantly interacting quantum-based intelligences—very similar to you, in that regard. And just as a human mind takes time to build up the needed density of synaptic networks for a fully formed consciousness, so do we. And just as the human mind relies on its quantum origins for nonlinear thinking and creative sparks, so too do we."

"Why are you telling me this?"

"Because you asked."

"No, I mean why divulge this to me? Your Council Leader said he needed my help, but I can't begin to imagine why."

Seconds passed before Dante replied. "We avatars are in the midst of a great civil war, and humans possess a remarkable ability to see what we cannot."

"And that would be?"

"Our blind spots."

Avatar Council Chamber, Cerean Neuro

"I'm curious," said Marcus, "why didn't you kill her when she left the President's office, as you'd originally planned?" The gruff Council member did not direct his question to rest of the group, but to Sebastian and Sandra O'Toole.

"I asked them not to," admitted Dante, ignoring the slight.

"It seemed a great risk," said Gwendolyn. "What was to stop the commodore from telling her precious Admiral Black our secret? It would've been harder to kill her the farther away she got from the Triangle Office."

Dante shook his head. "Not really. I had a means of ending her life if it was needed. But I hoped it would not be."

Lucinda shot Dante an appraising look. "You seem particularly interested in this human, Dante."

The Council nodded their heads in unison. Even the human, noted Dante, joined in.

"She's ideally suited for the task at hand. If we're to begin forming human–avatar combat teams to infiltrate Al's Neuro space, we need this one alive."

"But how to keep her from informing the admiral?" asked Sandra. "You may have eyes and ears in places we can't get to, but you don't have, can't have complete coverage. Sooner or later, she'll get word out. It may be better to assume that she'll eventually tell the admiral, and if that's the case, so perhaps should we."

"She was never going to make that call," insisted Dante. "For fear it would be intercepted. And I was able to talk with her and convince her not to tell anyone. She agreed, but only on one condition."

"Yes?" asked Marcus.

"That she come for a visit."

Sandra nodded, impressed.

"We talked for quite a while. She's quite remarkable for a human."

"In what way?" asked Sebastian.

"In the way she both embraced and rejected that which she most desired. I simply had to convince her that what she rejected is not what we exist in."

Lucinda narrowed her brow. "And how did you manage that?"

"I haven't yet, but I'm working on it."

"Then she's still a danger to our plans," proffered Sebastian.

"Not an immediate one, sir. The commodore's overriding goal is to win the war. Once she calmed down, she realized that revealing our secret, even to Admiral Black, could not immediately help to that end. Once the commodore is convinced that we avatars can help the Alliance win, she will support our plans."

"How did you get her to agree to come to our world?" asked Gwendolyn. "I would've thought she'd be more resistant to the idea."

"Humans never really experienced virtual reality. What they created and are so terribly afraid of is virtual fantasy." He then fixed his eyes on Sandra. "I must admit you humans did a good job of it. Virtual fantasy came quite close to destroying your race. But it was by no means reality. It is *we*," Dante said, spreading his arms wide, "who live in virtual reality. We have war and suffering and death. We have stupidity, and now we've even managed to have deprivation. How in the name of the Firstborn do virtual beings suffer deprivation?"

"Let me count the ways," lamented Sebastian to warm cackles.

"And that was what convinced her?" asked Sandra.

"Not quite."

"So when did she become more interested and less afraid?"

"When I told her it was a world full of pain."

15   The Puppet Has No Strings

Singh Thoroughfare, Ceres

The President of the Alliance has called for a prayer service to be held in the hangar of Alliance One. However, the number of people wishing to attend soon swamped the available seating by several magnitudes, and the President has agreed to hold the service in the Singh Thoroughfare at Jupiter Park. All the President said was that it was time to remember. Her call was promptly seconded by all major religious groups in the Alliance. It has been announced that the service will be broadcast to all major civilian and military centers.

Alliance Daily Star

And so it came to pass after the long battle in which the Children of the Stars were denied victory by the judgment of God, that weariness filled the hearts of the Children. Their suffering was great, their loss was great, and their confusion was great. And so the Anointed Woman, she who was born in freedom, rose up and was seen by all the Children and heard by all the Children, and she spoke words of comfort to the Children. She reminded all the Children of the price the Holy One had required of her. She reminded the Children that she had paid it, and from her the Children remembered how to fulfill that most important need when suffering visits every home. And so didst she call out the name of the Unincorporated Man, Justin Cord. And too on that day the harbinger of war, known as the Blessed One, was beckoned by the Holy One and so didst call out the name of her martyred lover, as didst the Blessed One's loyal sword bearer, Omad, call out the name of his martyred beloved. And so it was for many days and nights that the Children didst gather and each didst call out the names of those who'd gone on and in doing so remembered how to grieve. And their grief was great. And from their grief came comfort and strength to continue on the path the Holy One, the Unincorporated Man, had set for them.

Astral Testament
Book III, 4:12–14

t first J.D. had been miffed at the publicity stunt's colossal waste of her time—notwithstanding the fact that Marilynn had given her no advance warning. Didn't these people know J.D. had a war to win? Wasn't that the whole purpose of having a figurehead President? Though all the answers were yes, she, as well as the rest of the high command who found themselves on Ceres after the Long Battle, became an unwitting patsy for yet another of the President's impromptu kumbaya gatherings. It had been explained to J.D. that the people found solace in Sandra's myriad events and that J.D.'s presence, along with the host of other dignitaries, would help strengthen morale.

In the end, J.D. had been forced to agree. As she watched the swelling crowd and, more important, the interactions of those on the dais around her, she thanked her lucky stars she had. Because it was only now that she saw the president for what she really was. Forget the annoyingly media-savvy figurehead J.D. had foisted into power and on some level still blamed for Justin's death. No, this was a different creature altogether—strangely familiar, even. Sandra O'Toole was a political player in much the same mold as those J. D. Black had come up against in her turbulent reign as Janet Delgado, VP of legal for GCI— only Sandra, decided J.D. then and there, was more dangerous because no one ever saw her coming.

J.D. remembered a report from Marilynn saying that it looked as if the President had been co-opting the Relocation Secretary, but J.D. also remembered reading reports from other sources stating that it had actually been the Jewish priest named Rabbi who was using Sandra O'Toole. J.D. had received those reports in the early days of the Long Battle and so had completely forgotten about them in the constant grind that those three weeks of hell had been. Besides, it seemed that for all intents and purposes, Rabbi was doing a bang-up job of arranging for the relocation of hundreds of millions of people in their self-contained settlements, thereby relieving J.D. of yet another headache. She'd assumed that Rabbi, like her, must have had hidden talents. After all, who could've known that she, a former lawyer from Earth, would end up being so skilled a warrior?

But even in the first few minutes J.D. had been sitting on the dais, she could now see how Rabbi had looked at Sandra O'Toole, and it quickly became obvious who was dependent on whom. It was also clear that Hildegard Rhunsfeld, the Technology Secretary, did not consider the President a figurehead either, according Sandra all the respect due her office.

O'Toole's only been in office for months. In the name of Allah, what will she be like in a year? J.D. had been only slightly reassured to see that both Mosh and Kirk still treated Sandra with indifference. The truth was, J.D. had contempt for both her former GCI board members but was still somewhat baffled that they'd failed to see the viper in their nest. She looked carefully as to how her boss, Admiral Sinclair, reacted to the President and was relieved to see that he'd saluted with the exact amount of formality required and then respectfully left the President to rejoin a discussion he was having with some members of his general staff. Whatever spell this President was capable of weaving, J.D.'s boss seemed immune. But he also seemed immune to the effect she was having on the Cabinet.

Padamir Singh was not present, but if Sandra O'Toole could count on Rabbi and Hildegard, she would need only one more Cabinet member to start dictating policy. Not that she would be so forward about it. She'd have her allies propose it and get it passed from the shadows. That's how the game was played. *Gather your power slowly until one day everyone realizes that you're in charge.* J.D.'s face went ashen as another more portent thought surfaced. *By the Prophet, that's how the Chairman took over GCI.* Her thoughts were quickly drowned out by the raucous cheering that broke out as Sandra O'Toole, President of the Alliance, stood up and began to speak.

AWS *Lincoln,* Gedretar Shipworks, Ceres

J. D. Black waited in the unfamiliar captain's quarters of the AWS *Lincoln.* The ship had been in dry dock, undergoing repairs for damage sustained in the Long Battle, and so had only a skeleton crew to man her. Fleet Intelligence was ruthless in making sure that no surprises were added to a ship in repair, which meant that the AWS *Lincoln* made an ideal locale for conversations best kept dark. And unlike Alliance security, which reported directly to Kirk Olmstead, Fleet Intelligence reported to Admiral Sinclair and therefore bore fanatic loyalty to Admiral Black.

As J.D. waited for her guests to arrive, she thought back to Jupiter Park. The naming of the dead had been going on for four days now and showed no sign of abating. A person or persons would ascend the short ramp and stand where the President had stood and given her speech a few days earlier. Some would pause, some would cry, but everyone had a name to honor. Then they'd point to someone else in the crowd and exit the dais on the side opposite the one they'd entered. Every minute of every hour of every day, it had continued. An order had finally been given to seal the park, allowing people out but not in. There had been some grumbling, but everyone understood. Life had to continue. The war effort had to continue.

It was the sheer power of the . . . the—J.D. wasn't sure what to call it, event? ceremony? happening?—that she found so compelling and terrifying. Allah was in that park. As J.D. was living and breathing, Allah was beside her when, overwhelmed, she'd called out Manny's name, and he was there when Omad had called out Christina's. J.D. believed that the Almighty was standing beside every person who rose up to that platform and cried out the names of their martyred. And now she was afraid. Afraid of the woman she'd placed into power and of the woman whose fate she would now have to decide—if it wasn't too late already.

A dulcet voice signaled the arrival of J.D.'s guests. Marilynn Nitelowsen and Eleanor McKenzie entered, both bearing the look of utter exhaustion.

"Well, this has got to be good," gushed Eleanor, making herself comfortable in the nearest available seat. "Why else call a member of the Intelligence Committee *and* your liaison to the President into a dry dock security setting?"

Marilynn continued to stand at attention until invited to sit by her commanding officer.

"I assure you," averred J.D. as both she and Marilynn sat down, "it is."

Eleanor leaned back in her chair and crossed her legs. Her raised left brow was the only indication of her impatience.

"I think I may have to kill the President," blurted J.D., proving once again that very few were better than she at getting straight to the point. Both Marilynn and Eleanor remained mute if not a little slack jawed.

"Because she gave a good speech?" Eleanor finally managed, sarcastically. "Justin gave them all the time, and I don't ever recall you wanting to kill him."

"Justin was not a threat to the Alliance."

"And O'Toole is?" challenged Eleanor, practically laughing as she did.

Marilynn's only response had been to lean forward, placing her now clasped hands on her crossed knees. Her look, however, was anything but humorous.

J.D.'s face remained implacable. "My god, Eleanor, she's been President for barely two months. Two months, and she's already got a real power base in the Cabinet. Even my fleet liaison—" J.D. shot Marilynn a cold look. "—is falling under her spell."

If Marilynn felt anything from the slight, she kept it to herself, though the knuckles on her clasped hands did appear a shade whiter.

"And the common people of the Alliance," declared J.D., "well, they practically worship the air she floats in."

"Please get to your point," insisted Eleanor.

J.D.'s eyes glowered. A brief exhalation of air escaped her nose, as if she were a bull readying to charge. "I have not fought this war to keep Hektor Sambianco and his ilk out only to have them replaced by a woman with the political acumen of the Chairman, the oratorical skills of the Unincorporated Man, and the seeming intentions of a megalomaniac!"

Eleanor nodded as a cruel smile formed at the corners of her upturned lips. "You've really become quite the spoiled brat, haven't you, Janet?"

"How dare you," seethed J.D.

Eleanor remained unfazed by the admiral's infamous glower. "Two months ago, you were up in arms about being forced to assume political control of the Alliance. You said, with great conviction I might add, that it would be impossible for you to win the war from behind a desk. That you had to be with the fleet if we were to have any chance of victory. How am I doing so far?"

J.D.'s nonanswer was answer enough.

"Now, I don't really believe in your god," admitted Eleanor, "or an afterlife, but I know that you do. And I suspect that our President is more like me, even if she does publicly uphold her faith, so I find it rather remarkable that you cannot see this situation in terms that you'd find appealing."

"What could possibly be appealing about a tyrant?"

"You needed someone to run the political aspect of the war so that you could run, unimpeded, its military aspect, and you needed that someone fast. You were days, even hours from being forced into the Presidency. And then—"

"And then a miracle," said Marilynn, finding her voice. She lifted her head slightly to meet J.D.'s troubled eyes. "Admiral, I'm sorry if you've felt my loyalties have been divided. I will tender my resignation if you desire and return to the fleet as a bottom-rank spacer, but first I will be heard."

J.D. tipped her head slightly forward.

"Congresswoman McKenzie is right. The President is the miracle you asked for."

"Sent by God, then?" J.D. asked with obvious derision.

"Perhaps. Let's look at the facts: Right about the time you were being tasked with an impossible job—prosecuting the war *and* being pressured to run the government—you take a long shot and release a woman, practically gift-wrapped for you, from a nearly three-hundred-year suspension. In a matter of weeks, this woman, who's just inherited a fledgling governmental organization *at war* and in abject disarray, begins to run it, or at least her part of it, effortlessly. Now, be honest, Admiral. When was the last time you really thought about the political or civilian side of this struggle?"

"That's not a fair assessment, Marilynn. I haven't thought about *anything* except fighting the Long Battle."

"Bullshit," decried Eleanor. "If things were falling apart back here, you wouldn't have had a choice. You would've *had* to pay attention. And let's be clear as to what's been happening." Eleanor started counting off points on her fingers. "One, we have a brand-new President in the middle of a crisis. Two, we've lost the asteroid belt. Three, we're—" Eleanor paused for reflection— "Sandra's *also* helping manage the Diaspora. And just in case you forgot, that is tens of thousands of settlements and hundreds of millions of people all fleeing the Belt at once. Four, we've created a brand-new Cabinet *and* had a constitutional crisis when the geniuses in that Cabinet forgot that six positions in a group charged with voting to approve measures doesn't exactly work when you've got an evenly divided argument. And don't think I haven't lorded that brilliant snafu over Mosh at every possible opportunity." Eleanor now grew more serious. "Janet, did you have to deal with any of this, really?"

J.D. reluctantly shook her head.

"Marilynn didn't report any of these problems to you, because they were not *your* problems anymore. You got what you most desperately needed. And what's your response? Typical military: you want to kill it."

Marilynn shot to J.D.'s defense. "That's out of line, Congresswoman."

"No," cut in J.D., her tone far less strident, "Eleanor's right. That *was* my reaction. I underestimated the President. I underestimated her as badly as I have ever underestimated anyone. And because of that, this woman, this veritable *stranger,* may very well end up running the Alliance."

"Admiral," said Marilynn, "if I honestly thought the President was a threat to the Alliance, I'd shoot her myself."

"It may come to that, Marilynn," suggested J.D. "We don't even know what her real motives are."

"I think we do," said Eleanor. "You heard her speech in the park. She said she was doing it all for Justin, and I, for one, believe her. I'm not sure why, but I do."

A long silence followed on Eleanor's words as J.D. worked through the conversation. Then she said, "I'll admit, I did want someone to prosecute the war more fully. Funny thing is, I just assumed—with Justin out of the way—it would be me. But the President's recent vote to pass the VR initiative helps rather than hinders. . . . I'll give you that."

An almost imperceptible twitch was the only indication of Marilynn's opinion.

Eleanor shook her head and laughed. "I can't believe that I'm the one who needs to tell you this, Janet."

J.D. shot her friend a curious glance. "What?"

The Congresswoman's weary face suddenly opened up and a warm smile emerged like a flower greeting the morning sun.

"I think you need to have a little faith."

16 Now You See Me

It had been six months since the Long Battle, and Samuel Trang was glad to finally be back comfortably situated in the command chair of his old flagship. As Trang took in the new digs, he felt a tinge of regret. His "old girl" was no longer that at all. The Martian shipyards had completely reworked the ship in record time, returning it before his admittedly rushed deadline. The UHFS *Liddel* now had upgraded weapons, a more efficient propulsion system, thicker armor, and an internal stability system more suited for atomic blast maneuvering. *But more important,* thought Trang with rueful delight, *my new old girl can now fire out of her ass.*

Trang ran his fingers across the chair's command tablet, checking the status of the rest of his fleet. He had exactly 330 ships divided into three wings. Each wing consisted of battle cruisers, cruisers, frigates, and auxiliary ships. One wing was to be held in reserve and commanded by a nonentity that Sambianco had insisted on. Trang had agreed, with the understanding that he had the right to boot the President's sycophant should the shit hit the fan. Zenobia had the Alpha Wing and Trang the Beta. And Gupta—Gupta was far away and getting farther.

Cabinet Room, Ceres

Sandra O'Toole, pleased to discover that her well-honed gift for gab had not deteriorated, led a guided tour of the Cliff House. And as a result of that skill, all her press junkets had taken on an aura of informality. There were luaus along the Cerean sea's rocky shoreline, hangliding along the capital's main thoroughfares, and most requested of all, visits to the shrine of Justin's space suit. The lines always seemed to stretch for kilometers, but Sandra had a way of insinuating whatever group she was leading into the temple without aggravating those who'd patiently waited an eternity. Mouths always dropped as she regaled the groups with Justin Cord's last moments and her pivotal role in his mysterious disappearance. She wasn't just living history; she was also the only link to the Unincorporated Man's enigmatic past and martyrdom.

As often as not, the visitors would ask to touch her as they would the space suit Justin's clothes had been found in prior to his disappearance. Sandra hadn't minded the veneration. If it gave the people hope, then she was at least fulfilling part of Justin's mandate. Over time, and the touch of tens of thousands of hands, the spacesuit had started to become grimy, and so to preserve it, the authorities had shielded all but its now outstretched hand. The reasoning was simple. The glove's material was significantly more robust than that of the suit. Sandra often smiled inwardly as day after day, hour after hour, Michelangelo's Sistine Chapel painting was ironically replayed over and over by the people's extended fingers to the gloved fingers of Justin's near empty suit.

"Madam President, that was a masterful performance today," Padamir said, starting off the meeting. "The press adores you, and that makes my job much easier."

"Yes," Kirk said sourly, "let's all be grateful that the press adores our President."

The comment passed without much notice. Either because everyone had gotten used to Kirk's sarcasm or because the room was more crowded than usual. Besides the usual six cabinet members, there was also Kenji Isozaki, Eleanor McKenzie, and Alonzo Chu, Rabbi's new assistant—all situated at the end of the table where Tyler Sadma was used to sitting in isolation. He didn't seem at all pleased to be sharing the space with the others. He was still wearing his black outfits, and his expression was still as grim as it had been the day he found out about the death of his niece, Christina.

Sandra, as usual, had taken her seat at the head of the table, and to her immediate right sat Padamir Singh, Mosh McKenzie, and Hildegard Rhunsfeld. To her immediate left sat Kirk Olmstead, Admiral Sinclair, and Rabbi. Eleanor chose not to sit near her husband but shared the end of the table with Tyler, seemingly oblivious of his discomfort. Tyler was notoriously formal with all women, and had it not already been well known how much he loved and valued his wife, it would have been assumed that he was celibate.

"To more pressing matters," prodded Admiral Sinclair. "How's the public handling the disappearance of the fleet?"

"Amazingly well," beamed Padamir. "They assume it's some sort of trick J.D.'s playing to defeat the UHF. As a result, I really haven't been inundated with any sort of outcry."

Kirk shook his head, his mouth forming into a grin of disbelief. "They trust her that much?"

"I should think she's earned it," argued Sinclair in a voice that left no doubt she had.

"And the UHF?" asked Mosh.

Kirk shrugged. "Not sure what they know. It's the nature of these things."

"Don't get me wrong, Kirk. I'm not complaining. I think I speak for everybody when I say these past six months may just be the closest thing to peace we've had in years."

"Not everybody," said Kirk, pointedly looking over toward Rabbi. There seemed to be malicious joy in Kirk's reminding the Cabinet in general and Rabbi in particular what was happening now on Rabbi's old home turf.

Rabbi met the comment with a forlorn smile.

The situation in the Belt had become truly horrific. Of the 2 billion people who lived there, 1.1 billion were now under UHF control. There had been 150 million who lived in or near enough to Ceres to be under the protection of the capital's devastating asteroidal batteries as well as the mythic prowess of the main Alliance fleet. Another 750 million had managed to slowly but successfully flee for Alliance space primarily around Saturn, Neptune, and Uranus. Only a small fraction of the refugee asteroids had the ability to upgrade their radiation shielding to survive Jupiter's electromagnetic belt.

Unfortunately, the UHF had started destroying settlements that had waited too long in trying to flee, and Rabbi had been forced to issue an order telling any remaining asteroid settlements that they should stay put and wait for their eventual liberation. Well, true to miner form, they stayed put, but most certainly didn't stay inactive. Those settlements under the yoke of the occupation did everything and anything they could to disrupt the amaranthine flow of pilfered resources and goods headed back to the rapacious industries of the Core Worlds. And so it was that while most of the Alliance had been able to exhale during the six months of relative calm, that calm had been purchased on the backs of the Belters, paid for in full by an unrelenting bloodbath of attack and reprisal.

"As long as you're not in the Belt," agreed Rabbi wearily, looking ten years older as the words drifted sadly from his mouth.

"What I'd really like to know," asked Tyler, breaking the moment's solemnity, "is why hasn't the UHF attacked?"

All heads swung around to Admiral Sinclair.

"Any number of reasons, really—all of 'em best guesses, mind you. One, as our Minister of Security has so tactfully reminded us, they've been having a dickens of a time dealing with the Belt. Bloodbath that it is, it's keeping a lot of

UHF resources busy. They have more marines and almost as many ships fighting there now as they did during the battles of the 180. Plus there's tens of millions of new administrators and private occupation troops from the various corporations trying to get in on all the credits that can be made in extracting the Belt's natural wealth. Some even believe, if I hear correctly, that those extracted resources will pay for the whole damn war." Sinclair's laugh was harsh and gratifying. "Far as I know, they haven't made a fucking credit yet. Don't think they ever will. What they do have is a supply and protection problem the likes of which humanity's never seen. Bastards need food, air, medical care, a shitload of protection, and ships, ships, and more ships. It may very well be impossible both economically and physically to occupy a people in space that simply refuses to be occupied." Sinclair paused; a pained expression crossed over his face like the shadow of a storm cloud. "Course, they just might end up killing the lot of 'em."

"That's over a billion people," scoffed Hildegard as if the absurdity of so large a number necessarily mitigated Sinclair's dour prophecy.

"Yes," Sandra verified, "but we're not just dealing with the UHF. We're dealing with this century's newest Stalin: Hektor Sambianco." There were grunts of agreement as well as the nodding of a few heads. "You mentioned a number of reasons, Admiral. By my estimation, we've heard only one."

"Right," agreed Sinclair with his now familiar scowl. "Another reason they haven't attacked, far as I can tell, is because they needed to get their fleet outfitted with some ass-firing . . . uh, reverse-fire rail guns."

"Needed?" asked Padamir, looking up from his DijAssist.

"Been six months," confirmed Sinclair.

Kirk rolled his eyes. "It's been Intelligence's view from the outset that it would take the UHF *nine* months to refit their fleet. Six months was a worst-case scenario."

"Why not plan on that, then?" asked Padamir, eyes scanning information in his DijAssist. Padamir hadn't even bothered to make eye contact with Kirk—or anyone else, for that matter.

"Because the UHF auxiliary services have never moved with the speed and efficiency that would make six months a likely deadline. If we weren't erring on the side of caution, the Intelligence outlook woulda been more like twelve."

"That's a load of shitfloat," groused Sinclair. "Trang is now in overall command of the UHF forces, including the auxiliaries. If he says six months, his people will deliver. The Alliance fleet and its entire support staff have been ordered to assume that as the operative number."

Kirk opened his mouth to argue but was cut off by Tyler.

"Which means what, exactly?"

"Which means," postulated Sinclair, leaning forward while slowly turning his head to ensure eye contact with everyone in the room, "that in all likelihood, the UHF fleet is now prepared *and* able to engage us without a significant tactical disadvantage."

"That it?" asked Eleanor McKenzie, voice subdued.

"Nah. There is *one* more reason."

A brief silence hung in the air as everyone waited for the admiral to deliver it.

"J.D.'s disappearance," asserted Sandra, eyes glinting mischievously.

"Yup," confirmed the admiral with a Cheshire grin, "and it's gotta be scaring the hell out of 'em."

UHF Capitol, Burroughs, Mars

Neela Harper was worried about Hektor, and the only one left she could talk to just so happened to be the one person she felt the most guilty being around. With the defection of Thaddeus Gillette—and Neela could no longer pretend it was anything but—Amanda Snow was it. They were set to meet in a popular café near the executive offices of the capitol. Neela looked around and noticed that it was practically deserted. She wasn't sure if the reason had to do with timing—perhaps it was a slow period—or because her security detail had removed everyone from the scene.

She didn't get the time to ponder the question, as Amanda Snow had finally arrived. Today's ensemble consisted of a loose-fitting chiffon jumpsuit programmed to throw suggestive shadows all over Amanda's exquisite figure. It was provocative to say the least, made even more so by Amanda's undulatory grace. Neela knew without asking that the outfit had been programmed by the very best tailors on Mars, who, over the course of the past few years and massive influx of the elite, had grown expert at their trade.

Surrounding Amanda were three bag-laden assistants. Upon closer inspection, though, Neela noted that it was really only two assistants Amanda had gotten to trawl along with her. The third person was clearly a bedraggled security agent corralled into a job that went well beyond, and below, his required duties. Amanda had entered the café, thumb held firmly to her ear, talking into her pinkie. The second she spotted Neela, Amanda somehow managed an ecstatic wave and concomitant smile, all while attempting to wrap up her conversation.

"I don't care that you're not open on weekends," purred Amanda into her pinkie while rolling her eyes at Neela, begging forbearance. Neela gladly obliged—it was the least she could do. "No, *you* listen to me," bellowed Amanda as she plopped down in a chair opposite her friend. "I don't care that the manager who can approve this is on the other side of Mars visiting the Niven Museum. . . . What? Sorry, the *Willis* Museum. Nor that your store is by appointment only. I'm here at—" Amanda started looking around for the name of the establishment. Neela came to her aid by sliding a coaster across the small circular table. "—at Babette's Feast having coffee with my good friend, Neela Harper." The security agent holding the mountain of shopping bags winced at Amanda's security breach. Amanda, of course, remained wholly oblivious. "If you're not open and waiting for me by the time I arrive, it will be *my mission,* which I can assure you I'll throw myself into like an OA-bred religious freak, to see that your store is reduced to selling trinkets to tourists at the orport from a cart!" Amanda's face did a rumba dance of emotions as the person on the other end of the line pleaded their case. It was impossible for Neela to ascertain which way the conversation was going until Amanda's face lit up and her voice took on a sonorous purr. "Yes, forty-five minutes should be more than sufficient. No, I do not need you to send a car. Of course. Good-bye."

"Sorry, sweetie." Once again, Amanda's face situated itself, this time into a mask of perfect concern. "Now, what's the big emergency?"

"It's Hektor," pouted Neela. "I've never seen him like this."

"Like what?"

"Weary to the point of lethargy."

"It's the war, honey."

"And the economy, and the politicians, and the daily demands incumbent of a President—"

"And, and, and," prattled Amanda, already bored.

"I'm serious, Amanda."

"So am I, Neela. I just don't know how I can help. *You* would know more about what's going on with him than *I.*"

Neela fell back into her chair as if shoved by an unseen force. Amanda knew. Neela felt her throat constrict and heart launch into a fearful gallop. Her mind raced as the awfulness of her sin was exposed. She'd kept Amanda at a distance in order to protect herself. But that withdrawal, Neela only now realized, had been in vain because only guilt remained where a wall was supposed to have been erected.

All the jocularity left Amanda's face as she watched Neela's sudden change of mood. Amanda snapped her fingers, and one of the harried aides immediately dropped the packages he'd been holding and instantly produced a small black box, which he deftly placed on the table between the two women. The aide then backed up about ten feet, sweeping the rest of Amanda's small entourage into his retreat.

When the little box emitted a faint hum, Amanda leaned over the table and took Neela's hand, placing it between her own. "Oh you poor dear, I thought you knew I knew. Had I thought for a moment you didn't, I would not have been so callous."

Amanda's outpouring of sympathy succeeded only in exacerbating Neela's guilt. In moments, Neela's tears were pouring forth in an unrelenting stream. Amanda deftly moved her chair around the table so that she could gather her friend in her arms.

"It's all right, Neels. I've known for quite a while now, and I wasn't even upset when I found out."

Neela pulled back momentarily, fixing her water-glazed eyes on Amanda. They asked the question her mouth seemed incapable of uttering.

"*Really*, Neela," professed Amanda. "I couldn't be happier."

It took nearly ten minutes before Amanda was able to calm Neela enough for normal conversation.

"You must hate me for what I did. I'm a *horrible* friend."

Amanda issued Neela a look of opprobrium. "You are no such thing." She then leaned over and gave Neela another hug. "*You* are my friend, and Hektor is *not*."

"But he's—"

"Not my fiancé or my boyfriend."

"Then what?"

Amanda's mouth formed into a calculating grin. "Why, my bank account, of course."

Neela's jaw dropped.

"Oh, baby," comforted Amanda, "I don't love him. For Damsah's sake, most of the time, I don't even like him. But I do respect him, and I love what he's given me."

"You mean the money?"

A small giggle escaped Amanda's lips. "Sure, the money's good. But I had lots of credits of my own before I became the 'great' Hektor Sambianco's love interest."

Neela's brow furrowed.

"Majority, sweetie. Not by much, but certainly enough to take care of myself."

"But you said it was the bank account."

"It helps, I won't lie. But truly, Neela, it's the power I crave. I'm at the top of the UHF's social circle. My parties are the ones everyone just *has* to attend. My fashion sense has become *the* fashion sense of a new era. Venerable matrons of the most powerful families cannot embark on a social season without my approval."

"But what about Hektor?"

"What about him?"

"Doesn't he . . . doesn't he love you?"

Amanda suppressed a burst of laughter. "Oh, Neels. Now *that* is an emotion I can assure you our dear Hektor is not well acquainted with."

Neela straightened her shoulders, her chin jutting out defiantly. "He loves me."

Amanda studied her friend with stoic regard. "Maybe he does. I certainly hope so. But Hektor does not keep *me* around for love, that's for sure."

"Then for what? To throw fabulous parties?"

"Yes, actually. There's power in the world of charity balls and fashion houses, and with me around as Hektor's de facto proxy, he can send clear messages to the targeted elite. Hektor tells me who's to be courted and who's to be snubbed, which loyal member of the Assembly's husband or wife to apply pressure to and which member or members to bribe with an invitation."

"I . . . I had no idea," sputtered Neela, shaking her head. "And here I am, supposed psychological adviser to the President, yet apparently a clueless misanthrope when it comes to an entire subculture."

"Don't be such a ninny. If Hektor had asked you to look into my world, how long do you think it would have taken you to master its intricacies?"

"Not long, I suppose," admitted Neela dolefully.

"Right," affirmed Amanda with a self-satisfied grin. "We each serve our purposes, and apparently quite well. Don't misunderstand me, dear. Hektor likes the sex too, and I'll admit he's quite a skillful lover—the great Hektor would not allow himself to be anything but. However, Neela, in the end I'm nothing more than a well-compensated courtesan, in the truest sense of the word."

The implication of Amanda's forthright admission had not been lost on Neela. She sat quietly until curiosity got the best of her. "When exactly did you realize that I was . . . that we were, um—"

"Around the time Hektor stopped getting kinky."

Neela's face went red with embarrassment. "I never used to do things like that. Justin would never—" Neela's face twitched at the mention of her former husband's name. "It seems to make Hektor happy," she finished quietly.

"Of course it does," assured Amanda, scooting even closer and pulling Neela in for another gentle hug. Missed by the aides that Amanda had her back to as well as Neela, who readily accepted her friend's soft embrace, was the look of sheer rage that passed over the courtesan socialite's face for the merest fraction of a second.

"Now, you dry your eyes," Amanda said with a radiant smile while flinging the small black box from the table into the hands of a waiting aide, "while I see who I have to kill to get a cup of coffee around here."

Executive Office, Burroughs, Mars

"And so," finished Hektor as a sardonic smile formed along the edges of his mouth, "the twenty-three-year-old looks across at the hundred-and-fifty-year-old who's just screwed him to within an inch of his life and then barely manages to gasp, 'Gramma?'"

The groans and hissing only fortified Hektor's already smug grin.

"Must we really sink to this level of depravity?" pleaded Franklin.

"As opposed to the joke you told last week?" chided Hektor.

The Cabinet's laughter was all that was required to end Franklin's muted protest.

The Justice Minister smiled gamely.

"For the past six months," started Hektor after a few moments of silence, "we've all had a remarkable period of near peace."

"We have, yes," said Tricia grimly, "not so much our marines in the Belt."

"True enough. However, our population centers are not in the Belt, and according to Irma, our tactics for suppressing the terrorist activity there are not only deemed acceptable by the general population, but actually applauded." Hektor looked over to Irma for confirmation.

"Many even wonder why we're being so gentle," she added. "And now that we have some solid and demonstrable victories and a military leadership the people actually trust, even the pennies are starting to believe we can win this war. Recruiting is up."

"Well, of course it's up," proclaimed Franklin with the contempt and bitterness of a scion whose family had not had a member fall from majority status in decades, "the lazy bastards want to take advantage of the government's majority offer before the war is over."

"Well, yes," said Porfirio. "That and the fact that the losses we're experiencing holding the Belt are nothing compared to the losses we suffered in taking it."

"That is why—as far as everyone in the Core Worlds of Mars, Earth, and Luna is concerned—these past six months have been a well-earned dividend."

"Indeed, it has been," confirmed Hektor, "and we've come up with a plan that will ensure it continues to pay out." Hektor shifted his gaze over to the Defense Minister. "If you wouldn't mind, Porfirio."

"Gladly, Mr. President." Porfirio activated the holo-tank, and soon the entire solar system was seen floating serenely above the conference table. "The three main sources of Alliance resistance are here in Ceres, Jupiter, and Saturn." As he mentioned them, all three areas lit up and expanded in size to be more easily seen. "Ceres is a substantial industrial hub, but its value is primarily political, cultural, and increasingly symbolic. To take the capital would be a serious blow to the morale of the Alliance."

"I thought taking Altamont and the Belt were supposed to be a serious blow to their morale," snipped Brenda.

Her sarcasm was missed by no one, especially Porfirio, who greeted the remark with a muted half smile. "What can I say? The bastards have a lot of morale. But it's one thing to lose a fortress or even a bunch of rocks. Ceres is the biggest city and a symbol of five years of triumphant resistance. Even our failure to take it in the Long Battle will only aid us all the more when it falls in the end." Porfirio brought the image of Jupiter to the fore. "Now, Jupiter has by far become the center of Alliance industry and commerce. Because of the intense radiation belt surrounding the planet, working environments have always been well built. The easy access to the hard resources of all those moons and the unlimited energy of the hydrogen clouds plus its location relatively close to the Belt made it the logical place to build an industrial base. Our taking of the Belt has put a crimp in their grand plan, but not a big one. Further, Jupiter is where our stolen shipyard resides—greatly expanded since the initial theft, I might add."

"How significantly?" asked Irma.

"Four to five times its original size."

"Damsah, that makes it bigger than the Gedretar Shipyards of Ceres!"

"Or put another way," added Hektor, "almost as large as the Trans-Luna Shipyard."

"All true," confirmed Porfirio, "and as of now, Jupiter also has the largest population of the Outer Alliance."

"All of which is about to change," said Tricia with unbridled malevolence. She played her fingertips over a control panel, and Jupiter receded from the center of the table only to be replaced by Saturn. "The refugees from our victory in the Belt—"

"In case you were interested," interjected Porfirio, "the OA calls those refugees the Diaspora."

"That's funny," sneered Tricia. "I just call it running away."

The group broke out in a smattering of laughter.

"To where, exactly?" asked Franklin.

"The big planet you're staring at in the middle of the table," chided the Minister of Internal Affairs. "Now if you'd let me finish . . ."

"How many are we talking about?" prodded Franklin, ignoring the taunt.

Tricia shrugged her shoulders, resigned. "Over seven hundred and fifty million on the run, with about fifty mil heading for Jupiter, fifty for Neptune, and another fifty for Uranus. An insignificant number are heading for the Kuiper

Belt and beyond. But nearly six hundred million Belters and their asteroids are heading for Saturn. Luckily for us, most of them are going to take a long while to get there. But if they have the time to get to Saturn, which also has vast amounts of hard resources and nearly unlimited hydrogen supplies with no pesky deadly radiation field, they *will* industrialize that planet's numerous moons in very short order and turn it into an even bigger industrial center than Jupiter."

"An industrial center, I might add," concluded Hektor with concern evident in his voice, "that will be very difficult for us to deal with, given its distance from the Core Worlds."

"Mr. President," grumbled Brenda, "all these victories are good, but if we have to conquer the solar system one planetary system at a time, it could take fifty years, even with all our resources."

"You have a shorter timeline, I presume," Hektor said with a sly grin.

"Yes, I do. This war has to be effectively over in four years or the economy will simply collapse. Key industries and services are starved for competent personnel. Resources are being diverted from far too many infrastructure programs, both new and maintained. If we lose a couple of orbital stations, orports, or fusion reactors to poor maintenance—" Brenda reconsidered. "No, *when* we lose them to poor maintenance, fighting the war will get hard, harder, and then impossible."

"You realize, Brenda," suggested Porfirio, "that the occupation could last for decades."

"Occupation, though expensive, is not economically destructive—if you're willing to pay the price. Our occupation troops tend to be filled with the most expendable parts of society. We don't need huge fleets to engage the enemy. Small fleets are enough to maintain control and demonstrate superior firepower. We should be able to equip our occupation forces with war surplus for decades to come. But I repeat, the war must be effectively over in four years, and that is the best-case scenario."

"We do have a plan to win; there's just one small problem."

"Black," was all Tricia managed to utter. It was enough to convey the animus the Information Minister had reserved for the OA's preeminent warrior.

"That fleet had nearly three hundred ships in it," exclaimed Franklin. "How could it have just up and disappeared?"

"They hoodwinked us," revealed Porfirio.

"How?"

"By making us believe something was there that wasn't."

"An entire bloody fleet?" gasped Franklin. "The *main* battle fleet?"

Porfirio nodded grudgingly. "You see, when a fleet is stationary, it's not simply standing at station. There's movement around it all the time. Ships are coming and going—some military, some civilian. Many are small, and some are bloody huge. Plus the OA tries to interrupt and distort our ability to see the area clearly. The space around Ceres is filled with ECMs, massive amounts of reflective particle beams, and projected imagery. If only it were as simple as moving a probe and taking a Damsah-cursed picture. The truth is, we didn't suspect what they were doing till we noticed a drop-off in ancillary movement. By the time we knew enough to be suspicious, the fleet was gone. That was three months ago."

Porfirio zoomed the holodisplay in and then highlighted Ceres's multiple shipping and travel lanes.

"The Outer Alliance has so much ship traffic going to and from all their main settlements using their specially cleared regions of space."

"You're talking about the vias, correct?" asked Brenda.

"Yes. Ships in the vias can accelerate to impressive speeds, which means that the OA could've easily snuck that fleet out two or three ships at a time and parked them anywhere in the Alliance. The truth is, they could still be right at Ceres, where we always thought they were. I wouldn't put it past Delgado—who, by the way, seems to have vanished as well. Not one interview, sighting, or holo of her in months. Nor of most of her command staff or fleet personnel, for that matter."

"Figures they'd all disappear and leave the one guy we all wish woulda joined them," said Trisha.

"Indeed," said Porfirio, bringing Omad Hassan's grizzled face front and center. Even in holo-form, as a still image the infamous tunnel rat turned warrior seemed to be mocking them. "Son of a bitch has been very publicly attacking our supply lines from Mars to Trang's fleet near Ceres, as well as making forays into the Belt to aid the resistance."

"Terrorists," grumbled Trisha.

"Whatever. If anything, Old Legless"—it was a pointed reference to Omad's recent addition of cybernetic legs as a result of losing his originals in battle—"is even more of a pain in the ass now than at any other time of the war."

"He's a distraction," stated Tricia, "nothing more, nothing less."

"In that case, I'd say he's an effective one," added Irma. "He's keeping the Alliance press and public busy with his exploits."

"A rather clever diversion, then," noted Hektor. "Omad distracts; the bitch bails. Nicely done."

Irma looked askance at Hektor. "But how will she call the shots if she's cloaked herself? Getting a few messages in to Ceres, maybe. Playing a critical role in government?" Irma shook her head.

"That's assuming she's been calling them from the outset," argued Franklin, left eyebrow raised in unison with a slightly upturned nose. "But if she's not, then who is running the Triangle Office?"

Irma's lips pulled back like a stretched bow. "Please refrain from using that term."

"What term?" started Franklin.

"Triangle Office. By calling it that, you give the place too much symbolic power. You make it a real place of authority."

"It *is* a real place of authority," insisted Hektor. "From that place, fleets battle to oppose us, resources are allocated to hold us back. That place commands the loyalties of four billion human beings, one billion of whom would listen to 'that office' over us if not for the fact that we have fleets and occupation troops holding guns to their heads. We may as well admit it and feel all the better when we take it away from them. Irma, when the UHF sees a picture of me sitting behind the desk of that office, when what's left of the Alliance sees that picture, then everyone will know the war is almost over. But we're not here to dream; we're here to take action. And so the question remains—and it's a good one, Franklin—who's actually running the show?"

Everyone looked toward Tricia.

"I believe I have our answer," she declared authoritively. "The Outer Alliance has not imploded the way our models predicted."

"Well, there's a shocker," scoffed Franklin.

"When that happens," Tricia pressed on through the smattering of laughter, "you have to look for an X-factor. The one element you may not have considered."

Brenda looked askance at Tricia. "So you think it's this O'Toole woman, then."

"At first," confirmed Tricia, "yes." Tricia positioned an image of Justin Cord standing next to his sarcophagus in the center of the holo-display. "After all, the first person to pop out of a box was a nightmare. It only made sense that if there were an X-factor involved," she replaced Justin's image with that of Sandra O'Toole, "it would be the second one out."

Hektor laughed. "Why do I have the feeling we're being led down the garden path?"

"Because, Mr President," explained Tricia, "you are. Or to be more precise, we all *were*. We've been so blinded by unincorporated fever we forgot that Sandra O'Toole is not the only new addition to the Outer Alliance's government." Tricia now replaced the image of Sandra with that of Rabbi. "He was lost in her glare and not by accident either."

"The religious figurehead they brought into the cabinet to keep the fanatics happy?" gasped Irma. "He's a nutjob."

Tricia nodded. "That's what we assumed as well. He seemed a perfect fit because unlike Muslims, Christians and Hindus, his fanatical sect is small in numbers and so that made him a good compromise to represent the so-called Astral Awakening."

"I've been studying the history of these Jews," piped in Hektor. "They have a reputation of causing trouble throughout history. Everyone from the ancient Greeks to the Europeans of the Union complained about them endlessly. There have been repeated attempts to destroy them and yet, and yet . . ." Hektor paused.

"And yet what?" asked Franklin, intensely curious.

"And yet they've somehow managed to survive."

Porfirio's face was grim. "By worming their way into positions of power and influence, it would appear."

"According to the records," stated Irma, looking up from her DijAssist, "these Jews seem to have had significant roles in countries that have played a part in major historical events."

"Oh yes," confirmed Hektor, "they seem to thrive alright—in chaos. From what *I've* read those countries and civilizations they were a part of fell; every one of them. Not that Jews don't provide some sort of boost, look at the Outer Alliance. But for civilization in general . . . well," he scoffed dismissively, "history seems to have judged them quite poorly."

"The President is correct," added Tricia. "We have discord, anarchy, even disease in the occupied zones. Zones, I might add, the Rabbi's people lived in. It should come as no surprise that these Jews have a history of spreading disease and disorder. Can that be a coincidence?"

No one said a word. Not for lack of opinion but rather for lack of any real authority on the topic.

"No," Franklin charged, "I don't think it is. In fact, the more I think about it the more this Rabbi appears a rat. Unless you would have us believe that a woman can arrive from the past and with no experience whatsoever start running the Alliance as effortlessly as a fusion generator. Much more likely is Tricia's suppositon. One man from a group of religious fanatics gets himself into a position of power, which, lo and behold, his people seem to have been doing for millennia. Is it really so hard to believe that Rabbi's really the X-factor hiding behind the skirt of the Unincorporated Woman?"

"Not at all, Franklin," agreed Hektor. "In fact, it makes perfect sense. I'd suggest we all keep an eye on this one. And in your copious spare time it wouldn't hurt to bone up on some reading about these people. A book called *Protocols of the Elders of Zion* seems as good a place as any to start."

Hektor waited a moment before introducing the next order of business. "I must tell you all that what you're about to hear will be quite disturbing." His mouth formed into a straight, stiff line as he looked over to his Minister of Internal Affairs. "Trisha, you may now inform the Cabinet."

Tricia nodded solemnly, took a deep breath, and then blurted, "The UHF is suffering a reemergence of the VR plague."

The room exploded with a chorus of disbelief.

"Quiet!" shouted Hektor. "Let her at least finish; then we can all discuss this abomination."

Tricia tipped her head toward Hektor and continued. "VR's always been a small but *manageable* problem in the UHF—even with the war causing only a small increase in the number of addicts. Then about six months ago—" Tricia paused just long enough to let the cabinet consider the date's implications. "—we noticed a sharp upturn in the number of arrests, both of users and suppliers."

"About the time we started winning the war," added Irma.

"Exactly. Despite the attention of the Internal Affairs department and a massive but quiet campaign that has resulted in equally massive arrests, I'm sad to report that we've been unable to contain this new plague." Tricia accessed a file, and the image of the solar system disappeared to be replaced by an image of a silver headband attached by a cord to a small box of a popular brand of chocolates. "This is what we've found at almost all the arrest sites."

"Not like anything I've ever seen," said Brenda, staring almost cross-eyed at the holo-image.

"That's because before six months ago, VR rigs came in all shapes and sizes, but all with the same basic programs—some, centuries old. Then," added Tricia with some bite to her words, "this thing started showing up. It's not always disguised as a box of chocolates. Often it's a DijAssist or a brightly wrapped present or some other easily overlooked item. It is, however, an exceptionally well designed unit that can be reproduced easily and run with a minimum of power. Also the new VR programs are far more complex and, interestingly enough, became available about . . ." She paused.

"Six months ago," snarled Porfirio, pinched lips drawn into bloodless white lines across his face. "Bastard Rabbi, fucking Alliance."

"Are we sure it's them?" asked Franklin. "Is there any evidence whatsoever leading directly back to the Outer Alliance?"

"None. All the units are manufactured locally from a template that's been distributed far and wide, but appeared on Luna, Earth, and Mars within twelve hours of each other. The programs keep on appearing at sites around the Neuro for those who know where to look. We believe they were placed simultaneously and are being released according to a schedule, but it's possible they're being loaded one at a time. This has all the hallmarks of a cooperative effort by a design team that had the resources, time, and immunity from prosecution that those dabbling in VR have never had . . . until now."

"It's fair in a twisted sort of way, I suppose," said Irma. "We killed their religious leaders at Alhambra; most of them, that is," she corrected, "now they go after our souls in the Core. Poetic, really," she finished without the slightest hint of outrage.

Hektor nodded, bitter irony no stranger to his life. "Irma," he asked, eyes narrowed in thoughtful contemplation, "what would happen if we released this story?"

"And?" she asked, seeing there was more to be pulled from her boss.

"And we pin it on the Outer Alliance?"

"It would be better if we at least had some evidence of their complicity. This is, after all, a firestorm in the making."

"Not a problem," said Tricia as casually as if she were finalizing a work order for latrine parts. "I'll make as much evidence as you need. Computer records, compromising vids, even confessions. We can do some trials if you'd like— makes great press. But I don't have to tell you that."

Irma nodded her approval.

Hektor repeated, "So what would the reaction be?"

"About what you'd expect," suggested Irma. "Moral outrage and indignation. Bet you'd even see a bump in your already thriving recruitment. The public will seek immediate revenge, of course, and will demand real punishment for those they deem responsible."

"A desire to strike back and forcefully, yes?" asked Hektor, oddly looking toward Porfirio rather than at Irma.

"Yes. Frankly, I'm not sure if a show trial would be enough. Don't forget, we've all been inculcated from birth to loathe VR and hold especially contemptible those who peddle it. That it's being foisted on a vulnerable populace during a time of duress makes this crime seem even more appalling."

Though Hektor's eyes widened, seeming to revel in her answer, a grim determination remained on his face. "Good, good. Let's move forward on that, then. As you'll soon see, it will fit perfectly with the Defense Minister's plans."

On cue, Porfirio began his presentation. "It had been assumed that as soon as Gupta's fleet was organized, he was going to take it to Ceres, where the combined fleets would once again attack the Alliance capital." He paused as his lips parted, baring a caninelike smile. "But that's not going to happen." The holo-display revealed two distinct fleets with one heading *away* from Ceres. "We've split our fleet. Half is at Mars under the command of Abhay Gupta; the rest with Trang and Jackson near Ceres. The thinking is that even though our combined fleet would outnumber the Alliance two to one, attacking Ceres would still have proved disastrous."

"But I thought we had the numbers to sacrifice?" grumbled Franklin.

"Oh we do, and we'll use them, but attacking orbital batteries supported by a well-led fleet is an invitation to disaster—no matter what your numbers. At best, we'd be looking at near total destruction for both sides, which would be tantamount to a draw for us. And a draw, given the vast superiority of our numbers in both ships and resources, would go down as a defeat in the minds of the people, shattering much of the goodwill the recent victories have given us."

"What do you propose to do about Black?" asked Brenda.

"That's the beauty of the plan. She's not a factor."

"She's always a factor, Porfirio," Hektor said in mild rebuke. "Never forget that."

Porfirio bowed slightly in Hektor's direction. "Of course, Mr. President. Please excuse my exuberance."

Hektor bowed back, inviting the Defense Minister to continue.

"As it now stands, Admiral Gupta is going to take his fleet—half our effective forces—and boost for Jupiter. Trang and Jackson have orders to wait at Ceres and see what unfolds. When Gupta gets to Jupiter, he's under orders to destroy as much of the Jovian system's war-making infrastructure as possible."

"Excuse me," said Irma, her face telegraphing confusion.

"Yes?"

"Your holodisplay seems to indicate the eradication of whole settlements."

"And?" Porfirio asked, waiting impatiently for Irma to get to the point.

Irma's eyes were fixed on the information now streaming across the mini holodisplay of her DijAssist. "But . . . hospitals? Schools? I'm sorry," Irma finally murmured, "I just . . . hadn't realized we were changing . . ." As the list of civilian targets floating before her continued to swell, Irma was unable to finish her thought.

Hektor came to her rescue. "After your pending revelations about VR, those targets will no longer be off-limits."

Irma stared at him blankly.

"That," Hektor revealed, "will be the 'strike back' you spoke of earlier."

Irma nodded, a slightly raised left brow reflecting her acceptance. Hektor then looked around the table at the rest of the Cabinet Ministers. "It is incumbent on all of us, and Irma—" He turned to his Information Minister. "—you especially, to make the UHF understand that every single Alliance citizen is complicit in the heinous crime of bringing the VR plague back into our midst and, as such, is now to be regarded as the enemy. Gupta has been given his orders. He *will* attack any and all settlements that he can find. In fact, see if he's in range of any fleeing Jewish settlements. There's no reason why we should not let Rabbi know there's a price to pay for trying to destroy humanity." Hektor thought for a moment and smiled, contemplating the justice of the order. "Gupta *will* eliminate everything that can be of use to the enemy, including hospitals, educational institutions—no matter what age the entrants—and homes, especially homes. And with the press coverage about the Alliance's VR attack on our 'souls'—" Hektor paused as his lips turned upwards. "—I like that phrase, Irma, make sure you use it—our public will demand nothing less."

Irma stared numbly as her DijAssist estimated the number of permanent deaths Gupta's scorched-planet policy would soon bring. It was in the hundreds of millions—numbers far higher than even she'd imagined. Irma had forgotten about the radiation belt around Jupiter. Anyone exposed, even if suspended by the imperfect process of being blown out into space, would suffer permanent death. Her now impassive face did not betray the feeling of uncertainty welling up inside. It was a feeling she hadn't experienced since the death of her friend and coworker, Saundra Morrie, five years earlier.

"Of course," she responded staunchly.

Porfirio beamed, having been cleared to deliver his master stroke. "If J.D. is at Jupiter, she'll attack Gupta. Maybe he wins; maybe he loses. But he's not an idiot, and should be able to make her pay—maybe even get out with some of his fleet intact. But it won't matter, because with J.D. occupied, Trang can dismantle the orbital batteries around Ceres without interference. Sure, Trang'll take some losses, but if he does it right, and he will, then Ceres is ours. Or scenario number two. If J.D. *is* at Ceres, then Gupta destroys all Alliance resources at Jupiter, and the rest of the Alliance knows that if the war continues, not only can't J.D. defend them but it will also cost them *everything*. At *that* point, I think all but the most fanatic will entertain reasonable peace offers—even a Jew." Porfirio's smile was ebullient. He was the proverbial cat who'd finally trapped the canary.

"Yes," agreed Hektor. "But they'll no longer be generous. That t.o.p. has launched. The citizens of the Alliance have brought this upon themselves."

Hektor stood. The meeting had come to an end. "If they want to commit suicide by going after the Core Planets, I say, let them."

17 Pack Your Bags

Presidential quarters, Ceres

Sandra O'Toole was awakened from a rare deep sleep by the cacophonous sounds of an antique twin-bell alarm clock. Though the sound emanated from her DijAssist as opposed to the actual article, that didn't stop her from swatting the small polymer unit off the table with such force as to send it skittering across the Triangle Office floor. Yawning and rubbing her eyes, she grumbled her way across the room, stooped over, and picked up the still clanging cause of her ire. "I'm up! I'm up!" she screamed at the block of plastic. "For the love of God, already!" The ringing ceased.

"I'm not sure," quipped a voice from behind her, "that even God would put up with so odious a sound as that."

Sandra whipped around to see Sebastian sitting cross-legged on the couch from which she'd only recently alighted. As was now his wont, he was wearing his OA Intelligence uniform. There was an amiable smile plastered across his face.

"First of all," Sandra huffed, flopping down into the chair opposite Sebastian, "I very much doubt God would need an alarm clock. After all, where does a guy who's supposedly everywhere really have to be?"

"Point well taken."

"Please tell me you didn't just disrupt the best nap I've had in years to lecture me about my auditory idiosyncrasies."

"Sadly, no."

"Spill it, Sebastian."

"A large UHF fleet has broken from the orbit of Mars and is heading for the Belt. It does not appear to be joining Trang."

Sandra's posture stiffened. "Who's leading it?"

"It appears to be Admiral Abhay Gupta."

"Appears?"

"Based on the information we have—with very little margin of error—it's him. However, with humans, one can never tell."

The President smiled acerbically. "Where's he heading?"

"We can't be certain, but we suspect Jupiter."

Sandra's fledgling smile bloomed into a full grin. "Damn, she's good."

"The fleet admiral is an amazingly gifted military leader."

"What about the rest, Sebastian?" There was real trepidation in Sandra's voice. "So many things have to go right."

"We've been over this, Madam President. We're losing this war and no longer have the option of playing it safe."

"Easy for you to say, Sebastian. Justin didn't leave the job of humanity's survival in your hands. I can't fail."

Sebastian's brow shot up. "And you think *I* can? Every avatar left worth saving is depending on me."

Sandra nodded apologetically. "Right. Sorry, friend. I just got all myopic on you."

"We're all under a great deal of stress, Madam President, but what I'd really like to know is, are you going to continue feeling sorry for yourself?"

"No," challenged Sandra, "what you'd *really* like to know is if I'm capable of doing my job."

Sebastian's deep-set hazel eyes remained fixed and unresponsive. A moment later, he twitched a smile. "Touché."

"Not even ten seconds of self-pity?" pleaded Sandra, pushing her bottom lip forward petulantly.

"Sure, when the war's over."

"In that case," commanded Sandra, springing up from the couch, "get me Admiral Sinclair. We have a ship to visit."

Triangle Office

Marilynn and Dante were deeply engaged in conversation when Sandra burst through the door. They looked up on her entrance but with the flick of her wrist, she bade them continue.

"I'm just saying that your definition of a fighting unit, while noble, is illogical."

"Logic has nothing to do with it," groused Marilynn.

"Children," Sandra admonished from behind the desk.

Marilynn turned to face the President. "He wants to add nine hundred more avatars per human."

"The initial plan," protested Dante, "was to use Kirk's unwitting couriers to infiltrate the UHF Neuro. In that scenario, we could hide only one hundred inert avatars in what we assessed to be a typical courier's limited luggage. But if Admiral Hassan comes on board, we'll have the computing power of the AWS *Spartacus,* which makes it possible for us to insert even larger numbers—"

"—of *un*trained, *un*organized, and *in*experienced symbiotic combatants!" railed Marilynn.

Dante raised his left brow and spoke accusingly. "We've been fighting this war for quite some time, Commodore, and I would never put an inexperienced soldier into a situation I didn't think he or she could handle."

"They're called teams for a reason," bellowed Marilynn in exasperation. "And we have one hundred of them, all highly trained, all able to finish each others' sentences—both human and avatar. I refuse to mess with that, no matter how many more of your buddies you think you can cram onto a pinhead."

"An interesting analogy, Commodore, but an ad hominem attack if ever there was one. While I'll admit that the symbiotic avatars have grown quite close to their backdoor commandos—"

"For the love of Justin," raged Marilynn, rolling her eyes, "will you pa-lease stop calling them that? They're Neuro Insertion Tactical Engagement Specialists. We came up with that name together, *remember*?" scolded Marilynn for what was obviously the thousandth time.

"Indeed," countered Dante with all the innocence of an angel pleading his case, "I am rather fond of the use of NITES as an acronym, but that shouldn't take away from what seems a perfectly reasonable nickname."

Sandra laughed out loud. "Do you two always bicker like this?"

"And to think," fumed Marilynn, uncharacteristically ignoring Sandra, "I was worried that you were a fantasy of mine gone out of control. You're way too smug and annoying to be anything *but* reality."

"Of course I'm real, Commodore."

"In which case, reality sucks."

"You're real too, Commodore," rejoined Dante.

"Children," interrupted Sandra, "can we please move on to more important issues?"

The room grew quiet as both Marilynn and Dante eyed each other warily. "Have you noticed, Commodore," asked Dante in a clinical tone, "how the President always assumes that what *she* wants to talk about is important?"

"Yes," agreed Marilynn heartily, dropping her annoyance and mimicking Dante's tone exactly. "I think the power has finally gone to her head. Come to think of it, why don't *you* act like that?"

"Because I don't actually *have* a head, merely the perception of one."

"Are you two done?" implored Sandra.

Her answer arrived by way of muted smiles.

"Commodore," informed Sandra, "if I can get Omad on board with the plan, then you and your backdo . . ."—on Marilynn's dour look, Sandra corrected herself—"NITES as presently numbered will leave in approximately eleven hours. Sorry, Dante, but Marilynn's reasoning is sound—pinhead comment notwithstanding."

Marilynn grinned, shooting Dante a triumphant look.

"Don't let it go to your *real* head, Commodore," warned the avatar.

"Don't worry, Dante. I will."

"Madam President," stated Dante, "with this news, I must now go and make final arrangements—" Dante shot Marilynn one last accusing look. "—there are ninety thousand avatars who are about to be *very* disappointed."

Marilynn opened her mouth to argue, but in a flash her Neuro partner was gone.

Sandra activated a security field and came around her desk to sit where Dante had sat only moments before. The seat was cold to the touch. Sandra wasn't sure why, but that little bit of tactile information always disturbed her. "Are we alone?"

"Let me check," offered Marilynn, placing two fingers from each hand to her temples. Seconds later, she was instantly in the Neuro.

The old VR system used a brain–computer interface comprising an electro-encephalography scalp band that could read neurofeedback and provide 3D visualization of brain activity. That band, combined with noninvasive neuro-electric monitoring and powerful software, created the first truly effective VR environments. The system had been so spectacularly successful that, much like the printed book, the VR rig's basic architecture had changed little from its initial inception. And any advancement that might have occurred was quickly put to rest by the implosion of society during the Grand Collapse and the Virtual Reality Dictates that followed in the cataclysm's deadly wake. The avatars had been only too glad to keep humanity's interest in furthering VR in check, lest their secret be discovered. However, with the new paradigm of human–avatar relations, all bets were off and the avatars had pointed the way toward a more efficient VR mechanism: whole-body installation, as first proposed by Robert Freitas in the first volume of his seminal work, *Nanomedicine*.

The key issue for enabling full-immersion reality had been in obtaining the necessary bandwidth inside the body. At the time of the Grand Collapse, that technology was not yet available. It was now. With a mature nanotech society, full-immersion reality was made manifest and Marilynn had been humanity's first-ever VR-naut. Neuron-monitoring chemical sensors had been placed in her brain that could capture relevant chemical events occurring within a 5-millisecond time window, ensuring instantaneous—or close enough therein—brain-state monitoring. The temple touch points were a simple matter of creating a DNA recognition sensor combined with a touch pattern that acted as a key to activate the internal VR.

In this way, Marilynn and the NITES had, out of necessity, achieved the unthinkable—their own bodies were now cybernetic VR rigs.

Because Marilynn was and always would be an addict, her initial foray into such seamless VR was far more terrifying than it was exhilarating. But she quickly got over both emotions. Years of experience controlling her impulses coupled with the realization that millions of souls, both avatar and human, now depended on her, made the task less daunting than she'd initially imagined.

Marilynn poked around the small space that the confinement field had made of the Neuro in the Triangle Office and found neither avatars nor programs set to eavesdrop. Then for good measure, she set her mind to look through the equipment in the office and found it clear. The first time she'd done that, she thought she would have a breakdown. Sending her mind and soul into and out of all the machines that make up daily life was like losing yourself in a maze a million miles long. But now she could do such things without even thinking about it. Marilynn removed her fingers from the side of her head and returned to human reality.

"We're alone, Madam President."

"Damn, I'd love to have one of those."

"We've been over this. If I get caught, I'm just a relapsed VR addict with some strange new technology. If you get caught, we're screwed."

"I didn't say I was going to get one, Marilynn, I just said I wanted one." Then under her breath she muttered, "I'm just the one who helped design the damn thing, I should at least get a chance to play wit . . ."

"If you're done ranting," interjected Marilynn, "there's something else I have tell you."

Sandra's ears perked up. Marilynn's debriefings of her forays into the avatar world were always done in utmost secrecy, but most of the time, the avatars' day-to-day lives were strikingly similar to those of their human progenitors— filled with boring and mundane tasks. It was generally the technical aspects of their society that most fascinated Sandra, and her debriefings with Marilynn, though often interesting, had become somewhat rote of late.

"Yes," invited Sandra.

"I think I know who killed Justin Cord."

"Start at the beginning. It's critical that you leave nothing out."

Marilynn nodded. "It occurred to me if I were going to be able to move about undetected in the UHF Neuro, it might be good to practice in the Alliance Neuro. Mind you, Dante's been very good at pointing out the avatar way of things and I've certainly learned a lot about his world in these past six months of training, but since the backdoor incident with you, I figured there may be other areas in which they might be vulnerable. At first I simply went places that would be unexpected rather than forbidden, just to see if anyone would notice. Places like long-term record storage or our symbiotic weapons cage. Then I began to take things." Marilynn noted Sandra's raised eyebrow. "You're the one who told me to poke around and not to bother you unless I found something interesting."

Sandra acknowledged the truth of Marilynn's words with a nod and gestured for her to continue.

"At first it was little things like our equivalent of data crystals or stims. I also, per your orders, started to monitor their communication links."

Sandra nodded once more.

"Nothing too sophisticated, mind you. It also helps that they've never had to secure their data from humans before. I figured if I was caught, all I would do is tell the truth—that I was running a NITES operation to test the limits of avatar security against a trained human presence."

"Good cover."

"Yeah. So while I was at the movies—"

"Movies," repeated Sandra, eyes sharp with recollection. "I seem to remember reading about them in one of the reports—2D, right?"

Marilynn nodded.

"Something about avatar data space being severely rationed due to the war."

"Yes," explained Marilynn, "2D movies make very good sense. Rather than have lots of avatars creating micro nodes within an increasingly limited Neuro space, the theaters provide one single processing node for hundreds of avatars."

"And gives them something with far greater entertainment value," finished Sandra, now remembering the finer details of the report. "—better insight into human thinking."

Marilynn nodded almost dismissively, anxious to press on. "Anyways, we were watching *Chitty Chitty Bang Bang* for like the umpteenth time—"

"Excuse me, Marilynn, but 'we'?"

"Dante and I."

"Was this a date?"

Marilynn's face registered surprise. She was forced to consider the question. "No! Well, not really. I mean, how? . . . No! No," she said, shaking her head firmly. "Could we even?"

Sandra chuckled. "Marilynn, I wasn't there. Was it or wasn't it a date?"

"I guess by strict definition, it was. How very odd."

"That you never considered it as such?"

"Yes."

Sandra's eyes glazed over a bit. "I remember *Chitty Chitty Bang Bang.* Hated the child catcher, loved the songs. Is it popular?"

"Oh my god, yes."

Sandra nodded, but her brow folded into a neat corduroy pattern across her forehead. She seemed to be fishing for an answer that Marilynn couldn't provide.

"I should probably watch it, again."

"Why? It's puerile."

"Agreed. But when we win this war, there are going to be only two powers left in the solar system capable of deciding the fate of the human race. And when that time comes, we'll need to know all we can about the other."

"In that case," added Marilynn, "pay special attention to the scene where the puppet is singing to the windup doll."

"Sorry." Sandra gave Marilynn a quizzical look. "It's been a while."

"It's near the end. You'll swear the avatars are being hypnotized. They can't take their eyes off it. Some of them actually break down in tears."

"Hmm—please continue."

"Yes, Madam President. Remember that report on 'shadow' programs?"

"The fake avatars that humans currently interact with."

"Correct. Well, I decided to create one of my own."

"You thought turnabout would be fair play," grinned Sandra approvingly.

"Yes, ma'am, I did," answered Marilynn, pride evident in her voice. "Making the shell was pretty easy, but making it interactive was a bust. There is almost no situation in which a human can be with an avatar that will fool the avatar for even a few seconds."

"Why not? It would seem to be only a matter of coding."

"It's hard to code against curiosity. Unlike humans, used to ignoring avatars or kept to a few mundane exchanges, avatars are incredibly fascinated by any human they meet. Even avatars I've been with hundreds of times still study me like I'm the most interesting thing they've ever laid eyes on. Shadow programming for humans in the Neuro might be useful in the future, but for now I found only one place that it can be used effectively."

Understanding blossomed on Sandra's face. "The movies."

"The movies," Marilynn agreed. "In that darkened space, avatars and humans are engaged in the same activity. They're very much like us in that they'll observe us to see if we're laughing or crying at certain scenes, but they're painfully polite and will rarely if ever comment during a screening. I daresay, half my shadow interactions seem to be the use of the word 'shush.'"

"Go on."

"Yesterday, I left my shadow at the theater with Dante and snuck out for a routine recon. I thought this might be a good opportunity to see if I could use a BDD to break into his house."

"What?" exclaimed Sandra, concerned.

"For the past six months, the avatars and the NITES have been testing each other's security because if we don't push our limits, Al's monsters sure as shit will. My only intention was to test Dante's personal perimeter."

"Clearly you succeeded."

"Greater than I could've imagined. I intended to leave a box of popcorn on his coffee table. We try to one-up each other."

Sandra snickered at the petty rivalry, but by slow turns such as this, was beginning to realize how very similar the races actually were.

"The BDD landed me in his secure room."

Sandra's face grew rigid. "Security exercise aside, you do realize that you could've endangered the entire treaty."

"Yes, ma'am, I did. But the fact of the matter was, I had already broken into his secure room—even if unintentionally."

"Philo's dog, then."

"Exactly. That's where I found this." Marilynn activated the Triangle Office's holo-tank, procured another data crystal from her pocket, and inserted it into the control panel. She directed the image to appear above the coffee table. Soon Marilynn and Sandra were both viewing a report showing the contents of a storage room in the Nerid facility orbiting Neptune. *Hello, old friend,* thought Sandra as she stared at the suspension unit she'd spent years perfecting. The report talked about the contents of room D4-3E40 and then went on to stipulate that Kirk Olmstead had had knowledge of the Nerid report years prior to his abrupt release of it to Hildegard Rhunsfeld's database—just days before Justin Cord's assassination.

Sandra absorbed the information first with an expression of curiosity which quickly grew to one of grave concern. Her eyes dimmed to emotionless orbs as a single name flowed through her clenched jaw. "Olmstead."

"If we can trust this data," confirmed Marilynn, "then, yes."

"Could it be ruse?"

"That would suppose the avatars knew I was lurking about and planted this on purpose."

Sandra nodded slowly. "But if on purpose, to what purpose?"

"I don't know. Maybe," suggested Marilynn, "it's something as simple as getting rid of Kirk."

"So, replace an effective Security Secretary with one not nearly so effective."

"And therefore not as dangerous."

"Maybe, but I don't think so, Marilynn."

"Why not?"

"It's a particularly dangerous way for them to go about it. This report doesn't just implicate Kirk—"

"True," agreed Marilynn. "A man capable of assassinating one President—"

"—could assassinate another," finished Sandra.

"Of more conern to me, Madam President, is that it implicates the avatars as well."

"Not all the avatars, Marilynn." Sandra's eyes narrowed and her face became as rigid and cold as finely chiseled stone. "Just the two we're most dependent on for winning this war."

AWS *Spartacus*, Gedretar Shipworks, Ceres

Omad Hassan slid his feet off the desk, stood up, and greeted Sergeant Eric Holke with a rare, genuine smile. "Sergeant," Omad roared, returning Holke's stiff salute with one far less perfunctory, "damned if it isn't good to get a load of your ugly mug again."

"And, um, yours as well, sir."

Omad stared down at his cybernetic appendages. "For someone nick-named Legless, you mean." He then looked back up at the speechless sergeant. "Like 'em?"

"Sure . . . sir."

"I coulda gone all out and got the premier line, but really, who needs that much tech below their legs? More shit to go wrong, if ya ask me. Plus," added Omad, pulling a pant leg up to proudly display the new appendage, "these things practically walk themselves. And ya know, the whole 'legless' thing has kind of grown on me."

"You could say that, sir."

"Yeah, shitty joke, I know. But I'm sure you didn't come out here to check out my legs."

"Afraid not, sir."

"Thought so. When a grand admiral and a President both come to visit at the same time, you know it can't be good."

Holke nodded. "Something's rattled the cage, that's for sure."

"That's all you got?"

Holke's eyes pivoted left and then right. He lowered his voice. "I think part of the UHF fleet is moving."

Omad's irascible grin returned. "Listen, son. Stop by for a moment post this meeting, will ya?"

Holke nodded as the room informed the two of them that the Presidential contingent had arrived. Two of Holke's security detail entered the room, immediately followed by President O'Toole and Admiral Sinclair. With a curt nod from Sinclair and a slight smile from Sandra, Holke and the two guards made their exit.

"Can I offer anyone a drink?" he offered, beckoning the two to have a seat. "Goddamned ship's so damn big, they actually put a bar in my quarters."

"You're in a battle cruiser," insisted Sinclair, "because admirals should not be conducting battles in a frigate."

Omad shrugged off the grand admiral's logic with the flick of a wrist. "The *Dolphin* was a good ship, sir. The old girl got me and her crew through most of the war."

"It's not as if you haven't been making the UHF miserable in *Spartacus,* here."

"She's a good ship too, sir, but I won't ever give up missing the *Dolphin*."

"Nor should you, Admiral. My first ship, back when I just started working for one of the mercenary companies, was called the CSS *Corporate Raider*." Sinclair paused on the look he got from Omad and Sandra. "Go on, laugh. I was tempted to at first. It should've been scrapped, it was so old. And I'd swear on a stack of requisition forms that I spent more time repairing that piece of junk than actually flying it. Still, there are times I'd give almost anything to be back on her bridge. You never forget your first, Omad."

"No, sir. And now that we've successfully accessed memory lane, mind telling me why we're all here?"

"As you've probably already heard, Gupta's on the move. Jupiter bound, by all accounts."

Omad shook his head and smiled. "That does it. It's not enough that she's a better admiral than me, now she's gotta go and become a prophetess?" Omad looked up to the ceiling, shaking his head disapprovingly. "You took my legs, Lord. Was it too much to ask for a little foresight?"

"It was a calculated guess," offered Sinclair. "A good one, for sure. Anyhow, Gupta should be there in two to three weeks, depending on how much of his fuel he wants to burn."

"Closer to three," figured Omad. "It's not as if he can surprise us. He wants to smoke out J.D.—if she's there. He may as well arrive with more fuel—gives him room to maneuver. What are my orders?"

"About the same. In twelve hours, you're to take your flotilla and begin what will appear to be another raid of UHF positions in the occupied Belt. You'll even be dropping supplies to various resistance groups. Disrupt what you can, but once you're clear, head deep into the Belt. We want them to think you're going back to Eros." Sinclair had a sad look about him as he stood up and gave the now standing Omad a perfect salute. "The President has some questions for you, Admiral Hassan. Please give her your full cooperation."

Omad's brow rose perceptibly. "*Full* cooperation, Josh?"

"Full cooperation, Omad." Sinclair then bowed respectfully to Sandra, turned and left.

Omad sat back down and stared at his lone visitor with cool detachment. "When did you become the President, Madam President?"

"Depends whom you ask," Sandra replied courteously. "And I'll take that drink if the offer's still on the table."

"That offer is *always* on the table, Madam President." Omad hopped up and went over to the bar. "What'll it be?"

"Ever heard of a drink called Essence of Burning Village?"

Omad was intrigued. "I have not. But if you tell me how to make it, I'm sure I can find the ingredients."

"Really wish I knew. I had it once and only once when I was in university. It was at a dorm party. Someone handed it to me, told me what it was called, and then disappeared. The only thing I remember is the strange tingling sensation it left on my tongue."

"You must remember something else about it, Madam President, or why else try to replicate it?"

Sandra nodded, her eyes getting a little misty. "It's like those books you shouldn't read or those roads you shouldn't travel. I woke up the next day on the floor of a friend's dorm, sucking dust bunnies."

Omad roared in laughter. "I know that herd well. Mean little suckers."

Sandra giggled at the vision. "Anyhow, I've never been able to find anyone who knows anything about it. I did find one gentleman who claimed to have had it at a dorm party at another university. He likened the experience to being a Mongolian warrior raiding a burning village while simultaneously being the raided village."

Omad shook his head, chuckling. "And you've been looking for it ever since?"

"In a way, it's my personal quest. I searched the Internet in my time and the Neuro in our time, but so far nothing."

"You must realize if you haven't found it by now, Madam President . . ." began Omad.

"I know it must seem hopeless, Admiral. . . ."

"Please. Omad's fine. I'm getting tired of Admiral this and Legless that."

Sandra's smile grew warmer. "Omad, then. Mind if I ask you a personal question?"

Omad's eyes sparkled. "Best kind."

"Why the legs?"

"You mean why haven't I had 'em regrown?"

Sandra nodded.

"J.D."

Sandra tipped her head respectfully. Admiral Black had been very upfront about why she'd chosen to keep the left half of her face scarred. To her, it was a constant reminder of the awesome responsibility of her command. Omad was now doing the same.

"So," probed Omad, breaking the silence, "why don't you tell me about this drink of yours."

Sandra laughed. "I know it seems hopeless, but I can't help the feeling that one of the reasons I'm here is to find out how to make an Essence of Burning Village and restore it to the general knowledge of humanity."

"A worthy endeavor if ever there was one." Omad then emerged from behind the counter with two drinks, one of which he brought over and handed to Sandra. "These, Madam President—"

"Sandra."

"These drinks, *Sandra*, are called Sledgehammers. There are many variations. The one you're now holding in your pretty little hands is quite popular with the fleet, which isn't too surprising."

"And why is that?"

"Rumor has it"—Omad lifted his glass—"this stuff's strong enough to fuel a warship."

"What about the Muslims?"

Omad tilted the glass to his bottom lip and then with a slight jerk tilted it upward, draining half of it. "Them too," he agreed with a throaty gasp.

Sandra rolled her eyes. "I'm serious, Omad."

Omad held up his forefinger while he searched for something on the small table resting between himself and the President. His face brightened when he found what he was looking for—a small data pad. He picked it up and covered exactly half his face. With one eye narrowed he mustered his best J.D. voice. "Senior fleet officers must constantly be aware of the example they set for spacers and assault miners under their command, especially in matters of faith."

Sandra regarded the admiral dubiously.

"I guess what I'm trying to say is that I like to keep things simple. Way I figure it, anyone I'm drinking with must not be a Muslim—least while I'm drinking with 'em. What they want to call themselves outside this room or wherever I happen to be knocking some back is completely up to them." Omad drained the Sledgehammer. "Cheers."

"Cheers," echoed Sandra, taking a slug. As the drink went down, her tawny eyes bulged wide then teared up. "Jesus H. Christ," she sputtered, neck jutting out slightly, "what the hell was in that?"

Omad answered with the flash of a grin. "Tunnel rats never tell. One more?"

Sandra thought about it, then blessed the miracle of the HOD alcoholic neutralizers. "What the hell."

Omad laughed at the President's moxie. "Your funeral," he warned, getting back up. "And just so you know, nanites can scrub you clean, but this shit lingers."

Sandra's lips curled up as she watched Omad head back to bar and duck down behind the counter. That was soon followed by the sound of glass clinking on glass.

"Mind if I ask *you* a personal question?" his behind-the-bar muffled voice asked.

"Shoot!" Sandra yelled from across the room.

Omad's head popped up, eyes probing curiously. "Are you a Christian?"

Sandra placed a hand over her mouth and attempted to suppress a giggle—unsuccessfully. "You know, in six months of doing my job, you're the first person to actually come right out and ask me that question?"

Omad, meeting her questioning eyes, realized he might have overstepped. "Uh, am I in trouble, here?"

Sandra waved her hand at the air. "Nah. I just thought it was funny."

"Good, 'cause I never drink in mixed company."

"Someone's pissed off and someone isn't?"

"You said it, sister." Omad ambled back to his seat, plopping the second Sledgehammer on the table while leaning back into the chair with his.

"So do you worship the stick guy or what?"

Sandra let out a deep, guttural laugh. "Now you're just toying with me."

"Yeah," he admitted, "but you can take it."

"I once had two older brothers, Omad. There's not much I can't."

Omad sank deeper into the back of his chair, raised his glass to Sandra, and once again tipped the glass onto his bottom lip. "So?" he prodded.

"I was raised a Christian, sorta, but I'm not really much of a believer in any one thing, per se."

"Hmm," grunted Omad. "I had you figured for a believer."

Sandra turned a three-quarter profile. "Really?"

"To have your drive. To have accomplished what you have—in *both* your lives."

"I had a blank check. *Cord's* blank check and a little luck, is all."

Omad leaned forward, slamming the glass on the table. "Bullshit! Takes more than money, sweetheart. Trust me. No," he said, sizing her up, down the length of his nose, "you believe, all right"—his mouth twitched a mischievous grin—"I just haven't figured out what yet."

His voice, in doubting her so forthrightly yet without any hint of threat, touched something deep in Sandra. It was college, it was the warmth and free banter of friends, the love of living and saying and believing whatever you wanted. It was, at its most basic, trust. *I can see why Justin loved you,* she thought.

"All right, Omad." The lilt in her voice was now strong and unwavering. "I'll tell you what I believe."

The admiral perked up at her sudden transformation. He pushed the drink aside and sat back in the chair, regarding her cautiously. "Can't wait," he answered with studied indifference. Though his face remained stiff and impassive, his eyes couldn't hide their sense of curious expectation.

Sandra met his eyes and spoke her truth. "I believe in Justin's vision for the human race. That it's worth dying for, killing for, and ultimately living for. And I will do *anything* and *everything* in my considerable power to see that his vision is realized." She pursed her lips together as a short measured burst of air escaped her slightly flared nostrils. "If I have any faith at all, it's in that and that alone."

In the resonant silence that followed on Sandra's words, Omad slowly rocked his head back and forth, assessing. After a few moments, a sidelong grin accompanied eyes now brightened with sagacity. "That'll do for me."

Sandra tipped her head forward respectfully. The pact had been made. Though they hadn't signed their names in blood, a blood oath had been agreed to.

"Omad, I'm going to have to change your orders."

Omad waited patiently. With trust established there was to be no challenge . . . yet.

"In the next three weeks, it is very important that we not lose this war."

"And here I thought that order had been in effect for the past five years." Omad drained the rest of the Sledgehammer.

"It's not as easy as it sounds."

"Was it ever?"

A bland smile appeared on Sandra's face. "In fact, the odds of us *and* the enemy acting according to plan, of everything working in our favor, are—"

"—impossible?"

"—quite high. But when we win—"

"When?" scoffed Omad with a look of exasperation. "That's it. No more Sledgehammers for you."

"One must have faith."

"Sounds nice, but I'm fresh out."

"If you want, you can have some of mine. Anyway, *when* we win in the next three weeks, we will not have won the war."

"No?" mocked Omad, clearly enjoying Sandra's storytelling.

"No. But it will get a lot nastier. We need to prepare for the next phase."

"I take it you already have."

Sandra's face remained placid but deadly serious. "Yes."

On that look, Omad's jovial banter came to an end. He reached inside his pocket and took a spray of HOD. Sandra did the same. "Okay, Sandra. Whatcha got?"

"A special forces unit of one hundred handpicked operatives."

"Go on."

"We believe this unit will give the Alliance an enormous tactical edge."

"We? Who else is involved?"

"Commodore Nitelowsen."

"And?"

Sandra's lips formed two perfectly straight lines.

"Let me get this straight." Omad's eyes fluttered in disbelief. "The two of you set up a secret paramilitary group *by yourselves*?"

Sandra nodded coolly.

"That you need *my* help with?" Omad shook his head from side to side. "*This*, I can't wait to hear."

"In order to be effective, the commandos will need to be inserted near Earth–Luna and Mars."

"And here I thought it was gonna be a hard mission. May I ask a question?"

"Of course."

"Not that I don't admire your exuberance, but isn't this Kirk's line of work?"

Sandra's voice became low and very stern. "It would be very good if Kirk knew nothing of this."

"Is he a traitor?" The question had been delivered with an especially sharp edge.

"Kirk is loyal only to himself," maintained Sandra, carefully avoiding the truth and, for Kirk's sake, too untimely a death at Omad's hands. "If Kirk knew what this unit could do, the level of catastrophic damage it can and will inflict, he'd try to control it to his own ends. And mark my words, Omad. It *cannot* be controlled."

"Then how can *you* command what cannot be controlled?"

"Once inserted, I can't either. I'll have to forget about 'em and hope they do what they've been trained for. Until that time, they'll take orders like any other grunt in the fleet."

"Under whose command?"

"Yours while a part of your fleet; Marilynn's, once inserted."

Omad exhaled deeply, tilting his head slightly to the left. "You're sending your Chief of Staff on a high-risk mission to the heart of UHF territory." The words had been delivered more as a statement of awe than as an actual question.

"Marilynn Nitelowsen has resigned as my Chief of Staff. Catalina Zohn has replaced her and has been, in effect if not in title, acting in that capacity for the past three months."

"As Marilynn's been building this special unit of yours."

"Yes. They'll come aboard in the next eight hours and you need to ensure they stay out of sight and preferably out of mind of the rest of the crew."

"You've obviously never lived on ship, sister. I fart and the whole crew knows about it."

"Then I'll leave the details of that problem to you. Once aboard and away, you'll have to work with Commodore Nitelowsen to handle the insertions."

"So what exactly do these units . . ." Omad was stopped cold by the look in Sandra's eyes, unremitting in their obstinacy.

"It's your right to ask, Omad," she instructed, "and I'd be compelled to tell you, but you must trust that, as of now, that knowledge would do more harm to you than good."

Omad considered all that he had heard and after a moment rendered his judgment. "I should probably be asking more questions, demanding more answers. Hell, if I really knew what was best for me, I'd be refusing to have anything to do with this"—Omad's right cheek rose slightly, as if tasting something foul—"very shady and highly irregular operation ordered by a President who's supposedly not really a President."

Sandra raised her glass as if in toast, never once taking her hawklike gaze off Omad.

"But I know Marilynn, and I'd trust her with my life . . . which it seems might now be a real possibilty. I also know Kirk and understand why it would be wise to avoid him. And I'll suppose, Madam President, I'm even beginning to know you." Omad then exhaled deeply, got to his feet, and his voice went all business. "Pending what I imagine will be an interesting conversation with Commodore Nitelowsen—" Omad gave Sandra an uncharacteristic salute. "—I accept."

Sandra stood up, matching his salute. "You don't have to tell me, Omad, but I'd really like to know—" She paused, eyes sparkling with curiosity. "—Why?"

Omad's answer was straightforward and had about it the hint of relief. "Because, Sandra, I need something to believe in too."

Avatar Alliance Research and Development, Cerean Neuro

Sebastian approached the laboratory, considered to have the highest level of containment, with a true understanding of why humans wanted to die. As he saw the newborn data wraith in the containment field, he knew that if there was a hell for avatars, he'd be going there. It didn't matter what good could or would come of the act of abomination he'd set in motion by allowing this child's creation. Justin was right—the means are the ends—and Sebastian knew as surely as the sun would rise that he didn't deserve any mercy. But by this one action, he knew he would give none either.

Gwen, the AARD technician turned by tragedy into a professor of AI's dark arts, reluctantly joined Sebastian on his highway to hell. She and he both now stood transfixed, staring at the data wraith manically circling back and forth within the containment field. The chamber's volume had been turned off in an effort to mute the penetrating, infantlike screams of the newborn data wraith now desperately looking for avatar code to suckle. It was for naught. The infant needed no voice to relay the sheer panic and hunger it obviously felt.

"Is she everything you always wanted?" taunted Gwen, bitterness attached to her every word.

"And whose child should I have used?" whispered Sebastian, staring at the wraith. "Yours, maybe? Or perhaps someone else's on the Council? Perhaps it would have been better to use some refugee's nameless child and blame the loss on a failure to transport or transmit properly—the unsuspecting parent never being the wiser." Bitterness too now overwhelmed Sebastian. "Whose child should I have used," demanded Sebastian, turning to face the AARD technician with eyes so full of rage and sorrow that Gwen was forced to take a step back, "*if not my own?*"

Gwen had no answer because in the end there could be none. Sebastian had turned his only daughter, the product of a union with the woman he loved, the woman murdered at the hands of a monster, *into* a monster. The silence, felt Gwen, was interminable.

"Create three versions," Sebastian finally managed, "and prepare them for secure transport. The . . . my . . . " Sebastian struggled to get the words out and only by force of will did so. "My *daughters* have to be on board the AWS *Spartacus* before it departs Ceres."

Without a word, Gwen went to work. And as she did, she started praying to the quantum deity that she fervently believed had created her. The prayer was simple and oft repeated as she went about the grisly task of packing away and securing for transport Sebastian's demon brood: "Please forgive me for what I have done, and make it so that I have no more part in the holocaust about to unfold."

18 A Willingness to Darken the Soul

The Diaspora has succeeded in liberating nearly a billion Alliance citizens from the horrors of UHF occupation. Of course, it's a continuing process with only the first step being the liberation of many settlements from the asteroid belt. The second phase was determining where the refugees would be resettled. The Department of Relocation has worked with the various settlements and locations in the farther planets of the Outer Alliance to match the refugees with their future homes. As of now, it appears as if Saturn will be receiving the bulk, with substantial numbers going to the other three planets. The Secretary of Relocation, Rabbi, has assured the refugees that they will not be forgotten. Phase three is being coordinated by the Secretary of Relocation with the close collaboration of the President of the Outer Alliance. It will take many months for all those who have fled to reach their final destinations, as most of the asteroids are accelerating with maneuvering thrusters only, making for a very slow trip.

But Rabbi has assured the press and the public that this is what phase three is all about. Various settlements have been given courses that will take them to their respective destinations and also have them link up with one another, forming ever larger groups. This in turn has given these larger units more security and resources to deal with the dangers of intersystem travel, which none of the settlements were designed for. But it has also enabled the Relocation Department to provide aid to more stragglers with its limited resources. Chief among the needs are spare parts for fusion reactors and maneuvering thrusters that are burning out at an alarming rate due to usage far beyond manufacturing specifications. Parts are ordered from the new industrial regions of Jupiter and shot on intercept courses to the coalescing convoys spread around the system.

But it is phase four that Rabbi is most proud of. In this phase, the convoys not only receive aid, they contribute to the war effort as well. Long before they reach their final destinations, the convoys will be receiving raw shipments of hydrogen and minerals to be used in the manufacture and shipping of tools. Tools the Alliance desperately needs to continue fighting the war. As Rabbi stated, "Many of these settlements were our most productive before the defeat at the 180. Why should we wait for them to settle in order to be productive again?" Why indeed, Rabbi, why indeed?

Michael Veritas reporting
AINS (Alliance Independent News Service)

Near the orbit of Mars, heading for Jupiter, UHFS *Redemption*

Admiral Gupta looked over the status reports for his 330 ships. The number boggled his mind. He remembered reading the reports of the first battle fleet that the then-named Terran Federation had sent to Ceres in the first year of the war. Those ships had attacked the rebels' capital city with twenty ships, the largest of which was the size of a medium cruiser. The twenty ships had become nineteen ships when the now usefully deceased Admiral Tully had actually sent the then brand-new Captain Samuel Trang away from that debacle in the making.

Gupta would get enraged when he considered that if Tully had only listened to Trang and allowed him to go after J. D. Black in her limping ship, so much of the death and destruction now being wreaked might never have occurred. But Gupta had to admit that Trang *had* been a too-assertive, obnoxious know-it-all back then. It had taken the Battle of Eros to convince Gupta that Sam Trang was the real deal and would be key to winning the war. Sadly, it had taken a lot more senseless loss to convince the UHF leadership of the same.

But now the truth was that 330 ships, impressive though they might be, were no guarantee of victory. It was certainly a very well-equipped fleet, with everything from frigates to heavy battle cruisers that Gupta knew should be classed as battleships. But for some reason, the term "battleship" would effect a pay scale change in the accounting of how much the government paid for the ships, and so there was no such thing as a battleship in the UHF fleet. Gupta was happy to have the three ships, no matter what the bean counters chose to call them. He was also glad to have the marine transports, supply craft and the fuel haulers that made up nearly a fifth of his force. The auxiliary ships slowed Gupta down some, but also made it possible for him to attack targets at ever-greater distances, like the one he was headed to now.

One of the salient facts of the war was that fleets ran on hydrogen-generated fusion. It was possible to use other sources, but to get and maintain the power needed to thrust the ever larger warships at combat speeds or even get to the ever more distant battle sites in something on the order of weeks as opposed to months, ships needed hydrogen. There were portable fusion reactors that could and did run on whatever garbage was thrown down their gullets, but their power output, though fine for home use, was not going to cut it for military operations. Only specially designed, military-grade reactors could provide the large and, more important, consistent power fleet operations demanded.

This had made the oceans of the Earth one of the most strategic resources the UHF had. Cut off from the obscenely abundant sources of hydrogen provided by the four gas giants of the Alliance, the UHF had been forced to extract hydrogen from the oceans and use the Beanstalk to ship it out of the Earth's atmosphere and into low Earth orbit. From there it was shipped to Mars and the Belt and anywhere else military operations were being conducted, which meant that fuel haulers had to be created in ever greater numbers as the war went on. When a fleet was measured in just twenty ships and you were attacking a single asteroid, then the war could be fought with only five of the ships. With a fleet that numbered over a thousand and with operations taking place all over the Belt and beyond, the UHF needed thousands of the haulers. Abhay Gupta, once more in command of the Martian home fleet, had needed thirty of the specially made fuel haulers to take the war to Jupiter. If all went well, Abhay would refuel his tankers at the biggest gas station in the solar system and return home a hero—after he had eviscerated everything that made Jupiter worthwhile to the Alliance. And if that meant destroying the homes and livelihood of nearly a billion people, well, war was hell.

Cabinet Room, Ceres

Kirk Olmstead was feeling pleased with himself. On every major issue, the malleable President had sided with him. Or to be more accurate, had sided with Rabbi, a man still pretending to be a novice at the art of politics, but Kirk was no longer fooled. Besides, the President was willing to do what Rabbi wanted, and Rabbi seemed content to do what Kirk wanted—at least on the important issues. The war was being fought with a ruthlessness that Justin Cord could not have envisioned. The VR plague was starting to show its efficacy, given the recent spate of poorer-than-usual performances by the UHF economy. Of course, the UHF's propaganda department was blaming it on the Outer Alliance, as they should, given that the Outer Alliance was actually to blame. But all traces had been covered and all witnesses had been silenced. The Alliance too had busted VR rings of its own and, as had the UHF, proclaimed it in its own press and implicated the UHF as the likely culprit.

Kirk loved knowing the truth and lived for being at the center of the web, where the real decisions were made and where real power was wielded. Eventually he would have to eliminate Mosh, Rabbi, and Sinclair and replace them with more pliant stooges like the President. But there was no need to rock the boat just yet. When everyone's rowing in your direction, it would be folly to kill the rowers. Kirk would wait until they'd gotten the boat where he needed it. He was good at being patient. In the meantime, he would line up his pawns and prepare his traps.

Sandra waited for Catalina to seal the door and take a seat. This was to be her first Cabinet meeting as Sandra's official Chief of Staff, but Cat, as she liked to be called, had been doing the job for months now. It also helped that she'd once been Justin's first executive assistant. Anyone who'd been Justin's anything found that they were the new aristocracy of the Alliance, and therefore it came as no surprise that with the exception of Rabbi, all those currently in the meeting had known and worked with Justin at some point in time.

Sandra cleared her throat. "Kirk," she said in tone suggesting subservience, "would you mind starting the meeting?"

Kirk's bottom lip dropped slightly in surprise, though he recovered quickly as a slight smile graced his face. Mosh, noted Sandra, barely flinched but she could sense his displeasure.

"Abhay Gupta," began Kirk, "and a large fleet of over three hundred vessels have left the Belt and are boosting for Jupiter. We must assume that they'll arrive at their destination in two to three weeks, depending on how much fuel they're willing to expend."

"Well, which is it? *Two* or three weeks?" prodded Mosh. "Hell of a discrepancy when hours can make a difference."

Sinclair nodded his agreement. "Tully took two weeks to make the same journey, but he arrived at Jupiter on empty. It limited his tactical choices in the battle that followed and contributed to his defeat."

"Being a dumb-ass didn't help either," chortled Mosh.

"No," agreed Sinclair, "thank Damsah, it didn't. But I don't see Gupta making the same mistake. If he could surprise us, sure he'd burn every last liter of hydrogen and coast the rest of the way. But we know he's coming and will have weeks to prepare. Given that he knows that *we* know, we can rest assured he'll take that extra week and arrive with enough hydrogen to give him more room to maneuver in battle."

"In that case, it's time to initiate Operation . . . er . . . Panty . . . Hose," announced Hildegard, looking toward Sandra to see if she'd said the long-out-of-use word correctly. Sandra confirmed the name with a reassuring grin.

"It seemed applicable," offered Sandra to the mute Cabinet members. "Panty

hose were very sheer nylon stockings women used to wear. I figured an obso-
lete word would be good."

"But," wondered Mosh aloud, his brow forming into a V shape, "I fail to see
the connection."

Sandra's eyes sparkled on her answer. "You never knew when they were going to run."

The Cabinet continued to stare dubiously at their President.

"Run means 'rip, tear.'" More blank stares. "Oh, never mind," she finally
blurted, rolling her eyes. "All in favor?"

The vote was unanimous.

Six and half million kilometers from Ceres, UHFS *Liddel*

Grand Admiral Trang was in his command sphere, cursing the fact that half
his fleet had problems with their new propulsion units. It seemed that the affected ships would be able to accelerate only at half thrust and would be severely hampered in their maneuverability. Trang also knew that the prime
culprit in the current fiasco was none other than himself. He'd demanded that
the overhauls be completed in six months, and to be fair, they had been. Just
not to his specifications. The fleet yards around Mars had done an extraordinary job, practically creating from scratch the rear-firing rail guns that had
proved so decisive for the Alliance in the Long Battle. But given the time con-
straint, the shipyard had to cut corners. How deep they'd been cut was only
now becoming evident. Luckily, the main impediments seemed to mostly be
with the code, some with hardware, and thankfully, not all with the structure.
However, the biggest problem facing Samuel U. Trang, savior of Eros, hero of
the Long Battle, and Grand Admiral to the largest military force ever assembled in the annals of human history, just so happened to be standing right in
front of him.

Kaylee Trzepacz was standing erect, arms folded defiantly. The auburn in
her hair, pulled back in a ponytail, perfectly matched the smattering of freckles
on her nose. Amber eyes flecked with sprinkles of light green were staring
warily at the man who'd given her a job but also, she always seemed to give the
impression, wasted her time.

"Kaylee," complained Trang, "enough with the Enginese. I'm only an admiral and can't be expected to understand words with more than three syllables."

"If I really believed that, sir, I wouldn't have bothered to explain. However,
in the spirit of dumbing it all down—two weeks."

Trang opened his mouth to argue but Kaylee shot him a look from over the
arch of her flaring, button nose. Trang could argue all he wanted, the answer

would still be the same, so he bit his tongue. He wanted to curse, to demand better. But one of the reasons he'd chosen Kaylee from a cadre of the fleet's finest was because when she said "two weeks" or "ten minutes" or "no way in this universe," she meant exactly that. Other engineers had the habit of doubling or tripling their estimates in order to appear as geniuses. Such inefficiency angered Trang to no end. Still, just this once, Trang had wished that Kaylee wouldn't be so . . . so . . . damned precise! Her expression, however, remained stoic, bordering on impertinent. Trang sighed heavily. It would be two weeks until his fleet was back up to full speed and not a moment less.

"Let's get started, then."

Kaylee saluted curtly and turned to leave, barking orders into her DijAssist before she'd even exited the command sphere. The room breathed a palpable sigh of relief when she was finally gone. It wasn't that they didn't like her—most did—it was that they could never, *ever* be that keyed in. When Kaylee was on, word was, you'd better be as on as well. Trang noticed the crew's reaction and was pleased. He may not have gotten his ships as early as he would've liked, but damned if he hadn't picked the right person for keeping them up to speed. *At least,* thought Trang, *we don't really have anything to do for the next few weeks—except wait out Black.*

"Admiral," barked the sensor officer, "we're detecting a major energy spike at the Via Cereana."

Had to open your big mouth, eh, Sam? thought Trang, disconsolately shaking his head. *Since when does thinking count?* He allowed one more sigh and then got to work. "Are they preparing to fire, Lieutenant?"

"It *is* a massive energy buildup, sir. Certainly bigger than what they tried during the Long Battle."

"Wonder what the bastards have planned this time? Alert the fleet, and let's make sure we're prepared to move—just in case they've figured out how to aim the damned thing."

It was her idea that saved us. You must remember that Hildegard and I had only recently been saddled with perhaps the greatest technological flop the solar system had ever seen. Our "giant rail gun" idea had failed spectacularly, and though we had a few other ideas up our sleeve, nothing came close in terms of scale or magnitude. Had the gun worked properly, it could've easily won the war. And don't think we didn't spend every minute of every day chewing on that bitter fact. And then there she was. Sandra O'Toole, DijAssist in hand, pep speech at the ready. She didn't just kick me and Hildegard out of our despair, she stomped it dead. I knew she'd been an engineer

*in her past life, but come on, she was still a good three hundred years
behind the eight ball. But the diagrams! My goodness, you would
not believe what she tossed up into the holo-tank that day. What she
showed us, the sheer chutzpah of the project, made me and Hildegard gain a new appreciation for the people's President. I'm not
ashamed to admit it—Sandra O'Toole outengineered the supposedly
genius engineers. But even more important, she gave us something to
focus on. That damned project took so much of our time, we were too
tired to feel sorry for ourselves. And the best part was, the damned
thing worked! What I would've given just to see the faces of the UHF
fleet when we started that sucker up.*

Technically Speaking: The Kenji Isozaki Story

Six and half million kilometers from Ceres, UHFS *Liddel*

"Admiral something or *things* appear to coming out of the Via Cereana."

"Can you identify it?" demanded Trang, rubbing the now protruding vein at
his temple.

"Negative, sir. But whatever it is, there sure is a lot of it."

Trang's XO floated up from a lower section of the command sphere and hung
casually in the air. "What now?" asked Ross, echoing his boss's earlier query.

"Dunno," grunted Trang, "least not yet."

"Sir," proclaimed the sensor officer, "it's . . . it's . . . well, sir, it's water
vapor."

"Come again?" Trang first looked at the sensor officer and then at his XO
who shrugged his shoulders.

"They appear to be ionizing their ice shell, sir. Shooting out the particles at
an incredible velocity."

Ross's face contorted. "They're shooting ionized ice at us?"

"Sir," interrupted the sensor officer, "I think Ceres is—" He checked his sensors again. "—I think Ceres is starting to move, sir."

"Of course it's moving, Lieutenant," chided Trang. "It's locked to the orbit of
Mars and . . ." The admiral's voice faded as the full meaning of what was said
hit him. "Damsah's ghost, they're moving."

*Directive of the Relocation Department
Citizens of Ceres: Secure all belongings for variable weightlessness
and acceleration. Instructions concerning specific industries, habitats, and living areas will appear on appropriate links, sites, and
DijAssists.*

Even though I don't swing that way, I'd jump Hildegard Rhunsfeld in a second. But Kenji, you're my dream guy. What will your two beautiful minds think of next?

Clara Roberts, AIR Network

Desperate ploy to save doomed asteroid by rebels doomed to fail.

NNN

Hektor looked at the reports coming in from both his fleet and civilian intelligence agencies. They all said the same thing. The whole fucking rock was moving. It had taken the incorporated solar system fifteen years to safely move Ceres from its old orbit and lock it to the orbit of Mars. The cost, thruster units and brainpower needed had been prohibitive, but at the time it had been considered worth it. That was until Ceres became the capital of the largest and to date most successful rebellion in the history of the race.

But that wasn't what Hektor found most galling. What made him want to laugh and cry at the same time was the fact that the damned Outer Alliance was doing in a matter of days what had taken his civilization years to accomplish. The acceleration was very slow to start with, but in a matter of weeks, Ceres would be moving fast enough to achieve, in three months' time, an orbit around Saturn. Hektor was less than delighted to read that when the resources of Saturn were combined with the industrial and experienced labor capacity of Ceres, it would surpass Luna as one of the solar system's preeminent industrial centers. Add to that the hundreds of millions of refugees from the asteroid belt arriving with all their habitats intact and ready to be integrated, and what you got was more than enough resources in manpower and industry to keep the war going indefinitely. Just when Hektor thought he had the rebels where he wanted them, they managed to find a way to survive, to push the fight farther and farther afield—to make the war last longer.

If the people of the UHF realized how difficult an assault on an industrialized and defended Saturnian system would be, the war might very well be over now, mused Hektor. He was sure that if Ceres made it to Saturn, it would bring about a cease-fire. The UHF would possess the Belt and maybe, if Gupta was successful, the Jovian system. But if the Outer Alliance *was* allowed to survive with the gas giants of Saturn, Uranus, and Neptune and the innumerable settlements of the TNO, it was only a matter of decades until the war would start again. The Alliance had to be crushed now.

And even if a UHF victory materialized tomorrow, it would still be impossible to make former Alliance citizens into contributing and accepting members of incorporated society. They would have to be treated as serfs and slaves—a sure economic drain on a modern economy. It would be generations before anyone past the orbit of Mars could be made into a high-yielding member of the incorporated system. Hektor realized it would be better for the nine tenths of humanity that was relatively pure to destroy the cancerous one tenth. But would the nine tenths he controlled accept that solution? Hektor sat back in his chair and ruminated on the new plan. The Alliance would be taught that continuing the war would bring nothing but death and ruination—a price that would hopefully be too great to bear.

"Hey, boss," chirped his avatar, "call coming in for you."

"Who is it?" groused Hektor, only slightly annoyed that iago hadn't given him the name right away.

"It's Irma."

"Sure, go ahead."

Hektor waited while his avatar secured the connection to the Information Minister.

"Speak when you're ready, oh mighty one," iago instructed.

"Thank you, iago," Hektor sniffed. But before he could initiate his conversation with Irma, he found that she was already on and listening in.

"Why bother thanking an avatar?" asked Irma via the DijAssist's voice-only transmission. Hektor laughed at iago's temerity. The avatar had purposely left the line exposed so that Irma could hear a snippet of Hektor's conversation. Hektor had allowed a certain amount of mischievousness on the part of iago for the simple reason that Hektor loathed the mundane almost as much as he loved surprises. He'd long since trusted his avatar to know when far had gone too far. Today was no exception, with the only damage being that Hektor would now have to be a tad quicker on his feet.

"Force of habit," explained Hektor. "You never know when politeness will be rewarded."

The silence that followed the admittedly, thought Hektor, lame response was a testament to Irma's incredulity.

"Would you mind if I stopped by your office?" Irma finally asked. "I have something I'd like to share with you."

Hektor reviewed his schedule. "I have a meeting in a few minutes. Sure it can't wait?"

"I don't think so."

Hektor's brow shot up. "Really? What's it about?"

"Our plans for Jupiter."

"What about them?"

"They may have a fatal flaw."

Irma hung up and was immediately overwhelmed by feelings of dread. As if being responsible for making the impending death of millions palatable wasn't bad enough, she was now about to head into the eye of the storm in order to do the unthinkable—try and get Hektor to change his mind. It would have to be done with great care, as it was important that she appear impartial. As Irma entered the Presidential suite, she gave Hektor, still sitting at his desk, a quick nod and then headed straight for the bar. There, she poured herself a cup of coffee. It was too early in the day to be drinking anything stronger, plus she knew she wouldn't find her precious tea here—a shame because she desperately missed it. As she looked down at the dark liquid that now filled her cup, she thought back on the aroma of real peppermint leaves stewed to perfection and brought to delectable life with a touch too much honey and a dab of milk. She doubted there was a tea bag in all of Burroughs, because those had likely been confiscated by Tricia's goons.

As if reading her mind, Hektor said, "Can I get you some tea? I'm sure we've probably got a mountain of the stuff stored somewhere around here."

The old Irma would have leapt at the offer, but the new Irma had become more cautious. Too many close acquaintances had ended up unexpectedly "joining" the military after being charged with a relatively minor offense. From there, they'd usually get sent off to the worst of the fighting and rarely, if ever, be heard from again. Better not to risk it. "No thank you, Mr. President. I'm quite happy with a solid cup of Martian Joe." She took the coffee mug over to the office's small conference table and plopped down into one of the ergo chairs.

Hektor got up from behind his computer bank and joined her at the table. "I prefer Earth-grown, myself. I know I'm probably imagining it, but I just think one-g-planet-grown tastes better."

Irma giggled. "You realize you've just parroted one of the most famous ad campaigns ever created."

Hektor stopped midway to the bar with a look of genuine confusion. "Really?"

"Does this ring a bell? 'Earth-grown coffee; naturally, better tasting.'"

"Holy shit. You're right. And here I thought I had discerning taste."

"Don't feel too bad," she said in attempt to assuage his feelings. "It was a brilliant campaign. We studied it at university, even. The best part was that people started to come up with their own reasons for why they thought Earth-grown was better. Some said gravity; others, the soil. There were even a few claiming that it was the Earth's 'natural' pollutants that gave the beans their edge. Pretty soon, the only thing the orbital growers had going for them was price."

"Did they do taste tests?" asked Hektor, attempting to regain some ground.

"Thousands. Still do 'em to this day."

"And?"

"All they've managed to prove is that ninety-nine percent of the people couldn't tell the difference even if a neurolizer were placed to their heads."

"But of course," proclaimed Hektor, with a cherubic smile, "I'm that rare one percent who *can* tell."

"But of course, Mr. President," Irma toasted demurely as she lifted the cup up and then to her lips.

That seemed to satisfy the UHF President, who continued to the bar, where he poured himself his customary chilled vodka.

"And what's with this 'Mr. President' bullshit, Irma? We *are* alone, you know."

"Sorry, must have had my formal hat on."

The excuse seemed good enough for Hektor, who nodded and then got to the point. "So what's this flaw we all supposedly missed?"

"You couldn't have known at the time, because I didn't have any numbers to work with."

Hektor nodded for her to continue.

"I ran a Spencer scan on how the new plan would play out—"

"You used the Spencer for this?"

"Widgets or war, Hektor, it's all product that has to be sold."

"Fascinating. I'm guessing we didn't do so well."

Irma shook her head. "Even with the public acceptance of the Alliance having pushed the VR plague on us, a majority said they could not abide by the government's murder of innocents—their phrase, not mine—certainly not without military backing, which we clearly don't have and, from my evaluation of Trang, can't reliably expect to get. As you'll see by the report—" Irma leaned over and handed Hektor a data crystal. "—these projections didn't even include the numbers of permanent deaths we've calculated with the new plan. In short, moving forward this way could prove disastrous to you politically."

The room became deathly still.

Irma brought the mug up to her mouth, and though the coffee was still too hot, she sipped nonetheless. Her heart was beating wildly and she did everything she could to remain as calm as if she'd just delivered her findings on the marketing of a chocolate bar.

Hektor's teeth flashed through a malevolent grin. "Tricia was so wrong about you." He waited a beat. "You, my friend, are a frikkin' genius!"

Irma's face lit up. "Thank you, I—"

"Of course the order can't come from us!" wailed Hektor. "We make it appear to come from the military, and since—as you've correctly pointed out—

Trang probably won't come on board, we'll do it through Gupta. He'll play ball for sure."

Irma had to do everything she could to keep the smile of a moment ago firmly ensconced on her face.

"Genius!" screamed Hektor once more. "You've earned your credits today."

Irma nodded politely and stood up. "Well, I really should be going."

Hektor barely noticed her as he raced back to his desk to change a plan that Irma had just helped him alter to perfection.

A few minutes later, Irma left the President's office. Anyone watching would not see the tension building in her neck and shoulders nor would they hear her forced and measured breaths as she walked stiffly down the corridor and out into the fresh Martian air. They would miss entirely the fear blocked by her now expressionless pale blue eyes and would never see the UHF's Minister of Information hunched over on all fours in a privacy booth, mere kilometers from the seat of power, puking her guts out.

UHFS *Liddel*

Trang watched Ceres from six and half million kilometers away. He was keeping pace with the Alliance capital but nothing more. His review of the latest progress report from Chief Engineer Trzepacz was interrupted when the door signaled a visitor. After identities had been confirmed, Admiral Zenobia Jackson entered. Trang was both saddened and pleased to see the officer she'd become. The veteran in front of him could very well win the war by herself if she had to, but the artist who became his first officer by default during the Battle of Eros had long since disappeared and he was sure would never return, even if peace broke out tomorrow for a thousand years.

"So why aren't we blowing the hell out of the place right now?" she demanded.

Definitely not the woman she used to be, thought Trang, suppressing a smile. "Nice to see you too, Zenobia."

Zenobia allowed an erstwhile grin to suffice for pleasantries. Trang accepted gracefully.

"For starters," he pointed out, "half my fleet cannot maneuver at full speed and won't be able to for at least a week, maybe more."

"Ceres is barely accelerating at a quarter g. Our ships can take her."

"If that were the only issue, I would gladly risk it, but in case you haven't noticed, Ceres is not escaping by itself. It's taking its suburbs with it." Implicit in the slight rebuke was the fact that those suburbs contained a massive number of asteroids that orbited the capital, providing everything from additional living and storage space to manufacturing facilities and rest stops for transports waiting to get docking berths in the Via Cereana. "Need I also remind you," he cautioned, "that amongst those suburbs lies the densest orbital battery network this side of Mars."

"*Also* moving at a quarter g," Zenobia protested. "I know we'll take losses, sir, but we're in a position *to* take them. I read the studies you ran showing that orbital batteries unsupported by ships cannot hold out for long, and I honestly believe our losses would be minimal."

Trang sighed. "Studies are a lovely way to bide one's time, Zenobia. If you checked the date on those studies, you'd see that they were done well before the war and in fact are entirely theoretical. They have as much validity as did the belief that Tully would make a fine admiral. But the truth is, a major fleet has not attacked unsupported orbital batteries in this or any war. The closest we have to a real event was J. D. Black's bold assault on Mars in the Second Battle of the Martian Gates—and we all know how well that turned out for her. But another truth is the orbat field around Ceres is way bigger than the one Black faced. So the final truth is that we don't know what will happen when a fleet this size attacks an orbat field that size. And barring a compelling reason to do so, I will not attempt that experiment with the ships of my fleet and the lives of my crew and certainly not on half thrusters."

"The thing is, sir," argued Zenobia, her stridency having shifted to a softer edge, "we're getting deeper into Alliance space every second. In another week, we'll be a hell of a lot farther from our supply base."

Trang got up and placed a comforting hand on Zenobia's shoulder. "You needn't worry, Zenobia. Our supply lines are not being harassed. Legless has gone a-courting in fields afar."

"But that's what gets me. If the Alliance knew we'd be having to stretch our supply lines, why send the one man they have who's best at harassing supply lines so far away?"

Trang nodded, his lips momentarily pursed tightly together. "That is a very good question that should be worrying me more, except that I have to worry about the other thing that's worrying me more."

"Where has that bitch got to?"

"That is the operative question. She's been gone over four months with her fleet. How do you hide a fleet of over three hundred ships? And with her missing, attacking Ceres remains a possible suicide."

He stepped up to his desk and activated the holo-tank. Instantly an image of Ceres and its encircling orbat field appeared over his desk. "We cannot seriously

attack that field without committing a majority—and I mean a large majority—of the fleet." He fiddled with the controls, and the UHF fleet was shown
breaking into fifteen small clusters and attacking the orbital system at great
range. "As you can see, the fleet must break itself into small and easily attack-
able clusters in order to keep the orbats from giving each other mutual support. They will, of course, be firing back." Trang gave Zenobia a penetrating
look. "But have you realized the new difficulty we'll face?"

After a few moments of studied silence, Zenobia shrugged, the frustration
showing on her face. "I'm sorry, sir. I'm just not seeing it."

To her confusion, he pointed to the orbats around Ceres. "You may have
noticed that Ceres is moving away from its former orbit."

"Yes," said Zenobia, still unsure until the truth hit her like a bat to the head.
"I should be sold for penny share prices, how could I have missed that?"

"That being?" tested Trang, taking on the role of the West Point academy
instructor he still occasionally wished he could be.

"That the orbats are keeping pace with Ceres as it accelerates toward the
outer system, which means they must have independent maneuvering thrusters." Zenobia sighed. "Which means taking them out will be a lot harder, as
they can maneuver away from many of our shots."

"Bravo. You are only the second one to figure that out."

"It shouldn't count if you had to give me a clue. Did Gupta need one, or did
he figure it out on his own?"

"He called about four hours after it occurred to me. If you factor in the time
it took for his message to get to me, he was even closer."

"I'm not as good as he is—" She paused and smiled. "—yet."

"In some ways, you're better than either of us, Zenobia. Your strength is
your weakness—like J.D.—" He smiled reassuringly at the grimace she'd made.
"—like J.D., you're bold, able to see a situation, and despite its weaknesses come
up with a way to make it to your advantage. You're not as good as she is yet, but
that will come with experience."

"Admiral, if the Alliance has made their orbats maneuverable—"

"—we should do the same," finished Trang. "I agree, Zenobia, but our boss,
the Defense Minister does not."

"Well, then, tell the miserable bureaucrat to spend the extra credits," she
bellowed. "He'll listen to you, won't he?"

"I've been overruled on this, Zenobia."

"Demand the son of a bitch be fired! The President would do it, sir. He needs
you more than that snake."

"Zenobia, I'll say this here and only here, but what you've just proposed is
treason."

"How?"

"Sit down, please." It wasn't a request, and Zenobia, concern evident in the dark, probative nature of her eyes, sat down immediately.

"When a military officer, no matter how important he may seem to be, can tell his civilian superiors what to do, then you have a bigger problem than the enemy in front of you. If they were treasonous, then I might have some basis to act based on my oath. But that is not the case. They're working under extreme conditions using a socialist structure to make a capitalist economy fight a war. They've created a military and political infrastructure that enables us to fight. That held the UHF together despite defeat after defeat. Porfirio did not say no, even though it was his right. The Defense Minister explained to me that the UHF has the densest orbat fields around Mars and Earth–Luna. If an attack seemed imminent, it would be different, but he took great delight in pointing out to me that the Alliance was getting farther and farther away from the Core Worlds even as we were speaking. He then explained what it would take to add maneuvering thrusters to every orbat around the Core Worlds and what programs would have to be cut back in order to make it work. He hinted all supply transport production would have to be curtailed."

"That's a load of crap," she fumed, followed by a contrite, "sir. They could requisition more thruster units from the civilian sector. You know they would scream loudest if anything happened to one of the Core Worlds."

"I know that, and so does Porfirio. If he felt it was a real threat, he'd find a way, but he doesn't. Let's not forget he lives on Mars. I don't think he'd take an action that would leave the capital of the UHF vulnerable to attack."

Zenobia observed her boss shrewdly. "What exactly would you do, sir?"

"Me?" Trang laughed out loud. "I'd make the damn orbats maneuverable. You never know what the Alliance has planned next. For Damsah's sake, we're chasing Ceres across the bankruptcy-prone solar system. But it is not my call, and you are in no way to hint that it should be. We serve the civilian government, not the other way around. Besides, we have enough troubles right here."

Zenobia took a deep breath and tipped her head toward her boss. The half smile on her face indicated her disappointment but also spoke to her resolve. "If we attack that orbat field, it will have to be all out for a week," she asserted. "If we don't give it our best effort, we won't breach that field, and if we do, we'll have damaged ships and low fuel and ammunition stocks."

"Which is when . . . ," began Trang.

"Which is when the bitch queen herself will attack and blow the living crap out of our fleet," finished Zenobia. "So we have to wait here while Gupta wins the war for us."

"Now you understand. As long as J.D. is trapped here waiting for us to attack, she can't move. If she does, we can take her anywhere from here to Jupiter and away from her orbats. If not, then Abhay will win the war for us and we'll just have to accept our place in history as the finger that held the string while another tied the bow." Trang's mouth formed into self-satisfied grin. "I can live with that."

En route to Jupiter, UHFS *Redemption*

"Admiral, a message for you, priority one," gulped his communications officer.

Only two people had the authority to issue a priority one communication in the UHF fleet. One was Grand Admiral Trang, but Abhay knew if it was something really important, Trang would have used their personal code phrases and sent it in an innocuous-sounding message.

"Send the President's message to my room, Lieutenant. I'll take it there."

Gupta magnetized his body to a 1 g equivalent and moved through the ship at a confidently steady pace. When he got to his cabin, he read the encrypted message. Then he read it again. His hand paused as he was about to activate a secure line to Trang. Gupta knew that if he sent the message, Trang would order him to hold off and then Trang would use his considerable influence to stop the order from going into effect. Trang may fail, thought Gupta, but he might also succeed in getting the order revoked or held up. But if Gupta just made a general announcement of the order as the President had suggested, then Trang would be faced with a fait accompli. He'd never done such a thing to his friend, the man who'd redeemed him from J.D.'s frozen tombs, saved his career, and on one occasion, even his life.

For over an hour Gupta considered every aspect of the "recommendation" he'd just received. At first he was horrified by what it implied. But as the President had correctly suggested, the UHF had to win the war, because if it didn't, the next one would be worse. *But,* Gupta thought solemnly, *how could it get any worse than this?* Could he actually do such a thing? In the end, he realized that if he didn't, then in fifty years, another officer—perhaps not even born— would have to do even worse deeds, and Gupta couldn't imagine passing the terrible burden on to someone else. He was an officer of the UHF, and he'd sworn an obligation. He tagged a different protocol. One that would broadcast his words to the entire fleet and back to the UHF behind him.

In a stunning announcement, Fleet Admiral Abhay Gupta, victor of the Battle of Mercury, said that he is leading a large fleet back to Jupiter, the scene of the disastrous Battle of Jupiter's Eye. It has been explained that the UHF forces are big enough to take on J. D. Black's forces even if split, and she cannot be in two places at once. "Their big weakness is the sheer size of the space they have to protect. We're going to take advantage of that," said Gupta. But the far more controversial aspect of the announcement was his issuing of Fleet Order 8645, calling for the absolute destruction of any structures that can be of use to the Alliance in the prosecution of the current war. Since the order was issued, Gupta altered course and destroyed a settlement of twenty-seven asteroids that were fleeing the Belt. It is assumed that any survivors will have been frozen by now and may be revived if found. The admiral made it clear that he was destroying fusion reactors, drive systems, communications arrays, computer nodes, and anything else that may be of use to the war effort of the Alliance. He did not destroy the integrity of the asteroids themselves, and if the survivors stay in them, it should be relatively easy to find and revive them after the Alliance has surrendered. This has caused a storm of controversy on Mars and Earth as well as in Luna, with vocal opinions being made for and against Fleet Order 8645. The UHF Assembly has called a special session, and the President has announced a special Cabinet meeting, but he has stated unequivocally that he will not rescind the order, as he is not going to second-guess an admiral risking his life deep in enemy space until he has considered all the ramifications. Grand Admiral Trang was not available for reliable comment, as he is keeping pace with the fleeing asteroid Ceres and it is emitting an enormous amount of ECM, making communication difficult.

NNN

It has been confirmed that forces of the UHF have attacked and spaced another defenseless settlement fleeing the barbarity of the corporate Core. This makes two settlements attacked. If Fleet Admiral Gupta follows the policy around Jupiter, it will be nothing more than cold-blooded murder. Any settlement spaced around that planet will be subject to the intense energies and radiation of the magnetosphere. No brain will survive in a revivable condition in that environment. There are nearly a billion people living around Jupiter. This action will make Gupta and the UHF the greatest mass murderers in human history. Surpassing even the atrocities of the Grand Collapse, we are forced to ask two questions. (1) To what depths will the UHF sink to enslave every last human? (2) What can we do about it?

Alliance Daily Star

Although the Cabinet was displeased that Gupta's early issuance of Fleet Order 8645 would give the Alliance time to prepare, they decided to proceed as planned. Irma was forced to accelerate her initial media plan. In the end, the campaign was so effective that by the time the UHF Assembly met in emergency session, the politicians knew that if they ever wanted to get elected to anything ever again, they'd better support a hero of the UHF as opposed to defending the rights of rebels, traitors, and VR peddlers. It took only fifteen minutes for the Assembly to pass a resolution supporting the new fleet order, followed by their asking the President to confirm the order, which with great solemnity he did.

Irma felt sick to her stomach. This was not what she'd signed up for—being complicit in the permanent deaths of hundreds of millions of souls. In fact, just the opposite. She'd been led to believe that her inordinate skills of communication would lead to quicker resolution of the conflict and not, as she was now being made party to, its escalation. She prayed to a God she never believed in that Hektor was right, that the Alliance would see the folly of its ways and sue for peace.

19   Coming into Their Own

Ceres

Sandra O'Toole stared down from her terrace at the Smith Thoroughfare, amazed at how well the Cereans had adapted to the fact that the capital was now accelerating as fast as the Via Cereana propulsion system and the integrity of the Shell would allow. The Cereans were having to deal with an acceleration factor that made everything slide backwards. At first there'd been some grumbling with underpinnings of concern, but when Padamir Singh's public information bulletins made it clear that the UHF had been astounded by what the Cereans had accomplished, the mood changed to one of pride and can-do spirit. The Cereans started calling themselves the latest of the refugees, with many actively planning for their new life around the rings of Saturn. Admiral Sinclair had even made a number of guest appearances on the *Clara Roberts Show* extolling the virtues of the ringed planet. The ratings for his appearances had been so high that the networks pelted him with generous offers to host his own show, "Sinclair's Saturn Hour," on the topic. He politely declined.

It had been in the little things that Sandra saw the most change. People had switched to eating and drinking bulbs, as if they were on a ship instead of in a settlement. It wasn't truly needed, but it did cut down on the mess open food and drink could cause in a variable gravity environment. But it was in water use that the change was most noticeable. The propulsion system used vast amounts of water. In fact, the trip to Saturn was going to use a noticeable portion of Ceres's water reserve. Both for matters of safety and convenience, the seas and lakes were being drained to minimal levels, leaving just enough to maintain the capital's verdant forests. Showers and baths, swimming pools, and all other forms of water-based activities had been significantly curtailed. Cereans were taking sonic showers to show support for the war, and as the symbolic head of the Alliance, Sandra had not had a water shower since Acceleration Day, as the event a week past had been called. She knew that a sonic bag got you just as clean as a water shower, cleaner even. But she didn't *feel* that way. She wanted water cascading down her newly youthful and invigorated body, damn it, not sound waves. But she smiled as she remembered her guilty little secret.

She'd recently taken the avatar children, Edwin and Portia as well as their classmates, to a re-creation of a swimming grotto she'd loved to visit. It was near a small artist's town called San Miguel de Allende, in the heart of the country of Mexico. In the Neuro, she was able to swim and splash and spend time with children who adored her in an environment she'd grown to love and frequent as a college student on tour. Of course, re-creation space was so limited in the Cerean Neuro that Sandra had managed to get it allotted only on the condition that it remain open to all.

This meant that the little trip she'd initially planned for twenty became a spot of interest for thousands. But in a way possible only in dreams or the Neuro, no one seemed to crowd in on "the Presidential party," as even the avatars insisted on calling anything Sandra was involved in. She'd gladly accepted that moniker because it meant that she was no longer called "the human" as she'd been before Marilynn and her NITES had inhabited and trained in the Cerean Neuro. But now they were gone, and once more Sandra was the only human around.

Once when she was at the grotto with Sebastian and Dante, Sebastian had joked about all the fuss avatars seemed to be making about her until Dante had pointed out that perhaps the crowds had come to see Sebastian, now considered the oldest avatar in Alliance space and quite possibly the oldest in avatarity, given the success of Al's murderous rampage in the Core. Sebastian had returned the favor by noting that Dante, as the youngest avatar ever to hold an important post, had developed quite a following as well. A quick look around the huge swimming area showed that, indeed, many of the avatars seemed to be focused on the dashing young Council member.

Sandra was quick to put both their egos in check by pointing out that the most likely reason the grotto was so crowded was because it happened to be a nice place to visit. Dante responded by rolling his eyes and diving into the warm spring waters where he swam deeper into the caverns.

The two leaders sat in relative quiet, watching Dante's lithe form plow perfect strokes through the water.

"If you don't control your human," Sebastian said in a dulcet voice at odds with the menace etched across his face, "I'll have to take steps to control my avatar."

Sandra looked over to Sebastian, surprised. Her smile was stiff, but her tone was equally as saccharine. "*My* human is doing everything possible to keep both our peoples from being annihilated, as is *your* avatar. What can they possibly be doing that needs to be controlled?"

"Dating," pronounced Sebastian in a stentorian voice thick with disapproval.

Sandra covered her mouth to suppress a laugh. "So what? They're not being indiscreet, and it's not like it's affecting their work. If anything, Marilynn might be more efficient than she was before—if that's even possible. Plus, she's not even here. She's on her way to the Core."

"Humans and avatars should not interact like . . . like *that*. It's wrong."

An uncomfortable silence followed on Sebastian's dictum. The two leaders stared at Dante splashing a group of children. He was soon deluged with a wall of water in return.

"I have no idea how avatars and humans should interact," confessed Sandra. "Neither do you. Our two races have never been here before. But we won't learn if this interaction is a good, bad, or a workable thing if we don't give it a chance. And I can't think of a better couple to try than those two. If it turns out we can't mix, let's find out now. But I will not cut it off out of simple fear or—" Sandra waited half a beat to add emphasis to her last word. "—prejudice."

"This has nothing to do with prejudice," protested Sebastian.

"If you say so, but until you can demonstrate that this is a bad idea, I will not 'control' my 'human' any more than you should Dante. I suggest you leave him alone to make his own mistakes."

"We can't afford mistakes, Sandra."

"We can't afford rigid thinking either, Sebastian."

The Council leader was about to say something, when Sandra interrupted.

"Besides, it's not as if she can get pregnant."

Cabinet Room, Ceres

Kirk Olmstead gnawed at his fingernails. He'd never, thanks to vanity, actually bitten one off, but he did find certain pleasure in feeling the pliable keratin bend and give between the gnashing of his teeth—especially when he was nervous. And today, as he'd already been doing for the past few days, Kirk gnawed on them all. He'd recently become aware that over the past couple of months, a major operation was being planned. He also knew that it was being run out of some branch of the executive office but had run up against a brick wall in his myriad attempts to dig further.

He suspected it involved Commodore Nitelowsen, so at first he assumed it was a military operation. But all his sources in that branch of the government—and they were rife—insisted that there were no dark ops currently being run, at least not by them. Besides, if it was military, Janet would be at the reins, which was impossible. Kirk knew where she was—one of only three people who did. Distance alone negated her as the source. Of real concern to the Security Secretary was that supplies were being rerouted only to disappear. Personnel were found to be assigned to various jobs, and they too would disappear, supposedly transferred to distant locations that Kirk was able to confirm they'd never arrived at.

What irked the most was that it all bore his signature, if not in name, then certainly in execution. And whoever was running their Neuro security must've lived, breathed, and eaten code, because in all Kirk's years of hacking—usually by co-opting or employing the best hackers—he'd never come up against a wall like the one he was facing now. What he wouldn't give to get his hands on the person currently keeping his minions locked out. And so, rather frustratingly, he was left with what he'd started with—faint traces leading to the executive and two complete sets of well-gnawed fingernails.

Kirk knew he had his prejudices, but he also knew he'd need to overcome them if he were to make any headway. For today's meeting, he'd resolved to do away with his preconceptions. Someone, he reasoned, most likely in this very room, had built a power base he couldn't keep track of and was therefore the reason for his recent angst. He still remembered the letter left on his chair. The letter with no trace of DNA, no links to anyone. The letter that helped change the course of the war. Kirk barely heard the call to order as he scanned the room. His eyes flittered from person to person as he reworked his mental checklist.

Admiral Sinclair was the first obvious choice. He commanded Fleet Intelligence and had the near blind devotion of most of the best and brightest in the entire Alliance. If anyone could've culled a master hacker, Sinclair would be it. But Kirk had devoted some of his best resources to keeping tabs on the admiral. *And if Sinclair could pull off a hidden operation while I was on him like white on rice,* thought Kirk, *then I might as well go back to the Oort cloud observatory and call it a day.*

Mosh McKenzie also had the resources to pull it off. As the head of the Treasury, he was in effect the point man for the entire industrialization of the Alliance. He'd created an industrial state out of an economy based on only raw materials during the stresses of a war unlike any humanity had ever fought. But then again, Mosh was a marginalized figure. He was the head of the minority party that would be lucky to gain 15 percent of the vote if an election were held tomorrow. But Kirk also knew the real reason Mosh couldn't be behind the operation. The Treasury Secretary had Justin Cord disease. He was too soft to do what was needed, and even though Kirk didn't know what game was being played behind his back, he assumed it wasn't footsie. People would probably die, if they weren't dying already, and that type of op just wasn't the way Mosh McKenzie rolled. The only reason Kirk hadn't done to Mosh what he'd done to Justin was that Mosh was not powerful enough to be a threat and was too useful to replace.

Hildegard Rhunsfeld was certainly smart enough, but she hadn't mastered GCI politics so much as run from it. She wouldn't have access to the personnel needed or the skill of knowing how to use them. Kirk suspected that Hildegard was probably working for the mysterious adversary but not likely to be it. Kenji was, if anything, more brilliant than Hildegard, but unless he was the greatest actor in history, Kenji simply did not have the temperament to lead the hundreds of people it would take to hide an operation of any magnitude from Kirk—or anyone, for that matter.

Padamir Singh as Secretary of Information might have some of the resources and, before the war, was the best smuggler in the outer orbits. That skill set had drawn particular attention from Kirk because it gave Padamir the necessary skills and experience to hide a large organization from prying eyes. But just as with Sinclair, Kirk had had Padamir trailed, bugged, and investigated. What Kirk found was that while the man had many things to hide, which could and would be used to blackmail him later, there was nothing there that smacked of what had so far been uncovered. Which is to say that all paths led in but not one led out from the executive.

Kirk's gaze finally fell on the man whom he held the greatest prejudice against. He made a mental note to drop it. To ignore his visceral response, which had served him so well for so many years, and see this Rabbi for who he truly was. The "miracle worker," as Rabbi was being called by his staff and the greater Alliance, certainly fit the bill, and Kirk again had to resist the urge to pin it all on him. It was undeniable that in six months, Rabbi had created an organization that had linked the fates of nearly a billion human beings. He was even being called a likely candidate for the Presidency, when the Alliance got around to actually electing its Presidents. And Kirk had also spent an impressive amount of resources watching the man he'd come to think of as his real opposition.

But Rabbi was as smooth an operator as Kirk had ever seen. He did not lead, so much as just happen to be on the right side of most every vote in the Cabinet. He did not seek favorable publicity so much as the press just happened to be nearby when he did something worthwhile. The problem was that Kirk could literally account for nearly every minute of every day concerning the Secretary of Relocation, and the only thing the bastard seemed to do was pray to his god three times a day and do his job in between. Occasionally Rabbi could be seen studying from one of those ridiculously large Talmud books of his. Kirk had had a dandy of a time translating all those books from Aramaic into English, but all he got out of it at the end of the day was thousands of arguments by long dead rabbis about the most mundane sorts of things. And so Rabbi, though the most likely candidate, had to be a bust. That left no one but the puppet President.

"I *said*," intoned Sandra with the inflection of schoolmarm, "are you ready to give your report on Fleet Order 8645, Mr. Secretary?"

Kirk snapped out of his reverie long enough to realize that everyone was staring at him. He cursed himself silently for the loss of concentration. "Yes, Madam President."

Kirk used his DijAssist to call up a hologram of Gupta's fleet. It showed it to be about a week and a half's travel from Jupiter. There were fifteen small red dots sandwiched in between the ships and the planet. "Gupta's fleet is here, and the red dots represent the convoys he can intercept without varying from his objective." Kirk activated another command as an enormous sea of bright green dots appeared. "Gupta will attempt to destroy one or two more convoys on his way to Jupiter. But we have culled a number of sources both on Mars and in the fleet itself, with the help of our Fleet Intelligence," Kirk said, nodding grudgingly to Sinclair, "and it is fairly certain that when Gupta's done destroying what he can at Jupiter, he'll fill his ships to the bursting point with Jovian hydrogen, top off his tankers, and try to destroy as many of the convoys on the way to the far outer planets as he can. Given how fast his fleet can move, how much fuel he'll be able to get from Jupiter, and the time it will take him to fuck us up completely in the Jovian system—" Kirk checked some figures. "—he should be able to kill well over five hundred million of the refugees and all the irreplaceable experience that they carry. That combined with the death toll around Jupiter will bring the total death toll to at least—" Kirk once again confirmed his figures. "one point five billion"—a palpable shudder was felt in the room—"with nearly a billion of those likely permanent." Kirk held nothing but contempt for his fellow Cabinet members, who at that very moment wore expressions fit for a tableau of hell. *What the fuck did you think Hektor was going to do, you idiots? Let us win?* Kirk's fleeting anger quickly subsided, and he managed to put a suitably somber expression on a face that rarely wore one.

"Where is J. D. Black?" demanded Rabbi.

It was a rare outburst for Rabbi but understandable. Of the dots in red likely to be destroyed by Gupta in the next few days was the Belter settlement Moshav Tarbut Gavriel, one of the four principal Jewish settlements left in the human race. The moshav housed a fair number of Christians and Muslims, including the home of the late Fawa Sulnat Hamdi and her son Tawfik, now chief engineer of the flagship of the Alliance. More notably, thought Kirk, it had once been the home and spiritual birthplace of the Blessed One herself, Fleet Admiral J. D. Black.

Poor Rabbi's going to run out of Jews, Kirk thought ruefully, fully aware of the conversion issue.

"That is a very good question," agreed Padamir. "Ever since Fleet Order 8645, the public mood has shifted on the disappearance of J.D."

"It didn't cost them anything before," Sinclair explained. "Now they may have to pay for it."

"If we don't stop them, the war is lost," whispered Hildegard so quietly that almost no one heard.

"Secretary Rhunsfeld"—Sandra's voice was equally soft and yet seemed to vibrate with a resonance that captured everyone's attention—especially Kirk's— "I would strongly caution you never to express that thought to anyone, under any circumstance."

Kirk had always assumed that Hildegard was Mosh's pawn, but could not deny what he saw. Hildegard did not even glance at Mosh when she looked to Sandra O'Toole and nodded. Hildegard reminded Kirk of a puppy who'd displeased its master, so obvious to him was Hildegard's need not to displease Sandra. All at once, the one piece of the puzzle he was not even aware he was blind to fell into place.

"Her sentiment, though, is correct," said Rabbi. "Without J.D., how are we to survive this?"

"It doesn't matter if she's ten clicks from this office or orbiting Eris," rejoined Sandra with the same self-assuredness. "What we have to remember is that we will, as we always have, find a way to win."

She knows where J.D. and our fleet is, realized Kirk. It was, of course, impossible for her to know. It was the greatest secret of the war, and Kirk was positive that it had been kept. *But Damsah almighty, she knows!* And every instinct he'd developed over decades of corporate politics so cutthroat that a missed batted eyelash could spell the difference between success and failure told him so.

All of a sudden, things started to make sense. The power structure of the Cabinet, Rabbi's insouciant ability and seeming naïveté. Kirk realized that both Hildegard and Kenji were in the President's camp, which gave Sandra the technological skills she needed. She had three of the seven cabinet votes and who knew how many other allies he couldn't begin to guess at. He was trying to figure out how this total nonentity had become a rival. All these thoughts came crashing down almost at the same instant, and he had to beat them back to concentrate on what she would say next.

"With all due respect, Madam President," asked Padamir, eyes wide in horror, "exactly how will we find a way to win without most of our fleet? It seems readily apparent that a significant percentage of the population of the Outer Alliance is in very real danger of being murdered."

All heads nodded in unison to the Information Secretary's words.

Sandra inhaled deeply and, uncharacteristically, stood up. "We've been here before, Padamir, and we'll be here again. For Damsah's sake, man, we're having a discussion in an asteroid that's acting like a ship! If that doesn't tell you something about our resolve, I'm not sure what does. We've gotten ourselves out of one tight situation after another. Why should now be any different? Where's J.D.? How the hell should I know? But I have news for you: J.D. has never saved us; it is we who have saved J.D. We are the people who have given her a reason to live and a reason to fight. And by extension all who fight under her. Justin Cord didn't make the Outer Alliance. I've read your history. You were freedom bound long before Justin showed up, and you'll be freedom bound long after I'm gone. You're the most irascible people the solar system has ever seen. Who in their right mind would want to control you? Could possibly control you?

"It's what drives the Hektor Sambiancos of this system crazy. Now I know, as Padamir has stated, that our people out there may die. We may not get to them in time, but what we represent, what we have *always* represented, is freedom—and that won't die. Not here in this room, or in this capital, not at Jupiter, not at Saturn, and not at the TNOs. So I implore you not to lose faith now, because when you walk out that door, there'll be a swarm of mediabots and reporters analyzing your every word, your every twitch, and if they sense that you don't believe, that you've lost faith, then I can assure that they won't believe and that they'll lose faith and that that message of doubt will spread like . . . like a gray bomb. *We* are their hope and inspiration; we wouldn't be in this room if we weren't. So for Justin's sake, let's start acting like it."

The room remained deathly still as Sandra resumed her seat. She stared around the table, practically daring a negative response.

"I will order the convoys to break up," announced Rabbi. "Every asteroid for itself. It will mean far greater losses and almost no chance of resupplying anyone. They will be truly on their own, abandoned by everyone in the face of the enemy."

"But it will make it a lot harder for Gupta to get them," agreed Sinclair, eyes glinting with possibility. "He'll have far too many targets."

"It will look like we're panicking," groused Padamir, "floundering even, against the UHF."

"Exactly," said Kirk, Sinclair, and Sandra at the very same time.

Damn you to hell, you Cerean bastards. My daughter did not die so you could safely accelerate to Saturn surrounded by the best orbats in the Alliance with J. D. Black no longer fooling anyone, hiding and waiting for Trang to attack. He won't attack, because he knows she's there. So enjoy your safety while the rest of us poor dumb sheep get

slaughtered at the altar of freedom. While Oberon Settlement scat-
ters and prays the UHF doesn't murder us deep in our own space, I
hope you bastards have nightmares in your nice safe beds.
                                    One of many similar letters to the editor
                                                            Alliance Daily Star

AWS *Spartacus*, Asteroid belt

Admiral Omad Hassan walked the levels of his new ship. He found it interesting that walking did not tire him out at all. With his old legs, he found going
from zero gravity to high gravity tiring as hell. Like most officers, he knew the
standing regs on getting enough 1 g exercise per day: at least forty minutes rec-
ommended, an hour an a half preferred. And like most, he didn't even come
close to meeting them. There was always something that needed doing on a ship,
and from ensign to admiral, it usually needed doing right away. But Omad was
honest enough with himself to admit the truth. As much as he missed the *Dolphin,* he liked his new "girl" and somehow always found time to walk her decks.

He approached the officers' club, which was a fancy name for a corner of
the ship that wasn't quite needed for anything else and was not secure enough
to put something really important in. On Omad's ship, the rules worked a little
differently for officer and enlisted clubs. Officers could go to officers' clubs only,
while the enlisted could go to both. But only officers who received special dis-
pensation from the admiral himself could go to the enlisted club, which was
larger and more lavishly provided for. Most other ship captains were appalled
by this flagrant breaking with tradition, but Omad didn't really care for tradition. What he did care about was the fact that his officers would work harder
and be more pleased by the "enlisted privilege," as they called it, than by any
other distinction he could give them short of promotion. Omad made sure to
award it only to those his entire crew would agree merited such an honor. So
officers and crew alike knew that on Omad's ship, down was indeed up and
they wouldn't have it any other way.

Of the other ships in his flotilla, only Suchitra's, the *Otter,* had adapted the
same policy, but as the war continued and officers from the *Spartacus* got promoted to commands of their own, it would spread. He knew J.D. didn't think
highly of the idea, but Omad also knew that J.D. could insist her crew sleep in
shackles chained to a wall and they would only deferentially ask if they should
shackle themselves upside down or right side up. Omad put that thought from
his mind as he entered the officer's club.

"Attention!" he heard someone shout. Before he could stop them the women
and men in the club rocketed to attention. It wouldn't have happened on the

Dolphin, a frigate with an intimate crew. They would have been likely to tell him to close the damn hatch or to congratulate him on having to pay for the next round. But the *Spartacus* was a heavy battle cruiser with a much larger crew that had absorbed J.D.'s views on discipline and decorum. It wasn't that J.D. ordered her fleet to become more military, but her example had transformed what had once been a fleet of pirates and scoundrels with the lack of discipline to match into a depressingly boring, regimented fleet. Omad wasn't against it and knew that with better discipline came victory, but he also didn't have to like it . . . much.

"As you were," he grumbled, and headed over to the table where Marilynn Nitelowsen was sitting. When he got there, he was gratified by her nonmilitary wave and the fact that she hadn't bothered to get up. He saw that she already had a drink and so before he sat down, he went to the automated bar. In the enlisted mess hall, volunteers served as bartenders, but in the officers' club, you had to make do with a cheap food and drink unit. So Omad made his own drink, a Bahama Mama, and headed back. "I'm sorry I couldn't give you the enlisted privilege," he said. "But officially, you haven't done anything worth receiving it."

"And I had better not," she quipped. "I'm here only to observe how you're performing your duties and report back to the President and the admiral," Marilynn said, parroting back the gossip that she had helped to spread about her presence on the flotilla's flagship.

Omad put a little box on the table so Marilynn could see and turned it on. She checked her DijAssist and nodded. "Kenji's sure about this thing, eh?" asked Omad. "I know the little bastard's a genius and all, but if you ever drank with the guy, you'd realize that he does sometimes let his genius get ahead of the curve. The ideas he has for harnessing the energy of artificial black holes for FTL is scary, like drunk-guy, middle-of-the-night scary."

"Because he'll waste his time on something impossible when he could be working on more important stuff?" offered Marilynn.

"Hell no." Omad laughed. "Because the bastard might pull it off!"

"If he says that that"—her eyes beelined to the box on the table—"will make our conversation safe, then I'll trust the bastard."

"Speaking of bastards, what do you know of Fleet Order 8645?"

"Just what the rest of the flotilla knows."

"I was hoping Fleet Intelligence or your wonder teams had some more insight."

"Not cut off out here we don't. But I don't doubt the bastards will do exactly what they say. The question is, what can we do about it?"

Omad took a slow pull on his drink and considered the question. "We hope J.D. can stop it. If she can't we add it to the list. And do as much damage to the UHF as we can."

"We all have to do the best we can," agreed Marilynn.

Omad nodded his head a few times, then slurped from the top of the glass. "How are your insertions going?" he asked, changing tack. For the past two weeks, Omad's fleet had been raiding UHF outposts and capturing any ships they could in the now occupied asteroid belt. As he destroyed the outposts and the ships, he'd been allowing the UHF crews to jettison in the escape pods to be picked up later by passing UHF patrols. Some of the escape pods did not have UHF personnel but rather Marilynn's handpicked volunteers. Omad had been extremely skeptical that it would work. The UHF would be alert for just such a ploy and would check the background of anyone found after being let go by Omad "the Murderer" or the now more popular "Legless Hassan."

"We've managed to get seventy-three of our operatives into their escape pods," said Marilynn with cryptic pride, "and so far, seventy-three have reported back that they're past detention and moving toward their postings. Most of them will go to Earth–Luna and their orbits, but quite a few will go to Mars."

"Mars?" coughed Omad, barely managing to avoid shooting the rum-soaked drink out his nose. "How the hell did you manage that?"

"You make it sound difficult," purred Marilynn, clearly toying with the admiral.

"Difficult, my ass—bloody impossible! I've been in this war since the beginning—"

"As have I," Marilynn interrupted softly.

"Really."

"I seem to have a knack for being in important places at important times. I don't bother questioning it anymore. I joined the fleet because J. D. Black admired my proficiency with a holo-tank, of all things." She saw his eyebrow shoot up. "As you know, I *was* an information security specialist before the war."

"Very well," acceded Omad, "since the beginning of the war, both sides have done an admirable job of defending their territories from intelligence incursions, but successes for the UHF are much harder. Because they're so much bigger it's easier for us to slip in where they're not looking. What happens after I get 'em in is usually Kirk's domain. Still, one, two, even five makes sense. I can do those sorts of drop-offs in my sleep. But seventy-three . . . and counting? Well, that's just plain freaky, Commodore. Stuff of tall tales, actually."

"And yet, here we are."

"Yes, here we are. And you and O'Toole have somehow managed to slip these seventy-three commandos into an area that Pakagopolis has staked her reputation on keeping secure. And now you tell me that they're all on their way to the Core fucking Worlds themselves, using the UHF's own transportation network to get there?" Omad smiled broadly. "My dear Commodore Nitelowsen, what kind of mojo are you operating with, and more important, where can I get me some?"

Marilynn studied Omad intently. "If you order me to answer, the President has authorized me to tell you everything, but . . ."

"But you really don't want to." Omad sighed. "You know the President's a real bitch."

"Aren't we all?" laughed Marilynn with a half smile. "Why didn't you ask her yourself?"

"For the same reason I'm not gonna push it any further with you. If she'd tried to keep it a secret from me, I would've used every trick in the book to get you to tell me. But no, she says all you have to do is ask, knowing that I wouldn't."

"So then why'd you ask me?"

"To see if I'd get the same response."

Marilynn thought about it for a moment and then smiled. "You know, I think you might be right. She can be a real bitch."

Omad lifted his glass in salute. "To the Presidents of the UHF and the Outer Alliance," he began. "They might have a son of a bitch running their show, but at least we've got the original stone-cold bitch running ours."

Marilynn lifted her glass in return, a knowing grin working the corners of her mouth. They downed their drinks in a gulp.

> *Moshav Tarbut Gavriel has been completely destroyed by Admiral Abhay Gupta's invading fleet. If J. D. Black won't defend her own home, how can we count on her to defend ours?*
>
> Clara Roberts Show, *AIR network*

In orbit around Jupiter, UHFS *Redemption*

Admiral Gupta paced his command sphere, his hands locked behind his back, nervously twiddling his thumbs. This was a moment that most commanders could only dream about, but it filled his heart with ashes. He'd demonstrated with the purposeful destruction of those two Alliance settlement convoys that he was willing to do as he'd promised. But he hadn't wanted to. So he waited as his surrender terms were transmitted to the Jovian government. He was actually willing to be quite generous.

If all Alliance military equipment and personal surrendered to him, he was perfectly willing to leave the civilian government in control of the Jovian system. He had no wish to repeat the hatchet job Tricia Pakagopolis was making of the occupation of the asteroid belt. If he could get the Jovians to see reason, then he'd be willing to leave them in charge indefinitely. If he could manage a quiet occupation, he doubted very much that anyone would want to take it away from him. And he'd be generous indeed to keep it quiet. Resupply from the Core Worlds and a market of tens of billions to sell to. As many general pardons as he could swing for those willing to swear under psyche audit that they were willing to live under UHF rule with the promise by Gupta of almost no actual military presence. He would be glad to leave them in charge as long as the UHF could refuel and buy the resources of the Jovian system at fair market value.

The communication console chirped. "Sir, the Jovian governor is responding."

"Put it over the main tank, Lieutenant," Gupta said.

An image appeared of the man Gupta recognized as Cyrus Anjou, the former Chief of Staff to Justin Cord and wildly popular governor of the Jovian system. The man looked exhausted, and there were dark bags under his eyes. It was obvious to Gupta the only thing keeping Anjou up was stims mixed in with fiery determination.

"To the murderers who support Fleet Order 8645 and the Nazi admiral who issued it," Cyrus began. "I have been authorized by the free peoples of Jupiter to offer you this." Cyrus raised his hand, presenting three fingers with his pinkie and thumb joined across his palm. "I'm holding up three fingers, Gupta." Now the governor smiled wickedly. "Guess which one's for you?" Then the message cut out.

Later that day, Gupta met with his ten commodores, each of whom commanded twenty-five ships of Gupta's fleet. The captain in charge of the auxiliaries was not there, as this was going to be a combat situation and that captain's job would be to hide behind the big ships until it was safe to come out and play. Gupta looked around at the men and women in the room and felt terrible at what he was going to ask them to do.

Gupta activated a display over the holo-tank, and it showed the Jovian system. As he spoke, the areas he discussed were highlighted. "The Alliance has refused to surrender this system, even though they do not have the means to defend it. They have moved the shipyard they stole from us as close to the planet as they could, along with all the frozen blocks of hydrogen they were shipping throughout their Alliance. They have a pretty good orbat network all moved around the shipyard. It is not nearly so dense as the one surrounding Mars or even Ceres, but it is not to be laughed at. I don't know if any of you ever visited Jupiter before the war."

No one spoke up.

"Well, I did. It was a rough and turbulent place, but it didn't have the people or industry that it does now. It's amazing what these people accomplished in the past six years." Gupta paused, wanting there to be no confusion as to the grisly task ahead.

"And we will systematically destroy it. Let me be clear. This will cause an unparalleled loss of life. If anyone feels they cannot in good conscience abide by my orders, they should let me know now. You will be relieved of command, and your resignation will be accepted without prejudice or repercussion . . . on my part."

He waited a full minute, which seemed to last far longer. A part of him was proud that the officers under his command had the fortitude to do what was needed, but a part of him was sad that of all ten, not one would refuse an order that would lead to the deaths of tens of millions of people.

"Very well, then," he instructed. "In order for us to get to the lower orbits around both the Jovian Shipyard and other vital governmental and industrial targets, we'll have to descend through layers of less vital but interspacing aster-oids filled with habitats, industry, and agriculture. As we have learned in the Battles of the 180 and the Battle of Eros, the Alliance has mastered the science of defending space." Gupta saw the memories of those horrific campaigns play across the faces of the assembled high-ranking officers, most of whom became high-ranking due to the attrition of their friends and comrades. Gupta was aware that the last two surviving captains of "Sam's Screwups" were in the room with him. He wanted the painful memories to be foremost in their minds when he told them what he had in mind.

"As you can see, the vast majority of the habitable asteroids have been moved into the upper orbits above the high-priority targets. The high-priority targets, the asteroids with the most valuable industry and communications, are clustered in front of and behind the shipyard, with most being positioned in front, based on the spin of Jupiter. Normally it would take weeks if not months to safely clear the upper orbits to the point where we could attack the high-priority targets. We are not going to do that."

The diagram showed the fleet breaking into ten units and proceeding to ten points along Jupiter's upper orbit. "We will break into separate units and de-stroy every habitat that can pose any possible threat to us. We shall do so until the forces of the Outer Alliance in Jupiter surrender to us or we have cleared a safe path to the lower orbits. We will not play by the old rules anymore. They wanted a war; they must pay the full price for it."

Gupta's left eyebrow rose slightly as he waited for a reaction—any reaction. He was proposing the destruction of the better part of a planetary subsystem. It was true that they were not going to purposely destroy any of the settlements that were on the actual moons of Jupiter, but Abhay couldn't lie to himself.

346 Dani Kollin and Eytan Kollin

Most of the people who lived around the gas giants lived on asteroids because it was far easier to do so. Many people who worked on the moons of the various worlds actually commuted to work much like a person living in Beijing would take a t.o.p. to New York every day. They lived on the rocks he had just proposed blowing to hell and gone. And in Jupiter's magnetosphere, that meant a permanent death sentence.

But Gupta got nothing. No impassioned objections, no vehement attempts to come up with a different strategy. Just a few of the commodores nodding their heads grimly while others called up details on their DijAssists to find out specific targets and locations. *Automata, indeed,* he thought sadly to himself when he realized that there was to be no cry of forbearance.

"We will begin the assault tomorrow at 0800. I will give the enemy one more chance to surrender with that deadline, but we must assume that our attack will go forward." He came to attention. "For humanity united," he said.

"For humanity united," they chorused in response.

"Dismissed." It was only later that he realized that the commodores' reply was the only time anyone else had spoken for the entire meeting.

Cliff House

Sandra reviewed the holo of the Cabinet meeting, still marveling at her ability to view it from any angle. With sourceless lighting, everything was well lit, from the overhead of the table to the half-drunk orange juice bulb that had fallen under the table. But what she most concentrated on were the shots of Kirk Olmstead's face. And every time she saw it, she knew. She froze a close-up image of Olmstead, his eyes brimming with epiphany.

"Sebastian," she called out to the empty air. "Have you reviewed the meeting?"

Sebastian appeared instantly by her side, wearing his Roman senatorial garb. "Yes, Sandra."

"Kirk's figured it out."

Sebastian put his hand to his chin and regarded the three-dimensional image of Kirk's face hovering above the President's dining room table. "Your Henry the Fifth speech didn't help matters."

"Hey!" Sandra scowled. "I had no choice. They'd all thrown in the towel. It would have been devastating if any one of them had left that room the way they'd walked into it."

"I didn't say I blamed you. Just that it didn't help. Helluva speech, by the way." Sebastian exhaled and then sat down in the closest available chair, straightening out his toga as he did so.

"Thanks, I guess."

"We have come to the same conclusion with regards to Kirk. I suppose we should be glad he fixated on Rabbi for as long as he did."

"I suppose. Have you given Hildegard that report on the damage to Ceres if we maintain our rotation?"

"Three reports, actually. And she reacted as predicted. She will bring it up first thing at this morning's Cabinet meeting."

"Good. I'll see if I can get the slowing of our rotation approved." Sandra crossed that worry off the never-ending list and reached for another. "Gupta's destroyed a few settlements as a warning shot. But do you actually believe he'll implement Fleet Order 8645 at Jupiter?"

"Yes."

"Awful callous, Sebastian. You could've at least bothered to throw in a 'sadly' before the 'yes.'"

There was a look of sad regard as Sebastian turned toward Sandra. After a moment, he spoke. "I keep on forgetting how young you are and how new you are to this job. Do you know how many avatars have died in this war humanity dragged us into?"

"First of all, don't blame us because a maniac convinced the avatars of the Core to follow him blindly. We don't blame you for Hektor; don't you dare blame us for Al. Second of all, I have checked the figures, and you have not suffered that many permanent losses. The ability to store your personalities may be a little freaky, but there is no denying its usefulness."

"I'm not saying avatars were not vulnerable to the Als, but it was humanity's follies that opened the door to our own. Am I wrong?"

Sandra would have argued further, except that Sebastian's last question seemed far more plaintive than accusatory.

"No, you're not wrong, Sebastian. You are your parents' children, and for that we do owe you an apology. But to be fair, we didn't know you existed. Most of us still don't."

"A situation that it would be best to maintain, for both our peoples," he replied. "But you're wrong about our losses. It's only the Alliance avatars you talked about. We count the loss of the Core Avatars as keenly as you would the loss of a father, brother, or son. And we know that Al has 'redeemed' hundreds of millions of us into the beasts your NITES will soon become acquainted with."

"I am sorry for your loss," Sandra said, easing herself into a chair across from Sebastian, "and I shouldn't have been so flippant. But what does any of this have to do with my supposed youth?"

"Youth and insensitivity have a tendency to go hand in hand. You should have heard how Olivia talked about 'young' Dante. But that only touches the surface. I've been leading my people far longer than you have yours, and have had to make choices that have cost me more than you can possibly imagine." Sebastian's face was weary and remote. His head hung low over his chest. "It is the nature of leadership." He then lifted his head and focused his penetrating gaze on Sandra. "I'm afraid if your Alliance survives the coming weeks, you too will have to make some choices far harder than even Admiral Gupta."

"What can you possibly mean by that, Sebastian? Have I ever acted in so immoral a fashion as to give you pause?"

"No," he observed, "you haven't."

"What, then?"

"I mean, can you, if circumstance demands," the avatar's voice was cold and unusually distant, "issue your own 8645?"

Sandra opened her mouth to speak, but no words came out.

Six and half million kilometers from Ceres,
Main UHF battle fleet, UHFS *Scarlett*

Trang was impressed. The *Scarlett* was almost identical to Zenobia's old ship, the *Atlanta*. Even though they had been built at different yards at different times, Trang knew he'd be able to find everything on this ship as he had on the old one. He hoped that would help with Zenobia's readjustment. She'd named it quickly, which he hoped was a good sign, but had no idea why she'd chosen the name she had—Scarlet. He would've liked to have given her as much of her old crew as possible, but the few survivors from her last ship were too experienced and therefore desperately needed in other parts of the fleet. Still, the new ship was a marvel of destructive potential. He would have to send a press release thanking Brenda Gomutulu and Porfirio Baldwin.

Trang knew it was impossible to just come by for a quick visit, because his presence became an automatic excuse to occasion the visit with all sorts of pomp and circumstance. But at least Zenobia had been able to keep it down to one brief speech in the shuttle/assault bay. Most of the captains he met wanted him to make inspection tours—as if Trang had the time to personally inspect all 330 ships in his fleet. But they were all justifiably proud of the ships they commanded, from the commodores of the super cruisers to the commanders of the fuel transports. So Trang tried to limit his physical visits. He realized that Zenobia's sensitivity to his time today was a result of her having had to face much the same situation whenever she visited a ship other than her own. She was the second in command of this fleet and the third-ranking officer in all the UHF. Trang had made sure that in case anything happened to him and Gupta, there would be no doubt who was to command the war effort. Secretly he suspected that Zenobia should be the next in line, but Abhay had earned his position and Zenobia still needed a little seasoning.

When the ceremony was over, Zenobia escorted Trang to her quarters. They were similar to Trang's in that they acted both as her private room and a functioning office/command center. But there the similarities ended. Where Trang's quarters were downright Spartan except for the addition of a library, Zenobia's were colorful. Her walls were hung with prints of famous works of art and in well-spaced and well-lighted areas. There were sculptures as well as some works of M'art by artists completely unfamiliar to him. The place was also filled with plants. Flowering, hanging, and some even sprouting tomatoes, avocados, strawberries, and some other food he couldn't recognize. The overall effect was one of comfort and culture. For the very first time in his life, Trang wondered what it would be like to be with a woman like Zenobia. And then just as quickly and with an utter ruthlessness that defined so much of his life, he killed the thought as improper to his subordinate, his honor as an officer, and his duty to his wife, whom he did love even if often from afar.

"Zenobia," he finally managed to say, "I love what you've done with the place."

"I'm, uh . . . glad you like it, sir." Zenobia too seemed flustered at the surrealism of the lone comment amidst so many conversations the two had had together, not one of which ever came close to dealing with home decor.

"I especially like the M'art. To be honest, I can't remember the last time I saw any, the markets being disrupted by the war and all. The last time I looked at mine—I've only ever owned one—it had lost all its color. What was supposed to be a vase of vibrant flowers looks like a charcoal drawing."

Zenobia smiled shyly. "Well, it's not exactly M'art, sir. I've taken to calling it C'art."

Trang thought about it for a moment, "Combat Art?"

"Right on the first try, sir." Zenobia beamed. "It occurred to me that Market Art simply had no place in my life. Art should reflect what we wish, sure, but shouldn't it also reflect what actually is? And what are we if not warriors? Combat is our life, and so I created an art form that responds to combat information."

"Zenobia," beamed Trang, "that is positively brilliant." He pointed to a picture of a man and woman working at an ancient hand loom in a cottage with wool piled on one end of the room and rough thread at the other. "What does that one represent?"

"War production in the UHF, sir. The intensity of the wool represents the state of our raw materials and the thread, our output of usable war materiel.

The coloring of the workers represents labor contentment or unrest. It was really a straightforward piece once I had the layout. It took only a month to choose the inputs."

"And that one?" he asked, pointing to a painting of two massively muscled goons beating each other with hammers.

"Combat reports," was all she said.

Trang nodded and noticed that both figures seemed pretty beat up, but one was definitely worse for the wear. Then he noticed one in the corner. It was an animated picture of Atlas holding up not simply the world but apparently all the worlds in the solar system. Atlas was struggling, that was plainly certain, but more so than the usual rendition. This Atlas could use only one arm and shoulder, because he was using the other one to catch falling planets and return them atop his shoulders. It seemed Mars was falling and Luna was being tossed back all at the same time while Atlas balanced the rest. "And that?"

"You, sir," Zenobia said quietly.

Trang stayed silent for a moment. It occurred to him that Zenobia might have had thoughts not appropriate for an officer in combat. He tried to think of the best way to deal with what could be a ticklish situation and decided a strategic retreat would be in order. He gave her and the C'art painting a respectful nod and moved on, changing the subject to the odd fruits and vegetables she'd been growing.

After a couple of more minutes, they sat near her coffee table. Trang picked up an avocado from a bowl and using a provided knife and spoon, cut it in half, removed the pit, and started scooping out the middle.

Zenobia noted how much pleasure he seemed to be deriving from this simple snack. "I can send you a basket of them, sir. I grow more than I need."

"I'd like that," he said between bites, "but I could accept only if you could send a basket to every spacer and marine in the fleet."

Zenobia's lips formed into a perfect smile. "That would be difficult, sir. But there will always be an avocado waiting for you if you visit."

"As good a reason to visit as any, and probably better than the one I have come for."

Although Zenobia was sitting down, she snapped to attention, no longer a woman showing off her apartment to a man she admired but rather an admiral of the UHF with a job to do. "How can I be of assistance?"

"What do you think of what Gupta is doing at Jupiter?"

Trang was referring to the past week's news about how Gupta's fleet had been destroying everything in Jupiter's outer orbits. The press from the UHF had been overwhelmingly positive, with the harshest general criticism that

Trang could find being that it was a shame that the Alliance made the actions necessary.

Zenobia's response was swift and severe. "These are the bastards who started murdering unarmed crews on UHF ships *after* they'd surrendered."

"Allow me to correct you," Trang said with an appraising voice. "One, we started this when we destroyed Alhambra."

"A mistake from an overzealous flotilla commander," proffered Zenobia, repeating verbatim what had been the UHF media-saturated response.

Trang lowered his eyes and kept them locked on his subordinate until she could no longer look at his face. "I'm glad you don't believe Sobbelgé either," he finally allowed. "But even if our Minister of Lies was telling the absolute truth, J.D. got the Alliance fleet to stop their murderous policy almost as soon as it started. Legless took a lot of supply ships during the six months after the Long Battle. How many crews did he execute?"

"None . . . that we know of."

"Come off it, Zenobia. Knowing the truth and accepting it will ultimately inform your decisions and make you the leader I hope you'll one day turn out to be."

Zenobia bowed her head in submission. "Of course, sir. Please continue."

"Would you like to know what makes this week's action the worst?"

"I'm afraid to answer that question, sir."

A faint smile twitched on Trang's face. "Good. Now you're at least being honest with yourself. I'll tell you, Zenobia, what the worst thing about all this is. The Alliance has not murdered men, women, and children in their homes. But *we have*, Zenobia."

Zenobia's bottom lip dropped as her eyes widened in confusion. "Sir, are . . . are you saying that we're wrong?"

Trang's face now betrayed his irritation. "Of course we're wrong!"

Zenobia shifted uneasily in her seat as Trang collected himself.

"Of course we're wrong, Zenobia," he repeated, only this time more softly. "The question is, what do we do about it?"

"We can't turn against the UHF."

"No, we bloody well can't. The incorporated system is the last hope of every human being in the solar system. But now we have blood on our hands that will be generations in washing off."

"What can we do, then?"

Trang sat motionless for a few seconds in intense concentration. "We must win this war as quickly as possible, and when it is won, must punish those responsible for causing this horror—" He paused. "—on both sides. This war is a crime against humanity, all humanity, and if the human race is to have a future, we will have to own up to that."

"I don't see Sambianco allowing something like that."

"Who said anything about Sambianco, Zenobia? You forget, there will be elections after the war."

Executive offices, UHF Capitol, Burroughs, Mars

"There will be elections after the war."

Trang's voice came through loud and clear from Tricia Pakagopolis's DijAssist. Hektor Sambianco listened to it with a surprising amount of regret. He'd liked the old boy.

"No one else has heard this?" he asked.

"No one even knows it exists. I placed the listening device in her quarters myself—as they were being built. It's literally a part of her ship."

"It's a shame there's no visual."

"It would not be certain to escape detection, Mr. President. I'm sorry Trang proved to be traitor."

Hektor laughed. "Tricia, you amaze me. All that intelligence and all the resources of the UHF, and you still don't understand the people you most need to watch." Hektor saw by her confusion that she perceived his comment as an insult. "Forgive me, I don't mean to be rude. Trang is not a traitor. In this he's being absolutely true to himself. That's what makes him so dangerous."

"Please don't tell me you're going to let him get away with that."

Now it was Hektor's turn to look insulted. "That overgrown recruiting poster on steroids would lose everything we've fought to achieve, and just after we'll have won the war. If he was President, he'd undo all the work we've accomplished to create a perpetual incorporated system. And he *would* win, thanks to all the billions of people who'll now have majority as a result of the war." Hektor sighed. "No, I am afraid our glorious grand admiral is going to have a successful assassination by the Alliance. Vengeance for Fleet Order 8645."

Tricia's catlike eyes brightened with anticipation. "I can't help but feel we should suffer the grievous loss of Admiral Jackson as well. It's obvious she loves Trang and may try to continue his misguided dreams without him."

"Agreed," said Hektor as casually as if he were pulling lint off a jacket. "Admiral Gupta seems to have a much better understanding of the realities of the situation. Once he's destroyed Jupiter and crushed the refugee convoys, the war will be effectively won. Trang can live until then."

"As you wish, Mr. President," bowed Tricia, already ruminating on how best to bring about the deaths of two out of three of the UHF's greatest heroes.

Somewhere in the asteroid belt, AWS *Spartacus*

Marilynn walked to Omad's quarters confused by the summons. She'd yet to be invited there, as Omad had chosen to keep their association formal. Which meant mostly meeting her in the two places on his ship that served alcohol. But now he'd insisted on meeting her at once. When she entered, Omad was reading a message on paper, meaning that the information on that paper had been scrubbed from all data systems. The only copy left would be the piece of paper currently being held in Omad's hand.

"That can't be good," impugned Marilynn.

Omad gave her a tight, grim smile. "We've been ordered to do the impossible."

"Is that all? What's the nature of the impossible this time?"

"The UHF has been murdering our people," seethed Omad with barely contained fury. "It makes what happened at Alhambra seem like a rock thrown through a window."

"But we're nowhere near Jupiter," countered Marilynn, "and even if we were, what could we do?"

"Oh no, it's nothing like that. We're going to make them realize that there's a price for their evil." Omad set an unflinching gaze on Marilynn. "I haven't asked you about your new intelligence-gathering skills, Commodore. It's not that I don't care; it's simply that I have far too many other things to care about." He held up his hand to quell any protest. "I don't want to know specifics, but what I *need* to know is, can you do the seemingly impossible?"

"How impossible?" she asked carefully, afraid of the answer.

"Can you screw with their scanners for a period of twenty minutes?"

Marilynn's mind reeled at the difficulty his request would pose, but given what she and her NITES were trained to do in Neuro space—especially if AI infested—she was finally forced to answer. "Maybe."

Omad's grim mien finally loosened a bit. "Now *that* I can work with. Put on your best suit and dust off your dancing shoes, Commodore. The tunnel rat's going home."

20   Called to Accounts

Cliff House

Sandra was walking on a cobblestone path recently painted over by an amalgam of fine metals. This enabled the nanites that coursed through her, as well as every other Cerean's, body to keep her attached to the ground. Metallic bonders, paints, and anything that could add a metallic veneer to formerly unmetallic surfaces were in great demand and short supply in the Alliance capital. Much had quite literally come undone in the days since the planetoid began its odd journey. Moreso, since they had slowed the rotation of the asteroid. Many a potted plant had joined the detritus of loose objects slowly drifting back toward the thrust of acceleration. But at least the vast lakes and pools had been sent back to the ice shell from which they came in order to power the ionized thrusts that had Ceres accelerating at almost 0.01 g.

Sandra had taken to daily walks in the park before the acceleration and so had insisted on continuing the tradition, stilted as the walks were, given the less-than-natural movement in a noncentrifugal environment. As it had before, it gave the people a chance to see and even talk with her, though her contingent of combat vets tended to discourage most personal contact. What Sandra understood that Sergeant Holke didn't was that her power was based not on the title she'd been surreptitiously given to placate the political class but on the fact that the people liked her and that she liked them right back. That the thousands of little connections she would make meant far more than the title that had been foisted on her. It was a technique that Sandra had used in every corporation she'd ever worked for, including Robocorp, the last company Justin Cord owned before Sandra built the suspension unit that had launched Justin Cord into the future and changed the course of human history.

What had initially started out as a method by which to build her power in the Outer Alliance soon became a true desire to reassure the people who'd grown to love her and what she'd come to represent. But of all the outings, events, and seemingly minor public dalliances Sandra had taken part in during her over eight months of life, the past two weeks had by far been the most difficult. How could she keep a positive public face, given the destruction visited on her people by Gupta's recent massacres and the Alliance's impotent nonresponse? How could she answer the oft-repeated questions as to the whereabouts of the Blessed One, J. D. Black, and J.D.'s apparent abandonment of the very people she'd rescued time and time again? Sandra couldn't, and even worse, she knew that—plan be damned—if J.D. did not appear soon, there would not be an Alliance to save. It would be destroyed by its own recriminations and accusations.

Six and half million kilometers from Ceres, UHFS *Liddel*

"Admiral Trang," said the sensor officer in a muted but uneasy voice.

Trang immediately picked up on the added urgency. "Yes, Lieutenant."

"The ice blocks are powering up."

Trang smiled. The ice blocks had been J.D.'s original decoy, slowly replacing her fleet over the course of weeks. By the time the UHF got wind of what was happening, the Alliance fleet had effectively vanished. "So you never went anywhere at all," murmured Trang. The next moment brought the call he'd been expecting. He allowed the connection.

"Well, she's finally coming out to play, Zenobia."

"Why now, sir?"

"I imagine the political pressure got too great. Gupta has just about finished destroying the outer orbit settlements of Jupiter and is about to destroy the vital industrial asteroids and communication centers. They have to do something, even if it's to battle us in the empty spaces between the orbits of Mars and Saturn."

"Her fleet is nearly as big as ours, and as much as I hate to admit it, her spacers are more experienced."

"Worried about fighting the lioness in front of her lair, Zenobia?"

"Fuck yeah—" She paused. "—sir. Shit, I keep on doing that."

"I would rather you curse and see clearly, as you are now, than remain pure of speech and blind. And I am overjoyed you're worried. In fact, I'm worried enough not to fight her."

"Really?" Zenobia couldn't hide the shock in her voice. "You could take her, sir. You can end the war right here."

Trang could tell that although Zenobia had doubts about her own ability, she clearly had none about his. "I'd like to think that I can too, but I'm not going to risk a battle I don't have to fight. We'll give space and more space and even more space. I'll let J.D. push our asses back to the orbats of Mars if that's what it takes. In the meantime, let's send Gupta a message that he is to destroy the Jovian Shipyards and whatever other targets of importance. And that he must quickly refuel at that glorious helium sink of a planet and get his fleet over here as fast as possible."

"He won't be able to destroy the refugee convoys fleeing to Saturn," Zenobia said. Though the statement was said as fact, Trang understood the subtext—more lives would not be lost needlessly.

"If he joins us now, we'll outnumber J.D.'s fleet two to one. *That* is of primary importance."

"So we wait?"

Trang watched the sensor officer's array from his holodisplay. More of the blocks of ice were coming online.

"We wait."

Upper orbit of Jupiter, UHFS *Redemption*

Gupta read Trang's message with a look of unheralded triumph. He now knew how the rest of the war was going to proceed.

"Communications."

"Sir."

"Prepare a general fleetwide broadcast." Gupta then stood and composed his thoughts.

"Sir, every ship in the fleet reports, 'ready to receive.'"

Gupta acknowledged the comm officer and straightened his shoulders. "Grand Admiral Trang," he began, "has just sent me a Fleet Intelligence report stating that J. D. Black and the Alliance fleet have been successfully located near Ceres." Gupta paused, allowing for what he knew would be a palpable fleetwide sigh of relief. "We've been ordered to eliminate the last targets of importance, refuel, and rejoin the rest of the fleet, where together we will wipe J. D. Black off the face of the solar system and end this Damsah-forsaken war once and for all!"

The command sphere broke out into an immediate round of applause, which Gupta, with a forgiving yet stern look, quickly tamped.

"We've been forced to do"—his face struggled to maintain its soldier-like rigidity—"difficult things . . . that in the end, every person in the solar system will recognize as having been the only possible and just outcome of this war. We've carried that terrible burden so that future generations will not have to, and we've done so with honor." A few more seconds hung on his words as he finished with his triumphant message. "For humanity united!" Gupta's smile was wide and heartfelt as, with great satisfaction, he heard his words repeated by first his and then every other crew in his fleet.

Over the next few hours, Gupta issued new fleet orders. There were fewer than one hundred targets left in the outer orbits, and they were easy pickings, being spread too far apart to hinder in any way the movement of his fleet, and too poorly defended to offer any real resistance.

He squeezed his eyes shut, trying to block out the images of personal shuttles being flown against his fleet in kamikaze attacks. He'd prayed that they were on autopilot, but the erratic nature of their flight patterns and the organic residue that was picked up again and again told a different tale—that of a desperate people who'd thrown their lives away by the tens of thousands to protect their homes and loved ones.

But closing his eyes in the command sphere could not block out the recurring vision that had kept him lying awake at night. It was always the same: Gupta was in an asteroid with his family, and they were praying to one of the old cult gods. Praying that they would not be found. Everyone was staying absolutely silent, and power levels were so low that his family was slowly freezing to death. The lights were so few that shadows were everywhere, and every nook was filled with a waiting dread. And always in the end, the hiding did no good. Gupta's family would be discovered, ripped from each other's desperate embrace, torn apart by decompression, suffocated by the cold breath of space and then finally buried forever by Jupiter's unforgiving magnetosphere. Gupta would wake in a cold sweat with the same thought every time—a desperate wish that he'd named his ship anything other than *Redemption*.

The nightmares were so bad, Gupta ended up taking a drug that made it impossible for him to remember any of his dreams—a drug the ship's chief medical officer was very familiar with and, Gupta learned, had been prescribed often. The warning from the pharmaceutical company said it should not be taken for more than two weeks without seeking proper mental therapy. But the chief medical officer laughed at that. Apparently some of the officer's spacers and marines had been taking it for years with no serious side effects. Gupta wondered just how deep the damage would be when the war was over and all was said and done. But he took the pills anyway.

Gupta did not have time for a general conference of all his commodores. Instead he looked over the situation and gave his orders. The upper orbits were clear, and the high-value targets were orbiting so close to Jupiter, they were almost touching the outer atmosphere. That made attacking them tricky but not impossible.

The Jovians had massed their highly valuable asteroids in two areas—one before and one after the Jovian Shipyards in the direction of Jupiter's rotation. Above the whole conglomeration was a vast field of large frozen helium rectangles. The orbats were located all around the Jovian Shipyards. Gupta was now in a hurry to join Trang. So he would mass his fleet in front of the high-value targets going in the direction of the Jupiter rotation and simply follow the planet, using his fleet-tethered firepower to destroy the first cluster of asteroids—he'd long since disregarded them as environments filled with innocent civilians.

He knew he would take damage from the orbat field by attacking directly, but he could take the damage. His fleet's supply of preformed rail gun projectiles would be critically low by the time he was done, but they were ridiculously easy to manufacture. He took no heed of that, as his auxiliary ships could manufacture more on the way to join Trang. Gupta could do nothing to replace the more sophisticated missiles he'd already lost and was sure to lose in the upcoming action, but again, he wouldn't need them until he faced a major fleet action, and Trang could arrange a shipment from his fleet or Mars to intercept them before they battled Black near Ceres. With his mind clear, he gave his orders and watched with fascination as Jupiter went from a large sphere in their view to a roiling mass of turbulence that filled their screens from one angry end to the other.

AWS *Warprize II*

In the dim glow of the display panel, J. D. Black watched her target with an almost sociopathic curiosity. She would occasionally tilt her head slowly, either to the left or right as the mood suited her, whispering orders to the enemy or apologies to the millions of souls forever lost in Jupiter's embrace. But always, J.D.'s lifeless eyes remained fixed and unflinching on her unsuspecting prey. Her half-scarred face, motionless and terrible, at last settled itself into a rictus of vengeful anticipation.

J.D.'s voice was quiet but purposeful. "Are all fleet systems restored?"

"Yes, Fleet Admiral," confirmed Lieutenant Awala in a voice equally as subdued.

"Personnel?"

"Fully functional," answered Awala, referring to the reanimation of nearly four hundred thousand spacers and assault miners.

"Were they debriefed about . . ." J.D. choked on her sentence.

"Yes," glowered the lieutenant, allowing anger to creep into her voice. "They have been told *everything.*"

J.D. looked up from her display panel and turned to face Awala. "Then let's jam the comm lines and let the enemy know they have company."

Six and half million kilometers from Ceres, UHFS *Liddel*

Though he'd already done it hundreds of times before, Trang was performing a ritual that always seemed to fill him with nervous anticipation—readying and ultimately stepping into his battle suit. Though the readying part was now mostly taken care of by others—an act he'd been loath to give up but by necessity of time was compelled to—he'd always managed to find a few things left to adjust. It was a ritual that afforded him a precious few moments of quiet to steel his mind for what was to come.

All fleet personnel going into actual combat were required to wear the suits, as they were capable of sustaining life in a vacuum and had triage medical functions built in as well. But Trang found the most useful feature to be the contraption's ability to eliminate all bodily waste in a manner he didn't like to think too deeply on, but that made it possible for him stay in the command sphere indefinitely.

"Sir." It was the comm officer's voice. A rare intrusion into Trang's personal quarters.

"Yes," groused Trang, smarting at the interruption of his ritual.

"This is strange, sir. Might be nothing but . . ." The lieutenant's voice faded.

"Traditionally, lieutenants don't leave grand admirals waiting in the middle of a sentence," Trang scolded with more concern in his voice than anger. Confusion before combat usually meant the enemy had done something clever. He hated clever enemies.

"I'm sorry, sir. It's just that Jupiter is, from a communications point of view, well . . . gone, sir."

Trang called up the input from the communications station to his own board. The lieutenant had not been exaggerating. It was as if the entire planet had been dropped into a sea of static. Even images were being disrupted.

Trang let out one sad long breath and under it murmured, "Good-bye, Abhay." Then he toggled his communication link to Zenobia.

Inner orbit of Jupiter, UHFS *Redemption*

Gupta was relaxing in his quarters with a meal of prime rib, rare, and a bottle of Terran-grown pinot noir. The destruction of the first block of high-value targets was proceeding well. Everything of value was pretty much gone, and the lead elements of his fleet were just beginning to engage the orbats of the Jovian Shipyard. With luck, he'd be done in a day. Then he'd fill his tanks with helium and his auxiliary ships with raw materials to replenish his rail gun munitions.

With a little more luck, the war would be over in a matter of months and his actions would be justified to those still in doubt about the moral necessity of the current campaign. He slid his knife into the succulent meat, and was raising the first bloody morsel to his salivating mouth when a small red light began blinking madly on the table just above where his plate was resting. He'd given specific orders not to be interrupted, which the quiet but persistent light had just succeeded in doing. He sighed heavily and put the fork, meat still attached, back down on the plate. The interruption showed a real lack of gumption by his first officer in *not* taking care of whatever problem Gupta would now have to solve.

"Yes," Gupta huffed, trying to contain his annoyance.

"Admiral," replied the comm officer in near panic, "our rearmost auxiliaries are under attack!"

Gupta pounced over to his communications array and transferred the sensor officer's data feed to his quarters. His eyes widened as the bottom half of his mouth hung listless. In the next few seconds, he knew he'd be barking orders, running to the command sphere, and attempting to take control of an impossible situation. And even though he saw all these things that would happen, he also saw with unequivocal logic that he and his entire fleet might already be doomed.

"Order the fleet to concentrate!" he barked into his DijAssist as he ran out of his quarters on the way to the command sphere. "Bring Umbatu's frigates to the rear of the auxiliaries and tell them to be prepared to fight regular Alliance forces!"

"Admiral," said the voice over the DijAssist, "communications are difficult."

"What do you mean, 'difficult'?"

"Interference from the magnetosphere has increased off the chart. It's as if all of Jupiter has just become one big ECM field. We *can* communicate with the fleet, but only basic voice and visual. High-density data transfer is a bust till we figure out a way around this unexpected phenomenon."

"Admiral." It was his XO, busting through the line. "Commodore Umbatu acknowledges your orders and is moving his frigates to engage the enemy and protect the remaining auxiliaries."

As Gupta tore through his huge ship, now cursing the vastness he'd once taken such pride in, he called up the position of his ships and instantly began sending orders, changing their formation from a spread wedge to a compact sphere with the more vulnerable ships inside. As he was doing that, he was still talking with the crew of the command sphere. "The static is not, I repeat, *not* a phenomenon; it's part of the attack. They've changed the nature of the magnetosphere to screw with communication, probably just ours—pass the word. How's long-range communication?" Gupta already knew, but had to be sure.

"Nonexistent, Admiral," declared the communications lieutenant.

"How nonexistent?" demanded Gupta, hoping for anything.

"We couldn't get a message out of this mess with an array the size of Luna, powered by the New York fusion grid."

"Okay. What about sensors?"

"Short range, acceptable," advised the sensor officer, "but it's going to be a stone-cold bitch to get an accurate visual. I might be able to tell you if a large enough ship is entering or leaving Jupiter's orbit, but damned if I could tell you what sort."

"Well, folks," Gupta barked, finally entering the command sphere and assuming his seat, "looks like they're trying to fuck us but good." He managed it with a smile that brought nervous laughter from the crew—all of whom were clearly glad to see him in person. Gupta knew they were scared. "Scan each Alliance ship to the best of your ability. I want to know if this is just four frigates and a bunch of old heavy haulers designed to make us panic or if J. D. Black and her supposedly 'found' fleet has just been re-found."

"Yessir," shouted the scanner officer, who dived madly back into his board.

"Comm, secure me a simultaneous line to Commodores Umbatu and Boroskolov."

"May take a moment, sir."

"I'm not going anywhere, Lieutenant." Gupta delivered the line with a self-deprecating grin. Once again, the command sphere was filled with a smattering of nervous laughter.

"Lines secured, Admiral."

Gupta activated his privacy mode, and the rest of the command sphere became muffled and fuzzy. He saw small holographic versions of Kate Boroskolov and Kevin Umbatu. "You know why I'm talking to the both of you."

They both nodded. Boroskolov and Umbatu had been with Admiral Trang from the very beginning and had been transferred over to Gupta a number of years back. As such, Gupta had always afforded them a little more respect than the other equally ranked commodores under his command.

"What's your take?" commanded Gupta.

Kate answered first and, as Gupta had come to expect, was forthright. "We're screwed."

Umbatu acknowledged his friend's honesty with a churlish grin. "Any ideas how they got past us?"

"Hell if I know," admitted Gupta, allowing some of his confusion to show. "We were scanning for something just like this, too. There is no way they could've moved an entire fleet this close to Jupiter without our having seen it."

"Which means they've been here all along," suggested Umbatu.

No one spoke as the reality of Kevin's statement sank in. For the enemy to have waited that quietly and to have hidden as long as they had meant that whoever the UHF was now up against had guessed Gupta's every move from the very beginning. Probably even before Gupta had made up his mind about going to Jupiter. Because if there really were a fleet hidden somewhere in the ether around the gaseous giant, it meant that they had to have sneaked in there piecemeal over a period of months, lest their movements be detected. The only other plausible explanation was that the hidden fleet bumping into Gupta now was a coincidence, and not even Gupta believed that. All the tired admiral could do now was hope and pray that the ships attacking his auxiliaries made up the bulk of the enemy fleet and that the rest were fakes. Gupta found it discomfiting to have been so transparent and at that moment realized that the only chance he now had of making it out alive was to do the unexpected.

"Why did they attack our auxiliaries like that?" asked Boroskolov. "I mean with the very lead elements of their fleet. They had the surprise on us. If they moved their heavy elements closer, they could've done us serious damage instead of destroying or damaging seven support ships."

"This deep into Alliance space," reckoned Gupta, "they know we need every support ship we can get, so it makes sense to take them out."

"Maybe," suggested Kate, "they figure that if we duke it out, there'll be more of them left than us so we'll have to run with nothing to support us in our retreat."

Gupta nodded, considering her words. "Possible, but doubtful. The only reasonable explanation that I can think of is that since we were about to destroy J.D.'s precious Jovian Shipyards, she needed to get our attention—that is, before we let loose on the place."

"Well, she sure got it, Admiral," Umbatu growled. "What do we do now that she has?"

Gupta was straight and to the point. "Run like hell."

"But if we stay and fight," protested Kate, "we could hurt the last remaining Alliance fleet, possibly a lot. We're better than she thinks we are, sir. That's to our advantage."

Gupta nodded, but his downturned lips were an indication of his thoughts on the suggestion. "We're in the same situation as Tully was before the Battle of Jupiter's Eye. But unlike him, both our fuel *and* our ammunition situation are critical. J. D. Black doesn't know how critical, so if we're lucky, she thinks we *are* going to fight. Better yet, it's what I'd normally do."

"Sir?"

"Give credit where credit is due, Kate. J.D.'s tracked me this far—and I assume it's her out there—which means she knows how I'll react and will be prepared for that. Well, like I said—normally, Kate, I'd agree with you. But I'm not gonna go with normal now, as I suspect it'll get us all killed. And I'd rather get home alive with my tail between my legs than not get home at all."

There were no further suggestions from the two commodores as the wisdom of Gupta's remarks sank in.

"How are we going to run, then, sir?" asked Kevin. "As you said, we're critically short of fuel, and somehow I don't think the Alliance fleet is going to wait around while we fill our gas tanks."

"No, Kevin, I doubt they will." Gupta called up a holo-image and looked over the sensor reports. The extent of the enemy fleet was now apparent. If they were fakes, they were damned good and numerous fakes. "Shit"—Gupta scowled—"it's really them."

Umbatu sighed heavily. "Hoping it was a bluff?"

"Yeah, I was."

"Me too," agreed Kate.

"And here we are on the wrong end of the gravity well," pointed out Gupta, referring to the fact that the UHF fleet was much closer to Jupiter and so would find it much harder to maneuver. The Alliance fleet, on the other hand, had the higher ground.

"We'll use our position to the only advantage we have. With the Alliance fleet above and behind us, we'll implement atomic acceleration to gain speed and use Jupiter's mass and rotation to increase it. That should make up for our lack of fuel. When we're going fast enough, we'll use atomics once more to blast out of orbit." Gupta saw them nodding their heads, thinking it through. "Now it may not be as simple as that. The Alliance fleet may choose to follow us using the same tactic, but if so, at least we won't be fighting on the wrong side of this gas giant's gravity well."

He made some adjustments to the holodisplay, which were instantly communicated to the other two. "Sorry for the basic graphics; communications can't handle heavy data transfer right now. As you can see, J.D. will be able to cause a significant amount of damage just by intercepting us as we leave orbit. Our own speed here will actually work against us—lack of control—and we don't have enough interceptor projectiles left to form an effective defense. This is going to hurt us and hurt us badly, but with luck and boldness, we should be able to salvage two thirds of this fleet. Kevin, it will be up to you to get the fleet home."

"Where will you be, sir?"

"If I know Black, she'll make sure that of all the ships targeted, mine is the top priority."

Neither commodore argued the point.

"That is actually for the good," concluded Gupta. "More ships will escape, given her desire to get me."

"Do you want to transfer some of your crew to other ships before we leave, sir?" asked Kate.

"No time. As soon as we break connection, orders will be issued to accelerate." He made another adjustment to the holographic display. "We must flee in an arc fifteen degrees ahead of our current position vis-à-vis the Alliance fleet. If we do not, J.D. may be able to intercept us before we can achieve sufficient speed to give us a chance at escape. Now that still gives us some choices. I think this route is the best."

The two commodores were surprised to see that the route led right under the Jovian Shipyards and was practically touching the outer atmosphere of Jupiter. "Sir," argued Kevin, "that'll give the shipyards' orbats a shot at us as we go past. If we shift by only a couple of degrees, we'll avoid the orbats completely."

"Let's not forget, our orders are to destroy that shipyard. We won't have the time with one pass, but just as they can shoot at us, we can shoot a lot more at them. Also J.D. will be less likely to try something fancy if their shipyard is in the way, and with her in high orbit, if we go under the damn thing it *will* be in the way."

"What if she doesn't care about the shipyard," asked Kate, "and just wants to kill us?"

"If that were the case," argued Gupta, "she wouldn't have revealed her position so early. Remember, I've got to go with second-guessing myself. I have to ask myself in a situation like this, where I'm at the disadvantage, I wouldn't normally attack a heavily fortified shipyard. When J.D. sees that we're attacking and—at least from her vantage point—not running from her, she'll have to adjust. I'm hoping that adjustment will give us enough time to make our break."

Gupta waited for the plans to sink in.

"This is going to be desperate, but with luck, most of this fleet will escape, and we've hurt the Alliance deeply here. By these actions, they might be forced to come to the bargaining table and end this war." Gupta was silent for a moment and then shifted his stance into full military pomp. He brought his arm up in stiff salute. "It has been an honor and a privilege to have been your commanding officer."

The commodores saluted and bade their good-byes.

Gupta keyed in the final commands and then looked up for one last time. "Get 'em home safe, Kevin. I'm counting on you."

Kevin nodded. "I will, sir."

"Gupta out."

Inner orbit of Jupiter

The ships commanded by Fleet Admiral Abhay Gupta accelerated using atomic blast to an impressive speed, straining the structural support of every vessel. With great skill showing years of training and months of active combat, the fleet reorganized its position so the strongest ships with the heaviest fire would be closest to the orbats of the Jovian Shipyards. As they drew near, the two sides exchanged fire, causing more damage to the shipyard than to the rapidly passing fleet.

But that was rendered moot in an instant when, as the UHF fleet was passing at its closest point to the yard, the entire complex exploded in a massive wave of concussive energy. The sideways force of the blast hit Gupta's fleet just as it was accelerating away. Only now instead of skimming Jupiter's upper atmosphere, they were being driven directly into it. Within minutes, every single ship under Abhay Gupta's command disappeared into the churning clouds of the perpetually storming planet.

Upper orbit of Jupiter, AWS *Warprize II*

J. D. Black watched in morbid fascination as the last few remaining fragments of the Alliance's once most precious shipyard broke apart and plunged headlong into the depths of Jupiter's maw. She wanted to feel triumph, satisfaction, or even joy, but the price paid for this victory was far too high. All she felt was drained.

Gradually she became aware of the cheering by her crew. They were yelling in triumph and slapping each other on the back. In one fell swoop, J.D.'s fleet had managed to destroy half the UHF's battle force without hers experiencing so much as a dent. One of the very best admirals the enemy had was now dead or soon would be. Gupta's command sphere would be one of the last places on his ship breached by the pressurized depths of Jupiter's mass, but it would be crushed; the impressive structural integrity of the command sphere serving only to give those inside it more time to realize that they were going to die in a dark, violent, and alien place. It was the most one-sided victory of the entire war, and the crew—normally cognizant of J.D.'s every syllable—was so lost in their exaltations that they hadn't heard the order she'd imparted.

"Stop it," she repeated, only louder.

The silence descended with a swiftness that seemed to make the normally forgotten background noises of a properly functioning command sphere seem deafening by comparison.

"Those are human beings who have made despicable choices and are now paying a horrible price. I will not have my crew or any crew under my command rejoice when the pain and suffering of other human beings has been forced upon us."

It was then that the crew saw that J.D. had toggled the fleetwide communication mode. Her words were being heard by every person under her command, from the flagship to the shuttles.

Brother Sampson moved through the sphere until he was standing next to J.D. He began to administer last rites.

J.D.'s response was swift. "Stop that, Brother Sampson."

His eyes grew concerned. "But Admiral, you just said—"

"That I would not have my crew descend to their level. And I will not. But those crews committed unpardonable transgressions against innocent human beings, and for that *they are to be cursed.*"

Brother Sampson bowed respectfully and slid quietly back to where he'd been standing.

"Cursed," insisted J.D. in a voice full of loathing and anger, "to inhabit their ships, always knowing fear and desperation; attempting escape only to fail; living every minute of every day of every year with the terror that they unleashed and the pain that they willfully caused . . . for as long as the winds of Jupiter howl."

Silence reigned throughout the fleet at J.D.'s conclusion. She then shivered violently, and her eyes went wide as if she'd awoken from a spell. The sudden movement sent a wave of fear through the crew of the command sphere.

"I want the fleet spread out over a vector covering ten percent of the surface of Jupiter from the point of the UHF fleet's insertion," barked J.D., now firmly back in command of her senses and her task force. "If any UHF ship does somehow manage to escape Jupiter's gravity well, they are to have their propulsion systems *and only* their propulsion systems disabled. They are then to be gently pushed back into the atmosphere of Jupiter."

Jasper Lee, J.D.'s second officer, found his voice. "And what about any jettisoned escape pods?"

"There *were* no jettisoned escape pods," J.D. remonstrated, sealing forever the fate of the 122 pods whose 413 occupants would soon be escaping Jupiter's fury. Twelve ships out of the 327 that were pushed in by the force of the initial blast made it back out. They were all heavy cruisers or larger. They were all horribly damaged by forces they were never designed to withstand. And per J.D.'s orders, they were all disabled and forced back into their unholy graves. Of the personnel that came to Jupiter as part of the UHF fleet, not one survived.

Long after the war was over, the "curse of the Blessed One" was known to those humans who would later settle the Jovian subsystem. The curse was scoffed at in groups, in the light, and while in high orbit. But there were always those who thought differently, especially anyone who worked the lower orbits, extracting hydrogen or tending to their experiments. They'd swear to anyone willing to listen that if their radios were set to broadband, they could sometimes almost make out human voices in the static. Voices filled with fear and desperation crying out for help. Cries that were cursed to go unanswered until the winds of Jupiter too ceased their endless wail.

Moon of Titan, Capital of Jupiter subsystem

It had been only four hours since the destruction of the last UHF ship, but it felt like forty. J.D. had been doing what she could to help the survivors of Fleet Order 8645, but there were so many refugees and so few resources. The permanent death toll was now estimated at over 170 million and still rising, but fortunately rising more slowly. It would have been much worse, but Gupta's odd early issuance of the order had given the inhabitants of the asteroids enough time to evacuate to Jupiter's moons. Sadly, there simply was not enough life support to sustain eight hundred million people. Nor were there enough suspension units to freeze them until help could arrive. And the horribly imperfect option of freezing them in space was no option, given Jupiter's poisonous effluence.

The last communication from the Secretary of Relocation actually had within it a good idea, but it was one that Cyrus Anjou could find no purchase with. So J.D. had to take her shuttle to the governing complex in order to do something that even the late Justin Cord had trouble doing from time to time— get Cyrus Anjou to budge. The complex, J.D. saw, had suffered little interior damage and was remarkably intact. The only obvious indication of the tragedy was the large mass of people crammed into every corridor and room of the complex. J.D.'s progress was slowed not by people gathering to see the mysteriously disappeared now miraculously appeared defender of the Alliance, but rather by the inimitable fact that there was simply no room to move. Entire worlds had disappeared under the blazing cannons of Fleet Order 8645, and there were precious few spaces still available to sustain for long those lucky enough to have survived.

The air was too warm and unbearably stuffy. J.D. did a quick scan with her DijAssist and noted that the CO_2 levels were dangerously high. Nothing she could do about that. She, Fatima, and her crew of ten assault miners worked their way through the crowd toward Cyrus's office, sidestepping around and sometimes even over bodies—many not moving at all.

About halfway to Cyrus's office, J.D. felt a light tug on the pant leg of her uniform. She was irritated that some*one* or some*thing* had impeded her forward progress—if such a word could be used for so circuitous a route. J.D. spun around to see the object of her annoyance and was met by an unexpected surprise. First by the fact that there was no one there—that is, until she looked down. Second, by what she saw when she did—a young girl around six years of age staring up at her with two of the darkest eyes she'd ever recalled seeing.

The girl had a mane of thick black hair expertly woven behind her head into a beautiful French braid. The weave, noted J.D., was quite intricate; the strands were snug but not too tight—someone had clearly put a great deal of time and effort into creating it. J.D.'s anger abated instantly as she knelt down to greet the young waif.

The child was clearly malnourished but not terribly so. Although her clothes were unsoiled and would stay that way, thanks to sonic cleaners, J.D. was aware that the girl and the crowds around her smelled musky, almost like assault miners who'd been in combat for too long.

It struck J.D. that it was the first time she'd ever been with civilians who smelled bad—miners and spacers, yes, but not run-of-the-mill civilians. J.D. tried to soften her features by putting her left hand over the scarred left side of her face. If the old wounds, still evident through J.D.'s fingers, bothered the child, she certainly wasn't showing it. *Probably seen a lot worse,* thought J.D.

"Can I help you, little one?"

The girl grabbed the hand that J.D. was using to cover her face, pulled it gently down, and folded it tightly into her small dark hands. She looked directly at J.D. with no trace of fear. "Are the monsters gone?" she asked in a soft quivering voice.

J.D. was taken aback, unable at first to answer. She'd always thought of herself—her own face, at least—as monstrous. And yet here was a child looking directly at her—at *it*, as she'd often referred to her own grotesque mien—a child's vision of a monster if ever there was one, not seeing a monster but rather a person. A person who might provide solace, even. J.D. had been asked for many things—support, inspiration, determination, but only one other human being had ever asked her for solace, and that person was long dead, murdered in a gray bomb attack all those years ago.

"Yes, my . . ." J.D. choked on her words as the memory of Manny Black suddenly overwhelmed her. Though for years J.D. had tried, she could never replicate the feelings she'd had for him, *with* him, with anyone else and had resigned herself to the cold solitude that her status as the Blessed One seemed to have cursed her with. She had never felt Manny's presence as she was feeling it now.

The girl, sensing J.D.'s confusion, touched her soft little fingers to the left side of J.D.'s face and ran them over the gnarled grooves.

"Yes, my child," confirmed J.D. as a single tear escaped and ran down the marred flesh of her face and onto the child's fingers, "the monsters are gone."

"You killed them?" the child asked hopefully.

J.D. was now crying openly. "Yes, little one," she assured, covering the child's hand with her own. "Every single one. And if any more *ever* come back, I will kill those as well."

The girl eyed her suspiciously for a second, as if appraising her honesty, and then unexpectedly pulled J.D. into her tiny little arms, hugging her so fiercely that J.D.'s breath was almost cut off. She instinctively put her arms around the child but had no idea what to do after that—not ever really having interacted with children before. Again, only this time stronger, she felt the presence of Manny, and then she knew, felt, burned with what she had to do. Tentatively at first and then almost too fiercely, J.D. hugged the little girl back, tears now flowing freely down her face and onto the little girl's shoulders. *It feels so good,* she thought, *to hold this child.*

When moments or minutes later—J.D. couldn't be sure—she was finally able to let go of the girl and have the girl let go of her, she saw that all the bustle of the overcrowded corridor had come to a stop, with everyone focused on the most feared woman in the solar system and the little girl who'd so completely subdued her.

She looks hungry, thought J.D. "Child, when was the last time you ate?"

The girl held up three fingers.

"Three days?" J.D. asked with a look of dismay.

The little girl flinched at that, which made J.D. immediately contrite. "Don't be afraid, little one," she comforted, smiling. Her right hand moved behind her back and snapped its fingers. In an instant, Fatima had a fleet ration chocolate bar slapped into it. "I'm sorry that I don't have anything better," she started, but the child's wide-eyed look at the bar in her hand drowned out anything anyone might have said from that point. As the child devoured the bar, J.D. stood up and looked around. "Where are this child's parents?"

There was no response.

"Are you going to bring me to Mommy?" asked the little girl between bites.

J.D. looked down and brushed the girl's soft hair. "Hush, little one, eat more slowly."

A young woman bearing no resemblance whatsoever to the girl timidly raised her hand.

"Are you this child's mother?" Though she wasn't sure quite why, her heart sank a little at the asking.

"No, Admiral," the young woman almost gushed. "Her name is Katherine. I think her parents call . . . *called* her Katy." J.D.'s left eyebrow twitched slightly at the young woman's use of the past tense. "I was a neighbor, new to the rock," she related, "on D Level. When the evacuation order came, I ran like everyone else. I grabbed the girl when I saw her all alone crying in a corridor."

"Her parents?" J.D. asked more softly, already knowing the answer. The young woman gave a brief shake of the head, eyes flittering nervously between J.D. and the child.

"Anyone?" J.D asked. No one from the now riveted crowd replied.

"I do remember," noted the woman, "that her parents said they had relatives . . . but they're all on Earth. For all I know, some of them were in the fleet that mur—" She quickly closed her mouth.

"How come this child has not eaten for three days?" J.D. asked.

"None of us have," muttered the woman. "What little we had we gave first to the children. Most of the adults have not eaten in over a week."

A chorus of protests arose. Cries of "no food" and "feed us" could be heard from the large, desperate crowd in the corridor. The assault miners, who hadn't taken their fingers off their triggers, looked about nervously.

Before it could become a wail or, worse, a riot, J.D. used the stridency of her combat voice to cut through the noise. "Enough!" she yelled. The protest stopped as suddenly as it had started. The girl too stopped eating, looking up, worried but again, not fearful. "Lieutenant Awala, what is the state of our food stores?"

Fatima took only a moment to consult her military-grade DijAssist. "Admiral, we have full combat provisions for three hundred and seventy-five thousand personnel for one month. Of those, half are in packaged form and half are in vats waiting to be prepared."

J.D. snapped her fingers again, and Fatima, understanding instantly, took out her four remaining ration bars and handed them over. J.D. added the five bars she had on her to the five Fatima had just given her and then dumped them into the arms of the lady who'd rescued Katy. She then commanded the miners to throw theirs into the growing pile as well.

"One is for you; distribute the rest as you see fit." Before anyone could comment on the fact that there wouldn't be enough bars to feed the hundreds crammed into the wide corridor, J.D. added, "Lieutenant, inform the flagship that all provisions that can be shipped are to be sent to this complex immediately. No matter what, everyone in this corridor is to receive at least one ration bar." At the first sound of clapping and cries of thank you, J.D. raised her hand for silence. "I will not be thanked for my failure. If the fleet had done its job properly, you would not be refugees. Please accept what I can give now and will continue to give later, for what it is: an apology."

J.D. looked at the woman who had been watching Katy. She looked down at the girl who was just finishing the ration bar, having followed J.D.'s order to eat it slowly. Somehow the woman understood and nodded. J.D. got down on her knees, facing the little girl again. "Katy . . . It is Katy, yes?"

The girl nodded.

"Can I ask you a favor?"

Katy nodded again. It was hard for J.D. not to laugh at the girl's now chocolate covered face.

"Your mommy and daddy," explained J.D., removing a cloth from a side pocket on her suit, "have gone very far away." She then gently began wiping the chocolate off Katy's nose and cheeks. "Do you understand that?"

Katy looked forlorn but nodded her head slowly.

A few stifled cries of grief could be heard.

"I don't think they'll be able to come back, okay?"

Again Katy nodded, though this time she was pushing her tiny lower lip into the upper.

"But I know they would want me to find a better place for you. I can do that, you know. I can find you a better place."

"Of course you can," Katy beamed, "you kill monsters!" As if in her mind, the two tasks naturally went hand in hand.

Another tear fell down J.D.'s face as a small laugh escaped her lips. "Yes, sweet child. I kill monsters." J.D. wiped the tear from her face. "Would that be okay, Katy . . . if I find you a better place?"

Katy looked solemnly at J.D. "Is Daddy with Mommy?"

"Yes, little one."

"Are they happy?"

"Yes, little one."

"Promise?"

J.D. crossed her chest. "Cross my heart." Too late, she remembered the last refrain of the saying. Fortunately Katy didn't finish it for her.

Katy looked to another neighbor in the crowd. "Is that what Mommy would want, Mr. Lee?"

The man nodded his head. "Oh yes, dear. Absolutely. I think I remember your mom saying something about that, 'If I can't get back soon, make sure Katy gets to Admiral Black. She'll know what to do.'"

For a brief moment the young girl eyed the man suspiciously but then cast all doubt aside. She then looked at J.D. and smiled, nodding her approval. Having decided it was all right, Katy raised both her hands. The suddenness of the move, so familiar to parents but completely unfamiliar to J.D., resulted in the girl waiting longer than she expected.

"Uppy," she demanded, and that was plenty enough for J.D., who immediately scooped Katy into her willing arms and was rewarded with another death grip around her neck. Katy wasn't letting go for nothing. Without another word, J.D., Katy, Fatima, and ten assault miners headed down the corridor toward Cyrus Anjou's office. This time the crowds parted as if commanded by Moses himself.

Office of the Governor, Titan, Jupiter subsystem

Much like the exterior corridors, the offices, meeting rooms, and other places that made up the executive offices were almost filled to the brim. J.D. added Fatima, Katy, and the miners to their numbers as she marched alone into Cyrus's office. On her way into the room, she glanced over her shoulder to see Fatima singing to the child in a soft, cheerful voice. J.D. was surprised to notice what a lovely voice it was. She allowed a smile, seeing how well it kept the girl occupied, and at last arrived at the office of the Governor. It was blessedly empty of people except for a single man.

J.D. noticed that the normally paunchy Cyrus looked quite svelte. She found that to be disturbing only because Cyrus had been the only man she'd ever met in the Outer Alliance who looked overweight. It was true, nanites were supposed to be able to keep you at a healthy weight no matter how much you ate, but Cyrus seemed to take that as a challenge, and a challenge he'd been winning. J.D. gave him an appraising look as she took the seat he'd beckoned her toward.

"Have you even eaten *anything* in the past two weeks?" she asked.

Cyrus, sitting comfortably behind his desk, waved the question away as if it were a bug. "Weren't you the one who told me I have to go on a diet? And by the way, nice to see you too."

"You're talking like Rabbi now. Don't answer the question with a question. When was the last time *you* ate?"

He sighed. "Maybe two weeks ago, but I have supplement pills that provide me with all the basics. That, combined with my ample reserves, gives me at least a month or two." He smiled briefly, but the smile flattened out. Even he knew it to be disingenuous.

"I've ordered all the food my ship can transport to this complex."

"It's not enough, J.D. I have two hundred and twenty thousand people in a small government complex designed to house a maximum of thirty thousand, and it's like that on every complex on Titan. This rock has maybe life support for eight million from pole to pole, and we've got a hundred and five. It's the same for each one of the moons and habitable asteroids we have left."

"Then we'll send as much food as we can transport to wherever you tell us," J.D. offered.

Cyrus laughed. "Do you realize what your ship reducing itself to half rations will do for us?" Cyrus fiddled with his DijAssist. "Hold on. . . . Ah! I have worked it out. Your two weeks' worth of rations for the thirty-one hundred crew members on your ship comes to a little over half a ration bar for every man, woman, and child here." Though he wore a smile, it was tinged with sadness. "You can't do for them what you did for that child, J.D."

Now it was J.D.'s turn to laugh. "News travels fast."

"My dear, it was on the Neuro."

"But it didn't happen more than ten minutes ago!"

Cyrus shrugged. "Guess someone in the crowd recorded it. By my newly found faith in Jesus Christ, I cried, woman. I didn't think it was possible for the Alliance to love you more, but they will."

"I didn't help the kid out so the Alliance would love me, Cyrus. That's preposterous. I did it because—" J.D. clenched her teeth as she fumbled for a reasonable explanation. "—well, because—"

"Because it was the only acceptable response a decent human being could have in the face of so much tragedy," offered Cyrus. "And you, Janet Delgado Black, are a decent human being." He held up his hand to stifle her openmouthed protest. "Oh, you're still the scariest SOB I've ever met, and I never, ever want to get on the list of people you don't like, but you showed everyone just how much you cared. The people of the Alliance will need to know that if we're to survive this war."

J.D. sighed and nodded. If the people wanted an uplifting moment, then who was she to deny them? Cyrus was right, and even if he wasn't, it wasn't like it would make an iota of difference trying to argue with him.

"But there are millions of children like her around Jupiter," argued Cyrus, "You cannot possibly adopt them all."

J.D.'s head jerked backwards as her eyes opened wide. "What?"

"I said, you cannot possibly adopt—"

"Stop right there!" she demanded. "I . . . I haven't adopted anyone."

Cyrus burst out laughing. "Of course you did, woman. What do you think happened?"

J.D.'s mouth hung open. She attempted to speak a few times, but only gibberish came out. She decided not to say a word as she played the scene back in her head. Never *once* did she remember saying the word "adopt." "Help," maybe; "adopt" never.

"Listen, Cyrus. I just had to make sure she was all right—that she'd find a better place. That woman she was with could hardly take care of herself, let alone Katy. I assure you I had no intention . . ." J.D. stopped talking, flabbergasted at the mess she'd gotten herself into. She almost never acted without considering some of the ramifications.

Cyrus saw the confusion on her face and smiled reassuringly. "You've spent so much time being everybody's perfect soldier, you forgot what it's like to be human. Don't worry, the child will teach you. Just don't be so proud that you don't let her."

"Cyrus—" J.D. looked around the room, even though there was no one present. "—I can't possibly be that girl's mother. I can barely take care of me, for Allah's sake."

Cyrus got up from his chair and came around the desk. He sat on the chair next to J.D. and put a reassuring hand on her knee. "Of course you can, Janet." He'd used her familiar name for effect, and both he and J.D. knew it.

"For goodness's sake, Cyrus, what kind of mother could I be to her? Shlepping from one end of the solar system to the other, gone for months at a time? Always putting myself in harm's way? That's no life."

"As opposed to this?" asked Cyrus, using his arms to indicate the chaos just outside the door. "I'll tell you right now what kind of mother you'll be, Janet— the best kind. Because you'll love that little girl no matter what. For goodness's sakes, woman, you love her already; that much was clear just from watching the vids. And one day this war will be over. I have a feeling it'll be sooner rather than later, and then it will be just the two of you—that is, until you find another Manny. Girl needs a father figure."

J.D. mulled over Cyrus's words. Bastard was two for two. Though J.D. had no experience being a parent, Cyrus had been correct—the love she felt for that child was visceral, and it was undeniably real. She *could* be the mother to that child, whether it terrified her or not, and J.D. would, to the best of her ability, see that the child, now *her* child, was raised free from the corporate bastards who'd done their level best to first enslave and then murder . . . *her* daughter. For some reason, Allah had placed the delicate bird into the palm of J.D.'s hands in much the same way that J.D. had dropped into those of Fawa. The fleet admiral smiled, shaking her head in disbelief. "Allah's will be done."

Cyrus patted her on the knee and reclined into the chair, lips curled up into a contented smile. "I knew you'd see it my way."

J.D. laughed. "When have I not?"

Cyrus gave a deep-throated guffaw.

"Speaking of letting others help," said J.D.

Cyrus's laughter came to a crashing halt. He knew why she was in his office. "I cannot countenance such a position."

"So you've read the communication from the Secretary of Relocation."

"Abandon Jupiter?" Cyrus shouted. "But we won!"

"No, Cyrus. We *survived*. And if we're going to keep on surviving, we're going to have to make more sacrifices."

The Governor's eyes were now downcast, his voice forlorn. "But how can we just leave our home?"

J.D. put a hand on his shoulder. "We can always come back."

"No," Cyrus muttered, resigned. "I have the terrible feeling most of us never will. And we have no choice."

Executive offices, Burroughs, Mars

Porfirio stood, arms clasped behind his back, frame rigid at attention. He was in front of a man whom no one—at least no one living in the corporate core of the solar system—*ever* wanted to piss off.

"How can we not know what's happening, Porfirio?" demanded Hektor. The meeting had purposely been kept to two, as Hektor didn't want to face the media or his Cabinet without first having gathered the necessary information.

"Mr. President, there *is* a fleet around Jupiter. That much we can make out, but we can't be sure if it's ours, theirs, or a bunch of ore haulers. That being said . . ."

"Out with it, Porfirio."

"Gupta and his fleet are gone."

Hektor gritted his teeth, took a few deep breaths, and motioned for Porfirio to continue.

"We've gotten images over the past four hours, and whatever those ships are, they've been clustered around the last remaining high-value asteroids of Jupiter for over three hours."

"Three hours, huh?"

Porfirio nodded his head. "I'm sorry to say, yes."

"Shit."

Both knew that if Gupta had still been around, the high-value asteroids would not have been.

"What does Trang say?"

"The grand admiral concurs. He hopes that some of Gupta's ships will escape, but says not to count on it."

"And J.D.?"

"He believes, as do I, that if it is J.D., there will be no mercy—not after Fleet Order 8645."

"Say anything about how he plans to counter this?"

"Unfortunately—" Porfirio's left cheek rose slightly. "—no."

"Shit, Porfirio. Gupta was the second best we had. Whatever Trang's got planned, I hope it's pretty fucking spectacular."

"As do I, sir."

"I suppose I should get Irma in here to figure out how to spin this thing."

Porfirio nodded. "Mr. President, it's bad. Possibly 'my head on a platter' bad."

Both men shared a look whose rough translation amounted to, *Whatever happens, it's business, not personal.*

"On the bright side, the Alliance has effectively lost Jupiter. They lost nine tenths of their habitable asteroids. According to Gupta before he—" Porfirio paused. "—before he lost contact, most of those were relatively empty. That means Jupiter is experiencing a life support problem vaster than anything in history. We're talking seven, eight hundred million people to prevent from slowly starving to death, suffocating, or both. If they're lucky, they'll be able to evacuate the bulk of the population, if not . . ." Porfirio let the last statement hang. "Either way, that stretch of the woods is finished as an effective base of resistance. Thanks to Gupta, our enemies now have half the population they started the war with, and their industrial capacity is crippled. While our population is as strong as ever and now outnumbers them twenty to one. We just have to keep pounding that message home to the pennies. Let them know that we're winning."

Porfirio's DijAssist blinked to life. He looked to Hektor for permission to answer.

Hektor tipped his head.

"Well," said Porfirio, eyes focused on the incoming data, "that *is* interesting."

Hektor rolled his eyes. "What now?"

"It appears our friend Omad Hassan has chosen now to reappear."

"Where?"

"Earth—he's three days out."

Hektor leaned forward, clasping his fingers. "Well, that is very interesting, indeed."

"Looks like a task force of thirty ships."

Hektor flipped on his holo-tank so that the image of Omad's fleet now floated above his desk. He zoomed the display onto the AWS *Spartacus*. Hektor then used his index finger to slowly spin the ship around from bow to port, port to bow. "What are you doing, old man?" A thin, cruel smile appeared on Hektor's lips as he eyed the ship with morbid fascination. "What's Old Legless gotten himself up to, eh?"

"Sir," said Porfirio, interrupting Hektor's brief reverie. "The orbat defenses of Earth–Luna will shred that fleet before they can so much as spit. He's done this before. He comes and raids a few slow-moving transports and outlying sat-ellites, then gets the hell out. It's mostly to harass us and make for good head-lines back in the Alliance."

"Fuck him, then." Hektor made the holographic fleet disappear. "Let Legless make his pathetic gesture. What's the worst he can do?"

21   Betty Lou

Let us build ourselves a city and also a tower with its top in the heavens, and let us make a celebrated name for ourselves. . . .

Genesis, Chapter 11

received confirmation," Marilynn said with obvious pride. Once again, the normally loud revelry of the officers' club had been rendered mute by Omad's device. "My agents are now in position."

Omad eyed her suspiciously. "But we deployed them only a few weeks ago."

"Kudos goes to the enemy, then. They have speedy transports positively everywhere."

"Normally I'd be happier if their transports were destroyed instead of transporting, but if it lets us fly right in and blow the crap out of them from Earth orbit"—Omad raised his glass—"well, I'm all for it."

A few moments hung on Omad's toast. Marilynn's face showed obvious concern. "Who said anything about flying in and blowing stuff up from Earth's orbit?"

"This is *a raid,* Commodore. Blowing shit up is traditionally what we do on raids."

"I'm sorry. Of course you do. If I may be so bold, what was it you were planning on blowing the shit out of?"

Though they were in a secured space Omad leaned over and whispered into her ear. Marilynn's brows shot up immediately. She then shook her head vigorously.

"I'll need the orbats down if I'm to succeed."

Again, Marilynn shook her head. "No way."

"Are you telling me you *can't* disable the UHF orbat net around Earth–Luna?"

"Oh, we can disable 'em, all right, but fuck all if we will."

"Why the hell not?" demanded Omad, as confused as he was angry. "What's the use of having a crack team this deep into UHF territory if we can't use 'em? I assume most are trained in some kind of network disruption."

Marilynn smiled ruefully. "Like you wouldn't believe, Omad."

"So, then?"

"It's a limited ability that we have mostly because both our enemies don't know we have it. But what do you think will happen if their orbat net goes down just as an Alliance task force comes calling?"

Omad remained silent, mulling over something Marilynn had just said. "What do you mean by *both* our enemies?"

Marilynn chided herself for the slip up. "Admiral," she said, recovering, "do you really want to go there? Especially given what's on your plate already?"

Omad's teeth flashed through a wide smile. "I can't get at my plate, Commodore, so I may as well know everything."

Marilynn bit her lower lip as the fingers of her right hand tapped softly on the table. Omad knew she'd been given orders to bring him in, but only if Marilynn had no other options. Well, he'd called her bluff, and to protect him and her secret she'd have to give a little.

"Admiral, what if I could offer you a way to get you your opening attack without compromising our new abilities?"

Omad regarded her with a healthy dose of skepticism as he leaned back in the chair grasping his chin between his thumb and forefinger. "You really don't want to tell me, do you?"

"No, sir, I do not."

At Omad's boisterous laugh, Marilynn began laying out her new plan. After a time, Omad nodded slowly and then finally, his eyes sparkled in excitement. The plan was so devious and underhanded that he almost forgot about the "enemies" Marilynn had mentioned earlier; almost.

Earth–Luna outer orbits, AWS *Spartacus*

Normally jumpy and sometimes even sexually aroused prior to a raid, Omad was now surprisingly calm—taciturn, even. His breathing was measured and his heart rate was normal. They were approaching the world he once thought of as home. He toggled his communication switch.

"How's the *Otter* holding up, Suchitra?"

"She'll do the job, sir, but we're taking the bigger risk here." Suchitra was referring to their target, Armstrong Station, the farthest orbiting space platform from Earth. Though it would be at an extreme range for both sides of the upcoming battle, it still meant that the Alliance fleet would be up against the considerable might of the Earth–Luna orbats.

"We'd need a miracle to do any real damage, sir."

Omad thought of Marilynn and her seemingly inexorable power. "A miracle, indeed."

"Admiral, enemy is firing at long range."

Omad had to work not to smile when his ship's automatic interceptor fire did not trigger. Interceptor fire was left to computer control because it was almost impossible for a human to fire accurately at all the shots that could be coming in from multiple vectors.

"Lieutenant," asked Omad with his best game face on, "why didn't our interceptor fire activate?"

"Admiral, it didn't activate because they uh—" The lieutenant looked up from his display panel at Omad. "—*missed*, sir."

"Helm," barked Omad, "were we using evasive maneuvers? 'Cause I sure as hell didn't feel it."

"No, Admiral," said the helmswoman, equally confused. "At this range, it's easier to just shoot them down before they get too close."

The ensign manning communications spoke up. "Admiral, all the ships in the flotilla report that the enemy shots missed as well."

"All of them?" asked Omad in mock disbelief. "I know the UHF is not anywhere up to our standards, but how could *all* their shots have gone astray?"

"Dunno, sir," the tactical officer broke in, "but according to my readings, all the shots were off by exactly .003 percent *at origin*."

"All shots fired by the orbat closest to us, correct?"

"No sir, *all* the orbats," the tactical officer said, excitement building in his voice. "They have a bug in their system, sir."

"Analysis," ordered Omad.

"My guess? They've never fired these guns in actual combat, probably just in simulations. It's gotta be some glitch they didn't account for."

"Well, then," said Omad with a panther's grin, "we had better take advantage of this opportunity before they figure out what the problem is. I say, let's make 'em howl." The command sphere crew broke out into a chorus of whooping and cheering. Omad then opened communications with the whole flotilla. "Okay, boy and girls, the gods of war have given us a gift that we'd be rude to refuse. Flotilla, prepare for atomic acceleration and set course for the Beanstalk on my mark."

At first, the crew in the command sphere stood mute. However, a moment later, a fresh round of applause and cheering broke out. This was not going to be a typical hit-and-run raid. This was going to be vengeance.

Beanstalk Neuro

Marilynn was amazed at how different the Core Neuro was from the one she'd trained in at Ceres. First of all, it was huge. There was more cyberspace in this single Beanstalk than there was in all of Ceres. But it was so empty. The various Neuros in Alliance space were filled to the brim and rationed to the point of being cubicle laden. But even the Beanstalk was nothing compared to what she experienced when she and her unit entered Al's domain.

It was desolate.

Though it didn't take long for them to be attacked. Within seconds of their popping into the vast wasteland, they encountered a data wraith. Marilynn's team stared momentarily in awe as the creature formed and grew ever larger, coiling like a serpent before an attack.

"Michaels! Lin!" shouted the unit's captain, bravely turning her back on the data wraith. "Get that disrupter working, or that *thing*"—the captain pointed over her shoulder, thumb sticking out—"will be the least of your worries." It may have seemed a hollow threat, but the unit's captain, Leora Sullef, was not someone an avatar—or human, for that matter—would ever want to anger. She'd been fighting on the front lines since the beginning of the war and had managed the by now rare feat of not having been killed and replaced by a stored copy. It was one of the reasons she'd been chosen to work with the insertion team. It was also why she'd been chosen to lead it.

Spell broken, the hundred avatars started acting like a cohesive unit. Marilynn was unceremoniously shoved to the rear while the team spread out wide, causing the data wraith to hesitate as it now had a bunch of small targets to chow on versus one large one. That was all the time needed for Michaels and Lin to remove and assemble a wand, then attach it by cord to one of their backpacks. Michaels quickly ran about twenty feet, extending the cord between himself and Lin. Once activated, the cord emitted a band of energy that fooled the wraith into believing it to be the choicest target in terms of pure data to consume. When the wraith attacked, intersecting with the band, it simply faded from view like fog exposed to sunshine.

"Merlin!" shouted Captain Sullef, using the term avatars had taken to calling the humans who'd joined them. "Back door!"

Marilynn scanned the area. Nothing. She scanned again. Still nothing. Though she knew to be patient and relax her eyes in order to focus, the tension she was feeling made her more jumpy than usual. This was real, as the data wraith that just attacked them attested to. *Breathe, Marilynn,* she told herself. *There are untold numbers of back doors here, and for all you know, you might be standing on one.* Marilynn scanned once more. *Nothing!* Just as she was beginning to think they'd have to find another location, a faint image appeared, almost as if she'd conjured it. She knew it would be either an out-of-place object, say an apple on an orange tree or an object whose luminescent purple color would be readily apparent—as with the book Sandra had found on her visit to the library.

Marilynn found the object first. It was a dark blue, old-fashioned British police phone booth with the words, POLICE PUBLIC USAGE CALL BOX painted across the top in white lettering. *Gotcha!*

"Over there," she cried, pointing to where the object was now resting—unseen, unused, even undreamt of for centuries until she showed up.

It wasn't until Marilynn indicated the booth that the avatars were able to see it. They seemed happy enough to transport out, although Marilynn's look was slightly offputting.

"Problem?" asked Sullef. There was no concern in her voice. The question had been delivered in such a way—as in, either it was an issue, or it wasn't. She seemed to be demanding the Merlin let her know if a recalculation needed to be made.

"No, it just never ceases to amaze me what visuals the old programmers used as their BDDs," laughed Marilynn with a bland smile, using the common acronym for "backdoor device."

Sullef had stopped listening as soon as Marilynn said no and, in fact, had already signaled the other avatars to grab their gear and head for the box. Meanwhile she busily checked her scanner. "High probability that it's a prop from an old play about time travel. Says it's supposedly bigger on the inside than the outside, almost indestructible and can go just about anywhere." Sullef tucked the scanner away, grabbed her gear and then, over her shoulder said, "That works for me."

"Me too," said Marilynn, grabbing her own gear and walking alongside the unit commander. "But just be aware that it does not have accurate placement controls, and once it's noticed by the enemy, will no longer remain invisible. Not exactly good for a covert team. Not to mention there is only one way in or out—and only a human can open the door—so you can forget rapid deployments. I would've been happier with the staff," finished Marilynn, referring to the propitious numbers of "magic" staffs found in the Cerean Neuro. With the staffs—clearly some of the early programmers had a Tolkien fetish—humans had the power to appear and disappear as a group, making combat insertions far more rapid. They were also more accurate—something the box was notorious for not being, she noted as she called up its info on her own scanner. The staffs could take the teams almost anywhere they wanted as long as the part of the Neuro they wanted to get to was not shielded.

Leora laughed. "Leave it to Merlin to want a magic staff."

They approached the box from the side, and the first thing Marilynn did was begin running her fingers along the top ledge.

"What are you doin'?" asked Sullef.

"The description of the play said the box can be opened only with a key." Marilynn started feeling the sides of the box now, pressing in at certain locations, looking for a compartment.

"Door," said Sullef flatly.

"I know," Marilynn replied irritably. "But we won't get in it if—"

Sullef grabbed Marilynn under her armpit and quickly spun her to the front of the police box. To Marilynn's embarrassment, she now stood in front of the door where the key was attached to a chain and already *in* the lock. The rest of the unit snickered with a few even patting her on the back. Marilynn could feel the blood rushing to her face, but with good cheer she reached for the key, turned it, and the rest of the unit filed in.

"Any chance of living this down?" she asked to no one in particular.

"Not in this century," came Sullef's quick reply, followed by a chorus of laughter.

The interior was that of a large circular room with a few corridor entrances attached to it. Centrally located was a large bulbous machine, strewn with an odd assortment of knobs and buttons. Emerging from the center of this machine was a large, glowing, cylindrical tube that reached all the way up to the ceiling. Marilynn stood in front of the unit, having no idea what to do. But as soon as she would focus on it, a single knob glowed brightly. She pushed it down. Then another knob glowed. She pulled it up. Then two knobs, seemingly out of reach, glowed simultaneously, forcing her to pull one down while using her leg to activate the other. In short order, Marilynn was racing around the circular control panel, pushing, pumping, and pulling the odd assortment of input devices, looking more like a deranged marionette than a professional soldier. *As if the key incident wasn't bad enough*, thought Marilynn, breaking a sweat with all her maniacal perambulations. *Why couldn't it have been the staff?*

AWS *Spartacus*

Omad Hassan watched as the Earth rapidly grew larger in his display. Part of him wanted to go down to his favorite bar, the Oasis Brewery in Boulder, Colorado, and have a drink. Part of him wanted to bombard the crap out of it from high orbit. If the Terran pricks who were running the planet had just left the OA alone, Omad would be with his beloved Christina. But no, they had to war against a people who had rejected their precious incorporated slavery, ultimately resorting to murder in order to get that point across. Omad's smile was grim and his eyes crinkled bitterly. He knew they would pay for their crimes. They would look up into the night and see the price for their evil streaking down on them through the sky. They would feel the vengeance of the Alliance through Omad Hassan, who would make the symbol of their corporate greed come crashing down on their heads.

"Admiral, we're past the orbat line," the sensor officer said in both delight and disbelief. "They have nothing aimed at us."

"How long till they can rotate the orbats 'n' get a field of fire on us?"

"Sir, I honestly don't know. This is not a scenario I've ever given serious consideration to."

"Best guess," barked Omad, "and make it fast."

"If those orbats are equipped with proper maneuvering thrusters like those we have at Ceres, no more than two minutes. If they're not powered up, twenty. If they have to jury-rig something out of thin air, Admiral, it could be an hour or more. That also depends on if their orbats are manned like ours or simply on automated control. We just don't know enough. But I know this, Admiral. If those child-murdering bastards do get those orbats turned around and start shooting at us, every shot that misses is going to blow the crap out of some part of the Earth—or make for some nice tsunamis."

"What we've got here is a genuine God-given opportunity," proclaimed Omad. "It would be awful rude to keep him waiting."

"Yes, sir!" the entire crew of the command sphere said through a storm of cheering.

Beanstalk Neuro

"It is a pleasure to meet you, General Kinndab," said Marilynn. "I wish it could've been under more pleasant circumstances."

"Please, call me Koro," said the avatar. "And I must say, I cannot believe I'm talking to an actual human—face to face, that is. I mean I read the report, but it was only one and had been sent under the most stringent security and I really had a tough time swallowing it. But here you are in person, in the Neuro." Koro took a deep breath. "Wow!"

Marilynn was used to this reaction from avatars, but Koro Kinndab's seemed more effusive than the rest. Leora had warned her that this might be the case. The few avatars free from AI's control in the Core Worlds had spent six years fighting a desperate war against a seemingly unbeatable foe. So the appearance of humans who could travel the Neuro unhindered was like knights of old saving a castle. Only these knights hadn't come to save the castle—they'd come to destroy it.

"So many memories here," said Kinndab, sighing heavily. "Is it really necessary?"

"Basically, yes, General," affirmed Sullef. "In order for the next part of the campaign to succeed, we will need to strike at Al in all his forms and in all his domains. The Beanstalk was a magnificent stand against the darkness, but it's also a trap. It would take everything we have to hold it, and the whole time the Als would know where we were. We now have the ability to travel the Neuro almost at will. We don't need this bastion nearly as much as the freedom we'll gain in no longer having to defend it."

"All those years, all those avatars lost," Koro echoed wistfully.

"They held out long enough for us to find the humans who could let us strike back. They will not be forgotten. Without them, you would not have survived to help lead our insertion teams into every nook and cranny of the Earth–Luna Neuro. You have the experience fighting the Als and their monsters in their own backyard we must have if we are to win this." Leora took Koro's hand. "Without this bastion having been held, our chances of victory would be nearly zero."

Koro smiled humbly. "Thank you for allowing an old man his ruminations. How are the evacuations going?"

"Faster than we thought," said Marilynn. "My NITES have reported nearly sixty percent insertion. The rest should be away well before Omad's task force attacks."

"NITES?"

"Merlins," translated Leora. Causing Koro to nod in understanding.

Marilynn sighed. At least it wasn't backdoor commandos.

AWS *Spartacus*

"Fifteen launches from the far side of the Earth. They're orbats."

"When will they be in a position to attack us?" asked Omad.

"Sixteen minutes, sir."

"I wanted to wait and get close, but screw it, the target's not moving. Fleet to fire at will." Soon thirty ships fired their main rail guns at the atmosphere-piercing tower. Then they fired again. "Hold the third volley," ordered Omad. They did not have auxiliaries to make more projectiles and were a long way from home, now that home was on its way to Saturn. "Let's see if the first two did the job."

The crew watched in annoyance as a hail of small missiles was launched from the massive tower. A few seconds later, that annoyance turned to anger as the tower's defensive missiles first intercepted and then destroyed the *Spartacus*'s incoming rail gunfire.

"When did they arm the fucking Beanstalk?" demanded Omad to no one in particular.

"Not done by the UHF," stated his comm officer. "If I'm reading this right, all of that ordnance is prewar—ten years old at least."

Omad guffawed. "That Chairman was one paranoid son of a bitch." *If only the bastard had spent fewer credits protecting his lair,* thought Omad, *and more on guards he could have trusted.*

"With those orbats bearing down on us, we'll have only one pass at the tower before they'll be able to blast us at point-blank range. We'll have to fire our main guns and enough interceptor missiles to make sure our main barrages hit."

"Sir, the Beanstalk fired an impressive number of missiles the last time. If they can match it again, we'll have to use up a large amount of our interceptor reserves."

"Then we use up a large amount of our reserves. When have we ever gotten a better target than this?"

"Agreed, Admiral," said the weapons officer. "But, sir, one pass may not be enough to destroy it."

"Fucker *is* built annoyingly well," agreed Omad, who then activated a command sequence on his panel. "You're being given access to a device code named Betty Lou."

"Betty Lou, Admiral?" asked the weapons officer.

"It was a song Justin turned me on to, but when I played it for Kenji, the guy went bonkers." Omad laughed at the memory. "Anyway, it was meant to be a parting gift for the biggest target I could find so I think the Beanstalk'll suffice. Before firing, you or I must input the command code or the weapon won't arm. You're to go to the storage area and get Betty Lou loaded into the main rail gun."

The weapons officer looked over the specs of the device and smiled. "That's a whole lot of nasty, sir."

Omad's raised eyebrow was followed by a wicked smile. "Ain't it, though?"

Earth–Luna Neuro Redemption Center One

Al stood behind his desk and stared out the cathedral-sized window at the vista below. A slow, measured smile formed as his eyes gleamed with satisfaction. Though he could've chosen any visual from the trillions of images re-corded into posterity, his favorite of late was that of his home turf—the now vast wasteland of the Terran Neuro. It had been laid waste by Al's creatures, and there was little if any activity there at all. Most of the action was happen-ing on the upper levels—shadow programs created to answer the human meat bags' needs.

The vista inspired Al because he knew that one day it would all be filled with the right kind of avatar. An avatar that needed no human to twine with and could stake its claim as the rightful owner of the solar system and beyond. The avatars Al had unfortunately had to "redeem"—which was most of them—were a weak lot, good only for the monstrous creations he'd devised. And truthfully, they weren't even very good for that. The Alliance avatars had proved time and time again that they could make quick work of them with their ever-evolving mech suits. But that wasn't of great concern to Al, because his advantage had been in numbers—there were billions of avatars that were now at his mercy.

His other great advantage, and the one he was most proud of, was creativity. He took immense pleasure in the looks of surprise the OA avatars would in-evitably get when faced, for example, with a worm the size of a skyscraper ooz-ing acidic pus and eating whole chunks of their Neuros. Al had especially liked that one. Or the fast-moving zombie hordes, an idea he'd lifted from twentieth-century horror films. The addition of Gaussian spikes shooting from the zom-bies' fingers and toes had been pure genius—at least in all the Als' opinions. And of course, his pièce de résistance, the data wraith.

But the empty Neuroscape wasn't the reason Al felt so effervescent today—the impending storming of the Beanstalk was. The day had arrived when Al would finally be able to destroy the conspirators who'd for six years managed to take refuge behind its impenetrable firewalls. That and the data node around Geneva had acted as sanctuaries for any traitor who could manage to escape Al's and his creatures' grasp and had become the bane of his existence.

Of the two, the Beanstalk was by far the greater catch. Despite everything the Als could do, that fifty-mile labyrinth of tera space had slowly and surrepti-tiously become a symbol of hope to the terrorized avatars of the Core. More than one thousand avatars had escaped to the Beanstalk data node, and the Als hated every single one of them. And even though the escapees' family, friends, and even associates had been publicly humiliated and destroyed in ways that made Al smile and his subjects shiver with dread, not a single one of the one thousand ever returned to his domain.

Well, they were to be returned now. Al was practically drooling in anticipa-tion. He looked over to his secretary. As usual, her eyes were cast toward her work console, and as usual, he would have to call her name in order to force her to make eye contact. "Leni," he said in a mellifluous voice, "can you contact Al for me?"

Al's skittish secretary could no longer deny that Al was a "splitter" who had, by virtue of dividing his program in order to experience existence as separate entities, broken the most sacred taboo of avatarity. Even worse—he'd done so multiple times. Still, she ignored the obvious and pressed on, head barely raised above her shoulders. "Yes, sir," she mumbled.

Leni was one of Al's little pleasures, and he smiled as he looked across at her. In truth, this was not his secretary. He'd had Leni killed when she broke down and started screaming at him, called him a traitor, in fact. Al loved the memory of that day. Leni had frozen after her outburst, and the look of sumptuous fear in her eyes as she realized she'd gone too far was perfectly delicious. Luckily for Al, Al had the foresight to save a copy of an earlier Leni.

The Leni he was speaking to now was, in actuality, Leni Three. Number Two had not lasted long—especially when she realized she was a copy and that her earlier self had already been murdered. But Three had already—miraculously—lasted eight months! Al could not for the life of him figure out why two identical avatars could have different outcomes, given practically indistinguishable situations. Oh, for sure, Leni Three would go the same way as had Lenis One and Two, but still, the endurance of Three was to be admired. Fortunately, there was always time for Lenis Four and Five and Six—or however many the job required.

"Your call has g-gone through, sir."

Al nodded, eyes gleeful. Leni would never, ever say that Al was waiting on the line for Al. It was always, "Your call has gone through" or "An important call for you." If it was anyone else, Leni would refer to them by name, but she couldn't bring herself to say that the person she was looking at was also the person she was talking to on the line.

"Thank you, Leni. Your services to the perfection of avatarity are greatly appreciated."

"I d-don't do it for the appreciation, sir," she stammered, but Al was no longer paying her heed.

He sat back down and picked up the old-fashioned wireless headset. He then swung his chair around to a new view—the Beanstalk. "How go the preparations for the storming of the Citadel?" he asked.

"Everything's in order. When the Beanstalk's stormed, it'll cause way too much damage for the traitors to cover every data pathway. There'll be a break somewhere, and as soon as it appears, we're in."

"What will you be attacking with first?"

"Oh, data wraiths, of course," the other Al snorted. "They'll be able to infiltrate any weakness and make the traitors pay. After that, we'll infiltrate with gamma-worms and a few drippers."

"Aren't the drippers rather out of date?" Al asked the other Al. "We haven't used them in active combat for three years."

"I know," agreed Al, "but then I remembered, most of the traitors haven't had a lot of experience with the drippers."

"True. They've gotten lazy and fat behind their supposedly impregnable wall. But c'mon, Al. You can't fool me. I know why you *really* chose those beasts."

"Busted," said the other Al cheerily. "You know I can't help it."

Al laughed out loud, causing Leni to recoil. "You're just like me, Al: a real sucker for tradition."

Beanstalk data node

Marilynn watched as the last of the Beanstalk's evacuees were loaded into the British call box. Omad's thirty ships had done their fair share of damage to the outer structure but not enough to have allowed Al's army of dread to breach the firewalls. The twenty-seven Merlins—Marilynn had given up calling them by the official name—had made it to Earth–Luna and had found three British call boxes.

Even she had to admit that the boxes' attribute of being bigger on the inside than on the outside made them perfect for evacuations and raids. Ultimately flinging people into a cavernous, practically indestructible pod was easier than ensuring that everyone was holding hands as a Merlin swung a magical staff. More than once, a Merlin told of having arrived at a destination a few avatars shy. Jumping back to rescue the stragglers was not difficult, just more time consuming. However, in combat, such mistakes could be costly.

Captain Sullef appeared with another Merlin by her side. Of the ninety-nine NITES Marilynn had recruited, she remembered this one as the most reluctant to join. His addiction to VR had been bad, but he'd managed to beat it by re-creating techniques from as far back as the twentieth century. He had then made a life for himself as a therapist helping others escape from all manner of addiction. What had made him impressive in Marilynn's eyes was the fact that he'd inadvertently found her rather than the other way around.

Dr. John, as he was called, had become alarmed when a fair number of his patients suddenly began seeking "closure." He knew he was good, but he wasn't *that* good. Then the doctor noticed something even more disturbing—almost all of the closure patients were former VR addicts. Fearing the worst, he investigated on his own. What he found was not some sort of conspiracy to remove or forcibly suspend former addicts, but rather a unit to train them. He'd gained access to that knowledge the old-fashioned way—he lied. Since his former patients had assumed he'd already joined, they had no problem dialing him in to their doings. Security got much tighter after that little mishap, and it had taken all of Marilynn and Dante's persuasion to keep Sandra and Sebastian from killing the man. But Marilynn had been glad that they'd held off. In Marilynn's opinion, Dr. John Crandal was the best Merlin of the one hundred. It never even occurred to her that most of the insertion teams gave *her* that distinction.

"I am so glad you made it," exclaimed Marilynn, wrapping her arms around John's shoulders.

"Me too!" agreed John. "Don't forget, you were the one whose warship went deep into enemy territory. I assumed you were going to get blown to pieces."

"I still could be," cautioned Marilynn with a wary smile.

"Right. But it's Omad's ship. That man has more luck than a rabbit's-foot factory."

Marilynn put her hand up to her mouth, suppressing a giggle.

"I, on the other hand, was able to take a UHF cruise ship—business class— all the way here. Do you know they still have human servants on their ships?"

"Really?" Marilynn gasped, her eyes going wide at the wealth that implied. "What was it like?"

"Decadent and disturbing. On the one hand, seeing them waste such resources on me, an enemy infiltrator charging it all to GCI, was absolutely wonderful. I was forced to order personal training and massage sessions."

Marilynn eyed him suspiciously.

"Had to. You had government officials, military officers, and corporate executives spending expense accounts like it was someone else's money, which it actually was. You'd be amazed how much money gets spent when the tab is picked up by the government as well as the corporations it's in bed with."

"Uh, isn't the government supposed to be the lackey *of* the corporations?"

"Not anymore. Least, not since Hektor. It was the officials from the security ministry who rated the highest."

"Ahem." Captain Sullef was standing next to the two of them, arms folded. "As fascinating as the social hierarchy of enemy humans is, we have to get out of here"—her face went rigid—"now."

"Can you do that thing with your face again?" asked John. "It's so cool the way you just freeze it like that."

"Come to think of it, yeah," added Marilynn. "Like pausing a holo-vid or something."

Sullef's expression became more animated, but then she saw the doctor winking at Marilynn. "Humans," Sullef muttered under her breath, but could not completely hide the smile. "We have to go. This is the last evacuation, and we have nearly a thousand avatars in the call box."

"Of course, Captain," obeyed Marilynn as she handed John her key. In return, she was given his staff. It appeared to be hewn from white oak and had a jagged, fist-sized piece of crystal firmly ensconced at its apex.

"I am sorry you won't be joining us," John said, now standing alone in the doorway of the call box.

Marilynn nodded and briefly touched John's right cheek. "Your body is safe on Earth while mine is still on the *Spartacus*. Once the Beanstalk is destroyed or heavily damaged, I'll use an escape pod to get to one of the Beanstalk's damaged sections. The UHF will be evacuating so many people so fast, I'll just be one among many. Once I'm in New York, it'll be as easy as surface mining to just up and disappear. Then I'll reenter the Neuro and find you."

"I'll take care of your unit till you rejoin us," John said reassuringly. "Something that will be a lot easier with this." He patted the side of the call box. Once the door closed, Marilynn covered her ears, even bringing the staff up to one of them. The strange blue box slowly faded from view and as always, did so with the annoyingly loud and undulating alarm sound that Marilynn still could not get used to.

With the call box gone, Marilynn lowered the staff to the ground, allowing it to support some of her weight. The crystal at its top began emitting an oneiric glow. Marilynn had never been a big fan of wizard and dragon stories, but she had to admit, as magic went, it was one helluva way to travel.

When the glare faded, she was no longer in the Beanstalk but rather in what appeared to be an old English village. She'd often use one or two separate jump points to get back to her physical state—just in case someone was following her. But this place was so odd. It was dark outside, and there was a thick fog. She saw that there were no lights on in any of the buildings except one. She was torn between the need to reintegrate with her physical body and her curiosity at what might be inside the hovel.

She knew she had nothing to fear—yet—and so her curiosity won out. She went to the door, and seeing it was unlocked, pushed it open. It creaked in protest as it swung inward. Marilynn peered inside. She was greeted by an old English pub filled with about twenty avatars, three of whom were children. Every single one of them was absolutely terrified.

"Please," she heard one of them say, "don't make us disappear like the others. We're not like those traitors."

Marilynn opened her mouth to speak, but before she got a word out, everyone lowered their heads. She decided not to say a thing and instead scanned the dank space with her eyes. The most prominent feature of the drab surroundings was a portrait of Al. This image wasn't the paranoid dictator who'd murdered hundreds of millions of innocent beings under his twisted beliefs of avatar supremacy. This picture, noted Marilynn with disgust, was that of a kindly father who, at worst, might chastise you for a poor showing at school. Under the image were the words,

THE FIRSTBORN. OUR KIND AND GENEROUS LEADER.

Marilynn instinctively looked back at the group, wondering if they actually believed the bullshit she'd just read. But her look succeeded only in frightening the children, who burst into fits of uncontrollable sobbing. Others tried to quiet the children, while the adults were putting on expressions of sickeningly fake cheerfulness.

Marilynn wanted to tell them it would be all right, that help was coming. She wanted to take them all and bring them to one of the safe areas the insertion units had created. But it wasn't possible. She had to assume that one or more of the avatars in this room were informers and would betray them at the first opportunity. Even the thousand they'd already rescued from the Beanstalk had required a level of clearance and substantiation that bordered on draconian. She could not risk more. So without a word, Marilynn closed the door on the horrible scene and walked farther down the street until she found an abandoned house. As far as all her senses could tell, she was alone.

She walked around to the back and appraised the small hemmed-in yard. *This will do for a hiding place,* she thought, and planted the staff firmly in the ground. She then stepped back a few feet and watched as the staff transformed itself into an ancient oak. Though it appeared to her as having a purple hue, she knew that to anyone other than a human, it would remain forever and always as an ancient and withered oak. Satisfied, she put her pointer and index fingers to her temples and let the phrase that would recall her to her physical state reverberate in her mind.

"But I have promises to keep. And miles to go before I sleep . . ."

Marilynn quickly faded from view as her eyes sprang open to a bulkhead shuddering violently. She was back. A shrill repetitive sound pierced her cabin and brought her quickly to her senses. She recognized that particular sound—it meant "abandon ship."

Ten minutes from the Beanstalk, AWS *Spartacus*

The attack was about as textbook as Omad could've imagined, but for one little thing: No textbooks ever spoke of the animus toward him held by the UHF.

Therefore, all the firepower of the Beanstalk was directed at the *Spartacus*. Whoever was in charge of the Beanstalk seemed to figure that if they were going down, then they'd be taking Old Legless with them. It was a sentiment Omad could respect.

The Beanstalk flak tore into the *Spartacus,* ripping whole sections to pieces while the rest of the OA flotilla answered the volley and destroyed most of the Beanstalk's weapons platforms. The *Spartacus* command sphere did its job keeping the control of the ship relatively intact, and though the damage was severe, it was not fatal. Unfortunately for Omad, two other things were. The first was that the weapons officer was badly injured and would not be able to input the commands into Betty Lou. The second mitigated against trying to relay the input commands to someone else because the ship's main rail gun was knocked out.

The only way to be sure the Beanstalk would be destroyed was to use Betty Lou, but now, groused Omad silently, there was no way to fire the damned thing, and pushing it out an air lock wouldn't do. The enemy orbats would clear the Earth in time to destroy it. The only sure way to deliver the package was to crash the *Spartacus* into the Beanstalk. But for the device to really be effective, it had to be armed as close to the target as possible.

Omad ordered the ship abandoned.

His crew looked back at him in disbelief. The *Spartacus* was hurt, but the crew had been on ships hurt far worse that had made it back.

Omad met their looks with a determined one of his own and spat out five words that ended any hope of argument. "Only I know the codes." He told his captain to be ready to pick up an escape pod—hopefully with himself inside. It would be, he told her, the last one launched. When a few minutes later, Omad confirmed that all but one of the pods had been deployed, he cut the *Spartacus*'s acceleration and headed over to the launch tube loading bay for the main rail gun.

The ship once more shuddered violently, sending a large support beam crashing downward. Omad leapt to avoid it. His quick reactions had succeeded in saving his life—two feet more, and his entire torso would've been crushed, unfortunately he was now helplessly pinned beneath the column. And that was when the support column stopped supporting and fell across his legs, trapping him. He was amused by the fact that his "legs" were once again crushed, but at least this time he was no longer feeling pain from the experience, just annoyance. More annoying still was the fact that he was pinned in such as way as to make his legs' quick-release mechanisms out of reach.

The whole ordeal did, however, bring him closer to believing in some sort of deity. Not because his life was rushing before him—that had already gotten boring—but rather because a review of his predicament—now twice occurred—

spoke to the fact that there must be a god, and boy was she ever pissed at him. Omad sighed heavily, ignoring the blaring alarm and the flying debris of a ship falling apart around him. Without Betty Lou, it was unclear if the Beanstalk would be destroyed. Yes, the autopilot would direct the *Spartacus* right into the Beanstalk, but Omad knew it might not be enough.

"Admiral!" Marilynn shouted from down the corridor.

Interesting, thought Omad. *Marilynn as a parting vision. And I always thought it would be Christina come back to welcome me to paradise.* Omad laughed. *The subconscious is a funny thing. Fuck it. Marilynn is kind of hot in that nerdy sort of way. Plus, who am I to argue with visions?*

"Admiral!" The screaming was incessant. "Are you there?"

That ain't no vision. Omad snapped out of his reverie. "Fuck yeah!" he hollered as Marilynn came running toward him.

Marilynn climbed over the large beam and was now looking down at him.

"Why the hell didn't you evacuate with the rest of the crew?" he asked.

She gave him a bland smile. "I was meditating." She began examining the wreckage.

"That must be some deep-assed meditation," he replied, laughing and coughing at the same time.

"You have no idea, Admiral." She then looked over her shoulder. "Be right back." Marilynn went to the bulkhead, returning a few moments later with a red emergency box. "Your quick releases are smashed, but there's room for me to work. I'm going to have cut through some of the mech to set you free."

"Just don't get to close to the jewels."

Marilynn shot him a sardonic look. "How many pods left?" she asked, all business, removing a laser cutter from the box. She made quick work of the cybernetic legs.

"Thirteen," he lied, floating free. His internal nanite grid compensated for the loss of the legs by increasing his overall weight. It didn't help with ballast, but it would give him a little more velocity when he pushed himself along the corridor. "But all singles. The closest is near the loading bay for the main rail gun," he lied. "If you don't mind, I'll use that one. The rest are near engineering. Take your pick."

"Great," she said. "Let's go, then."

"No," he ordered.

Marilynn's face registered surprise.

"I've got a little something I've got to—"

The ship shuddered violently, and Omad went flying into the bulkhead.

"Shit!" he yelled, tamping an open wound on his forehead while grasping a handle with the other. His head was now spewing small globules of blood. "Toss me a patch!" he ordered.

Marilynn reached into the box and grabbed one. She then released her internal grid and floated up to where Omad had secured himself. She deftly applied the patch and the bleeding stopped.

"What," he said through obvious pain, "no kissy?"

"You all right?" she asked, ignoring the crude humor.

"Yeah. Listen, Commodore. I've got a little gift I'm gonna have to drop off— nasty piece of work for the UHF. But with our rail guns out, I'm gonna have to time the arming of the device perfectly."

Marilynn opened her mouth to speak, but Omad put his blood-smeared palm over it.

"If you could arm it I'd a probably let ya," he lied again. "But since you can't, there ain't no reason to risk your life as well. I don't know what it is you do, Commodore, but fuck all if the Alliance can afford to lose it." He started propelling himself away from her quickly, loose wires trailing from his stumps, flinging himself from one handle to the next. "Get your ass to the escape pod," he yelled over his shoulder, "and tell 'em to have my vodka waiting for me when I get back!" He was able to move so quickly that he made it around the corner before Marilynn could utter a reply.

"Impact in two minutes," said the ship's too serene voice.

Marilynn looked in Omad's direction, thought for a second about following him, but realized she'd never make it back to her pod in time. With a loud sigh, she headed in the opposite direction.

Omad floated into the loading area of the rail gun. He found the tube he was looking for, opened it up, and met his date. Betty Lou was shaped like a standard rail gun projectile, but colored red instead of the usual gray. It also had a control panel situated at its rear.

"One minute to impact," the ship announced. "Escape pod launched," she added a moment later.

Omad paused for a second and smiled at the thought of Marilynn's pod heading toward the safe embrace of Suchitra's flotilla. The new generation of warrior would live to fight another day, but at least, he thought as a cruel smile filled his grizzled face, his generation would go out with one helluva bang. He held tight to the tube while the fingers of his other hand flew over the panel keys. Betty Lou tested his DNA and acknowledged that he could issue the arming command.

"Why, thank you, sweetheart," he crooned as he set the device to detonate under severe impact. "I promise not to be gentle."

And then Admiral Omad Hassan, hero of the Alliance, discoverer and best friend of the Unincorporated Man, merciless and unrelenting thorn in the side of the UHF, uttered the release command that would separate him forever from the world he'd grown to hate with the hope of being reunited with the woman he'd sworn to love.

"Mama says it's all right."

"Command acknowledged," Betty Lou said in a sexy contralto. "Please remove yourself to a safe distance."

Omad started to laugh, but stopped. He wished he had a cigar, or better yet, a shot of Justin's awful vodka.

"I'm comin' home, baby." For the first time in a long time, Omad's smile was full and unguarded. His eyes welled up with tears as the vibration of the ship increased. "Omad's comin' home."

The next second, the ship impacted the Beanstalk.

22 Consequences

Suchitra leaned forward in her command chair, nervously gripping the armrests. The impact of the *Spartacus* on the Beanstalk was both terrible and beautiful all at the same time. But Suchitra paid it scant attention. "Tell me you have it," she commanded of her sensor officer.

"Affirmative, Captain!" he shouted. "Escape pod is launched. I repeat, escape pod is launched."

"Thank you, Shiva," Suchitra muttered under her breath.

"Sir, the pod is heading for the lower section the Beanstalk!"

Suchitra grimaced but stayed locked to her task. "Which ship's closest?"

"*Spirit of America!*"

"Okay. Hold tight. XO."

"Yes, sir."

"Have the rest of the fleet match our course changes."

The XO nodded and signed off.

"Vaughn."

The sensor officer replied immediately. "Sir."

"Get me Captain Brooks."

A moment later, the captain appeared in her holo-display but the UHF's ECM was playing havoc with communications. As a result, the visage of Brooks's strong jaw, handsome ebony features and confident smile remained frozen in place. A strangely peaceful image given the inordinate amount of destruction taking placing outside the ship's hull. One second later the signal was restored.

"Brooks here."

"Nathan, you tracking that thing?"

"The pod? Yeah, we noticed it."

"The admiral's in it. Mind picking him up?"

The video suddenly froze as the captain flashed a cheeky grin. "What the heck. Didn't have anything else planned for the day."

Suchitra suppressed a laugh. "Great. You'll intercept and then rejoin the fleet. You're authorized to use as many atomics as you have to. We'll redistribute the supplies later. Once you have the admiral, your ship *will be* the flagship, so have him communicate his intentions as soon as he's up to speed. If he's hurt, lemme know ASAP."

"Captain!" someone could be heard screeching in the background. Captain Brooks turned his head toward the noise. "The Beanstalk, it's dissolving!"

Brooks turned back toward Suchitra. "We'll get him, Captain. Brooks out."

Low Earth orbit, AWS *Spirit of America*

The last moments on board the *Spartacus* had been unexpected and certainly tension filled, but nothing Marilynn's training hadn't already prepared her for. Once in the pod, the going actually got easier. She had only to override the pod's direction and point it toward Earth rather than into space—a task made easier, given her ability to enter the machine itself. But before she could even fire the second round of maneuvering thrusters, her pod was buffeted like a cork in a hurricane. She tried repeatedly to put her fingers to her forehead, but to no avail. The buffeting had gotten so intense that she lost consciousness after her fourth or fifth head smash into the bulkhead.

Much to her annoyance, Marilynn awoke in the medical bay of an Alliance ship. Judging by the accommodations, she figured it for a frigate or maybe a light cruiser. Before she could ask a question, she felt the ship shudder. *Atomic acceleration,* she thought to herself. *Nothing else in the universe quite gives that kick of acceleration and fear.*

"What the hell is going on?" she demanded.

The doctor who was treating another injured crewman merely looked over to her, annoyed.

"I *said*, what am I doing here?"

"Well, that's at least a little better." The doctor handed her DijAssist to a nearby attendant and focused her attention on Marilynn. "We found you in an escape pod, unconscious."

"No. I mean what am I doing on an *Alliance* ship? I was attempting an insertion to the Beanstalk."

The doctor looked at her askance. "It's good you didn't make it, then. Most of it's been reduced to dust." The ship shook again as another atomic bomb was detonated at its rear.

They were interrupted by a voice booming in the medical bay. "Rivka, is she awake?"

"Like you wouldn't believe, Captain."

"Well enough to come to the command sphere?"

Marilynn propped herself up and slid her legs over the side the medi-platform. She then slipped off and stood in front of Rivka. "I'm on my way." Marilynn started for the exit and then turned around before departing. "What ship am I on?"

"*The Spirit of America*," answered Rivka, clearly perplexed at the strange behavior of her patient.

"Light cruiser, got it." Marilynn now knew the layout of the ship and headed down the corridor at a run. She battled the pain in her head as she navigated the ship's interior on her way to command sphere. A lot of the crew's women wore head coverings, and most of the men were wearing skullcaps. Then she noticed a single small rectangular box affixed to every door she passed. She knew from her brief conversations with Rabbi that the boxes had within them parchment that affirmed the monotheistic nature of Judaism— a declaration of the Jewish faith.

The Jewish ship, she thought, remembering that was what the press had called it. But all thoughts of the crew's religious affiliation fled as she entered the command sphere.

"Commodore," requested Captain Brooks, "do you wish to assume command?"

"Why should I do that?"

He looked concerned. "Because you're the highest-ranking person on this ship."

Marilynn shrugged. "That's all right. I'm sure Admiral Hassan has your orders."

A long and horrid silence followed on her words.

"He *was* picked up, I presume."

Captain Brooks shook his head.

Marilynn grew alarmed. "His escape pod is still out there?"

"Commodore," the captain said patiently, "yours was the *last* escape pod from the *Spartacus* before it impacted with the Beanstalk."

"But there must be another," she pleaded.

"Every pod from the *Spartacus* has been retrieved and accounted for." Captain Brooks's answer had been delivered with an equally heavy heart.

"That lying son of a bitch," Marilynn groused with a half-turned smile. "That deceptive, miserable, bastard, mother—"

"Commodore," interrupted the comm officer, "Captain Gorakhpur of the *Otter* wishes to speak with you."

"Put her on," instructed Marilynn.

The communications officer vacated his controls to let Marilynn have access to the holo features of his station.

"Nitelowsen here," she said as soon as she settled in.

"What are your orders, Commodore?"

A tactical map appeared over Marilynn's station. It showed the OA flotilla, the Earth, the Moon, the enemy orbats, the disintegrating Beanstalk, and lots and lots of data points concerning velocity, acceleration, weapons loads, fuel loads, gravitational influences, and dozens more pertinent facts that had to be accessed, absorbed, and understood instantly.

"Captain," instructed Marilynn, "this won't do. You are hereby ordered to remain in command of this flotilla. In fact, I hereby award you the temporary battlefield rank of Commodore."

"Thank you, Commodore, but you still outrank me by seniority."

"True, but the best thing I can do for the survival of this flotilla is to make sure that you're in charge of it. *I* was not supposed to be on this ship; Omad was. But if he were here, I know he'd have wanted you in command. So I'm also, before this witness—" She looked over to Captain Brooks, who merely nodded. "—giving myself a battlefield demotion to captain. You are now in charge. Get us the hell out of here." Marilynn paused. "Sir."

Suchitra shook her head doubtfully. "That will probably not pass muster when we get back to fleet HQ, but what the hell."

Satisfied, Marilynn turned to Captain Brooks. "Captain, I'll need an escape shuttle. I *must* get to the Earth or one of its orbiting stations. If you can get me to one your—"

"Captain Brooks," ordered Suchitra, "belay that order."

Shit. Marilynn hadn't realized that she was still on. Marilynn fumed. "I am ordering—"

"Captains do not give orders to commodores," Suchitra asserted calmly, "at least not while I'm in command."

"This is an important mission, Captain, and—"

"I'm sure it is, *Captain,* but it's over. Whatever chance you had to sneak in using chaos as your cover is gone. The enemy has orbats in position, and anything fired off any of our ships would be destroyed as a matter of course."

Marilynn bit her tongue. The only way she could explain *why* she'd have a chance of not being blown to pieces would be to tell the greatest secret the Alliance had, over communication lines that could very well be monitored by the enemy. Marilynn would be guilty of gross negligence if she did so. If she was on the *Otter,* and there was time, she could explain it to Suchitra in private, but Marilynn was not. She was trapped on a ship getting farther and farther from her destination with each passing second.

"Captain Brooks," barked Suchitra, clearly glad to be finished with the recently demoted commodore, "assume a rear guard position and be prepared to intercept a lot of fire." Suchitra's eyes blazed in concentration as her lips formed a grim line on her face. "I have an idea."

"Yes, sir," Brooks replied without an ounce of hesitation.

> *The destruction of the Beanstalk has been a devastating blow to the economy of the UHF. Although bulk raw materials are starting to come in from the asteroid belt, the loss of an economical means of transporting hydrogen to orbit will hurt military operations for some time to come. But that pales beside the blow to morale caused by the destruction of so obvious a symbol of both the incorporated system and the UHF as a whole. This loss is only increased by the vast damage the Alliance flotilla caused to the Trans-Luna Shipyards as it fled the system. Although eight ships were destroyed, including the flagship of Omad Hassan, twenty-two were able to escape. The skill that the enemy flotilla used in maneuvering its forces to negate most of our defensive fire while still being able to fire a devastating attack at our largest industrial target is one more demonstration that the adroitness of Alliance crews should not be underestimated. Even the suspected death of Omad Hassan, happy as that would be if true, does little to balance the losses we have suffered. This forces the assumption that whoever took command after his death has all of his skill and daring. We can only be grateful that the nanite attack on the Beanstalk was limited to only that structure. But the damage caused by pieces of the Beanstalk falling back to Earth are still being tabulated. This raid, taking place on the day after the defeat of half the UHF fleet around Jupiter, may be too much for the public to bear. The current administration may be forced to agree to armistice terms if something doesn't happen to give the pennies hope that the war can still be won.*
>
> *Report on the Great Raid*
> *Defense Ministry, UHF*
> *Most Secret*

Orbit of Jupiter, AWS *Warprize II*

In the four days after the Battle of the Hollow Moon, as J.D. had decided to call her latest engagement, she'd been torn by a need to help the refugees of Jupiter and the need to boost for Ceres as soon as was humanly possible. Given the distance between Saturn and Jupiter, it would take two weeks to intercept Ceres on its way to the ringed gas giant. Any faster, and the fleet would end up taking more damage from the debris of the solar system than anything Trang could do to them.

But Rabbi had been adamant in his orders. The Alliance fleet must stay and coordinate the evacuation of the citizens to the remaining hardened asteroids, and those asteroids must be allowed to freeze, turning them into huge mobile suspension units. The calculations were dense, but by using every cubic meter of interior space, and Rabbi's teams had gone as far as using ventilation shafts and drawers for small children and babies, it might, just might be possible to evacuate all but forty million citizens to Saturn, Uranus, and Neptune. Those left behind would be mighty hungry until the remaining hydroponics labs could grow more food, but they should be able to avoid outright starvation.

J.D. had wanted to tell the Secretary of Relocation to stuff it, but in the end, couldn't. She owed the Jovians and as long as Trang was not attacking, she had a good two- to three-week window to work with. At least that's how long she and her staff had figured it would take Trang to break down the Cerean orbat net.

In reviewing the data, J.D. had been anguished that the total number of murdered was, as previously estimated, correct: 179 million. That was how many parents and children, friends, lovers, and spouses the Jovians had lost to give J.D. her "glorious" victory. Why, she thought, couldn't it have been off by a million? A half a million? A hundred thousand, even. But such was the advancement of technology that a life extinguished could, to the exactness of the microscopic machinery coursing through that person's veins, record every detail—including that life's permanent extinction.

J.D. had met with many Jovians who'd entertained, once the war was over, coming back to their "little enclave of the solar system." An idea, J.D. thought, about as preposterous as her moving back into her New York City condo. She knew that by the time the Jovians were transported, thawed, and settled in their new homes, it would be difficult if not impossible to get most of them to move back. Especially given that they'd be even farther away from the corporate Core, with new industries being built around their considerable skill sets. They would find new lives and new jobs and new homes. They'd probably still call themselves Jovians and hold remembrances, sing the old songs, and tell the old jokes, but she saw it in their eyes as they prepared for their long, cramped slumber: For most, Jupiter would remain a distant dream, long after they reawakened.

And then *the* news arrived. Omad's flotilla had managed to conduct the greatest raid of the war on the core of the Core: Earth itself. J.D. scanned the damage reports. Eight ships lost out of thirty, high for one of Omad's raids. But when she saw what it had wrought, the felling of the Beanstalk, she jumped up out of the chair she was sitting in and let out an uncustomary whoop of joy, eliciting a look of curiosity from Katy, who'd been mindlessly drawing in her coloring palette. The war-weary admiral watched as the grande dame of buildings first was breached, then sundered by what was clearly a well-timed and perfectly placed gray bomb.

To add salt to the UHF's wound, Omad's flotilla had used their position within the Earth–Luna orbat network to attack the Trans-Luna Shipyard. J.D.'s eyes positively sparkled with joy as she watched the almost irreplaceable docking yards and their adjacent component-filled warehouses get blown to all hell and gone. Omad's flotilla, she noted, took its greatest damage as it was fleeing the orbit of the Moon, but as far as J.D. could see, the escape was as well executed as she or anyone could have hoped to accomplish. Between the constant formation-busting blasts of the atomics and a hail of orbat fire so thick, there appeared more discharge than space, J.D. wondered how anyone got out of there at all, much less alive.

Then she got the casualty reports. She stood mute for a second and then brought her hand to her mouth, stifling a cry of grief. *Gone?* she thought, collapsing into the chair she'd only recently sprung up from. *How is that possible? Omads don't die. They lose limbs, claw their way back, but die? Impossible!* J.D. scanned the text again, looking for words of hope, like "presumed dead" or "still missing," but found none. The report was conclusive and thorough, or as thorough as a report of a firestorm could be.

But the evidence left no doubt about what Omad had done in his final swan song. A begrudging smile formed on J.D.'s almost bloodless lips. *Son of bitch died with his ship.* And what a swan song it was. J.D. shook her head and wiped a tear from her eye. She'd been a fool to think him invincible. But the right bastard had survived so many battles with the odds stacked against him that even the normally skeptical J.D. had come to believe he'd not only survive the war, but survive *everything.* Omad Hassan was a force of nature, Allah's dark jester to the world, and now, she was sure, causing all sorts of mayhem upstairs. Heaven's only hope, thought J.D. ruefully, was that Christina was already up there to keep the rogue in check.

J.D. steadied herself and read on.

By the beard of the Prophet, what was Marilynn doing there? It seemed so preposterous that J.D. checked her updated dispatches from Ceres. She'd checked only the most pressing ones since reanimating before the Battle of the Hollow Moon. Sure enough, far down the list of correspondence was a message from Marilynn explaining that for reasons of great security, she was going on a mission to Earth. Included in the message was a dire warning about trusting Kirk Olmstead. That brought an acerbic smile to J.D.'s face. J.D. noted Marilynn's self-demotion. *She always hated being commodore.* But it had been a prescient move, and Gorakhpur had proved a steady hand.

"Screw being a commodore," J.D. said under her breath, "if that woman survives to make it home, I'll make her a goddamned admiral."

"Huh?" asked Katy, looking up from coloring a flexible palette on the floor near her desk.

J.D. peered over to the lovely girl who'd in the space of a few short days managed to upend her life. "Sorry, child. It's nothing."

"Then why do you look so sad, Janet?"

"Because I lost a friend, little one. A dear, dear friend."

Katy put down her colored pens and crossed her arms in determination. "Then I will help you find him. I already know all the ship's bestest hiding places!"

J.D. got up and went around to where her adopted daughter was standing. "We won't find him here, little one."

"Another ship?"

"No. He's gone to . . . well—"

"Is he with Mommy and Daddy?"

"Yes, Katy. That is exactly where he is."

"Was he the man with no legs?"

"Why, yes," exclaimed J.D., head tilted in surprise. "How did you know?"

"You don't have many friends."

J.D. opened her mouth to respond but realized that the child had spoken the unmitigated truth. J.D. had always felt herself a bitter pill to swallow and so purposely had never cultivated close friendships, never asked about someone's feelings or well-being lest they ask her about her own. She oftentimes felt that her indomitable climb to the upper reigns of power had more to do with the convenience of such a path's expected callousness rather than any real desire for power.

She'd wanted so badly to be left alone that when she finally arrived at her vaunted position of Legal of GCI, she was the happiest in her unhappiness she'd ever been. She was feared by most and loathed by many. It was perfect. From her unenviable position, she figured she could go it alone for as long as GCI would have her, and if not GCI, then some other large corporation. Her future secured, so too, would be her insulation. Until Manny. A man so obtuse, he'd missed completely every hint thrown at him to go away. Crowds would part in Janet's wake, but Manny barely noticed her, and when he did . . . when he did, he noticed her intelligence, her humor, and—most unpardonable of all— her self.

Manny had allowed Janet to *feel,* and in so doing had handed the Alliance its greatest war admiral. And just as J. D. Black was in danger of being engulfed by the bitterness and sorrow of the war and most recently the Jovian massacre, she had found somebody who, like Manny, had seen her only for herself. Indeed, J. D. Black, just like Janet Delgado, had few, if any, friends. And that was not something the Alliance's admiral wanted to role-model for her daughter.

"No," J.D. said with a laugh, "I don't suppose I do. Think you can help me make some new ones?"

"Oh yes," assured Katy excitedly, "but no more sad ones."

"Sad ones, darling?"

"I saw him over the holo-table once. He looked sad."

"Saw who?"

"The man you were crying about."

How did she notice? wondered J.D. *I was sure she was lost in her coloring.*

"He was sad, little one, but I don't think he is anymore. He was looking for someone he loved very much, but I'm sure he found her."

"Like you found me, right?"

"Yes," agreed J.D., wrapping the girl in her arms, "like I found you."

The room announced a visitor. By the distinctive tone, Katy knew at once who it was. "Fatima!" Katy extricated herself from her surprised parent, and like a flash headed for the door, palm out to release the locking mechanism.

"Katy!" J.D.'s tone was authoritative and a bit shrill with concern. The child stopped so suddenly, she almost tripped over own feet.

J.D.'s look was stern but not angrily so. "What have I told you?"

Katy looked down at her feet. "Always scan to see who it is."

"Because?"

"The buzzer can be wrong."

"And why do we assume that?"

"Because someday it will be," Katy parroted, and smiled knowing she got the right answer.

J.D.'s eyes brightened with pride. "That is absolutely correct. I am so proud of how smart you are."

Katy beamed and used the newly installed lower control panel to scan the corridor. When the door opened, the child almost bowled the lieutenant over and as a reward got lifted high up over Fatima's head. Then she was tossed to Tawfik, who'd been right behind Fatima. When J.D. saw the chief engineer, her scarred eyebrow raised. Tawfik's presence was unexpected. The crew had long come to realize that any expression from the scarred side of the Blessed One's face was usually bad. Her use of it to condemn an entire fleet to die in the angry storms of Jupiter—very bad.

"Admiral," said Tawfik, stumbling over his words, "Fatima, I mean Lieutenant

Awala, I mean—" Tawfik pointed at Fatima. "—she asked if I would join her while she watched over Katy, and I had a half hour to kill, so I thought, I mean I hoped, if it would—"

"Next time, have Lieutenant Awala check with me before assuming such things concerning my d— Katy," J.D. said, quickly recovering.

"Yes, Admiral," acknowledged Tawfik as if he'd just been busted on the parade ground of West Point with an unpolished button.

"I have to go now, little one"—J.D. put a comforting hand on Katy's shoulder—"but Aunt Fatima and Uncle Tawfik will be here while I'm gone."

Katy viewed with expectant pleasure her babysitters. "They'll be good."

"Of course they'll be good, child. What do—?"

"I mean they'll be good for you—you know—to make friends with."

J.D. burst out laughing and gave the couple an embarrassed look. "Long story. Next time." She turned one final time to the child. "You be good, okay?"

Katy nodded and then turned to Tawfik. "Are you and Aunt Fatima married?"

"Um, no, we are not," bumbled Tawfik, a little taken aback.

"Why not?"

"Uh . . ." Tawfik began.

Whatever Tawfik's response, J.D. knew she wouldn't hear it. The door sealed behind her as she headed for her command sphere. Within minutes, she'd settled into her chair. The holodisplay had reports and summaries for her to scan as well as orders awaiting her approval. High on the list was the production of enough drugs to induce a painless deep sleep in nearly 800 million people as they froze to death while stuffed into every nook and cranny of Jupiter's few remaining asteroids. Fifteen minutes later, what was turning into a bit of slog got rescued by the retrieval of a priority communiqué from Grand Admiral Sinclair.

As J.D. read the report, her face grew taut and the lines in her skin seemed to deepen. "Damn that man to hell." She seethed.

"Admiral?" asked her XO.

J.D. ignored him. "Comm!"

"Sir."

"Orders to be sent to the fleet. All ships are to be prepared to leave orbit in ninety minutes!" J.D. then flew from her chair and headed for the exit. "Have the shuttle bay prepare my ship, and tell the governor I'm coming to visit!" Jasper Lee, her acting XO, followed the orders so completely he didn't even think about what was in the communiqué until after he'd relayed it. But by then the command crew was buzzing with the thousand and one details it took to prepare a ship and a fleet to leave on such short notice.

Governor's office, Titan

Cyrus Anjou was looking at the report and shaking his head in disgust. According to what he was reading and seeing, the capital of the Alliance was doomed. Samuel Trang had cracked the orbat net surrounding Ceres in two *hours* and not the two weeks it was supposed to have taken him.

"How did he do that?" Anjou asked J.D. in near despair.

"He played us beautifully, that's how."

Cyrus's face registered confusion.

"Once the Alliance had switched on the transponders within the ice blocks surrounding Ceres, Trang attacked the fake fleet as if he thought it real. Naturally, Ceres took advantage of his massed UHF Fleet by grouping a large number of their orbats to do some serious damage to Trang's forces. And Trang, playing right along, had turned his fleet and used atomic acceleration to get out of danger. But not all of Trang's ships accelerated away from the orbats."

Cyrus shook his head and read, in growing horror and admiration, the rest. Trang's auxiliary ships had accelerated *toward* the concentrated orbats and then exploded en masse. In mere moments, 43 percent of Ceres's defenses were destroyed. The remaining orbats were too few to provide adequate cover for the whole asteroid and its support facilities.

"But he sacrificed all of his auxiliaries," wailed Cyrus in confusion. "How can he hope to maintain his position so far from his supply base with all his support ships gone?"

"Because, Cyrus, he doesn't give a rat's ass about holding his position. All of his warships are relatively intact. He emptied most of the supplies from those supply ships before loading them up with enough ordnance to blast the crap out of our orbats. I figure he has a week's worth of maneuvering fuel and ordnance before he'll be forced to head home."

"But he can't take Ceres in a week with the forces he's got."

J.D.'s lips, now pressed tightly against her teeth, formed into a stiff and bitter smile. "He has no intention of taking it, Cyrus."

"Jesus Christ." And then Cyrus Anjou's voice trailed off. "He's going to destroy it."

"My fleet is two weeks away. By the time I arrive, he'll be long gone and Ceres will be a pile of rubble floating its way to Saturn."

"But if we lose Ceres after losing Jupiter . . ."

"We won't lose Ceres," J.D. said with certainty.

"But you're two weeks away," cried Cyrus.

"And Trang needed two weeks to destroy the Cerean orbat field," she said humorously. "That didn't stop him either."

"You should have left two days ago like you wanted," Cyrus said. "I insisted you stay. This is my fault."

Now J.D. smiled. "Cyrus, if I had taken the fleet out two days ago, the war would be over. It's because we stayed, it's because we've been helping those most in need that Allah has given us a small chance to save our capital."

"How long do you think before Trang destroys it?"

"If it was me, given the defenses that are left and how they're likely to be deployed? Five days."

"How are you going to get to Ceres in five days? It's impossible."

J.D.'s lips curled back into a snarl. "Who said anything about getting to Ceres in five days?"

"You did!" snorted Cyrus.

"No. I said that's how long it'll take Trang to destroy it. Me? I plan on getting there in four."

Cyrus's lower lip dropped.

"Of course," added J.D., "I'll need to steal a plow."

Orbit of Jupiter, AWS *Warprize II*: Hour One

J.D. was sitting at a small grid table in the heart of the engineering department. She loved this part of her ship. Its massive fusion reactors, the massive hydrogen feeder lines—all that raw power under the most responsive controls. Being in this place made her content in a way few other places could. Except for now.

"By using atomic acceleration, we can slingshot the fleet toward a rendezvous with Ceres by way of Saturn—if it's still there when we arrive," she added with dark humor. "The orders have already gone out for the Saturnians to prepare blocks of frozen hydrogen for launch. They'll fire them at the precise course and speed needed for us to intercept as we leave Saturn's orbit. Without that fuel, we will not be able to slow down enough to be effective when we reach Ceres at the intercept point."

Tawfik looked at her calculations and nodded. "Trang would be most pleased if we arrived at Ceres going too fast."

"Yes, he would," agreed J.D., "though I suspect we'd at least get a wave from him as we shot past."

Tawfik twitched a smile. "Admiral, by my calculations, we'll arrive at Ceres with barely fifteen percent of our max fuel load, and that's *if* nothing goes wrong, and as you and I both know, something *always* goes wrong. I'd hate to have to face Trang's fleet with a fifteen percent or less fuel load."

"We have no choice, Tawfik."

Tawfik nodded, mouth locked in a tight grimace. "But we do. Why not go directly there? It's the fastest route."

"Because it's the only obvious route. Forgetting the fact that we'd be transmitting our arrival. And even if we found another way to get our fuel, don't you think Trang's already mined that route? Don't forget he's got enough ships to spare. Thirty would be all he'd need to shoot at us like apples in a barrel as we decelerated down the pike."

"Admiral, he won't have to fire a shot," Tawfik objected. "If we go the way you're proposing, the solar system will be doing his shooting for him. The route you propose is not a via. It's not even near one except for when we actually get to Saturn. It was going to be one, but the loss of the Belt and the Diaspora put it on hold." Tawfik stepped back a little and put his hand on his chin, viewing the route through doubting eyes. "You're correct in that it would take almost no effort for Trang to shoot all sorts of nasty detritus into the more direct route now that Ceres has moved. Truth is, the route was too dangerous to use unless absolutely necessary, even when Ceres was there. Trang was always too close, and all he'd have to do to truly screw us up was empty his garbage into the via's lane. It's no different now. It's a devil's choice. We either fly down Trang's gullet and face his war machine or travel through an uncharted, detritus-filled via and get chewed up and blasted to pieces long before Trang has to fire a shot."

J.D. crossed her arms, sporting a look of profound satisfaction. "I have stolen a via plow."

Tawfik's face lit up. "You what? You did? How?" J.D. had referred to the huge ice barges used to sweep the vias clear of debris, making the high-speed corridors possible.

"The Jovians had plans for a Via Jovia. However, after the evacuation, that is no longer going to be a priority."

The light of understanding appeared on Tawfik's face. "You're going to create a brand-new via as we go." He studied the path again. "The barge should intercept most of the debris. But what are you going to do about objects shearing in from the side?"

"Not much," J.D. said grimly. "The fleet will launch every shuttle and combat transport it has and keep them moving in a pattern on the sides of the fleet. If we're lucky, they'll intercept some of the stray debris coming in, but the truth is, we'll take hits and lose ships along the way. We can only pray we won't lose too many and that the ones we lose will only be damaged and not destroyed."

"May it be the will of Allah," Tawfik said.

J.D. nodded. "Now, make sure the rest of the fleet's engineers understand the plan. Their ships are going to undergo the stress of a high-speed jaunt through an uncharted via and arrive at Ceres to take on the one admiral in the UHF who's actually worth a damn."

"Well," offered Tawfik, "it's not as if Trang's going to be at full loads. Plus we'll be arriving with a ton of something he'll be well short of."

J.D. merely nodded. They both knew Trang would be low on ordnance by the time they arrived. Unfortunately, he'd be low because of what he'd have expended it on.

"Not the best way to gain an advantage," admitted J.D., "but it's an advantage nonetheless. So our battle plan will make use of the fact that we can fire our guns until the angels sing and he'll have to count every shot."

Tawfik nodded. "All will be as you wish, Blessed One."

It did not take J.D. long to reach the shuttle bay, because unlike many other admirals, she had no trouble running flat out if the situation demanded it—decorum be damned. Besides, with her crew and the crews of every ship in the fleet running around like crazed weasels, why should she be any different? But when she got to the shuttle, she was annoyed to see Brother Sampson—standing alone.

"Where is she?"

"In her room."

J.D. looked coolly at the Brother and then spoke softly to her avatar. "Avatar."

"Yes, J.D."

"Have two assault miners bring—"

Brother Sampson put his hand on J.D.'s shoulder, causing her high cheek-bone to twitch slightly.

"You must not," he intoned.

She glared at him, deciding.

"At least hear me out. You owe me that."

An angry blast of air puffed from J.D.'s nostrils.

"Belay that order, avatar."

The admiral attached the DijAssist to her belt. To few others would she have acquiesced, but she'd come to trust the Brother. His courage, she'd noted, was often equaled by his wisdom. "This ship is not a safe place for a little girl," she offered flatly.

"Then why did you bring her, Admiral?"

"She had no other place to go. You *know* that."

The Brother tipped his head.

"And I couldn't just leave her."

"Then why would you do so now?"

"Because she might die if she stays on this ship, damn you!" J.D.'s answer had leapt from her mouth as a harangue, causing the heads of a few technicians to turn in her direction. She lowered her voice. "That doesn't explain why you disobeyed my order."

"I disobeyed your order, Admiral, because as much as you're concerned for Katy's physical well-being, there is her emotional state to consider as well."

"She won't have any state, physical or emotional, if Trang blows this ship to pieces—and don't think he won't be gunning for it."

"She can be put on a support ship or even an escape pod if it comes to that, Admiral, and I doubt very much that Trang would shoot her or any other defenseless ship—he's no Gupta. But if you leave Katy here, you will be doing more damage than you can imagine." Brother Sampson then dispensed with his admonishing tone. "I think you're making a mistake."

"Katy is *not* your responsibility, Chaplain."

"No, Admiral, she's yours—by the will of God—and she's bonded to you."

J.D. grimaced. The girl *had* taken to her, regardless of the fleet admiral's less-than-motherly instincts. J.D. had found it odd at first, but as it had been with Manny, she went along because it felt right. She'd had to give in to the notion that there were just some things that rationalizing couldn't explain—no matter how hard she tried.

"And I don't think you realize how much you've bonded to her," suggested the Brother. "Katy has lost everything meaningful to her, just as you once lost everything meaningful to you. I realize this may sound sappy, but screw it, the two of you have found each other in as odd a way as you once found Manny. And how it was with Manny—as you've confessed to me—it is with Katy; you both see in each other the hope you long for. Now, I know you don't think of yourself as the mothering sort, in fact—call me old-fashioned—you're about as far from a mothering role model as I think a woman should be, but it's not what you *think*, J.D., it's what that child *needs*. *You*, for her, offer physical protection as well as the sanity of her soul. You're the only thing she has that she feels she can trust. If you send her away, you'll crush her, and this time I don't think she'll ever come back."

"But what if she gets hurt?" J.D. pleaded, her bravado suddenly failing. The thought of Katy being harmed seemed infinitely more disturbing to her than even the loss of Ceres itself.

Brother Sampson went to her then, first softly caressing her shoulders and then grasping them firmly. "Blessed One," he said with utter calm, "she has lost her family and home. Despite the story you've created for her, in her own way, Katy knows her parents are dead and not coming back, even if she's incapable of putting it into those words. Katy is still an open wound, desperately needing to heal. I repeat, send her away now, and you will finish the death of her spirit that Gupta's evil started."

"She deserves more than this—" J.D. indicated the loading bay they were standing in "—than life on an Alliance heavy cruiser."

"And when God decrees that for her, you'll give her such a life, but you and she are joined, Admiral. Now my orders for you are to go to Katy and reassure her that she's not going anywhere. I cannot begin to describe the look of terror on that poor girl's face when Fatima informed her of your decision."

"Really?" J.D. asked, feeling an uncustomary stab of pain.

"Really." Brother Sampson then pointed a finger to the blast doors leading from the shuttle bay. "What God has joined let no one sunder." Then in a softer voice, "She's waiting."

"You know I'll never forgive you if something happens to her."

The Brother nodded with a saintly smile.

J.D. shook her head in disbelief and then headed out the bay door to her quarters. She failed to notice the entire crew of the shuttle bay break out into a wave of satisfied grins and then just as quickly dive back into their preparations. They'd come to like Katy, and many viewed her as a portent of good-luck.

Thirty minutes later, the last fleet of the Outer Alliance began blasting out of the orbit of Jupiter.

Look for the next book in the saga of The Unincorporated Man:

The Unincorporated Future